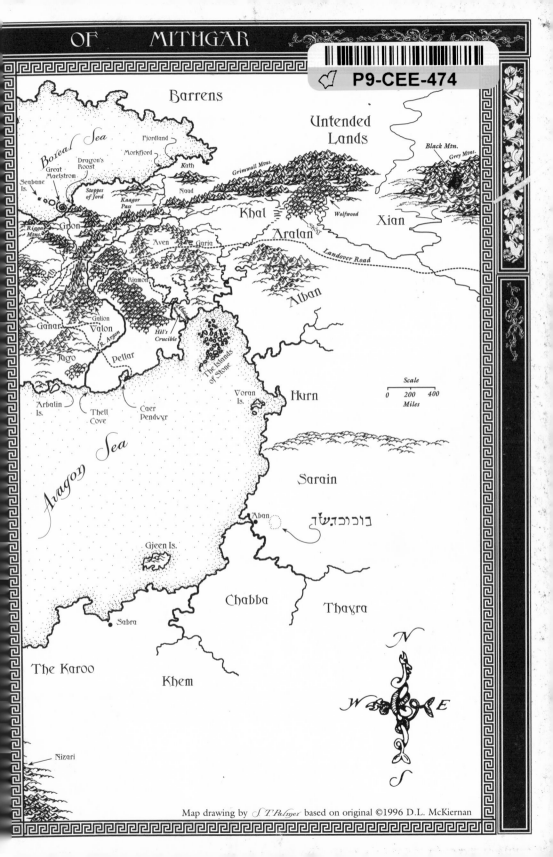

P9-CEE-474

Barrens

Untended Lands

Boreal Sea

Fjordland
Morkfjord
Kath
Naud
Dragon's Roost
Great Maelstrom
Seabane Is.
Steppes of Jord
Kaagor Pass
Rigga Mtns.
Gron

Black Mtn.
Grey Mtns.

Grimwall Mtns.

Khal

Aralan

Wolfwood

Shoé

Xian

Aven
Garia

Landover Road

Riamon

Ganar

Galion
Valon
R. Argon

Höl's Crucible

Alban

Jugo

Pellar

The Islands of Stone

Arbalin Is.

Thell Cove

Caer Pendwyr

Voran Is.

Hurn

Scale

0   200   400
Miles

Avagon Sea

Sarain

Aban

בוכוכהשלך

Gjeen Is.

Chabba

Thayra

The Karoo

Khem

Sabra

Nizari

N

W   E

S

INTO THE FORGE

INTO THE FORGE

HÈL'S CRUCIBLE BOOK 1

DENNIS L. MCKIERNAN

A ROC BOOK

ROC
Published by the Penguin Group
Penguin Putnam Inc., 375 Hudson Street,
New York, New York 10014, U.S.A.
Penguin Books Ltd, 27 Wrights Lane,
London W8 5TZ, England
Penguin Books Australia Ltd, Ringwood,
Victoria, Australia
Penguin Books Canada Ltd, 10 Alcorn Avenue,
Toronto, Ontario, Canada M4V 3B2
Penguin Books (N.Z.) Ltd, 182–190 Wairau Road,
Auckland 10, New Zealand

Penguin Books Ltd, Registered Offices:
Harmondsworth, Middlesex, England

First published by Roc, an imprint of Dutton Signet,
a member of Penguin Putnam Inc.

First Printing, September, 1997
10 9 8 7 6 5 4 3 2 1

![ROC] REGISTERED TRADEMARK—MARCA REGISTRADA

LIBRARY OF CONGRESS CATALOGING-IN-PUBLICATION DATA:

McKiernan, Dennis L., 1932–
    Into the forge / by Dennis L. McKiernan.
       p.   cm. — (Hel's crucible ; bk 1)
    ISBN 0-451-45458-8
    I. Title.   II. Series: McKiernan, Dennis L., 1932–   Hel's crucible ; bk 1.
PS3563.C376I58   1997
813'.54—dc21   97–12755
                                                                  CIP

Printed in the United States of America
Set in Trump Mediaeval
Designed by Leonard Telesca

To the writers and readers of fantasy
throughout the world
and
to that long chain of people in between.
Together, we make the magic happen

FOREWORD

*E*vents are like stones cast upon waters: they make an immediate splash and waves ripple outward in ever widening circles, diminishing as they go. Significant events, like large stones, sometime send waves great enough to engulf those immediately in the path, perhaps to completely overwhelm them if they are not far enough removed from the event. Sometimes the stone is so very large as to affect the entire world (as the dinosaurs literally discovered).

It depends upon the size of the stone and its entry velocity as to whether the initial wave is enormous or minuscule. Yet whether we sink or swim does not necessarily depend upon the magnitude of this initial wave, nor, to a great extent, our distance from it, for the water is full of expanding ripples, some large, some small, all commingling, reinforcing here, negating there, and several tiny ripples can combine a half world away to cause a great effect—a butterfly effect—just as other waves great and small can completely nullify one another.

This tale is about stones cast upon waters and the intermingling of waves.

—Dennis L. McKiernan
August 1996

AUTHOR'S NOTES

*I*nto the Forge is the first book of the duology of HÈL's CRU-CIBLE. Along with the second book, *Into the Fire*, it tells the tale of the Great War of the Ban, as seen through the eyes of two Warrows, Tipperton Thistledown and Beau Darby.

It is a story which begins in the year 2195 of the Second Era of Mithgar, a time when the *Rûpt* are yet free to roam about in daylight as well as night, although it is told that they prefer to do their deeds in darkness rather than under the sun.

The story of the Ban War was reconstructed from several sources, not the least of which were the Thistledown Lays. I have in several places filled in the gaps with assumptions of my own, but in the main the tale is true to its source material.

As occurs in other of my Mithgarian works, there are many instances where in the press of the moment, the humans, Mages, Elves, and others spoke in their native tongues; yet to avoid burdensome translations, where necessary I have rendered their words in Pellarion, the Common Tongue of Mithgar. However, in several cases I have left the language unchanged, to demonstrate the fact that many tongues were found throughout Mithgar. Additionally, some words and phrases do not lend themselves to translation, and these I've either left unchanged or, in special cases, I have enclosed in angle brackets a substitute term which gives the "flavor" of the word (i.e., <see>, <fire>, and the like). Additionally, sundry words may look to be in error, but indeed are correct—e.g., DelfLord is but a single word though a capital L nestles among its letters.

The Elven language of Sylva is rather archaic and formal. To capture this flavor, I have properly used thee and thou, hast, dost, and the like; however, in the interest of readability, I have tried to do so in a minimal fashion, eliminating some of the more archaic terms.

For the curious, the *w* in Rwn takes on the sound of *uu* (w *is*, after all, a double-u), which in turn can be said to sound like *oo* (as in spoon). Hence, Rwn is not pronounced Renn, but instead is pronounced Roon, or Rune.

*But Mithgar . . . Mithgar is yet wild,
tempestuous, unkempt, savage, turbulent,
exciting. We come here to feel alive.*

INTO THE FORGE

1

$W_{ha—?}$ In the chill dark Tipperton started awake—*What was that!* He lay quietly and listened, straining to hear above the burble of the Wilder River, the water running freely beneath its sheath of winter ice. *I thought I heard—*

shing

There it is agai—!

shing-shang . . . chang . . .

Distant metal striking metal. What th—?

Tipperton swung his feet over the edge of his bunk, and in the icy gloom stumbled from his bed and across the cold wooden floor—"Ow!"—barking his shin against a misplaced bench.

Shang-chang! Chnk! The clang of metal upon metal grew louder, as if coming this way.

He fumbled about on the table, knocking aside pots and pans as he searched for the lantern, while—*Ching-chang!*—the rattle and clash grew louder still, now mingled with guttural shouts and the thudding of feet.

At last among the trenchers and kettles Tipperton found the lantern, and just as he ineffectually flicked the striker, a high-pitched scream sounded, and something heavy thudded against the ground outside.

Tipperton flicked the striker again, and this time the wick caught. He lowered the glass and a yellow glow filled the mill chamber, illuminating the great overhead shafts and gears and wooden cogs that drove the massive buhrstones, all now at a standstill, for the sluice weir was shut and no current flowed through the millrace and over the grand water wheel.

Yahh! Chank! Dring! Clang! Tipperton stepped to the door and slid back the crossbar and flung the portal wide just as— *Thdd!*—someone or something slammed against the mill wall, the entire structure juddering with the blow, sending a shower of grain dust drifting down from the cedar shakes above.

In nought but a nightshirt and holding his lantern on high, Tipperton stepped out upon the porch—"Hoy, now, what's all this racket?"—and in the dimness just beyond the reach of the glow he saw black shapes whirling in melee.

"Get back, you fool!" came a shout, even as a dark figure broke free from the tumult and hurtled toward Tipperton.

"Waugh!" The buccan leapt hindward, slamming the door to and ramming the crossbar home just as whatever had rushed at him crashed up against the shut wooden panel.

Feet thudded upon the porch, and window glass shattered inward as Tipperton darted across the chamber and snatched his bow from above the mantel of the hearth. Amid thuds and tromping and screams and shouts and the skirl of steel upon steel, swiftly the buccan strung the weapon. Seizing his quiver and leaving the lantern behind, Tipperton scrambled up a ladder to the catwalk above and raced to a sliding door in the wall and jerked the panel aside. In the frigid light of diamond winter stars and in the frosty rays of the pale quarter moon riding upward in the southeast, he clambered out into the snow-laden run of the wooden sluice, the blanket covering a thin layer of ice.

In that moment there sounded a shriek and a heavy crashing down . . . and *lo!* except for Tipperton's own hammering heart and gasping breath and the burble of water below the ice, all fell silent.

Arrow nocked and crouching low, Tipperton made his way to where he could see the front of the mill. Several dark shapes lay scattered and unmoving upon the snow, and two or three were slumped on the porch. Cautiously, Tipperton crept to a point above a millrace support and waited, the buccan shivering in the frigid cold, for his feet were bare and planted in snow lying upon ice, and he was yet dressed in naught but a nightshirt. Long moments passed, and all remained still. At last he climbed down the support ladder, and with bow drawn taut, and ignoring his numbing feet, he moved through the snow to one of the sprawled shapes.

It was a Rûck. Dead. Hacked by some kind of blade. The now glazed-over viper eyes staring upward.

Tipperton moved onward through churned-up snow, his gorge rising as he cautiously stepped past a dead, hamstrung, eviscerated horse—steam rising through the cold air—and among more slain Rûcks: leather-clad, bandy-legged, batwing-eared, dusky-skinned. Their dark ichor seeped outward upon the snow, and weapons—scimitars and cudgels—lay scattered. Most of the dead had been cut or pierced by a blade of some sort, though the skulls of one or two had been bashed in. And here, too, vapor rose from gaping wounds and spilled entrails steaming.

Arrow yet nocked, Tipperton came to the porch. Half on, half off the planking, another Rûck lay dead. And to the left and slumped against the door lay two bodies. The one on top was a Hlôk—Rûcklike but taller and with straighter limbs—pierced through by a sword, his body yet impaled by the blade; he still clutched a bloody tulwar in his dead hand. As to the other body, the one on the bottom, it—

—groaned—

—His heart leaping in alarm, Tipperton yanked his bow to the full and—

Wait! It's a man, a Human. Oh, Adon, look at the blood flowing.

Tipperton set his bow aside and, straining, dragged the dead Hlôk from atop the Human.

Jostled, the man opened his eyes, then closed them again.

Got to get him inside. Tipperton lifted the door latch and pushed. It did not yield. *Nitwit! It's barred! . . . Wait, the window!* Swiftly, Tipperton stepped across the man and to the shattered jamb and broke out the remaining shards yet clinging to the frame. Then he clambered through, cutting a foot as he stepped on the glass fragments lying on the inside. *Twice a nitwit!*

Hobbling, he moved to the door and slid back the bar and raised the latch, the door swinging back as the weight of the man pushed it open and he slumped inward and lay half in, half out of the chamber. Struggling, Tipperton managed to drag the man the rest of the way inside. His heart yet racing, the buccan stepped back out and retrieved his bow and arrows, then scanned the landscape 'round—*Nothing.* He stepped back inside, closing the door after.

By the light of the lantern yet sitting on the hearth, Tipperton removed the man's helmet, revealing short-cropped dark hair, and he placed a pillow under the man's head. The man was slender but well built, and appeared to be in his mid-twenties—*Though with a Human, I can never tell.* Tipperton then ripped cloth to make bandages to bind the man's wounds, and he said aloud, "Look, my friend, I'd get you out of those leathers to fix you up, but I'm afraid that more jostling will only make the bleeding worse, so in places I'll just slit them apart where they're already rent." The man neither opened his eyes nor replied, and Tipperton thought him unconscious. The buccan then began swathing the man's cuts as well as he could—slicing open sleeves and pant legs, and unlacing the front of the leather vest and the jerkin beneath, all to get at the wounds to bind them—though crimson seeped through the wrappings even as he moved from one bleeding gash to the next.

Now the man opened his eyes, eyes such a pale blue as to seem nearly white. He looked at Tipperton and then whispered, "Runner."

"Wh-what?"

"Horse."

"Oh." Tipperton shifted to the next wound, then said, "I'm sorry, but the horse is dead."

The man sighed and closed his ghostly eyes.

Quickly, Tipperton bandaged the last of the man's cuts and covered him with blankets. Then he threw off his nightshirt, now soaked with blood, and began flinging on clothes. "I've got to get you some help. A healer. There's one nearby."

As the buccan stomped his cut foot into the other boot and

then stood and drew on his cloak, the man opened his eyes once more and raised a hand and beckoned.

Tipperton crossed over and knelt down beside him.

Staring deep into Tipperton's jewellike sapphirine eyes, the man seemed to come to some conclusion, and he struggled to unbuckle his leather gorget. With Tipperton's help, he at last got the neck guard free, and from 'round his throat and over his head he lifted a token on a leather thong. "East," he whispered as he pressed the token—plain and dull grey, a coin with a hole in it—into the buccan's hand. "Go east . . . warn all . . . take this to Agron."

Tipperton frowned in confusion. "Agron? Who—? No, wait. You can explain later." He slipped the thong over his own head and tucked the coin down his shirt. "Right now I'm going after a healer."

"'Ware, Waldan," whispered the man, his pale eyes now closed. "There's more . . . out there."

Tipperton drew in a deep breath, then said, "I'll take my bow."

The man did not reply.

Tipperton stood up to his full three foot four inch height and momentarily looked down at the man. Then he snatched up his bow and quiver and blew out the lantern light—*Don't want a beacon calling to Rûcks*—and slipped out the door, closing it behind. He slid to the right and paused in the shadows, his gaze searching for foe. Finding none, he glided upslope across the clearing and in among the trees, the buccan shunning the two-track wagon lane, seeking instead the shelter of the forest alongside. Then he began running, his black hair streaming out behind, his feet flying over the snow, Tipperton Thistledown racing in virtual silence, as only a Warrow can run.

*T*hd! *Thd!*

"Beau! Beau! Wake up!"

Again came the hammering on the cottage door and a rattling of the latch—*Thd-thmp-clk-clttr!*—followed by another call: "Beau! Blast it!" *Thd-thd!*

In the chill dark, Beau Darby groaned awake.

Thd!

"Ho—" croaked Beau, then, "Hold it! Are you trying to wake the dead?" Striving to not touch the floor at all, the buccan—"Ow, oh"—gingerly tiptoed across the cold wood to the door.

Thd! "Bea—!" the caller started to yell just as Beau clacked back the bar and flung open the portal. An icy waft of air drifted in. "Oh, there you are, Beau. Get dressed; grab your satchel. There's trouble afoot. I've a wounded man at the mill."

In the starlight and moonlight, Beau saw his friend of nearly two years—the only other Warrow living nigh Twoforks—standing on the doorstone of the cote, his bow in hand. They were nearly of the same age, these two, Tipperton a young buccan of twenty-three, Beau at twenty-two, though often in Twoforks they were treated as children simply because of their size.

"What is it, Tip?"

"I said, I've a wounded man at my mill."

"Wounded?"

"Aye. Rûcks and Hlôks. He's bleeding badly."

"Bleeding?"

"Yes, yes. That's what I said, bucco, bleeding." Tipperton pushed past Beau and limped into the cottage and began searching for a lantern. "They killed his horse. Tried to kill him, too. One even came at me. But he slew them all. Right there at the mill. Seven, eight Rûcks and a Hlôk." Tipperton caught up a lantern and lit it.

In the soft yellow light Tipperton looked across at Beau, that Warrow yet standing dumbstruck, his mouth agape, as was the door.

"Well, come on, Beau. Time's wasting."

Beau closed his mouth as well as the door and sprang across the room even as he pulled off his nightshirt. "Rûcks and such? Here? In the Wilderland? Near Twoforks? Fighting at the mill?" He threw the garment on the rumpled bed and looked at Tipperton, his amber eyes wide with wonder. "What were they doing at the mill? And are you all right? I thought I saw you limping."

"Cut my foot on a piece of glass. My own fault. You can look at it when we've seen to the man. And as to what they were doing at the mill, I haven't the slightest idea. Happenstance, I would suppose."

Beau slipped into his breeks. "Why would Rûcks and such be after a man, I wonder?"

Tipperton shrugged. "Who knows? And mayhap it was the other way about: him after them, I mean. But I'll tell you this: no matter the which of it, they're all dead and he's not . . . at least I don't think so. He was alive when I left him, but bleeding. Oh yes, bleeding. He took a lot of cuts, what with that mob and all. I bandaged him the best I could."

Tipperton agitatedly paced the room as Beau pulled his jerkin over his shoulder-length brown hair and slipped his arms into the sleeves. "Don't worry, Tip. I'm sure that if you bandaged him, we can save him."

"But what if those Rûck blades were poisoned? I mean, I've heard that they slather some dark and deadly taint on their swords."

Beau pulled on his boots and stood and stamped his feet into them. "All the more reason to hurry." He slipped into his down jacket and snatched up his medical satchel and turned to his friend. "I'm ready. Let's go."

Tipperton took up his bow and said, "Quash the light and leave it behind. The man said that there were more Rûcks and such out there."

Beau's eyes widened, then he nodded and blew out the lantern. In the darkness Tipperton stepped to the door and peered out. "All clear," he hissed, and slipped outside and through the shadows and across the clearing and into the woods, this time with Beau on his heels. And beneath the wheeling stars and the waning quarter moon nearing its zenith, two Warrows moved swift and silent among the trees.

"Wait a moment," hissed Tipperton. "Something's not right."

They crouched in the woods and peered across the clearing at the enshadowed mill as moonlight and starlight faded in the predawn skies.

Beau took a deep breath and tried to calm himself, tried to slow his rapidly beating heart. "What is it? I don't see anything."

"I left the door closed. Now it's open."

"Oh, my."

Still they crouched in the gloom of the trees, and then Beau asked, "The man, could he have opened the door? Perhaps he left."

"Perhaps, though I don't think so. He was cut to a fare-thee-well and quite weak."

They watched long moments more, but saw no movement of any kind. At last Tipperton said, "If we delay any longer, then the man will most certainly bleed to death. You wait here, Beau. I'll see what's what. If I whistle, come running. If I yell, flee."

Before Beau could reply, Tipperton glided away, circling 'round to the left.

Time eked by.

The skies lightened.

At last Beau saw a shadow slip across the porch.

Within heartbeats, lantern light shone, and Tipperton reemerged from the mill and whistled low, then stepped back inside.

Beau snatched up his satchel and trotted across the clearing, past the dead horse and the slain Rûcks. As he came through the door and into the mill, Tipperton grimaced and gestured toward the man and said, "I'm afraid there's nothing you can do, Beau. His throat's been cut."

The man lay in a pool of blood, his dead eyes staring upward, his neck hacked nearly through. His leathers had been completely stripped from his body and strewn about, and his helm and boots and gorget were missing, and the chamber itself looked to have been ransacked—with an overturned table and ripped-apart bedding and drawers pulled out and their contents scattered on the floor. Beau moved past Tipperton and knelt by the man and then sighed and reached down and closed the man's eyes. "You're right, Tip. Nothing I or anyone less than Adon can do at this time. What do you think happened?"

Tipperton's jaw clenched. "The man said there were more Rûcks out and about. They came when he was helpless and slew him." Tip slammed a fist into an open palm. "Damn Rûcks!"

Beau nodded and, as if talking to himself, said, "Back in the Bosky, my Aunt Rose, bless her memory, claimed that each and every Rûck—in fact, everyone from Neddra—is born with something missing: a heart. She said they only thought of themselves. Called them 'Gyphon's get.' She thinks He deliberately created them that way—flawed, no compassion, empathy, or conscience whatsoever, seeking only to serve their own ends. This cutting of a helpless man's throat wouldn't have surprised her one bit." As if coming to himself, Beau's eyes widened, and he raised his gaze to Tipperton, then glanced toward the open door. "Oh, my, Tip, do you think any of them are still about? If so—"

Tip shook his head and raised a hand to stop Beau's words. "No, Beau"—he gestured outward—"there's a large track beating westward, across the river and toward the Dellins. The weapons of the slain Rûcks and such are missing, taken, I think, by the others. The man's sword and helm and gorget and boots are gone as well. And as far as I could tell without actually going out there to see, a haunch has been hacked off the horse; rumor has it that's what Rûcks like best: horseflesh. No, I think they're gone for good."

Beau blew out a breath of pent-up air, and his shoulders slumped as he relaxed. "You're right about the horse, Tip: a haunch *has* been hacked from the steed, and the saddle and saddlebags are hacked up as well. I didn't see a bedroll." Beau stood and peered 'round at the disarray and finally again at the man. "Why did they ransack your mill? And rip off his clothes? And tear up the saddle and bags? What were they searching for?"

Tipperton shook his head, but suddenly his gemlike eyes flew wide. He reached down into his shirt and pulled on the leather thong until the coin came dully to light. "Perhaps this."

"And just who is Agron?"

"I don't know, Beau. The man merely said, 'East, go east, and take this to Agron.' I would have questioned him, but I thought it more pressing to get aid."

"But east? Hoy, now, there's nothing to the east but Drearwood . . . and the Grimwall. Awful places. Deadly. Filled with Rûcks and such." Beau's amber eyes widened. "Say, now, likely where these Spawn came from."

"Nevertheless, Beau, that's what he said—east. Besides, I hear that there's Elves somewhere 'tween here and the Grimwall. Of course, beyond, there's all sorts of lands."

Beau cocked an eyebrow and looked at the token again. "Well, I don't see how this coin could be significant. I mean, huh, it seems to be made of common pewter and of little worth. It's completely lackluster . . . and without device of any kind—no design, no figure, no motif. It's even got a hole in it." Beau shook his head and handed the drab disk and thong back to Tipperton.

"Well, it meant something to the man. And it'll probably mean something to this Agron, whoever he or she may be." Tip peered about at the disorderliness and sighed. "Perhaps you are right, Beau, and the coin held no significance to the Rûcks and such. Perhaps the Spawn were simply searching for loot."

Beau shrugged, then looked at the corpse. "We need to put him to rest, Tip. A pyre, I should think, what with the ground being frozen and all."

Tip sighed and nodded and glanced out at the dawn skies. "We'll build one in the clearing. Burn the Rûcks and the Hlôk as well."

"What about the horse? Cut it up and burn it, too?"

Tipperton pursed his lips and shook his head. "No . . . I think we should leave it for the foxes and other such." Tipperton took up his bow and started for the door. "I'll get an axe and break up some deadwood; you get some billets from my woodpile and build the base for the pyre."

Beau uprighted the table and set his satchel on it, then followed after, finding Tipperton stopped just beyond the porch.

"What is it?" breathed Beau, glancing about for sign of foe but finding none.

Tipperton groaned and pointed northwestward through the gap in the trees where the river ran. "Beacontor. The balefire burns."

3

*B*eacontor?" Beau's gaze followed Tip's outstretched arm. In the far distance atop a high tor nearly thirty miles away glinted the red eye of fire. A signal fire. A balefire. A fire calling for the muster of any and all who could see it throughout the entire region.

Now it was Beau who groaned. "Oh, my. As I said, what with Drearwood just to the east, and beyond that the Grimwall, and these Rûcks and such sneaking 'round, I think those of us hereabout are in for some hard times. I mean, look at what happened right here at your mill—the fighting, the dead man, the slain Rûcks and the Hlôk."

Tipperton shook his head. "If Beacontor is lit up, Beau, it means more than just troubles us folk 'round Twoforks've got. Look, you could be right: it might be a skirmish against raiders or such—Rûcks and the like. But if the alarm came from elsewhere—downchain from the north, or up from the Dellin Downs, well then—"

"Oh, Tip—regardless of this, that, or the other, it spells woe."

Tipperton turned to his comrade. "Well, Beau, if the

warning *did* come from upchain or down, it'll signify war as well."

Beau's eyes flew wide. "War? With whom?"

Tip gestured about. "Mayhap with Rûcks and Hlôks and other such."

"No, no, Tip"—Beau shook his head—"I mean, if it's war, who's behind it? And what would they hope to gain?"

Tipperton turned up his hands. "As to who or what would be the cause . . ." Tip's words came to a halt, and he stood and gazed at the glimmer of the balefire. Finally he turned to Beau. "All I can say is that fire on Beacontor not only spells woe, but it might spell wide war as well."

The blood drained from Beau's face, and dread sprang into his amber eyes. "Oh, my. Wide war. I wouldn't like that at all—ghastly wounding and maiming, to say nothing of the killing."

"Nevertheless, Beau, that may be what's afoot, in which case it's your skills that will be needed more than mine."

Beau glanced at Tipperton's bow and arrows, then looked back through the door toward his own satchel, containing his healer's goods. "You may be right, Tip—about there being a war and all, what with Beacontor lit—but I pray to Adon that you're wrong."

Tip's gaze softened, and he threw an arm across his friend's shoulder. "It could be just a false alarm, Beau, and perhaps by the time we take care of the pyre and then get to the town square, someone will know."

Glumly, Beau nodded, then said, "Speaking of the pyre, mayhap the balefire has something to do with our dead man."

Tipperton looked 'round at the slain Rûcks. "Or with these Spawn," he added. Then he eyed the distant balefire and said, "Well, let's get cracking, Beau. The sooner we finish, the sooner we might know."

It took most of the morning to build two pyres—one for the man, the other for the Rûcks. When the wood was piled high, Tip and Beau stepped back into the mill and prepared the dead man, washing him clean of blood and combing his hair and dressing him as well as they could in his hacked leathers. Struggling, they bore the dead man out and laid him upon the pine bough bed Tip had placed atop the pyre. Acting upon what Beau thought was tradition, the Hlôk and one of the Rûcks were laid on the wood at the man's feet—"Where a Human hero's slain enemies belong, I think."

Tip shrugged but added, "I thought it was supposed to be the man's dog, but perhaps a Rûck or Hlôk will do."

They turned away from the man's pyre, and one after another they began taking the Rûcks up from the ground and laying them on the other heap of wood.

As they lifted the last of the Rûcks, Beau exclaimed, "I say, look at this." On the ground where the corpse had been was a crumple of dark cloth.

They lay the Rûck aside, and Beau squatted in the trampled snow and took up the fabric. "Huah! What do you make of this, Tip?" Beau held up a square of ebon cloth. Crimson on black, it held the sigil of a burning ring of fire.

"Looks like a standard to me," said Tip.

"Yar," replied Beau, turning it about. "But whose? I mean, did it belong to the man or the Spawn or someone else altogether."

Tipperton turned up his hands in perplexity. "Mayhap when we find what the balefire is all about, then we'll know."

Beau stuffed the banner inside his jerkin and stood, and they took up the Rûck once more.

At last all was ready, and Tipperton lit two torches and handed one to Beau. They moved to the pyre where lay the man, and Tip said, "Even though I didn't know him well enough to grieve, he *was* a hero, you know, a powerful fighter. He probably saved my life, for if he hadn't slain those Rûcks and such, they might have come sneaking upon the mill when I was asleep . . . and it'd be my pyre you'd be setting aflame."

A stricken look swept over Beau's face. "Well, I'm glad he was around then, though I'm sorry he's dead."

Tip drew in a deep breath and slowly let it out, then said, "Let's get on with it, Beau."

And he and Beau stood with their heads bowed as Beau said, "Adon, receive this unknown but worthy man unto your care." The two buccen then thrust their torches in here and there and set all alight. They watched for a while as the wood blazed up, and when the whole of the pyre was roaring, they set the other pyre alight as well, the grey smoke of the two to

twine up into the chill winter sky, while far off to the northwest, the smoke of the balefire atop Beacontor did likewise.

While Beau peered out the window, keeping an eye on the
fires, Tipperton set about straightening the chamber and
washing the floor clean of blood, pausing only long enough for
Beau to bandage the minor cut on his foot, and then returning
to his task. When all was set to rights, he began packing a
knapsack.

Beau looked at him and sighed. "As soon as you're ready,
and the pyres burn out, we'll go to my place and I'll pack, too.
After all, Beacontor calls."

Tip nodded abstractly, his mind elsewhere.

In that moment—"Ho, the mill!"—came a call.

Beau turned and looked out the window. "It's Mayor Prell,
Tip. And he's got men with him. They're armed."

Prell cupped his hands to his mouth and shouted, "Hoy,
miller . . . Tipperton Thistledown. Are you there?"

"He's here," called back Beau. "Me, too—Beau Darby."

Tip moved to the door and opened it and stepped out upon
the porch, Beau on his heels. Just inside the snowy woods at
the edge of the clearing stood several men, Humans, all
armed—with swords or cudgels or longbows with arrows
nocked—a smattering of armor here and there—plain iron
helms or boiled leather breastplates.

Prell, a beefy man, said something to one of the others and
then stepped forward, a shortsword now in his hand. "Are you
all right, miller?"

"Indeed," called back Tipperton, moving out into the
clearing, out into the grim smell of the fire with its cloying
odor of burning flesh.

Yet wary, Prell waited until Tip and Beau were well clear of
the mill. Then he signaled to the men, and bowstrings were
relaxed, though arrows remained nocked.

Prell gestured to the fires and eyed the dead horse. "We saw
the smoke. And what with the fire atop Beacontor and the
muster, we came to see if somewhat was amiss."

"Yes, indeed, Mayor, somewhat *is* amiss," replied Tipperton. "Last night, you see, there was a battle here at the mill,
and a man—I don't know just who he was—slew eight Rûcks

and a Hlôk. But he took terrible wounds, and so I ran and fetched Beau. But when we got back . . ."

"And before he died he gave you this coin?"

"Yes. To deliver eastward to someone named Agron. And, oh, yes, he said to warn all. Warn them of what, he didn't say."

Prell unbuckled his helm and scratched his head. "Agron. Sounds Elvish." He handed the coin and thong back to Tipperton, who slipped it back 'round his neck and tucked it 'neath his jerkin once more.

One of the townsmen shook his head. "More like a Dwarvish name, if you ask me, Mayor."

Prell frowned at the man. "Elvish, Dwarvish, or aught else"—the mayor's gaze swung to Tipperton—"I mean, it doesn't have to be a person, you know, but instead could be a town, citadel, temple, realm, river, whatever. . . ." Tip's eyes widened at this conjecture, and he nodded in agreement.

Now Prell's eyes widened. "Say, now, miller, are you sure he said Agron and not Argon? I mean, the Argon River is to the east, just beyond the Grimwall. And they sound a lot alike. He *was* wounded, as you say, and might have garbled—"

"No, Mayor. It was definitely Agron he said and *not* Argon. Besides, if it was a river, what would we do? Cast it into the waters?"

Mayor Prell pursed his lips and shook his head. "Perhaps you're right, lad." With a sweeping gesture he appealed to all. "Regardless, does anyone here know just who or what an Agron might be?"

The gathered men looked at one another and shook their heads, some murmuring, *Not me.*

The mayor sighed, then said to Tip, "Describe this dead man again."

"Well, sir, he was about your height or so—it's rather hard for me to say, Humans being as tall as they are—but he was more slender. Slender but well built. Somewhat younger, too, or so I would judge. He had pale blue eyes, pale as ice, and dark hair—almost black—and was dressed in dark brown leathers. And, oh, I just remembered, he had a V-shaped scar above his left eyebrow."

Again the mayor looked about at the men, but once more they all shrugged or shook their heads.

"A stranger, then, I would say," said Prell.

"Hoy, Mayor," called one of the men—Gwyth, the tanner. "This horse. Mayhap it's got a brand."

"A brand?" The mayor and his men crowded about, and both Tipperton and Beau had to struggle through. No brand was in evidence.

"It's more likely to be on the mounting side," said Gwyth. "Let's roll him over."

Grunting and straining, the men rolled the horse. And there on the steed's left haunch was burnt the symbol of a crown.

"Lumme," breathed Gwyth. "That's the brand of the High King."

4

*T*he High King?" blurted Tipperton, his face stricken. "You mean the dead man was the High King?" A chill wind swirled through the barren trees and across the clearing.

Prell shook his head. "Not likely, miller. Unlike your man, High King Blaine has bright red hair, like my boy Arth, or so I've heard it said."

"But the brand on the horse—"

"Ar, all the High King's horses have such a brand," said Gwyth. "Hundreds of them. More likely this was someone in his service, a Kingsman of some sort—herald, messenger, warrior, or aught else. Who's to know?"

Beau looked at Tip. "Mayhap a courier bearing a message."

Tip's hand strayed to his neck.

"Oh, by the bye, Mayor," said Beau, fishing inside his jerkin, "we found this." He took out the square of ebon cloth, holding it up so all could see the crimson sigil it bore.

Now the mayor took it. "Hmm. A ring of fire on black." He looked up at the men. "Does anyone know whose sign this is?"

Men shrugged and shuffled their feet and looked at one another . . . and none knew.

Prell glanced at the Warrows. "Was this the man's or did it belong to the Foul Folk?"

Now the buccen shrugged, and Beau said, "It was lying 'neath a dead Rûck, but it could have been the man's."

Prell looked about, then glanced in the direction of Beacontor beneath the gathering overcast. "Well, lads, we're not going to solve anything here, and we've got to get back to town and see how the muster goes. My boy Arth should be riding back from the tor before dark with word as to why the beacon burns and whether or no we're needed. If we are, I'd like to start out first thing in the morning." He turned and fixed Tipperton and then Beau with his gaze. "As for you two, the muster's underway, and every bow and blade will count, as well as every chirurgeon."

"But I'm not a chirurgeon, Mayor," said Beau. "Just a plain healer instead. Herbs and simples, powders and potions, nostrums and medicks and salves and poultices, needle and gut: that's my trade."

Prell tossed the black banner back to Beau, saying, "Nevertheless, lad, you and the miller, you'll both be needed. So come to the square in Twoforks, and wear your winter eiderdown—warm socks and boots, too—for we may spend many a frigid night on the land with no fires to warm us, and it wouldn't do to freeze in the dark." He then clapped his plain iron helmet back onto his head and fastened the chin strap. "Besides, maybe someone there'll know who this dead man was, or know of Agron, or know of this dark flag. Regardless, the lads and I'll get back to the village and see just what's what. And you two come as soon as the fire's burnt down"—he glanced about at the winter-dry woods—"can't leave it untended, you know."

"We shouldn't be too long, Mayor Prell," said Tipperton, gesturing at the dwindling blazes. "Midafternoon or so."

It was, however, late in the day under lowering skies ere the fires fell into coals and the coals themselves began to darken. Tipperton and Beau took turns shoveling snow upon the embers, the cinders hissing, steam rising into the air. And even as they did so, a new fall of snow began drifting down from the overcast above.

Tip had nailed a square of canvas over the broken window, and after a look about, he latched up the mill and patted the door and said, "Well, eld damman, it may be awhile before I get back. Take care."

Beau cocked his head. "You speak as if the mill were alive."

Tip smiled. "If you ever heard her talking, grumbling as she worked, you'd think so, too, what with her creaks and groans as she grinds her teeth on grain."

Beau laughed aloud and hefted his bag, while Tipperton shouldered his knapsack and took up his quiver and bow, and together they set off through the whiteness falling down.

After a brief stopover at Beau Darby's cottage, where that buccan packed a knapsack of his own and changed into his down winter clothes, they made their way toward the town square in Twoforks. Night had fallen and the snow continued to drift down, muting the winter sounds, the furtive sounds, of the surrounding woods—now a vole scrabbling beneath the leaves; now a hare kicking up and away; now the pad of a fox; now the call of a distant owl—all amid the faint tick of snowflakes striking sparse dry leaves yet clinging to the brittle branches. Through this not quite stillness the buccen walked without speaking, each lost in his own thoughts: Beau mentally ticking off items he had packed, making certain he'd brought everything he needed to answer the muster; Tip fretting over the slain man's request. Trudging in silence, at last they could see lights from Twoforks up the lane, and the muted quiet was broken by sounds of activity ahead. As they came into the fringes of the village, the whole town seemed alight and abustle, with folks scurrying to and fro on unknown errands, their lanterns blooming halos in the snowfall. Cottages and houses were lighted as well, and through windows the buccen could see men packing goods, while some women helped and others wept, and children capered or cried, depending on how the mood struck them.

Among this flurry of activity, Tip and Beau made their way inward, toward the commons, and men with weapons slung and knapsacks on their backs made their way inward as well.

An oldster standing in the street and stamping his feet to ward off the cold stepped out to bar the buccen's way, saying,

"Here, now, you two, no children allowed. This is the work for—"

"Beg pardon, Mr. Cobb," called Beau. "But it's me, Beau Darby, and Tip."

The oldster bent down and squinted through the snow and then reared back. "Bless me, but it is you, Mr. Darby. And miller Thistledown as well."

"Mr. Cobb, you shouldn't be out in the cold, what with your bad joints and all."

The oldster waved a hand toward Beacontor. "Well, Mr. Darby, everyone's got to help in times like these. 'Sides, that willow bark tea laced with chamomile is just the thing for my achy joints and twitchy legs, and for that I thank you, and I'll drink some later. But for now I'm just doing my duty, directing folks of the muster where to gather."

"Why, the town square is where we're headed."

"Oh, no, Mr. Darby. It's down to the stables and out of the storm, what with this snow and all."

Beau glanced at Tip, then said, "We thank you, Mr. Cobb. But mind you, now, be certain to take that tea when you get home—a double dose."

The old man bobbed his head and stepped aside, and Tip and Beau trudged on. They hadn't gone for more than a few steps when Tip turned about. "I say, Mr. Cobb, is the mayor at the stables as well?"

The oldster hitched 'round and waggled a finger. "No, no, Mr. Thistledown. Last I heard he was over to the Fox, holding a war council, I believe."

Tip raised a hand—"Thank you, Mr. Cobb"—then turned to Beau. "I want to see the mayor. It may be that he's gotten some information concerning the dead man, or perhaps Agron."

Beau nodded, and they set out for the Red Fox Inn, located on the northwest corner of the town square, diagonally across from and marginally larger than the Running Horse, the only other hostel in town.

Shortly they arrived and made their way past a pair of blowing horses tied to the hitching rail. As the buccen stepped to the porch and stomped the snow from their boots, "Hmph," said Beau, nodding toward the chuffing steeds, "looks like they've been atrot."

Tip started to reply, but in that moment there came a roar from within. He looked at Beau and raised an eyebrow, and Beau shook his head and turned up his hands. Cautiously, Tip opened the door, and a clamor of rage bellowed outward. Together the buccen entered in among a press of shouting men. Above the din they could hear the pounding of a hammer or some such upon wood, yet down among the legs and stamping feet, there was little they could see, and less yet that they could make out among the shouted epithets and cries of outrage. But slowly the uproar subsided, and as Tip and Beau wormed their way among the men and across the common room, they could hear someone calling for order.

Now the buccen reached the stairwell to the rooms above, and they clambered up to a place where they could see, men making way for them once they saw who they were.

Behind the bar Mayor Prell yet banged a bung mallet down upon the wood, and called over and again for order. Before him stood two men in riding gear, their cloaks yet laden with snow.

Beau turned to Tip. "Do you know either of them?"

"One is Willoby," hissed Tip. "A crofter from up near the Crossland. I mill his grain. The other, I think, is his eldest son, Harl."

As Beau nodded, a sudden quiet fell, and Prell, glaring about, finally laid the mallet aside. Then he turned to the crofter and his son. "How many?"

"Not counting the Rûcks, five altogether," replied the older man.

Again a cry of outrage erupted, which was quelled quickly by Prell pounding the mallet upon the bar.

"Wot 'r' they doin' this far west?" shouted someone from the crowd.

Prell hammered against the bar once more and glared the man into silence, then turned to the crofters.

"It looked like a running battle to me, Mayor," said Willoby. "First we found the one man dead among the killed Rûcks—"

Tip sucked in air and looked at Beau, that buccan's eyes, too, gone wide, but he said nothing as Willoby continued:

". . . and a mile or two later another deader, and on down the Wilder they went, dead Rûcks and such and men. Hacked. Their horses killed too.

"We broke off the search and cut for here when we came nigh, seeing as how we were riding to answer the muster. 'Sides, we were both thinking that this might mean something to Twoforks, these dead men."

"Especially with the fire on Beacontor," added Harl.

The mayor shook his head. "I don't think—"

"Oh," blurted Harl, "'nother thing, the brands, couple o' them was ridin' King's horses."

A collective gasp and murmur rippled through the gathering, and again Tip and Beau glanced at one another, while Mayor Prell pounded for order.

"Do you suppose—?" began Tip, but the room fell to quietness as Prell asked Willoby, "Are you certain? King Blaine's brand?"

"It was the crown, all right," averred the crofter, "them horses that was layin' where we could see."

As if by intuition, Prell's eye found Tipperton and Beau sitting on the steps behind the banister. The mayor sighed and returned his gaze to Willoby and the youth. "Then there were at least six of these men: another one was killed by Spawn out by the mill."

This brought another grumble from the crowd, a voice or two rising above the others:

"Hoy, Mayor, wot would Kingsmen be doin' out this way?" called someone.

"Mayhap it's all tied up with this Beacontor business," declared another.

Speculation rumbled through the gathering, various voices calling out opinions and possibilities, and Mayor Prell, a pensive frown on his face, let it run on awhile. At last he pounded the bar again for quiet.

"Is there aught you would add?" he asked Willoby and his son. They looked at one another and shrugged. "Well then, I suppose that's it for now."

Now Prell addressed the assembly entire. "Men, as to what's going on, for the moment it's all spookwater and vapors. When my boy Arth gets back with word from Beacontor, then perhaps we'll know what to do, where to go, and even what these Rûcks and such are doing out here in the Wilderland. Till then there's nought we can do except stay vigilant. Now what I want you all to do is go down to the stables and get some rest, all but the ones assigned to guard duty. If aught happens, someone will ring the fire gong, and then we'll form up in our squads and meet whatever challenge or peril awaits. Any questions?"

"Hoy, Mayor, shouldn't your boy be back anow?"

Prell's face fell grim. "Aye, Redge, unless he was—"

"Oy, mayhap he ran into trouble," declared Redge, a beefy man. "Rûcks or some such."

"Here, now," protested the small man next to Redge, sketching a warding sign in the air, "there's no cause to bring trouble down on the boy."

The mayor banged his makeshift gavel, then said, "Arth is a good lad. He can well take care of himself. I think perhaps the snow has held him up. He should be arriving any moment now."

Redge cast a skeptical eye but remained silent. Someone else, though, asked, "When he does come, you'll let us know what word he brings, right?"

Prell nodded. "Aye, that I will."

"And if no word comes from Beacontor, Mayor . . . ?"

"Well, Redge, if no word comes, we march to the tor on the morrow."

Prell looked about to see if there was aught any wanted to add, but the men waited in silence. "Dismissed!" barked the mayor at last.

Muttering, the men began filing out from the Red Fox, speculation yet running high as to the fire on Beacontor, the slain Kingsmen, and the Spawn being this far west from their normal haunts. Beau got up to go, but Tip reached out a staying hand. "Not yet, Beau," he said. "I need to speak to the mayor." Beau cocked an eyebrow but said nothing as he sat back down.

At last the place emptied out, but for the buccen and Mayor Prell and three members of the elder council—two thin oldsters, Trake and Gaman, and robust Tessa, hefty owner of the Fox.

The council members moved toward one of the round tables

as Tip and Beau came down from the stairs and crossed the common room. Prell placed a ribbon-bound scroll and four small stone weights on the board and seated himself, saying, "It's a grim business, these Kingsmen. We need to make certain that they're taken up and given a decent pyre." As the others nodded, the mayor espied the Warrows. "Ho, lads, you two had better go on down to the stable as well. If things are as serious as they seem, I'm thinking we'll be marching tomorrow to Beacontor."

Tip shook his head and glanced at Beau, then said, "No, Mayor, not me. I'm not going."

"Not going!" blurted Beau. "Wha—?"

Tip turned to his friend. "Look, Beau, when I heard about the other slain Kingsmen, I made up my mind."

"Made up your mind?"

"Yes," said Tip, and he tapped a finger to his collar. "Instead of answering the muster, I'm going east to deliver this coin."

5

*B*ut Tip," protested Beau, "didn't you hear what I said back at the mill? It's much too dangerous to travel east. Drearwood lies that way . . . and the Grimwall."

"Nevertheless, it's to the east and Agron I go."

Again Beau started to protest, but Tipperton held out a hand to stop the buccan's words, saying, "Hear me out, Beau: that man and his comrades, Kingsmen all, died fighting Rûcks and such—mayhap over this very coin—and who knows how important the mission he gave me is? Perhaps very."

"And perhaps not," replied Beau, now holding out his own hand to stop Tipperton's retort. "Hoy, wait a moment, bucco, it's your turn to hear me out:

"Even well-armed caravans have problems getting through Drearwood. But a lone Warrow . . . ? I mean, you've got to sleep sometime, and then what? Even if some fool went with you, and you took turns guarding and sleeping, still you're not likely to make it through. But if by chance you did get past the Drearwood, still there's the Grimwall, where Spawn abound. Moreover, those mountains are impassable in winter. Oh, no, Tip, instead of haring off into the jaws of peril with nought but a worthless pewter coin, recall, Beacontor burns, seeking aid, and things have to be dead serious for that to happen. Our duty lies there. We can't forgo the muster here in Twoforks and the march to that far hill."

Tip shook his head and held his hands wide in appeal. "Look, Beau, if six Kingsmen died trying to deliver this coin to Agron, then it must be something that desperately needs doing. It's not that I don't want to join the muster, but one more archer among many will mean little. But you, Beau, they'll need your healing skills. I think you'd best answer the call. As for me, though, I'm going east with the coin, and that's that."

"But the coin may not mean a thing at all, except to the dead man," objected Beau. "And besides, we don't even know who or what an Agron is. I mean, to what or whom are you going to deliver it?"

Tip turned to Mayor Prell. "Did anyone know aught of this Agron?"

"No, miller," replied Prell, glancing at Tessa and Trake and Gaman. "We all asked, and no one knows."

"Well, then," said Tip, "I'll just have to find someone in the east who *does* know."

Tessa looked toward Beau—"You have the right of it, wee one: traveling eastward is dangerous"—and then she turned to Tip—"Yet, as you say, Tipperton, this mission, it may desperately need doing. So why don't you each pull up a chair and we'll talk it over. And by the bye, could we see that coin?"

As Beau dragged two chairs to the table, Tip fished the thong out from under his jerkin and over his head and passed the token to Tessa. The buccen shed their cloaks and took seats, their feet dangling and swinging from the man-sized chairs, their chins just level with the tabletop. Tessa examined the disk, holding it close to her ruddy face. Finally she shrugged and passed the token to Gaman, who squinted at it awhile and then passed it on to Trake, who said, "Humph. Doesn't look all that important to me." Last to take the coin was Prell.

After a cursory glance, the mayor scratched his head, then said, "It may be that you are right, Trake"—Prell looked up at Beau and cleared his throat—"harrum, and you as well, lad—

the coin may not be important at all. But then again, the dead man and his slain comrades *were* riding High King's horses—perhaps on a task of import. In which case you might be right, too, miller, in that the token needs to be delivered. But as Gwyth said out to the mill, who's to know? Certainly not I." Prell returned the coin to Tip. As the buccan slipped the thong back over his head, the mayor said, "But as far as letting you miss the muster . . . well now, I've been thinking it over and I'm going to need runners in my Twoforks army—"

"Runners?" protested Beau. "But I'm a healer, and Tip's as good an archer as any and better than most."

"Well, as to that," said Prell, "I've got Garven and Finch to do any healing, and you and the miller here, well, you can serve me best as runners."

Beau shook his head violently, amber fire in his eyes. "Not me, mayor. I'm not going to be a runner. As I said, I'm a healer."

Prell's jaw jutted out and he blustered, "I'm ordering you as your commander—"

The door burst open and a tall youth came striding in, casting back his cloak hood to reveal flushed features below a shock of red hair.

"Arth!" cried Prell, leaping up from his chair and rushing to embrace the young man. Then he held him at arm's length. "Where've you been, lad? We were fiercely worried that something ill had befallen you."

Panting a bit, Arth pulled off his gloves, glancing at the council members and the two Warrows as he did so. "The horse went lame on the way back, Father, up near the Crossland Road. Rolled her foot on an icy rock. I had to walk her the rest of the way."

Tessa leapt up, her brown braid flying. "Here, boy, you be seated while I mull you a good mug of dark wine."

The young man nodded gratefully and shucked his cloak, then jerked a nearby chair to the table and sat alongside his sire.

"Well?" said Prell, raising an eyebrow.

"Wilderhill is taken and Beacontor destroyed, Father—"

"Destroyed!"

"The buildings, Father, all but three or four. The tower, itself—smashed to bits."

"Who—?" snapped Gaman.

"Rûcks and Hlôks did it. Yesternight and -day."

"Yester?" blurted Beau. "But the fire, the beacon, is it—?" While at the same time Trake demanded, "What do you mean, Wilderhill is—?" and Gaman shouted, "The damned Rûcks ought to be—"

Wham! sounded a gavel on wood, and heads jerked about. "Hush, everyone," called Tessa, bung mallet in hand. "Let the boy tell his tale."

"She's right, lad," said Prell, glancing at the others. "Go on. Tell us all. We'll hold our questions till you're done."

"No, no," called Tessa, now at the blazing hearth, pulling a glowing poker from the coals and flame, "not yet, Arth. You wait till I'm there."

Moments later, wreathed in spicy aroma, Tessa came to the table, bearing a trayful of mugs of mulled wine. Passing the mugs about, Tessa sat and took a cup for herself, then fixed Arth with an eye and said, "Now. Tell us."

Arth took a deep breath. "Two nights past, a band of Foul Folk crept upon Beacontor. There were only two watchmen at the time—a man and his nephew . . ."—Arth frowned in concentration—"yes, Jörn and Aulf, those were their names, Aulf a year or two younger than me—sixteen summers or so. They were alone, there on the hill, them and a single mule, waiting for others to come all the way from Stonehill.

"Regardless, in the night, in the hours before dawn, the Spawn came sneaking, a great lot of them, forty or so. But the nephew heard them coming and he and the uncle—a veteran, they say, of the Jillians—they got away unscathed.

"They made their way across to Northtor and to the top and watched to see what the Foul Folk were up to. And in the moonlight the Rûcks and such took sledgehammers and iron rods to the watchtower and began to break the walls. By midmorn they brought it crashing down. Then they started on the cotes, ripping off thatch and breaking those walls as well, though they set three aside for their barracks and these they spared." Arth turned to his sire. "That's all that's left, Father: three cotes and the stables, and the low ringwall all 'round."

Prell shook his head and glanced at the others, resignation and rue in his gaze. "Go on, son."

Arth paused to take a pull on his mulled wine, but none else at the table said aught. Setting his mug down, Arth continued:

"Jörn and Aulf then discovered that a beacon fire north was burning—not the next one at Wilderhill, but the one beyond that—the one on the Weiuncrest.

"They knew that none of us down here could see the muster call, and they knew that they needed somehow to recapture Beacontor and light the balefire—"

Beau's eyes flew wide. "Two against forty?" he blurted, then clapped his hand across his mouth.

Arth nodded. "Aye. Two against forty. They waited until nightfall and beyond, coming back to Beacontor and lying low until the wee hours. And then they slew the ones they found on watch, and crept into the cotes where the weary Rûcks and Hlôks now slept, and in the dark and in silence they began cutting throats, their hands held tight across mouths that might scream."

Shuddering, Tip looked at grimacing Beau as Arth paused for another drink of spiced wine, and no one spoke a word.

Again Arth set his mug down. "But before they were done with the slaughter, they were discovered by a sentry they had missed, and the few remaining Spawn came awake.

"The nephew was killed, as were the Spawn, but the man survived and lit the fire—a funeral pyre for Aulf, a balefire for us." Arth looked at his sire. "And, Father, war has come, and we're all to report to Stonehill, and then march to aid the High King."

"Oh, my," breathed Tessa.

"War?" barked Gaman. "With who? Who's behind this bloody mess?"

"They didn't say," replied Arth. "Foul Folk, I suppose. Oh, they *did* find a standard of red on black."

"Like this?" said Beau, fishing out the banner from 'neath his jerkin.

"Aye," said Arth, his eyes wide. "Where did you get it?"

"Took it from beneath a dead Rûck," replied Beau, passing the flag into Tessa's outstretched hands. As the elders and Arth examined the banner, Beau turned to Tip. "Well, I think this sets one problem to rights: I mean, given that they found one of these standards at Beacontor, I would think it wasn't the dead Kingsman's out at the mill but a device of the Spawn instead."

Tip nodded. "I don't suppose it belonged to those standing ward atop Beacontor—Jörn and Aulf. No, not likely."

As Arth examined the banner, he looked at his sire. "Whose sigil is it, Father?"

Prell shook his head. "I don't know, but surely we'll find out when we get to Stonehill."

"Stonehill!" exclaimed Trake, taking up the scroll and unbinding it and rolling it out and placing the stone weights at the four corners to hold it open. It was a map, and he measured distances using his thumb. "Why, that's a hundred miles or more to the west—thirty-five leagues at least. I don't like this one bit, this going off to fight in foreign parts. Going to Bea-contor is bad enough, but now all the way to Stonehill?"

Handing the flag back to Beau, Arth nodded, then added, "And then beyond."

"To wherever the High King—" began Prell, but Gaman broke in:

"Say, just how do you know we're to report to Stonehill?"

"Huah!" Tessa barked. "What do you mean *we*, Gaman? Like me and the rest of us ancients, you're not going to report anywhere. Your fighting days are long past, and neither you nor I nor Trake here nor anyone else of our age should get in the way and be a burden to those able to do the fighting."

Gaman bristled at her words, yet said nothing in return. But Trake held up a finger. "What you say is true, Tessa, yet Gaman's question nonetheless needs answering." The oldster turned to Arth. "Tell me, lad, just how do you know we, er, rather, the muster needs to march off to Stonehill?"

"Because, Mr. Trake, just after dawn a squad of men came to stand duty on Beacontor, and they carried the word."

"Just after dawn?" said Beau. "This morning, you mean?"

At Arth's nod, Beau's face fell. "Oh, my. If they'd just been a day or two sooner, they could have helped Jörn and his nephew, and perhaps Aulf would still be alive."

"Then again, perhaps not," said Prell. "I mean, had the others been there, likely they would have stood and fought. And a small squad against forty Spawn in open combat . . . well, who knows what might have happened."

Beau shrugged. "Who can say, since it didn't happen? Regardless, what now?"

Prell's eyes narrowed. "Tonight we rest, and tomorrow we'll set off for Stonehill."

Tipperton shook his head. "You are forgetting one thing, Mayor."

"Oh? And what's that?"

"At my mill the tracks of a large force of Foul Folk headed west over the Wilder and toward the Dellin Downs." Tip stood in his chair and pointed at the map. "If their tactics hold true, I suspect that they've gone to the hills to capture one of the beacon knolls to stop the signal from going on down into Harth and beyond."

"Adon, but you're right," gritted Prell, gazing at the chart. "And if they break the chain of balefires—"

"Then no one south will be warned—" interjected Tessa, stabbing her finger down to the parchment.

"And they'll be taken unawares if the fighting comes south," added Gaman.

Prell looked at Tipperton, surprise in his eye, for clearly he did not expect someone no bigger than a five- or six-year-old child to think of it. "You've put your finger on a problem, all right, yet I reck' we can do something about it." He turned to Arth and clapped him on the shoulder. "Well done, lad, well done. But even though you're tired, I've another task for you. The men are mustering at the stables. I want you to go there and tell them what you found out—they'll want to know. Then bid the squad leaders to come back to the Fox—we've some planning to do. Then go home and get a good meal and some rest, for tomorrow we march."

Arth grinned and said, "Yes sir," and stood and swigged the last of his wine. Snatching up his cloak, he nodded to the others and stepped to the door and out.

"What about the Spawn in the Dellins?" asked Beau, that Warrow also standing in his chair to see the map.

"That's why I've asked the squad leaders to come back to the Fox," replied Prell, "'cause if the miller is right and the Spawn have taken one of the beacon hills in the downs, well then, it's got to be taken back. And so"—his finger traced a route across the map—"I'm thinking we'll follow their track into the downs and deal with whatever we find, and make certain the signal gets through so that other musters take place. Then and only then will we press on to Stonehill."

"Not me," said Tip stubbornly, his eyes fixed on the map. "I'm heading east."

"Oh, my." Beau shook his head.

"Look, Beau, I intend to carry out the Kingsman's last wish and find this Agron—whoever or whatever he or she or it may be—and deliver the coin."

"But the muster—"

"Don't you see, Beau, there's more to it now than just the Twoforks muster? I mean, you heard it right here: war has started and the High King is calling for all to aid." Tip turned to Prell. "You said it yourself, Mayor: it's vital that the war signals get through, the warning sounded, and other musters take place, not only south along the Dellins but everywhere else as well—and that includes the east. And that's what the dead man told me: 'Go east, warn all.' I mean, if war has begun, then all must be set on alert."

As Prell frowned, Beau's face fell, and he said, "But, Tip, there's nothing to the east but peril."

"Not true, wee one," said Tessa. "To the east, somewhere beyond Arden Ford they say Elves live"—her forefinger stabbed the map—"somewhere here between Drearwood and the Grimwall."

Tip's eyes widened. "I say, that's right, Miss Tessa. And someone out at the mill said Agron does sound like an Elvish name. Perhaps that's who the coin is intended for."

Beau held up a hand. "But someone also said that to his ear Agron sounded Dwarvish, and I know of no Dwarves living to the east—"

"'Cept those they say what live beyond the Grimwall," interjected Gaman. "South, now, that's a different matter, what with the Black Hole and the Red Hills and all. Are you certain, Tipperton, the man who gave you the coin and told you to warn all said to go east?"

At Tip's confirming nod, Tessa said, "Regardless, even if half of what I hear of Elves is true—what with their knowledge and all—if you do reach them with the warning and tell them of the call to arms, they in turn should be able to tell you just who or what or where an Agron is as well as who flies a black banner bearing a ring of fire."

At her words, Prell seemed to come to a conclusion. He turned to Tipperton. "As you pointed out, miller, I said it myself: the warning must go through. And since none of the Kingsmen themselves survived to carry the tidings on eastward, it's a task someone else must take on. But just who should go in their stead—"

"Huah!" Tessa burst out. "Come, come, Prell, I can think of no one who can move as quietly, as stealthily as a Warrow; and so I ask you, who better to sneak past the foe?"

6

 neak?" Prell raised an eyebrow.

"Well, surely you don't expect to send a large force of arms, what with the muster needed at Stonehill and all these Spawn lurking about, to say nothing about needing to make certain that the signal makes it through the Dellins," replied Tessa.

"A small force skirting 'round Drearwood, I was thinking," said Prell smugly, "with my boy Arth in command."

"But a small force has already failed," said Tessa. "Six Kingsmen lie dead as proof."

At these words, Prell sucked in a deep breath, finally connecting the facts.

"Oh, no, Mayor," continued Tessa, "I think this mission calls for stealth, and who better than a Warrow?"

Gaman and Trake nodded in agreement, for it was common knowledge that Warrow feet were light on the land—lighter than Elves, said some.

"Especially if he's going through Drearwood," Trake added. All eyes turned to Tipperton.

"Say, now," declared Gaman, "couldn't you go east by

traveling south first? I mean, down to Rhone and across and up? Skirt Drearwood altogether?"

"Hmm," said Trake, again laying his thumb against the map to gauge distances. "By travelin' down and 'round, it'd be some three hundred miles altogether, while going straight through would be, uh, right at two hundred." He looked across at Tipperton. "What I would do in your place, Thistledown, is—"

In that moment the door opened and some eight or ten men trooped in. Prell gestured at a large table across the common room and called out, "Over by the big table, men. We've a deal of planning to do."

As the men assembled 'round the long table, the mayor stood and fixed Tipperton with his gaze. "Miller, you can do as you please. Choose as you will—to march with the muster to the west, or to go east as the Kingsman bade. If you choose the latter, take whatever you need. As for me, I've got some important planning to do." Prell then turned on his heel and went to join his squad leaders.

"Hmph," grunted Beau, cocking an eyebrow at Tipperton, "as if what you're preparing to do, Tip, is completely inconsequential. I take it we've all been dismissed."

Gaman snorted and shook his head. "Prell, he's busy being commander, and if he doesn't watch out, likely soon he'll be swelled up as big as a toad."

Tipperton giggled at the image, but Beau just glared at Prell.

"Well," said Trake, gesturing at the map, "back to business. Which way will it be, Tipperton: straight through Drearwood, or down and 'round and up?"

"Aye," said Gaman. "Short and direct or long and roundabout."

"Well," said Tipperton, eyeing the chart, "it seems to me that—"

"Boy!" came Prell's call. "You. Darby. Run that map over here."

Beau's mouth dropped open.

"That's an order, boy."

Beau did not move.

Exasperated, Prell stormed to the table, glaring at Beau, and reached down and snatched up the map. "I'll deal with you later," he growled and turned on his heel.

"Hoy," protested Beau, "we need that to lay out our route." But the mayor paid Beau no heed and bore the map away. Incensed, Beau started to hop down, but Tip grabbed him by the arm and stopped him and turned the buccan face to face and mouthed, [*Our* route?]

"Never mind about the map," said Tessa, standing, "I've another. Use it to direct my traveling guests as to how to get to where they're wanting to go."

As Tessa stepped toward the bar, Beau looked at Tipperton, fire in his eye. "That settles it, Tip. I'll not serve under him. Instead, I'm coming with you."

"Coming with—? But the muster—they'll need your healing skills."

"Look, Tip, he said it himself: Garven the barber is going with them, and he knows stitching as well as I do. And as to herblore, there's Finch. Between them they can deal with the healing." Beau glared across the room at Prell. "Make a runner out of me, would he? Well he can just go pee up a rope." Beau turned back to Tip. "Besides, he said take whatever you need, and you need me, for with the two of us, one can stand watch while the other sleeps and, of course, conversely."

Tip raised a hand. "But you said that even if some fool went with me, and we took turns guarding and sleeping, still we're not likely to make it through."

"Look, Tip, I truly believe that one alone can't make it through, and since two are needed, as Tessa would say—and it's true—who better to sneak past the foe than two stealthy Warrows? Besides, if I want to be the fool who goes with you, that's my decision to make . . . if you'll have me, that is."

"But the peril—"

"Hang the peril, Tip. I can't let you go alone and that's that."

Tip's eyes glistered as he gazed at his friend, and he reached out and touched the buccan's hand. "Well then, Beau, if it's someone I need to take with me, I could choose none better than you."

"Heh!" cackled Trake, slapping Gaman on the arm, "I don't know who it is the High King is fighting, who's behind all this mess with the Rûcks and such, but if them what aid High King

Blaine are like these two, well, the foe doesn't stand even half a chance."

In that moment Tessa returned with her map.

They pored over the chart and discussed alternatives, and in the end at Beau's behest Tipperton finally chose:

"All right. It's long and perhaps safer against short and perhaps swifter." Tip fell into thought, his gaze on the map. At last he said, "Given that war has begun and the Foul Folk are on the move, as we have said, they could be anywhere and so no route is known to be safe. Too, it seems imperative that we carry the warning eastward as swift as we can. And since going 'round Drearwood adds at least a hundred miles to our journey just to find the Elves, it means delaying the alarm by a sevenday or more. So I choose to go straight through Drearwood, the most direct and swiftest way, even though the peril may be greater."

Beau let out his pent-up breath and nodded in agreement, while Gaman sighed and said, "Although I reck' the other way safer, so be it, Thistledown. But remember, build no fires and travel only after the sun comes up and hole up before it goes down, for even in dark Drearwood, things tend to avoid the light of day . . . or so they say.

"But look here, you two come down to my stables and take three of my best ponies, one each to ride, and the third one to carry supplies. That should shorten the time you are in the wood and get the alarm to the Elves all the faster."

"Ponies?" exclaimed Beau. "But then we can't go in stealth."

"True," said Tessa. "But Gaman is right: you *will* go faster."

All eyes turned to Tipperton, the buccan frowning in thought. At last he looked up at Gaman. "All right, we'll ride in the day and hide quietly at night."

"Good," said Gaman. "Be at the stables first thing in the morning."

Trake looked across at the Warrows. "Stop by my store on your way. You'll need food and grain for the ponies, extra blankets, whatever."

"And I'll throw in some of my best brandy," said Tessa, laughing, "purely for medicinal purposes, you understand."

Gaman raised his voice to be heard above the hubbub of men. "These are three of my best."

"But we don't have saddles or aught else needed," called Tipperton back.

"And nought but a few coppers to pay you," added Beau.

"Wellanow, lads, if it's the High King's business you're setting out to do, then I shouldn't quibble about payment, should I?"

"I'll work out something when we get back," said Tipperton. "Till then you can hold my mill in trust."

"And my herb garden," added Beau. "There's moonwrad and willowfern and bear's mint and a whole host of other such. If I'm not back to harvest it when it comes due, then you do so, and sell it for a pretty penny, too. Sell all but the moonwrad. Instead, dry the root and keep it for me; I've a special use to put it to."

"Ah, now, lad, I wouldn't know how to do such."

"Mister Trake'll know, I should think," said Beau. "He keeps herbs and the ones he can sell will help pay you both back for the ponies and tack and all these supplies."

"And if you can find someone to run it, you can use my mill whenever there's a need to grind grain," added Tip.

"Well, if you insist," Gaman grudgingly agreed. "Now let's saddle up these two and load your goods on t'other."

As shouting men tramped out of the stables to assemble in the dawn light, Tip and Beau and Gaman slipped halters onto all three of the ponies, then while the buccen saddled the steeds, Gaman fitted a padded rack on the third horseling and cinched it in place.

Quiet fell within the mews, but for the fading tramp and talk of the men moving off to the town square.

Tessa appeared with two flagons of brandy. "Did you sleep well, Mr. Darby, and you as well, Mr. Thistledown?"

"Oh, yes, Miss Tessa," replied Beau, glancing at Tip, who nodded in agreement. "The beds at the Red Fox are soft and warm, though a bit overlarge for the likes of us."

"Well, now, seeing as how you two are the only ones of

your kind nearabout, I think you'll just have to put up with such until more of my clientele are Wee Ones like you."

She shoved a flagon down into one of the saddlebags on Beau's riding pony, then did the same to Tip's. As she did so, from the commons they could hear Prell's shout calling for order, and then the drone of his voice—unintelligible in the distance—followed by a cheer.

"Have a safe journey, my friends," said Tessa, leaning down and hugging each, "and I'll say my good-bye now, for I've got to see the men off."

From the commons there sounded another cheer.

Gaman, too, stepped from the stables, leaving Tip and Beau to lash their goods to the pack pony's rack. At last they were finished, and Tip looked at Beau. "Ready?"

Beau looked back at Tipperton. "Ready."

Together they mounted, and Tip took the pack pony's tether in hand, and they moved out from the stables into the wan morning light. Turning easterly, they rode down a byway till they came to a north-turning curve, where they parted from the path and made their way into the trees marking the edge of town, the ponies' hooves soft in the new-fallen snow. In among the stillness of winter-barren trees they rode, neither saying a word.

And from far behind there came the faint sound of proud cheering as the brave men of Twoforks set out.

7

All that day the Warrows rode easterly, quickly breaking out from the shallow forest bordering along the margins of the River Wilder and into the long open wold beyond. Into the rolling land of this wide reach they fared, gently angling toward the Crossland Road, a tradeway which would carry them through the Wilderness Hills and into Drearwood beyond. But at the heading they followed, they would not intercept that route for a full two days or so.

Through a bleak winter 'scape they rode, two ponies side by side, a pack pony trailing after. Now and again the buccen would stop to relieve themselves, or to give the ponies grain, or to break through the ice sheathing streams and let the steeds drink and to take on water of their own. At times the two walked to stretch their own legs and to gain relief from the saddle. But in the main they rode, though at a plodding pace. And as they rode or walked or rested, at times they talked, at other times they were content to go without speaking in the airy silence.

"Tell me something, Beau," said Tip, as they resumed riding after walking awhile. "You mentioned to Gaman that you had a special use for some herb called moonwrad. Just what is this moonwrad?"

Beau laughed. "You planning on becoming a healer, Tip?"

"Who, me? Not likely. A miller's life is good enough I say."

Beau grinned. "Like your sire and his sire, eh?"

"Yes, though I wish my da hadn't set up in Twoforks."

"You miss our kind?"

Tipperton nodded. "Aye, though I can't say I've ever been around many, other than you."

"Well, Tip, when we're through with all this Agron business, and as soon as I'm ready, I'll take you back to the Bosky with me. There's always need for millers there."

"Go with you to the Boskydells?"

Beau nodded vigorously. "I mean, you told me that your da had a mill on the River Bog, there where it flows under the Post Road bridge, south and west of Bogland Bottoms and that's where you were born, and that makes you practically a Boskydeller already. I mean, the River Bog feeds into the Spindle, and the Post Road bridge is no more than twenty miles outside the Spindlethorn Barrier—less than a full day's walk—though to actually enter the Seven Dells you'd have to go up to The Bridge and through . . . or go in down at Tine Ford."

"But if I moved to the Boskydells, that would mean selling the eld dammen."

Beau nodded. "Aye. Yet I'm sure you can get another one there, one that'll grumble and groan just as loudly."

"Well, now, sell the mill and move to the Seven Dells? Not that it hasn't crossed my mind a time or two—moving away, that is. But my da, well, he built that mill, and I rather hate parting with it."

"How did he come to settle in Twoforks, Tip? I mean, in the year and a half I've known you, you never said why he moved."

Tipperton shrugged. "You never asked, Beau. It was after my dam died, and my da, well, he couldn't abide living there without her, what with the memories and all. And the folks of Twoforks, well, they had no miller at the time, and so he came here—I mean to Twoforks—in answer to their pleadings."

"Well, be that as it may, I still think you should move to

the Bosky. I mean, that's where most of our kind live, and besides, it's prettier than 'round Twoforks. It's even prettier than the countryside 'round your da's old mill on the River Bog."

"I wouldn't know about that, Beau. You see, I was just a wee tad when we lived along the Bog. I don't really remember much of that land. . . . —Adon, Beau, I can just barely remember my dam."

Beau let out a long sigh and glumly said, "I don't even have that, Tip—memories of my dam, I mean. She and my own da died when I was but a babe. Aunt Rose, she was the one who raised me, there near Raffin in the Bosky."

Tip nodded, for Beau had told him of Aunt Rose.

They rode in silence for a moment, then Tip said, "I say, what about my question? What is this moonwrad?"

Beau perked up. "It's because of moonwrad that I came to Twoforks."

"Oh?"

"Yes. You see, it seems that it doesn't grow very many places—the headwaters of the River Wilder being one of them."

Tip cocked an eyebrow. "Can't you take some of the seeds and plant them elsewhere?"

Beau shook his head. "The plant doesn't thrive elsewhere. Something about the Wilder soil, or perhaps the water, I believe."

Tip shrugged. "Well, I don't even know what a moonwrad herb is."

"It's not an herb, Tip, but a root instead."

"Oh . . . And just what do you plan to do with this root?"

Beau turned in his saddle and fished into a saddlebag, finally pulling out a thin book bound in faded red leather. "This journal, Tip, it contains nearly all I know about healing—a book about herbs and simples and medicks and potions and philters and physicks and healing, all to cure the ill."

Beau handed the book to Tipperton, who idly thumbed through the pages. Slowly a look of bafflement spread across his face. "Why, I can't read this."

Beau laughed. "There's a simple Wizard's trick to it, Tip."

"Wizard?"

"Oh, yes. This is the book, you see, given to me by Delgar."

"Delgar?"

"Uh-huh, Delgar the Wizard."

"Wizard!" Tipperton shrank back, trying at one and the same time to get away from the slender volume and yet not drop it. "You never told me about a Wizard."

"Take care, Tip, it's quite precious. And it'll not bite you."

At arm's length, Tipperton held the book at one corner by two fingers. "Yes, but a Wizard's book, magic and all."

Beau reached out. "Oh, it's not magic, Tip."

"Nevertheless . . ." Tipperton gingerly handed the journal back to Beau.

Eagerly, Beau flipped through the pages, finally stopping when he found what he was after. "Here it is: silverroot: to be dried and ground into a fine powder and then infused into a tea and given to those afflicted with the plague. To be taken internally to reduce the buboes and applied externally to any pustules as well. Recommended dosage: unknown. Cures one in six or seven."

Beau looked across at Tip. "They died of the plague, you know, my sire and dam."

Tip nodded. "Yes, you told me. —But say now, that was about something called silverroot, Beau, and I thought we were talking about moonwrad."

"They're two different names for the same thing, Tip; moonwrad is silverroot, though it took me years to find out it was so."

"And it only grows along the River Wilder?"

Beau nodded, adding, "And rare places elsewhere as well."

"Well, if it only cures one case out of seven, it doesn't seem to be very effective to me."

"One out of seven is better than the alternative, Tip. Without it, only one out of a hundred survive."

"Oh," said Tip, then frowned. "Still, there ought to be something better."

"Exactly so, Tip. You see, I believe that by mixing moonwrad with gwynthyme, we can make a more successful medick to treat the plague."

"Gwynthyme?"

"A golden mint which neutralizes poisons as well as promoting health. I think it grows high in the mountains in the summer, up near the snow. Although I'm not certain, if the plague ever comes again—Adon forbid—I'll mix it half and half with silverroot and then we'll see."

"Well, bucco, it's all quite beyond me," said Tip. "Wizard's work for certain."

"Not according to Delgar. He says that anyone with a good head on their shoulders and a passion to help others can be a healer."

"Delgar—the Wizard who gave you the book." As Beau nodded, Tip asked, "When *was* this?"

Beau grinned. "It was back in my stripling days, back when I wanted to be a Wizard. Oh, I did all sorts of experiments— mixing various forms of the five elements—trying to change lead into gold, or to transform insects into something else, or to learn to fly. But nothing I tried worked, though I did learn a great deal about admixtures and immixtures and such. All that was back before I had ever even seen a Wizard. But then one day in Raffin, I met Delgar on his way to Rood for the Mid-Year Festival. I asked him to take me on as an apprentice; he looked hard at me in a peculiar sort of way, then shook his head and said I hadn't the <sight>. But then he asked me a lot of sharp questions—mainly about my alchemistry—and he seemed to know how my parents had died. Finally he gave me this book and suggested I apprentice to Elby Roh—I told you about him—over in Willowdell and become a healer instead. Anyway, when Delgar gave me the book, it was as if a light had dawned, and that's when I knew what my true calling would be."

Tip smiled ruefully at Beau. "You can keep your Wizards and their books. Me, I'll stick to grinding grain."

They rode onward in silence for a mile or so, but at last Tipperton turned to Beau and said, "You know, bucco, there's a great deal more to you than meets the casual eye."

They camped in a grove at sundown. "Out of sight should a band of Spawn come tramping by," said Tip.

"Out of the bluster as well," said Beau, glancing up at the overhead branches rattling in the late-day wind. "I do wish we could build a fire and have a spot of tea."

Tip shook his head. "Gaman's advice was sound, I think: travel between dawn and dusk, and set no fires."

"In spite of him swelling up like a toad, so was Prell's," said Beau, "to wear eiderdown and warm socks and boots. I mean, with no fires it's like to be right chill in the night."

Tip smiled grimly. "In the day too, Beau, in the day too, especially should the wind kick up."

Beau sighed and finished currying the tangles out of the ponies' thick winter shag. As he cast the combs back into his saddlebags he asked, "How far do you gauge we've come?"

"Twenty-five miles, I would judge," said Tip as he set out the jerky and biscuits of crue. Then he fished into his own saddlebags and drew out the copy made of Tessa's map. After a moment of study, he said, "Tomorrow should see us to the Crossland at the edge of the Wilderness Hills, and two days after we should come to the Stone-arches Bridge over the River Caire."

Beau took a deep breath and slowly let it out and said, "And the day after that should find us in Drearwood."

In the dying light Tip looked across at his comrade and somberly nodded, while chill wind keened through brittle branches above to make them clatter like bones.

8

*T*he thin crescent of the moon had barely risen when faint light in the east heralded the glimmerings of frigid dawn. Beau, on final watch, awakened Tipperton, then turned to the ponies and fed them some grain. After the two buccen took a cold meal for themselves, they broke camp and saddled up and laded the pack pony and set out easterly once more. As they had done the day before, they rode and walked and now and again stopped to rest or to relieve themselves or to give the steeds a drink. And in late afternoon they espied a low range of hills standing across the way and stretching out beyond seeing to north and south.

"The Wilderness Hills," said Tipperton.

Beau grunted, but otherwise did not reply . . . and the ponies plodded on.

As the sun neared the western horizon they intercepted the Crossland Road curving down from the northwest and swinging back east and lying beneath a blanket of snow, the route hard-packed from centuries of slow-moving caravans and frozen in the wintertime cold. As it arced back easterly, the tradeway led them in among the snow-laden hills, the slopes barren and bleak but for a lone tree now and again, or an occasional small thicket of low-growing copse holding a handful of scattered thin trees.

Beau sighed and looked about at the desolate 'scape. "Why d'y' suppose they ever put a road this way, Tip? It seems a bad route to take, with Drearwood ahead and the Grimwall beyond. . . ."

"I suppose it's the shortest way to the other side of the mountains," said Tipperton. "I mean, you've seen the map. A trader would have to go far south to find another pass like Crestan."

"Yes, but with Drearwood along the way—"

"That's why they go well armed, Beau, and in a great cavalcade."

Glumly, Beau nodded, and they rode ahead without speaking. But at last Tip said, "I seem to recall that in the past there were several attempts to establish a fort at the far edge of these hills—a garrison of soldiers to escort wayfarers through—but each time they tried, the fort was burnt down . . . or torn to flinders."

Beau's eyes flew wide. "Torn to flinders? By what?"

Tip shrugged. "Who knows? Certainly not I."

"Weren't there survivors?"

Tipperton turned up his hands.

Beau shuddered and his gaze swept across the surround, as if expecting to find a massive unstoppable monster bearing down upon them.

Misunderstanding Beau's peering about, "Good idea," said Tip, glancing at the sinking sun. "We do need to find a place to stop."

Around the next bend they came to a draw with an ice-covered stream running through. As the sun sank into the horizon, they made their way well off the road and down into the shadows of the sparsely wooded gully, where they set a cold fireless camp.

"While standing a turn 'neath the stars last night, I was thinking," said Tipperton, as easterly they rode once again, the noon sun diamond bright but shedding little warmth.

"Oh? About what?"

"Well, Beau, every night we've camped, we've done nothing about our tracks. I mean, should another band of Spawn come this way, they could simply follow the hoofprints to find a couple more victims for their slaughtering blades."

Beau's features paled.

"I mean, it's not like we're mighty warriors or such," added Tipperton, "like the man who gave me the coin. The band who attacked him he laid by the heels, but we'd be short work for such. I think on this night and the ones thereafter we'd better erase our trail from the snow, at least for a way. A pine branch broom ought to do the deed."

Beau glanced about. Not a pine tree was in sight.

In late afternoon of the following day, beneath leaden grey skies they emerged from the bleak hills to see the road descending before them; down and across a short flat it ran and to the River Caire, the ice-clad waterway curving out of the north and disappearing in the south. A snow-laden stone bridge spanned from bank to bank, and the road rose up and out from the river valley beyond, where it entered a dismal tangle of forest, stark barren limbs clawing at the sky.

Reining to a halt, "There it is," said Tipperton. "Drearwood, straight ahead."

"Lor', but they named it right, they did," said Beau, taking a deep breath. "Dark, depressing, dismal . . . dreadful."

"And deadly," added Tipperton, glancing at Beau, "if what we've been told is true."

Beau swallowed. "How far to the other side?"

Tipperton twisted about in his saddle and fished out the map. "Hmm. Some eighty miles or so."

"Adon, but that's three or four days."

"If we push the ponies, perhaps we can make it in two."

Beau shook his head. "The best we've done so far is twenty-five."

"Even so," said Tip, "we've gone rather slow, and might be able to make forty."

Beau cocked a skeptical eyebrow. "It's not like we're riders from Jord, bucco, fiery steeds and all. I mean, these are just plain ponies."

"Time will tell, Beau. Time will tell," said Tipperton. "But for now, I suggest we go back into the hills and find a place to camp, and start our run through Drearwood on the morrow."

"I'll see if I can find a pine," said Beau, "and take care of our tracks."

As Tip awakened Beau for his next turn at ward, he hissed, "You'll have to use your ears, bucco, for there's no light whatsoever."

Beau sat up and peered about in the blackness, wondering how Tip had managed to find where he was bedded. Beau yawned, then looked overhead. "Not even a glimmer," he muttered.

"The overcast, Beau, it's blocking the stars," responded Tip, crawling into his own bedding. "And tonight is the full dark of the moon."

As Beau fumbled his way toward the boulder where he would take station, he found his heart racing with apprehension. *I can't see a bloody thing, for there isn't any starlight and tonight indeed is the full dark of the moon. . . . Oh, my, the full dark of the moon. Oh, I do hope that's not an omen of things to come.*

As dawn broke to a dismal day, an overcast yet covering all, Tipperton, on the last watch and weary, his eyes gritty and raw, stood and stretched. His entire being seemed at low ebb, and he knew that Beau would feel the same; neither buccan had rested well, but instead, turn in turn—three turns each— had slept in fits and starts throughout the long, frigid night. Regretting that he had to do so, Tip stepped over to awaken Beau. "Come on, bucco, it's time to go."

Groaning, Beau levered himself upward.

"You get the jerky and crue, Beau. I'll tend the ponies."

"Jerky and crue," moaned Beau. "Four straight days of jerky and crue, with who knows how many more days to come. Is anything else as tasteless as a crue biscuit? And jerky is called jerky 'cause it's so accursed tough that it'll jerk your teeth out by the roots just trying to gnaw off a simple bite."

Tipperton burst out in laughter, and Beau glared up at him through red-rimmed eyes . . . then burst out laughing himself. "Lor', Tip, you look like I feel—I mean, your eyes are ready to bleed to death. If I didn't know better I'd say we've both been dragged by the ankles through Hèl."

Again they both burst out in laughter.

Humor restored in spite of their weariness, the buccen watered and fed the ponies and took a meal themselves. As they ate, Tip said, "Shortly we'll be entering Drearwood, Beau, so keep your weapons at hand. We never know when we might need to make a fight of it."

"Weapons? I didn't bring any weapons, Tip. I'm a healer, not a fighter."

Tip's jaw dropped open. "No weapons! Lor', Beau, you thought I was mad for setting out on this venture, but here you are about to enter Drearwood itself and now you tell me you have no weapons?"

Beau turned up his hands and shrugged.

Tipperton blew out a puff of air. "Not even a dagger?"

Beau shook his head. "No, though I *do* have some knives."

"Knives?"

"The ones in my healer's satchel for lancing boils and the like, and of course the one I carry for eating and whittling and skinning game and such."

"Listen, do you know how to use *any* weapons? A bow, a stave, a sling, a long knife, a—"

"Say, I *did* use a sling when I was a stripling, though that was some years back."

"Well, bucco," said Tip, "you step down to the stream and gather up some slingstones while I fashion you a proper strap."

As Beau rummaged about in the streambed, kicking aside snow and breaking through ice and gathering suitable stones, Tipperton unthreaded a leather thong from one of the ties of a saddle cantle, then cut a swatch from the leather flap. Carefully trimming the swatch and piercing it at each end, he cut the thong into two straps and fastened one in each of the swatch holes. Then he tied a loop in one end of one of the straps, a loop sized to fit snugly over the thumb. "There, now," he muttered, "a proper sling for Beau."

Stepping down to the streambed, Tip handed the casting strap to Beau. "Here, bucco, while I saddle the ponies and break camp, you practice hurling stones."

"But, Tip, I had a time gathering these, and now you want me to fling them away?"

Tip threw up his hands and burst out laughing, and Beau grinned and took the sling.

As Tip strode back to the camp, behind him Beau set a stone in the looped strap and sighted on a tree trunk and whirled the sling 'round and let fly. The stone flew practically straight up. Beau watched it arc up and stepped hindwards out of the way as it came down to land in the creek.

"Huah!" grunted Beau, setting another stone into the sling pocket. "It's been awhile." Once again he sighted on the tree trunk and whirled the sling around. The rock hurtled upward at an angle to clatter through branches as it headed somewhere far beyond.

The third one smacked straight into the ground a handful of steps ahead. "At least they have all gone forward," muttered Beau, loading another rock.

Upslope, Tipperton shook his head in disbelief as he saddled the second pony.

"Don't worry, Beau," said Tipperton as they rode up out of the wooded draw and back toward the road, the pack pony trailing behind and laded with their goods, including the pine boughs Beau had cut for brooms, "you'll get the hang of it yet."

"Wull, I threw most of my rocks away and only managed to hit the tree trunk once. If it'd been a Rûck I'd've killed 'im dead had he been about eight feet tall." Beau grinned ruefully as Tip laughed aloud.

Smiling, they made their way up onto the Crossland Road and turned easterly, and then their smiles vanished, for in the near distance ahead they could see the dark tangle of Drearwood lying before them. Each taking a deep breath, they glanced at one another, and then down the slope they rode and across a flat to come the verge of the Stone-arches Bridge. Tipperton held up a hand and reined to a halt, Beau stopping beside him. Turning to Beau, Tip said, "Listen, bucco, I've been thinking it over, and you needn't go with me any farther. I mean, we've been fortunate so far, and I think—"

"Oh, Tip," broke in Beau, "shut your gob." And with that, Beau spurred his pony forward onto the span.

Shaking his head ruefully, Tipperton prodded his own steed and followed Beau onto the snow-covered stone pave of the bridge.

Above the frozen River Caire they rode, to come into the land of Rhone, the wedge-shaped realm known as the Plow, bounded on one side by the River Caire and on the other by the River Tumble, the rivers to ultimately join one another in the south to form the point of the plow, the land extending all the way north to the spine of the Rigga Mountains.

The road rose up again out of the river valley to strike straight through the grim heart of Drearwood, the bane of this region most dire. Hearthtales abounded of lone travelers or small bands who had passed into the sinister tangle never to be seen again; stories came of large caravans and groups of armed warriors who had beaten off grim monsters half seen in the night, and it was said that many had lost their lives to the ghastly creatures. This land had been shunned by all except those who had no choice but to cross it, or by those adventurers who sought fame, most of whom did not live to grasp their glory. Fell were the beast said to live herein, and fell, too, were the Foul Folk who reveled in its environs. And into this baleful place rode two paltry Warrows, following a road that would not set them free of its dread for eighty perilous miles.

Both Tip and Beau felt their hearts hammering with foreboding at the thought of entering this dread wood, for herein were said to live nightmares. Yet they had no choice and on they went, into the grim woods, and the wan winter light fell dull among the dark and grasping branches.

All about them clustered dim enshadowed woods, blackness mustering in ebon pools within. Stunted undergrowth clutched desperately at the frozen rocky ground, and barren trees twisted upward out of gloom-cast snow to grasp at the leaden sky, the jagged branches seeming ready to seize whatever came within reach.

Beau looked deep into the entangled dark galleries and hissed, "Lor', Tip, if ever anything held a black heart, this is it."

Tipperton nodded grimly, and urged his pony ahead.

Throughout the dismal day they rode, and at times walked, ever following the eastward trek, riding at a goodly pace or striding at a swift clip, for they did not wish to spend a moment more than necessary in these woeful woods.

They had not come to the central region when the unseen sun began to set, drawing gloom behind. Reluctantly they headed away from the road and in among the dark gnarl to find a place to camp. Neither one wanted to spend even a single night in this dreadful place, yet heeding Gaman's advice to travel only during the daylight hours, they searched for an out-of-the-way site. At last they came to a small clearing, and while Beau took the pine boughs they had saved and walked back to the road to sweep away the signs of their passage within, Tipperton tethered the ponies and unladed them and then fed them some grain.

That night during Tip's first watch, the slightest sound caused him to jerk up and peer this way and that for sign of danger, yet without starlight he could see nothing whatsoever. Even so, he listened on high alert. Whatever made these slight sounds—voles, a waft of air ticking branch upon branch, one of the ponies shifting, or something else altogether—he could not determine its cause. And he had visions of something unseen creeping upon them. But in spite of his foreboding, when it came his turn to sleep, exhausted as he was he immediately fell into a deep, dreamless slumber. Yet it seemed to Tip that he had no more than put his head down ere Beau was shaking him by the shoulder.

"Tip. Tip," hissed Beau. "Wake up. Something. A light. A sound."

Tipperton scrambled up. "Where?" he whispered, his heart pounding.

"East. In the east."

Tip faced eastward, and in the far distance, flickering among the dark trees, he saw a pinpoint of light . . . and then another mote, and another, and another, as more and more lights appeared afar. And there sounded a faint beat, muted by distance.

Tip sucked air in between his teeth, and he started to say, "What do you think—?" when there sounded a faraway blat echoing among the trees.

"Lor'," hissed Beau, "that was a horn."

With his heart in his throat, Tip fumbled about on the

ground and located his bow and arrows. Swiftly he strung the weapon, and slipped the harness of the quiver over his head and shoulder. "Get your sling, Beau. We may need it."

"I've already got it in hand, but whether or no I can hit anything in the dark, well . . ."

"Maybe it'll be eight feet tall."

Light after light continued to appear, and they seemed to be drawing closer.

"I think they're torches," hissed Beau.

"On the road," added Tip. "Torchlight coming along the road."

"Do you think whatever, whoever, they are, they're searching for intruders? Searching perhaps for us?"

"I don't know."

Behind them a pony shifted uneasily.

"Oh, Lor'," hissed Beau. "The ponies. We have to keep them quiet."

Using their scarves and a bandage from Beau's medical kit, quickly the buccen improvised blindfolds and covered the horselings' eyes.

There sounded another blat of a bugle, and still the beat pounded, as of a muffled drum.

More torches appeared—an endless stream, it seemed.

Tip and Beau held the ponies and murmured soothingly.

Yet the flaring brands drew closer, and now the buccen could hear faint chirpings, as of axles turning. And the drum grew louder, its beat augmented by the crack of whips.

Onward came the torches and drum and whips and horn and squealing axles, and mingled among it all, now the buccen heard voices, rasping and guttural, shouts and commands in a language neither knew. And the ground shook with the tramp of feet.

"Are we far enough off the road?" whispered Beau.

"If we're not," murmured Tip, "it's entirely too late to move."

Now the marchers drew abreast and could be seen through a gap in the trees.

"Adon," breathed Tip, "it's an army, a horde of Spawn, moving west along the road."

"But that's toward Twoforks, Beacontor, Stonehill— Oh, Lor', toward the Bosky, too. Oh, Tip, where are they going?"

"I don't know, Beau," gritted Tipperton. "Perhaps to one of the places you named, though they could just as well turn north and head for Challerain Keep in Rian, or south into Rell and beyond. But no matter where they're headed, there's nothing we can do about it now. Nothing whatsoever."

With hearts hammering, through the gnarl of trees Tip and Beau watched helplessly as Rûcks bearing torches tramped along the road, Hlôks lashing whips at any who strayed, driving them back into line. The muffled drum beat steadily, meting out the pace, and now and again a Rûcken bugle signaled a command, but what it might be, the buccen could not say.

Wagons hove into view—

"Adon!" gasped Tip, for the wains were drawn by huge, shambling creatures, ten feet tall and more. Like giant Rûcks they seemed, but no Rûcks were these.

"What *are* they?" sissed Beau.

"Ogrus, I think," replied Tip. "I've never seen one before, but what else can they be?"

Indeed they were Ogrus, called Trolls by some, but Ogrus nevertheless. And they drew the heavy wains down the road, axles chirping and screeching as the heavy wooden wheels turned 'round.

And then hèlish steeds passed by, bearing pallid riders the size of men, corpselike yet alive and wielding jagged spears. The steeds themselves resembled horses, but they were hairless and scaled, with long snakelike tails.

Now a foul odor drifted faint through the air, and it was all the Warrows could do to keep the ponies from squealing out and bolting, the stamp of their hooves unheard above the sounds of the passing Swarm.

And still the Horde marched past, feet tramping, drums thudding, bugle blats echoing now and again, armor jingling, hooves clopping, axles screeching, whips lashing, guttural commands barking out, and torchlight eerily casting flickering light among the dreadful recesses of dark Drearwood.

And the line now stretched beyond seeing to east and west.

Tip and Beau held onto the ponies and whispered soothing

words as the nighttide passed through its depths and began the long climb toward morning . . . and the end of the Horde was not in sight as more and more Spawn tramped past.

Yet, at last, just ere the sky began to lighten with the coming dawn, the last of the Swarm passed and the light of the torches and tramp of feet and squeal of axles and whipcracks and shouts and the beat of drums faded into the west until they could be seen and heard no more.

The Horde had gone at last.

And dawn came.

Exhausted from their all-night vigil, the Warrows groaned as dismal day broke upon Drearwood.

"We must go on," said Tip, "for I will not spend one moment longer than absolutely necessary in these dreadful woods."

"But, Tip, isn't there something we can do to warn the folks of Twoforks, Stonehill, elsewhere as well?"

"What would you suggest, Beau?"

"I don't know. —Something."

Tip shook his head. "I don't think so, Beau. I mean, we're on the wrong side of the Horde, and besides, there's our own mission we've got to complete. Look, we can't be everywhere, protect everyone at once. We can only pray that the pickets will see them coming and give due warning."

Grimly, Beau nodded, then stooped to pick up a saddle blanket to begin to ready the ponies. "How many Foul Folk do you think we saw tonight?"

"Thousands," replied Tip. "Thousands. . . ."

On they went, through the dismal woods, and the wan daylight fell dim among the clutching branches. Hours they rode, and at times walked even though they were weary beyond measure, ever following the eastward trek. The Crossland Road itself had been churned to muck by thousands of tramping feet and turning wheels and the cloven hoofs of steeds, and through this mire went the Warrows slowly, going the opposite way.

At last in late afternoon they came to a point where the Horde had entered the road—from the north they had come through the Drearwood, to turn west upon the way, and they left behind a wide track through the barren forest dire.

The Warrows did not follow this track northward into the woods, but continued on easterly along the Crossland Road.

Now they were back on frozen ground, frigid and hard and swift, though the exhausted buccen could pick up the pace but a bit.

Tip eyed the dismal sky. "As much as I hate to say it, Beau, it looks as if we'll have to spend another night in this tangle."

Beau groaned but made no reply, and on through the darkling woods they rode. Another mile passed 'neath the hooves of the ponies, and then the Warrows dismounted to give the ponies respite, leading them behind as they walked. As they trudged along the road, of a sudden Beau brightened. "Say, Tip, what with the Horde marching off behind us, don't you think that all the Rûcks and such are gone from hereabout? I mean, perhaps we can make a fire tonight, have some good hot tea— it'd be just the thing."

Tip shook his head. "I don't think so, Beau. Just as some good strong men were left behind to ward Twoforks, the Foul Folk will have left some Rûcks and such to guard these woods. No, I'm afraid we'll have to pitch a cold camp and do without any tea."

Beau groaned with disappointment, and after a moment said, "You know, Tip, in spite of my eiderdown, I think I'm growing colder with every passing day."

Tip nodded in agreement. "Me too, Beau. Me too. If we don't have a fire soon, well . . . —But we should be out of this dreadful place by tomorrow, and then we can have a fire, I would think."

Beau sighed and gestured at the frigid ground, saying, "I don't think people were made to spend their days traipsing endlessly cross-country and their nights sleeping in the dark on frozen ground. I mean, give me a good garden to putter in and a cozy hearth to sit by and warm bed to sleep in. And hot meals. Oh, yes, hot meals."

Tip grunted a noncommittal response but otherwise remained silent, and on they trudged.

After a while, as the sky grew darker, Tip said, "All right, Beau, let's begin looking for a place to camp."

Even as they peered off into the tangle, searching for a suitable site, a wind began blowing up from the south, the air slightly warmer than that in the surround. "Good," said Beau, licking a finger and holding it up in the breeze then glancing at the sky. "It seems that better things are due."

But as he said it, a chill rain began to fall, and wherever the water touched frigid trees or cold undergrowth, bitter rocks or frozen ground, it began to freeze.

"Oh, Lor'," groaned Tip, exhausted. "Just what we don't need—an ice storm."

9

The freezing rain fell throughout the nighttide, and Tip and Beau sat huddled and miserable beneath their oiled cloaks. The ponies, too, were distressed, for the only protection the Warrows could afford them was the buccen's own bedding: two ground tarpaulins—one on each of the riding ponies—and the Warrows' own blankets—spread over the little pack steed. They had all taken shelter beneath a gnarled black willow, but the barren branches offered scant relief from the falling rain, and down it came to freeze upon striking, and the Warrows could hear the breaking of branches near and far as overladen limbs crashed to the ground, and now and again there sounded a heavy rending and a massive thud as overburdened trees toppled down—all unseen in the utter darkness of the nighttime woods.

"Lor'," sissed Beau, shuddering with cold and leaning against Tip, "I do hope this willow doesn't crash down 'round our heads. —Or, wait, perhaps I wish it did. At least that would end our misery."

Some time after mid of night the rain ceased, but still limbs snapped and fell, and still an occasional tree shattered down in the blackness.

Shivering and shuddering and hugging one another for warmth, the Warrows attempted to take turns sleeping, but neither could even drowse, as wretched as they were.

Sometime ere dawn, the clouds began to break, and here and there stars glimmered through. And as the light of morning finally came, ice set the baleful forest aglitter with reflected sunlight, as of a world coated in brittle glass—bent branches and bowed limbs and glazed trunks straining against the weight of the sparkling layers, the tangle of undergrowth crammed under a crushing load, the rocks, the ground, the very land clad with treacherous, glittering armor.

Benumbed with exhaustion, Tip and Beau looked through gritty eyes out upon this ice-sheathed world and groaned.

"Tip, we can't go out on that. The ponies will break a leg."

"We've no choice, bucco, no choice at all, for we can't stay here."

Grunting, with aching joints they stood, ice crackling on their cloaks, shards tinkling to the layered ground. Then slipping and sliding and now and then falling to a knee, they readied the steeds for travel.

"We'll have to walk them," said Tip. "Else, if they tumble and take us down with them, it's not only their legs which might break but ours as well. —By the bye, you do know how to splint bones, don't you? I mean, you're liable to have to do so, given the plight of the land."

Beau groaned. "I've handled a bone or two in my time, Tip, but I'd rather not have to set one in these conditions, so take care. Small steps work best on ice."

"Tell that to the ponies," growled Tip.

Soon the steeds were ready, and Tip, glancing about, said, "Well, bucco, there's nothing for it but to set out."

And so, taking small steps and walking atop the ice, they headed for the road, the ponies clattering after, hooves now and again skidding.

Along the Crossland they crept, inching down the way, pony legs skewing, Warrow feet skating, slipping down even the most gentle of cants in the road. And as the land rose and fell, hills were a sliding struggle, whether going up or down. Occasionally they could take to the woods and make better time, for there the layers of ice were leavened with weeds and brush and the ponies' hooves broke through, though Warrow feet did not. But at other times the road was the only choice, for steep drops or upjuts in the forest barred the way, or the tangle of Drearwood was too close to break through. Too, travel by other than road was even more hazardous, for now and again, near and far, an overladen tree would finally give way and crash down, shivered ice flying wide and tinkling down like shattered glass bells, the sound echoing through the ice-clad land.

In all from sunup to sundown they gained at most ten miles.

"Lor'," said Beau, exhausted, "I'm nearly spent but can't we just go on? I mean, it can't be too far now to the edge of the wood, can it?"

"Another ten miles, I would judge," replied Tip. "But it has taken us all day to get this far, and it'll take all night just to reach it. Besides, it's simply too dangerous to travel in the dark, and I am too utterly bone weary to go any farther."

As the sun sank in the west, exhausted, they made camp in the woods to the north of the road and hoped no overburdened tree would fall on them. Tip took first watch, and only by standing and gazing at the new crescent moon sinking in the southwest and by counting the wheeling stars could he but barely stay awake for what he judged to be the requisite eight candlemarks.

Beau did likewise during his own watch—standing and counting the stars.

It was as Tip's second watch was drawing to a close that the tethered ponies began shifting restlessly, their eyes wide, their nostrils aflare. In the starlight Tip peered through the dark tangle of trees, yet he neither heard nor saw a thing. Even so, he awakened Beau, a finger to the buccan's lips.

"Wha—"

"Shhh," hissed Tip, "the ponies sense something. Ready your sling."

Setting an arrow to his bow, Tipperton stepped to the trunk of a tree and waited.

Still the ponies shifted about on the ice, their breath coming heavy as they cleared their nostrils.

Beau slid to a tree opposite Tip, his sling in hand and loaded with a stone.

Now both Warrows heard something heavy coming through the dismal woods, for the ice cracked and shattered under the steps of whatever approached.

The ponies squealed and skittered in fright, their hooves aclatter on the frozen surface. One pulled free and turned to run, only to crash down on the glaze, screaming as something *cracked* as it fell.

And branches shattered and ice clattered down as something huge came through the dark forest and toward the camp.

"Run!" sissed Tip, turning to flee.

"No!" countered Beau, slipping and sliding toward the wrenching steeds, the one on the ground struggling to rise, yet a hindleg flopped and dangled, bone showing through. "The ponies, we've got to loose them."

Cursing, Tip skidded after Beau, and slipped the knot on one of the tethers as Beau slipped the other one. "Now run!" hissed Tip as the ponies skittered away.

Slipping and sliding on the ice, Tip and Beau fled the opposite way. But they had gone no more than twenty yards when Beau cried out, "My book!" and turned.

"Beau, don't—!" called Tipperton, but the other buccan was already skidding back toward the camp.

"Damn! Damn! Damn!" cursed Tip, floundering after his comrade.

Beau reached the site and slid toward his saddlebags yet lying on the ice near the squealing, broken-legged pony. And just as he reached them and clawed inside, something monstrous and half-seen in the darkness crashed through the trees and loomed above the buccan, shards and splinters of ice raining down.

In that same instant Tip let fly an arrow, and the *thing* bellowed and reared up and back and clawed at this thorn in its side.

"Run, Beau!" shrieked Tipperton, and Beau skidded and slid

away, his precious red book in hand. Together the Warrows slipped and floundered across the ice and away, a monster's roars echoing behind. And then the woods rang with a high-pitched scream—like a female it sounded, but it was a pony's death cry—followed by the rending of flesh and crunching, slobbering, chewing sounds.

The rest of the night the Warrows lurched across the ice, the ponies gone, the bulk of their goods lost to the monster—but for the clothing they wore and Tip's bow and arrows and Beau's book and sling. Dawn found them floundering easterly, slipping and sliding upon the glaze in the glittering, frozen woods.

"Tip," panted Beau, "I'm totally spent. We've got to stop and rest."

Gasping, Tipperton agreed, able only to nod his head in assent. They sat on the ice beneath a tree and leaned back against the glassy trunk. In mere moments, completely exhausted, Tip was asleep and Beau nodding off.

Yet in that same moment Beau jerked awake, for from somewhere in the near distance to the west there came a dreadful howl.

10

*T*ip, Tip, wake up."

Beau Darby shook Tip by the shoulder, trying to rouse his companion.

Groggily Tipperton opened bleary eyes.

"Tip, listen. It's Wolves, I think."

Tipperton groaned but sat up.

Long moments passed, the Warrows listening in the silent, dismal wood. Somewhere in the distance another tree fell, followed by dead quiet.

"Beau, I don't—"

Again came a long, deep-pitched howl.

"Is it a Wolf?" asked Beau.

Tipperton drew in a long breath, then slowly let it out. "Sounds like one, Beau, though deeper, I think. But I don't believe a Wolf will attack the two of us, especially if it's alone."

"But what if it's a pack?"

"Look, Beau, at the moment it's some way off, and we need rest. But we also need to stand guard." Groaning, Tip struggled to rise. "I'll take the first—"

"No, you won't, bucco," declared Beau. "You stood the last watch. Now it's my turn. You sleep. I'll stand ward and keep track of the howls."

Tip slumped back. "Wake me in eight candlemarks, when the sun has climbed four hands."

Beau nodded and sighted on the sun. Holding his arms straight out toward it, he turned his hands inward, stacking one atop the other, counting upward four in all, and sighting on a limb directly in line. "All right, Tip, when the sun reaches that bough, I'll take my turn at rest." He looked toward the other buccan, to find him fast asleep.

Beau jerked awake. "What was th—?"

Another howl sounded, this one nearby.

Floundering up, Beau peered 'round. "Oh, Lor', I fell asleep, too." A quick glance at the sun showed it was midafternoon.

Beau turned to waken Tip, to find that buccan sitting up and rubbing his eyes. "Tip, I'm sorry. I—"

Tipperton's eyes widened, and he put a finger to his lips and held out a shushing hand, then motioned for Beau to duck down, Tip himself flattening against the ice-clad ground and pointing downslope toward the Crossland Road.

Beau's gaze followed Tip's pointing hand, and he gasped and dropped down, for there on the road and some distance away a band of Rûcks and a Hlôk slowly made their way easterly, following a huge black Wolflike creature. The size of a pony, no Wolf was this but a Vulg instead. The creature cast about, raising its nose in the air, then snuffling against the ice, and slowly, a pace at a time, easterly it stepped, only to stop again and snuffle and scour.

"We've got to go," sissed Tipperton. "I think it's tracking us."

"Where?" hissed Beau, squirming over to Tip. "I mean, which way?"

"We can't go back to the road," whispered Tip, glancing over his shoulder and back into the woods, "so north it is."

Down the back side of the slope they slithered, and when they were beyond seeing, they crept along, bending low, and moved silently deeper into the glassy tangle of Drearwood.

Finally they stood upright to make their way northward, moving as fast as they could over the slippery terrain.

"Try to touch as little as you can, Beau," said Tip, "for I think the ice is making it difficult for the Vulg to track us, and the less scent we leave, the better off we are. They say that Vulgs are mainly sight hunters, and so if we keep it from seeing us . . ." Tip's words fell to silence as he looked for a clear way around a thorny bar.

"Lor', I wish I had some gwynthyme," said Beau, following Tip as he crawled under a snarl of brittle ice-laden branches.

"Gwynthyme?" Past the obstacle, Tip stood up. "Why would you think of that at this time?"

"My book says that a Vulg's bite is terribly poison, Tip, but that gwynthyme will counteract it."

"Oh."

Northward they inched through the hindering tangle, their progress slow, their way blocked time and again, often they lost their footing on icy slopes and skidded down.

And the sun sank in the west.

Now and again in the south they heard the Vulg howl, and from the east, like howls answered.

Night fell.

"We'll have to keep going north through Drearwood," gritted Tipperton. "They've got us blocked off from escape."

"How far have we come?" asked Beau.

"A mile or two at the most," replied Tip.

And so they pressed onward into the night, their way lighted by the stars above and by a silvery crescent moon hanging in the western sky.

But then the moon set.

And under the light of the stars, still they made their way as cautiously as they could, slipping and sliding on the ice.

And *something* came slithering through the tangle nearby, breathing heavily. The Warrows froze and held their breath as the monstrous *thing* undulated past and away without detecting them.

"Lor'," breathed Beau, "what was *that*?"

"I don't know," murmured Tip, "but let's get the Hèl out of here."

Onward they struggled, and still behind them now and

again they could hear the Vulg howl, and so they pressed onward.

And off in the distance ponderous footsteps crunched, and branches shattered, and once again the Warrows crouched down, trembling in the darkness as Death stalked nearby.

Three more times that night the buccen scrunched down against the ground, holding their breath and moving not, as *things* were heard—two more massive creatures crunching through the ice, one flapping overhead on ponderous, leathery wings. What they were, neither Tip nor Beau knew—only that whatever they were, they were deadly and on the hunt.

Just after sunrise, weary beyond measure, at last the buccen stopped. Although creatures had passed unseen in the night, still they had not heard the Vulg howl since well before dawn, and so they deemed it safe enough to pause awhile. They clambered up a gentle slope along the precipice of a bluff, and when they reached a high point where they could see the approach from the south, they stopped to take rest.

As they sat beneath an icy tree along the rim, "How did the Rûcks and Hlôk get on our track?" asked Beau.

"The ponies, I think," said Tipperton. "They must have found the ponies."

Beau nodded in agreement, then added, "And after that, our goods."

"And then they set a Vulg on our trail," appended Tip. "But as long as we stay on the hard ice, I think it'll have trouble following."

Beau gazed out into the glasslike 'scape, ice sheathing all. "That shouldn't be too difficult."

Tip reached under his quilted down jacket and pulled out his waterskin. "Uh-oh," he grunted, shaking the skin, "I'm all out."

Beau felt his own water bag. "Me, too."

"I suppose we'll just have to eat ice," said Tip.

"Oh, no, we won't, bucco," objected Beau. "It'll just steal our heat, and we've no food to replenish it. And what with this sleeping on ice, I'm cold enough as it is, in spite of our eiderdown. No, Tip, if we're to get through this alive, we've got to find a stream."

Tip sighed. "All right, give me your bag. I'll look for water while you keep watch."

Beau nodded, and handed over the skin.

"I'm going down there," said Tip, pointing down the face of the bluff. "Likely if there's a stream, it'll be at the base of this precipice. If you spot anything, cast a slingstone down at me."

"I'll throw it by hand," said Beau, grinning.

Tip smiled back at the buccan, then started down the slope, following along the rim.

Beau stood and leaned against the tree. *And this time I'll stay awake.*

The later afternoon sun shone through the glass-brittle ice-clad woods as Tip said, "If you're going to pee, pee over the cliff. That way should any Vulgs come upon the scent, it'll be at the bottom rather than up here with us. But take care and don't slip over."

Beau groaned. "Too late, Tip, for while you were sleeping I . . ." Beau poked a thumb back over his shoulder and toward the woods behind.

Tip sighed and shrugged. "Oh, well . . ." He cast an eye toward the sun, then turned and pointed east and said, "Let's see if we can get out of these dreadful woods before dark."

"Oh, I do hope we can do so," said Beau. "Those awful things in the night . . ."

They set off easterly, but the icy terrain hindered their way, and the sun set and darkness fell, and it seemed they were no closer to escaping. Still they pressed on, bright stars and a quarter moon lighting the way. But then in the tangle ahead . . .

"Oh, no," Tip groaned, and pointed toward the glimmer of a fire in the distance.

"Perhaps it's a traders' caravan," murmured Beau.

"Not likely. A Foul Folk campsite instead, I would say."

"What'll we do?"

"Skirt around it. Leave it be."

Beau nodded. "Choose the way," he murmured.

And with Tip in the lead, the buccen swung northerly, keeping the campfire off to the right.

Onward they crept, and onward, but of a sudden Tip's feet

slipped out from under him, and he went hurtling down a slope, smashing through ice-clad underbrush, shards of ice shattering and tinkling in his wake. He crashed into an icy knot of thornbush at the bottom of the slide and, blundering, stood, his feet yet slipping, his bow lost to his grasp and arrows strewn out behind, all slithering slowly down the slope after. And in the moonlight and starlight, as Tip floundered to his feet a leather-clad arm snaked about his neck, forearm against the buccan's windpipe, and someone snarled and jerked Tip up off the ground and wrenched him back and forth, trying to break the Warrow's neck. Feet kicking, arms flailing, Tip tried to fight, but he could not bring his fists or feet to bear, and his throat was being crushed and he could not breathe.

"*Yarwah! Yarwah!*" the assailant yelled in Tipperton's ear.

Krnch! there came a sodden thud, and suddenly Tip was released, and he fell gasping to the ice. Slipping and sliding he turned, to see Beau standing over a dead Hlôk, the Spawn's temple crushed in, dark grume oozing across the frozen glaze.

"H-he was trying to m-murder you, Tip. Trying to break your n-neck," stammered Beau, his eyes wide and staring down at the slain Hlôk. "I had to kill him. Had to. There was no other choice."

"How?" Tip croaked, clutching his throat.

Beau looked up. "I hit him in the head with a rock."

Tip's eyes widened. "From your sling?" he rasped.

Beau shook his head. "No. I hit him in the head with a rock." Beau held up the ice-clad weapon—a rock the size of his fist.

From the distance there came a cry. "*Vetch! Vetch!*" and Tip could see torchlight bobbing through the trees.

"Adon, Beau," he said, struggling to his feet, "we've got to run."

But Beau, stunned, stood looking down at the Hlôk. Tip grasped him by the arms and shook him. "Did you hear me? We've got to run. The Rûcks, they're coming."

A bugle blatted, and from the east came a distant reply, and somewhere a great limb broke and ice crashed down.

Beau glanced around, then nodded, and Tip snatched up his bow and two of the loose arrows that had slithered to his feet, and together the two buccen fled northward through the wood.

* * *

"Down!" hissed Tip, and he and Beau wormed their way under an ice-laden gnarl of clutching vine. With racing hearts and pent breath they lay on their stomachs on the glaze and watched in the starlight as a spread-out line of searching Rûcks swept toward them. Spikes of crampons crunched into the ice as the Spawn came on, Foul Folk calling to one another in their guttural tongue. And Beau jerked as a horn blared, directly above, it seemed, and he gripped Tipperton's wrist, but otherwise moved not.

And then the widely spaced file moved on past and away, and as the crunch of boot spikes and callings of voices and blares of bugles faded in the dark distance, both Tip and Beau slumped in relief. Hearts slowed and breathing became regular again, and finally Tipperton said, "Come on, Beau, let's go." But as they crawled out from under, from the east and south they heard more distant horn calls and faint cries, so up through the woods they fled.

By early morning they could no longer hear the bugle blats and shouts from afar, yet they had been driven north and west, losing some of the ground they had gained the previous day. And still they struggled on.

Again they found a stream and broke through the ice and replenished their waterskins. And while Tip scanned the nearby 'scape, Beau lay down and drank from the stream. As he stood, he said, "Lor', but I'm hungry, Tip. I mean, I've been keeping an eye out for something, *anything* we could eat—acorns, pine cones with pine nuts, dried berries among the thorns, whatever—but everything is hidden under layers of ice. Y'know, right now even crue and jerky would be a feast."

But they had nothing to eat, and had had no food since the evening of the attack on the ponies, two days and a night past.

Now Tipperton flopped belly down for a drink, and as Beau stood watch he said, "Tell you what, Tip, if your bow will hold together long enough, you shoot one of those monsters in the night, and we'll eat the whole thing raw."

Tip choked on water and came up sputtering, hacking and laughing at one and the same time.

Too exhausted to go on, they struggled up a glassy slope to

the top of a low hill, where they could see the lay of the land all 'round, and Tip stood first ward as Beau slept. And it was during his watch that Tipperton discovered a long split in the upper limb of his bow. *Must have been cracked when I fell last night and may shatter if I draw it.*

"Barn rats," growled Beau upon hearing the news as his turn came to stand guard. "Me with a weapon I cannot cast and you with one that might break. A formidable pair we are, eh? The Rûcks must be shaking in their boots."

Rubbing red-rimmed eyes, Tip said, "Well, bucco, let's hope we have no cause to find out."

As Beau's first watch came to an end, Tip groaned awake and wearily stood and said, "Beau, we've got to get out of these woods ere nightfall. I think we should take one more warding each, and then go."

Beau haggardly nodded, and slumped down as Tip leaned against the tree and with bleary eyes scanned the dark glassy glitter of Drearwood.

East they went and east, steps skidding on the glaze and feet slipping out from under them now and again, more weary from trying to walk upon uneven icy slopes than they were from the travel itself. Tempers were short and they snapped at one another out of fatigue, and they were ravenously hungry and bone tired. Yet still they pushed on, and aided one another upslope and down, or helped each other to regain their feet after a fall. Stumbling, skidding, sliding, eastward they floundered on insecure feet, seeking an end to Drearwood, yet entangled within. And the diamond-bright sun shed little warmth and relentlessly marched toward the west. As evening drew nigh there sounded faint bugle blats echoing among the hard-clad trees, their direction completely uncertain.

The sun set and the short winter twilight fell over the icy gloom, and a quarter moon waxed overhead, shedding its light down through the glassy branches to glimmer upon the sheathed land. And as Tip and Beau struggled over a small rise, ahead through the ice-laden galleries Tipperton saw—"Beau, look! I think we've come to the end."

"It could be another clearing," cautioned Beau, yet his heart cried out for it to not be so.

Slipping and sliding, across the glaze they went, down a tiny vale, close-set trees at hand.

And the twilight vanished into night, leaving but moon and stars to dimly light the way through the dark and drear woods. Still the Warrows pushed on, striving to reach the clear way ahead, and the trees seemed to draw in closer, as if to block their escape.

Now they came to the pinch of the vale, where they could almost reach out to touch the thickly wooded sides, and of a sudden dark shapes hurled out from the trees and Beau was smashed down from behind as Tip was wrenched upward from the ground, seized in an iron grip, and the glimmer of sharp steel flashed in the moonlight.

Tipperton futilely clawed for the dagger at his belt, and he shrilled, *"Blût vor blût!"* an ancient battlecry in the old Warrow tongue of Twyll. Yet he could not get his dagger, as a gleaming long-knife flashed in the starlight, ready for the killing stroke.

"Kest!" came a sharp cry from one of the man-sized assailants, crouching over Beau and staring into the buccan's face. *"Slean nid! Eio ra nid Rucha tha Waerlinga nista!"*

"Aro?"

The knife moved away from Tipperton's throat, but still he struggled as a dark figure moved toward him and threw the buccan's hood back, then in Common said, "This one is a Waerling, too."

Now Tip was set to the icy ground and released, and the one who had seized him said, "Fear not, wee one, for we are Lian."

"Lian!" exclaimed Beau, looking up from the ground.

"What ye call Elves," replied one of the tall slender warriors, then adding, "from Arden Vale." And he cast back his hood to reveal golden hair to his shoulders tied back by a leather headband, and tipped ears and tilted eyes, seemingly green, though in the light of but stars and moon it was difficult to say. "I am Vanidor."

Tip buried his face in his hands, and he slumped to the ground.

Vanidor knelt at his side. "Art thou ill, wee one?"

Tip looked up, tears streaming down his face. "N-no. I-I mean, I'm fine. It's just that we have been trying to reach you and it's been so very hard."

The Elf reached out and put a hand on Tip's shoulder. "Weep not, wee one, for thou and thy comrade, ye have found us, whatever be thy need."

"I say," piped up a plaintive voice from behind; it was Beau, now sitting up. "Speaking of need, have you anything to eat? Even crue will do."

11

*T*his is delicious," said Beau. "What is it?"

"Mian," replied fair-haired Loric, the warrior Elf who had given the wafers of Elven waybread to the buccen. " 'Tis made of honey and oats and various nuts, and it will last long, several seasons, in fact, without turning."

Tip and Beau and two of the Elves made their way across an open wold, the slope gently rising and falling, the land yet covered by a sheath of ice, yet the buccen were steadied by their sure-footed escort. Free of the woods at last, they were headed for a campsite said by the Elves to be safe, and Loric and Arandar had been assigned to conduct them there.

"Well it certainly puts crue to shame," said Beau, taking another bite, "and I'm glad we ran into you, even though you did try to kill us."

"We thought ye to be a pair of *Rucha*, small as ye are."

"Well, that makes us even, I suppose," said Tip, speaking around a mouthful, "for when you grabbed me I thought you and your comrades were Hlôks."

"Lucky for us you were not," added Beau, taking another bite.

"Indeed, Fortune turned Her smiling face toward ye, for

Spaunen set ambush in that vale earlier," said Arandar, his dark eyes grim, his steady hand on Beau's shoulder.

"Lor'," breathed Beau. "We could have walked right in among them, just as we did you. . . . —Say, what happened to these, um, Spaunen?"

"They no longer enjoy life," replied Arandar.

"Oh, my," said Beau.

They walked for long moments without speaking, but at last Loric said, "It must be quite a tale as to why ye two were traipsing about in that dire wood—"

"*Traipsing?*" blurted Tipperton 'round his last mouthful of mian.

"—but it can wait until we reach the safety of our camp and *Alor* Vanidor and the others finish the patrol."

Tip looked up at Loric. "Alor? Alor Vanidor?"

"Lord," replied Loric. "Lord Vanidor."

Tip's eyes widened, but he said no more.

With the weary buccen flagging rapidly, the moon sailed another two handspans of nightsky ere the two Elves and two Warrows crossed a frozen stream, to pause at the far bank before a grove of ice-laden pine while Loric sounded the low chitter of a night-feeding winter-white weasel. A like chitter answered him, and together the four of them moved up the icy slope and in among the trees, where they passed a pair of sentries, who said nought but stared at the Waerlinga in wide-eyed wonder, for the Wee Folk were a most uncommon sight in this part of the world. Stepping through the grove, Tip and Beau and their Elven escort came to a hidden fissure jagging back into a low stone bluff, where another sentry marveled as the buccen passed by. They stepped into the cleft and 'round a bend, where they waited while Arandar lit a small lantern taken from a niche in the wall.

"Lor'," said Beau, stamping a boot to the dry rock of the cave floor, "solid footing at last. I'll tell you, I've had enough of slipping and sliding in my very own tracks."

Tip grunted a noncommittal reply as Arandar set off in the lead, the lantern hood but barely cracked, a thin slit of light showing the way. And they zigged and zagged through the narrow slot with dark stone arching above, and here and there both Loric and Arandar had to stoop, though Tip and Beau did not.

At length they came to the end of the rift and stepped out into a fair hollow where starlit sky stood overhead. All around, the bound of the basin rose up and inward, forming a broad overhang, and 'neath this sheltering jut and against the curved wall stood stone dwellings, ruins for the most part, though here and there an undamaged cote remained. To the left a small smokeless campfire flickered and Elves were gathered about, lounging on nearby boulders or sitting on the ground. Beau released a great sigh and Tip sagged in relief, their anxiety taking wing, for they had reached the Elven encampment and felt safe at last.

"Welcome to *Kolaré an e Ramna*," said Loric, "where Lian stand vigil on this one sector of the long Drearwood marge."

Tipperton looked up at Loric. "Kol-kol—"

"Kolaré an e Ramna," repeated Loric, "The Hollow of the Vanished."

"The Vanished?"

Loric gestured at the ruins. "Those who built these dwellings. We know not who they were, for they were long gone ere we discovered this basin, and other than these ruins, they left nothing behind to signify who they were—no symbols, no carvings, nought.

"But come, let us to the blaze—for warmth and hot tea at the least." Loric turned leftward and started for the fire.

Tears came into Beau's eyes as he followed. "Lor', a fire and hot tea. We haven't had either, or warmth for that matter, for, let me see . . ."

"Ten days," said Tip. "Or thereabouts. Ever since leaving Twoforks."

"Twoforks?" said Arandar. "On the River Wilder?"

"Yes," replied Tipperton.

"Then ye passed west to east through the full of Drearwood." His words were a statement and not a question.

Tip nodded.

"Ye twain and none else?"

Again Tip nodded.

Both Loric and Arandar looked at the two buccen in amazement, and Arandar exclaimed, "Ai, but indeed Dame Fortune *did* smile down upon ye."

"*Hál, Loric, Arandar!*" called one of the Lian at the fire. "*Ana didron enistori?*"

"*Hai!*" replied Loric. "*Waerlinga! En a Dhruousdarda.*"

"*Waerlinga?*" cried some voices in surprise, while others called out "*En a Dhruousdarda?*" Lian stood and peered toward these oncoming wee folk, waiting to see just who these Waerlinga visitors were who had come from the Drearwood.

A place was made near the fire for Tip and Beau, and mugs of hot tea were passed over to them. The buccen wrapped their hands around the warm cups and took long draughts and closed their gemlike eyes in bliss.

At a sign from Arandar, two steaming bowls of stew were passed to them, along with torn chunks of bread. Spoons were handed over, and with tears brimming, Tip and Beau dug into their first hot meal since the one Tessa had fed them back at the Red Fox Inn.

"From the Drearwood?" asked a ginger-haired warrior, shaking his head in wonderment and looking at Arandar.

"Aye," he replied. "In Vagan's Vale."

"Vagan's Vale, a bad place that, *neh?*"

Arandar nodded, and Loric said, "Had they come but a candlemark or two earlier, it would have been *Rûpt* they met and not us. But we came across the Spaunen first, and so those in the trap were trapped. None escaped."

"*Kala!*" exclaimed the Lian, making a fist, other Guardians doing likewise.

"They were lying in wait," said Arandar, "mayhap for us, mayhap for the Waerlinga, mayhap for reasons elsewise. Yet Alor Vanidor sensed the ambuscade, there in Vagan's Vale, and we divided and took them by surprise instead."

"Did any take wounds?" asked the ginger-haired Elf.

"Nay, Ragan," replied Arandar, then smiled grimly, "none but the Rûpt, that is."

"All fatal, I deem," said Ragan, his tilted eyes flinty.

"Aye, all fatal."

Ragan glanced across at the Waerlinga, both buccen using

bread to sop up the dregs of stew from their bowls. "And then . . . ?"

"And then these twain came along—we thought them Rucha come to join their brethren in the snare. We nearly slew them by mistake."

Wide-eyed, Ragan gestured at the buccen. "But what were Waerlinga doing in Drearwood?"

Loric held out a hand. "Let us wait for Alor Vanidor before having our guests answer that question, else they will be telling the same tale twice." Then he looked down at the Waerlinga and smiled, for warm and well fed, both were nodding over their empty bowls, sleep overtaking them.

Quietly Loric signaled the others, and they carefully took the bowls and spoons from lax buccen hands and gently lifted the two Waerlinga up and bore them to one of the stone cotes against the arched wall and lay them down on dry straw pallets and covered them with blankets of down.

Vanidor held the coin up to light. "And he gave thee this?"

Tip nodded. "And told me to deliver it to Agron and to warn all east. But the trouble is, I don't know who or what this Agron is, and I don't know what warning I'm supposed to give."

"But right after," added Beau, "that's when we saw the fire on Beacontor, and we thought it might have something to do with that."

Vanidor looked at the Waerlinga. "'Tis likely." Vanidor looked across at Loric. "With Beacontor captured, any alarm from Challerain Keep would be delayed."

Tipperton shook his head. "But as I said, Lord Vanidor, Prell's boy Arth brought word that all the Spawn who had done it were dead, killed by a man and his nephew. The boy was also killed, but the man survived and lit the balefire."

"But don't forget, Tip, the spawn that went by your mill, they might have taken one of the beacon hills in the Dellin Downs," cautioned Beau.

"Mayhap 'tis as we feared," said Loric, "that war has come. For something vile is afoot, with Hordes of Rûpt marching down through Kregyn from Gron and into Drearwood."

"Wull," said Beau, "Hordes marched out of Drearwood as well."

Vanidor's eyes widened. "Say on, wee one."

Beau glanced at Tipperton, then cleared his throat. "It was a sevenday back, the day we first entered Drearwood. On my watch a Horde began marching out. It took all night for them to pass where we were hidden. And they had Rûcks and Hlôks and Ogrus—"

"Trolls?" Again Vanidor's eyes widened. "Down from their mountain haunts?"

Beau nodded. "Only we call them Ogrus . . . pulling great wagons."

Tip cleared his throat. "Don't forget, Beau, there were also those ghastly men or some such—pale white they were, and riding horses that were not horses but were scaled—"

"*Ghûlka!*" hissed Loric. "On Hèlsteeds."

"I don't know what the men-things were," said Tip, "but the horses had cloven hoofs, or so the tracks showed us the next day."

"The men-things, thou wouldst call them Ghûls, wee one," said Vanidor, and Tip and Beau both gasped in alarm, "or corpse-folk, but by any name they are a terrible foe." Then he turned to Beau. "And thou sayest it took all night for the Swarm to pass?"

Beau nodded.

"Did ye see aught else in Drearwood?" asked Arandar.

"Well, *something* huge got our pack pony and nearly us besides," said Beau. He glanced at Tipperton. "But Tip feathered it with an arrow and we managed to escape."

Vanidor looked at Tipperton and smiled, and Tip said, "That was before my bow got cracked. But as to the monster, well, it was so big I couldn't miss, but I think my arrow only irritated the brute. Regardless, we ran away."

"Slipped and slid, you mean," said Beau. "The ice, you know.

"And speaking of slipping and sliding, the next night something monstrous slithered across the ice like a giant snake, but we didn't see what it was. Only heard it as it passed us by."

The Elves cast glances at one another but said nought.

"Something large flapped overhead," said Tip, "and we heard a couple more things stalking past, like the monster that got our pack pony. But except for the first, none of the others detected us."

"Ye were fortunate," said Arandar, "for ill things are awake out of season."

"Stirred by Modru?" asked Loric.

Both Vanidor and Arandar shrugged, and Vanidor said without elaboration, "Mayhap."

Suddenly Beau snapped his fingers. "Oh, I almost forgot." He reached into his eiderdown jacket and beneath his jerkin and pulled forth a crumple of ebon cloth. He shook it out and held it up for all to see, saying, "A dead Rûck was lying atop this."

It was the black banner enscribed with its circle of fire.

Vanidor, Loric, and Arandar all drew air in between clenched teeth, and Loric said, "Gron."

"Gron?" asked Tip.

"'Tis the banner of Gron, Modru's realm in the north," said Arandar.

Vanidor turned to Loric. "My sire need hear of this, Loric, and from the mouths of these Waerlinga. I would have thee take them there, for he may have questions to ask of them."

Loric canted his head. "Aye, Alor."

Now Vanidor turned to Beau. "Keep the flag, Sir Beau, to show to my sire, Talarin, for he will want to see it with his own eyes." As Beau stuffed the banner 'neath his jerkin once again, Vanidor handed the drab coin back to Tipperton and said, "As to the coin itself, Sir Thistledown, or as to the one who gave it to thee, I cannot tell thee aught. But the warning he asked thee to sound seems plain—that war has come, driven by Modru, or so say all the signs. Yet heed, as to the name of Agron, this I do know: he is the King of Aven. Across the Grimwall and past Darda Erynian and beyond the Circle of Rimmen in Riamon and farther still unto the city of Dendor, there thou wilt find his throne. It is to him the coin is intended, and it is to him thou must go."

12

*T*he next morning, as the Warrows and Loric prepared to set out, "Here," said Ragan, holding out a sheaf of arrows to Tipperton. "Twenty Lian shafts, trimmed to thy length, wee one. From the looks of thy quiver, thou didst use most of thine arrows in Drearwood 'gainst creatures dire."

Tip looked at the ground in embarrassment. "Actually, Ragan, I lost most of them when I skidded and fell and slid down a hill in the night."

Ragan laughed, then said, "Nevertheless, Sir Tipperton, thou wilt most likely need these."

"But my bow is cracked, even though you did wrap it last night, still it may break." Tip had awakened to find Ragan had wound a short length of thong tightly about the upper limb to keep the split from growing, and a second thong about the lower limb to balance out the throw.

"It may not cast as fair nor as far, yet it should hold for a while, and what good is a bow without enough arrows?"

Gratefully, Tip took the arrows and measured the bundle against a shaft of his own—an exact match . . . as Ragan had said, they had been trimmed to fit the buccan.

Now Ragan turned to Beau and handed him a small pouch, saying, "And thou wilt need these, Sir Beau."

Frowning, Beau opened the bag and reached inside and withdrew a molded slingstone. Made of lead, its ovoid form was shaped to fit a sling pouch. "Oh, my," said Beau, dropping the bullet back inside the bag and drawing the strings tight. "I cannot take these, Ragan. I mean, I'm not good enough for such. Why, I could but barely manage to hit that wall yon were I to try. You must give these to someone with the skill to use them." Beau held the pouch out to Ragan.

But the Elf shook his head. "Nay, my friend. They are for thee and none else."

Reluctantly, Beau tied the pouch to his belt. "If you say so, though I'll just manage to fling them away without hitting aught."

"Mayhap by the time thou need use them, thou wilt have the skill."

Beau sighed. "Perhaps. Nevertheless, I thank you, Ragan, and I do hope you prove to be right."

Arandar then stepped to the buccen. "My gift is not as worthy as that of Ragan's, yet mayhap 'twill do." He held out two pairs of crampons, saying, "For keeping thy footing on ice."

Eagerly, the buccen took the spikes and strapped them to their booted feet as Loric said, "These and the arrows were trimmed to fit as ye slept last night."

Tip stood and clattered about on the stone and, grinning, said, "Cor, but we could have used these in Drearwood."

Loric shook his head. "Had ye used such in Drearwood, ye both would now be dead, for they do leave scars behind by which the Rûpt would have quickly tracked ye down."

Beau's eyes flew wide. "And here all along I thought the ice to be our doom, when instead it probably saved our lives."

Loric smiled. "Hinder ye it did, yet it saved ye as well, for Vulgs found no scent by which to trail ye, and the Spaunen found no marks by which to run ye to ground. —Yet now these spikes will aid ye . . . though for a while ye need leave them off until we are well clear of Kolaré an e Ramna, for we would have no marks left behind to betray us to the Rûpt."

Quickly the buccen unstrapped the crampons and affixed them to their belts.

Now Vanidor handed the Waerlinga two packs fitted in new-cut slender pine-bough frames sized to suit their small forms, each provisioned with food and flint and steel and candles and a length of Elven-made rope and other such, as well as bedding tied atop. "Though it is but a short journey unto the Hidden Stand, ye mayhap will need these in the long days to come. And thy pack, Sir Beau, has some medicks inside, though not a great deal, to replace part of that which thou lost. Thou will be able to procure even more within Arden Vale, mayhap even gwynthyme, of which we here have none to spare."

Beau's mouth flew open. "*Gwynthyme*? Oh, Tip, the golden mint."

Bobbing their heads in thanks, the buccen shouldered the packs, each buckling the strap 'round his waist and snapping the clip across his chest to hold the shoulder harness in place. Then Tip fastened his quiver to his hip, and strung his bow. Looking up at Loric and then across at Beau, "Ready?" he asked.

"Ready," replied Beau.

And with Elvenkind wishing them well, following Loric, out through the crevice they went and into the ice-clad 'scape beyond.

For more than a mile they walked due south, feet slipping and sliding, but at last Loric relented and allowed the Waerlinga to buckle on the crampons. And after that the buccen had little trouble crossing the sheathed expanse.

Eastward they turned, and in the distance ahead they could see a high stone bluff jutting up out of the land, and beyond that and standing against the sky afar stood the Grimwall Mountains, dark stone rising up in jagged fangs to gnaw at the heavens above.

And across a frozen world and toward this forbidding 'scape they strode.

By midmorn they had come to the stone bluff, sheer rock rising a hundred feet or more and looming to their left. And beside this massif they walked, yet making their way easterly, now paralleling the Tumble River, the water cascading 'round and over rocks and swirling in rapids as it poured and spewed and rolled and surged within its ice-laden banks, the rage of the river giving it its name, and because of its churning and roiling, seldom did the water freeze but in those rare stretches along its length where the water ran placid, undisturbed by tumult.

With the river on their right and the sheer stone wall on their left, onward the hikers trekked, pausing now and again to rest or to relieve themselves or to take a meal.

And the winter-bright sun, casting no heat, slid up the sky and across and down again as the travelers trudged on, the stone wall to their left growing even higher the farther east they went.

Finally with the sun at their backs, in the near distance to the fore, they could see a cloud of vapor swirling into the air, the billow casting back a pale gold light in the afternoon sun.

"What is it," asked Beau, pointing ahead.

"Wait, wee one," replied Loric, his blue eyes atwinkle. "Thou wilt soon see."

Onward they strode, and now faintly they could hear a grumble above the crunch of spikes upon ice. And the closer they came to the roiling, rising vapor, the louder the rumble grew.

"I know what it is," said Tip, yet before he could say, they rounded an outjut and there before them and plummeting down roared a cataract from a high crevice carved in the sheer wall they had been following. Out from the stone hurtled the Tumble River, to fall thundering into a deep pool a hundred feet below. And a cloaking mist swirled upward to obscure the tall slot carved deeply down into the sheer stone rampart, shrouding what lay beyond.

Now Loric headed toward this cascade, calling out above the roar, " 'Tis Arden Falls, and the secret entrance unto the Hidden Vale lies 'neath."

"Oh, my, but what about our crampon marks?" shouted Tipperton above the roar. "Won't they point to the secret way?"

"Nay," called Loric back, holding out his hand in the swirling vapor. "When the mist falls in our tracks and freezes, it will hide all again. And speaking of freezing, hidden steps lie on this verge and by that way we will go, yet take care, for the mist will have frozen thereupon, and more wetness swirls constantly down. They will be treacherous."

With tilted wide sapphirine eyes Tipperton looked at Beau, only to discover the other buccan looking back at him, his own tilted amber eyes just as wide. And toward the roaring outpour they went, following Loric's lead up an icy slope alongside the sheer bluff.

And the closer they came to the cataract, the louder the roar, and by the time they reached the falls, they could only communicate with one another by hand gestures and facial expressions and the like.

Now they clambered behind the cataract itself, and Loric paused and pointed, and there shielded by the edge of the falls was a narrow ice-covered ledge, layered so thick as to be all but indiscernible against the sheath-covered vertical stone. A barely perceptible rising series of humps below the ice told that these were the steps Loric meant them all to climb, and Tip wondered if the Elf were completely mad. Yet even as the buccan thought so, Loric uncoiled a hank of rope and fastened one end 'round his waist and indicated to the Waerlinga they were to tie on as well, and with Beau in the middle and Tip on the trailing end, toward the steps they went.

And as water roared out of the slot some fifty feet above and plummeted down past them close enough to touch, plunging onward to thunder into the basin some fifty feet below, through churning mist and up the ice-buried stair they fared. Loric slowly clambered upward, seemingly without a concern, the buccen following after, trembling and clinging to knobs of ice jutting up or out of the mass whenever chance afforded. Yet Loric paused often to glance back, and this steadied the Warrows, and then he would turn and move on. But of a sudden the Elf disappeared 'round a jog, and Tipperton fleetingly thought that he and Beau had been cast adrift. And then Beau passed around the same bend, and Tip climbed all alone, with water bellowing past, and billowing mist obscuring the way ahead. Yet he came to the turn and 'round it to find Loric and Beau standing on an ice-laden road and taking up the slack on the line. The road itself came up a slant from the far side of the falls, and was broad enough to bear a spacious wain.

Trembling and weak-kneed, Tip stepped onto the wide surface and away from the brim, and Loric smiled and left them all lashed together as he gestured for the buccan to follow. Up the concealed road they went and into a tunnel beyond, to emerge moments later in a wide vale. And there on the edge of the mist and standing ward were two Elven warriors—silver bugles on baldrics at hand, scabbarded swords harnessed 'cross their backs, saddled horses standing nearby.

Loric gestured at the Guardians, and they signaled back, indicating that the trio was to pass onward. But Loric paused long enough to untie the rope from 'round his waist which bound him to his companions, the Warrows doing likewise, the buccen all the while gazing out upon this wondrous place they had come to.

They had entered a steep-sided gorge no more than a quarter mile wide at this point, through which the Tumble River flowed. And for as far as the eye could see, pine and fir and other evergreens marched away to the north. Yet the Warrows' wits were captured neither by the gorge nor the forest nor the fact that here in the vale the river was sheathed with ice but the snow-laden land was not, unlike the world outside. Instead what arrested their gaze was the tallest tree the buccen had ever seen. Hundreds of feet it towered upward in the near distance, and its leaves seemed somehow to hold a silvery-grey cast, as if twilight had settled within.

Loric finished coiling the rope and motioned them forward, and as the Waerlings passed by, the Lian warders looked on in wonder, for these were Wee Folk come into this Elven land. They strode away from the falls and toward the forest giant, and the rumble of the cataract diminished quickly, for the stone walls of the gorge arced 'round from each side to clasp the narrow, mist-obscured slot and shield the vale from the sound of the water cascading over the linn and thundering down into the basin below.

Soon they could speak to one another, though they had to raise their voices to be heard. But by the time they reached the immense tree with its Elven camp set among the roots at the base, Arden Falls was but a low grumble afar.

*   *   *

" 'Tis called the Lone Eld Tree," said Loric, gesturing at the nearby giant, "for of its kind it is alone in this vale," and his arm swept out toward the ravine with its evergreen-laden slopes.

" 'Twas borne here from Darda Galion as a seedling by Talarin and Rael to commemorate their pledge of troth," added Alaria, captain of the South Arden-ward. "And it is the symbol of the Hidden Vale and is borne on all our standards—green tree upon grey field."

"Hidden Vale?" asked Tipperton. "That's what Loric called it."

Alaria pointed back at the befogging vapor rising in the slot in the stone above Arden Falls. "Seldom does the mist clear, and none outside can see into this valley to know what passes herein. Yet we within stand watch upon the mountain bulwarks all 'round"—Alaria pointed high up on the stone wall above—"and relay silent signal to one another at need. That's why we knew ye were coming, for we watched thy progress from Kolaré an e Ramna throughout the day."

"You saw us on our march from the Hollow of the Vanished?"

Alaria smiled, brushing a stray lock of dark brown hair back from her eyes. "Every step of the way, wee one. Every step of the way, for ye did follow along the outer ramparts of the Hidden Stand."

"Why does it seem to hold twilight?" asked Beau, looking once again up into the dusk-laden leaves high above.

Alaria shook her head. "None knows, Sir Beau. There seems a mystic bond between Elvenkind and Eld Trees, Lian and Dylvana both, for when none are nigh the leaves lose the gloaming, yet regain it when Elves dwell near. It has been said that not only do Eld Trees sense the presence of Elvenkind, but that some Elves—not all, but some—can sense the eldwood trees."

Loric nodded. "When Rûpt felled the nine, 'tis said *Dara Arin* dreamt of the slaughter."

Tip frowned. "Felled the nine? —Say, now, is this the same as the 'Felling of the Nine'? The song the Bards sing?"

"Aye."

Beau turned up his hands in puzzlement. "What is this, um, 'Felling of the Nine'? It's a song I've not heard."

" 'Tis more than a song, my friend," said Loric, and his face fell grim. "Long past, in the time you call the First Era, Spaunen came down from the Grimwall and into Darda Galion and in malicious glee felled nine of the precious Eld Trees. I was among the March-ward along that sector of the marge, and when we discovered what had been done, we ran the tree-slayers to earth and in our rage slew them all. I bore word to Coron Aldor, and we mounted a force of retribution and took up the dead Rûpt and displayed their remains to Foul Folk throughout the Grimwall and gave warning that we would not tolerate such ravagement ever. Oft we fought, yet always we conquered, and never again did Spaunen set axe or saw or blade of any kind against the precious trees."

"This Dara Arin, is she the Lady Arin of legend?"

"Aye," replied Alaria. "Dara in Sylva means Lady in the common tongue. She was a Dylvana, and together with Egil One-Eye and Lady Aiko and others, she quested for the Green Stone of Xian."

"From my da I've heard the songs the Bards sing, songs of her as well as songs of the Felling of the Nine," said Tipperton. Then he turned to Loric. "But you say you were there, at the actual felling?"

Loric nodded.

"But that was back in the First Era, more than two thousand years ago."

"Nevertheless, wee one, I was there."

Tip's eyes widened, and he took a deep breath and slowly let it out, for although it had been bandied about that Elves upon reaching a certain mark aged no more, still to have it actually confirmed, well, what a marvel it was.

"And this Lady Arin," asked Beau, "she sensed the death of the Eld Trees?"

"So it is said," replied Loric.

"Oh, but I wish I could sense herbs and roots and flowers and mint and bark and various leaves and whatever else I need in my healing arts, for it would ease the finding a deal—but sense them alive, I mean, rather than when they die." Beau paused a moment, gazing up at the great giant, then said, "It must be grand to have a mystic link to such a great tree, for that would be special to my way of thinking."

Alaria nodded solemnly. "Special, aye, and this particular tree above many others, for 'tis said that when this tree is no more, then we, too, will no longer dwell in Arden Vale."

"Oh, my," said Beau, a stricken look on his face.

Just after dawn the next morning, Loric, mounted upon a fiery steed and trailing two behind, each with a Waerling astride, bade good-bye to Alaria and then set forth at a goodly pace, heading up through the wintry vale. Both Tip and Beau gripped the saddle forecantles tightly, for neither was equipped to manage such a great steed as a full-grown horse, Tip measuring but three feet four inches and Beau but three feet five. Northward they rode through the pine-laden glen, following alongside the waters of the River Tumble rushing southward, occasionally beneath thick ice. High stone canyon walls laden with winter snow rose in the distance to left and right, the sides of the gorge at times near, at other times two or three miles distant. Crags and crevices could be seen here and there, jutting up through the layered white, though for the most part the lofty walls were sheer granite and little snow clung to the steeps. In places where the canyon narrowed dramatically, Loric pointed out hewn rock pathways carved partway up the sides of the stone palisades that formed walls of the vale, the Elf remarking that in these straits when the river o'erflowed its banks in the spring, the valley below became a raging torrent, and so these courses along the walls were made for safety's sake. But they rode none of these snow-covered high pathways as on up the canyon they forged, at times passing through narrow slots and at other times crossing o'er wide valley floors, faring through snow and on stone and gentle loam alike, now and then clattering on a frozen stretch of the river itself, hooves knelling on the ice, but always returning to the verdant galleries of the evergreen forest carpeting the vale and reaching from side to side.

And northward they rode and northward, Loric leading the Waerlinga through fragrant pine, now riding swiftly where the snow lay shallow, now slowly where it drifted deep. And whenever they came to places where Loric judged the snow lay overdeep, he would dismount and bid the Waerlinga to do like-wise, and then he would lead the horses afoot, at times broaching the snow for the steeds, at other times having the steeds broach the snow for him, frequently trading off which horse took the lead and bore the brunt of the work. And always the buccen trailed behind, floundering through the drifts.

'Round a flickering fire they made camp that eve in a grove where the snow lay shallow, and as they waited for water to boil for their tea, Beau turned to Loric and said, "Yestereve you told us that two thousand years past you were standing march-ward along the Grimwall. And when we first saw you, you were standing march-ward along the marge of Drearwood. So tell me, Loric, is this all you do? Stand march-ward on borders, I mean. It seems that in two thousand years you'd get tired of such duty."

Loric laughed and looked at the wee buccan. "Ah, my friend, thou hast come upon a truth of Elvenkind, for indeed we would become weary of such constant duty throughout thousands of seasons, no matter the task. Whether Lian or Dylvana, none remain long at one calling—be it one summer or five hundred; eventually we change what we do, taking up other duties, other callings, other crafts."

"Five hundred summers? Five hundred years?"

Loric nodded but added, "We take note of the seasons more than we count the years."

Beau looked at Tipperton and in a hushed voice said, "Cor."

Tipperton slowly let out a breath. "But what about your kings and such—do they also take up other tasks?"

"Aye," replied Loric. "Though what you name king we call *Coron*. Alor Vanidar was Coron when the first Eld Tree seedlings were brought from Adonar and planted in the river-laden land which became Darda Galion. Yet his interest was drawn elsewhere and he gave Coronship of the realm over to another—Elmaron, I believe."

"Vanidor was Coron?"

Loric shook his head. "Nay, not Alor Vani*dor* but Alor Vani*dar* instead."

"Vanidor, Vanidar: they sound rather like one another if you ask me," said Tip, Beau nodding his agreement.

"Not to the Elven ear," replied Loric. "Vanidar means Silverleaf in Common, and Vanidor, Silverbranch."

"Oh," said Tip.

Loric leaned forward, ticking words off on fingers. "*Dor, dar, da*: branch, leaf, tree." He gestured about at the forest. *Darda* literally translates as leaf-tree, though it is the word in Sylva meaning forest."

Beau's eyebrows shot up. "Oh, I see. Like Darda Galion, it means Galion Forest, eh?"

"Darda Galion, Darda Erynian, Darda Vrka, exactly so. There is but one forest we name not Darda, and that is the Skög far to the east . . . an ancient wood, said to be the eldest in all of Mithgar."

"Skög, eh?"

Loric nodded, and silence fell upon the trio.

"So," said Tipperton after a while, "you haven't been at march-ward all of the days 'tween the Felling of the Nine and the capture of the twain, eh?"

Beau looked at Tip. "Capture of the twain? —Oh, you mean when they captured *us*."

Tip grinned and nodded.

Loric grinned too. "No, wee one, I was not at march-ward all those seasons. After the retribution, I turned my hand to silversmithing—two hundred summers or so—and thence to planting grain and harvesting it for a like while, and thence to shearing sheep.

"I lived in the mountains for seasons, sifting for gold, though not mining as do the *Drimma*."

"Drimma?"

"Dwarves."

"Oh."

Beau piped up, "All these things you name, Loric, seem close to the earth or seem to be common crafts."

"When faced with the span of Elvenkind, wee one, they are the only things of lasting merit—things of the earth and of arts and crafts and of home and hearth, and preserving all or leaving it better than when found. Crafting, husbanding, mastering skills, celebrating life and love—what better way to live?"

Tipperton glanced at the long-knife girted at Loric's waist.

"How does that creed reconcile with standing march-ward and the killing of Rûcks and the like?"

Loric sighed. After a moment he said, "Long past, Elvenkind nearly destroyed itself. In those days madness gripped us and we sought power, dominance, command over all, sought dominion even over one another. We cared not what we did to our world, plundering it just as we plundered our own kind. And as we stood on the brink, one came along who said, 'No more! If there is ever to be peace among Elvenkind, let it begin with me.' And he set aside his vile ways and walked our world spreading his message and asking others to take his pledge— Let it begin with me. Elvenkind was slow to learn, yet finally we grasped the truth of his words and turned away from the madness that once gripped us and began to revere life and love and to cherish the simple ways.

"Yet even though we revere life, there are those who would destroy all—among them the Rûpt. And we came to realize that in order to preserve life, we must protect it from those who would raze the world and turn it into an ash heap, protect it from those who seek dominion and maim and kill for their own gratification—those who slaughter in glee, ravage in delight, butcher for no reason other than the ultimate act of dominance and gain pleasure from doing so.

"And so when thou dost ask how standing march-ward reconciles with Elven doctrine . . . it is part and parcel of the whole. We are the Lian Guardians, each and every member of my folk, male and female alike, and when evil threatens, as in these times, we stand counter . . . though from what ye have reported and from what we ourselves have seen, Lian alone will not be able to stay the present menace."

Darkness seemed to fall upon the camp and little was said the rest of the evening, but as Tipperton and Beau took to their sleeping bags, Beau whispered, "Lor', Tip, think on this: if Elves' lives are timeless, what must it mean when one of them gets killed? I mean, with all of forever before them, why, no matter their age, their lives are just beginning. And to lose that endless life just as it has begun, well . . . what a terrible thing it must be."

A stricken look fell upon Tipperton's features, and he glanced at Loric, some distance away and sitting with his back to a tree. "Adon, Beau," Tip whispered back, "and still they take up the mantle of Lian Guardianship and put themselves in harm's way even though to lose their lives is to lose forever."

Loric, his eyes closed, turned his face away from the fire.

The sun had passed beyond the western rim of the gorge, and the glen had fallen into shadow, when Loric rode in among the thatched dwellings of the Elves of Arden Vale, the horse-mounted Waerlinga trailing after. The few Lian outside the candlelit dwellings looked up from wherever they happened to be, their eyes widening in wondering delight at the sight of the Wee Folk, for, excepting their gemlike eyes, Waerlinga resembled Elven children, though a bit sturdier of build. And for their part, Beau and Tipperton stared 'round in wondrous delight, for here was where Elven Folk dwelled in graceful though simple elegance.

Among cottages nestled amid the pines, down a path they wended, to come at last to a broad central shelter, a long, low building, its roof thatched as well. Loric dismounted and tied the horses to a hitching rail as Tip and Beau jumped down. All three stepped up onto the porch and past a door warden and entered the hall. Vivid colors and warmth and the smell of food and the liquid syllables of the Sylva tongue assaulted the buccen's senses as they entered the great hall, lambent with yellow lamps glowing in cressets and fires burning in hearths. Banquet tables with benches and chairs were ranged 'round the tapestried walls, but the center floor thronged with fair Elves smiling and filling the hall with bright converse and gay laughter. And through this cheerful crowd strode Loric, with Tip and Beau following, the trio travel-stained and Loric's face grim. Lian turned to see the warder and two Waerlinga striding past, and voices fell to hushed silence and the assembly quickly parted as Loric escorted the buccen toward the far end, where sat the Elven leader of Arden Vale with his consort at his side.

Finally they reached the dais and Loric bowed, saying, *"Alor Talarin e Dara Rael."*

"Alor Loric," replied Talarin, gazing at the Waerlinga and

rising to his feet. He was tall and slender, with golden hair and eyes green, dressed in soft grey.

But it was Lady Rael who captured Tip's wondering vision. Fair she was, and graceful, and dressed in green, and her golden locks were wound with green ribbons. And she smiled down at the Waerlinga, a sparkle in her deep blue gaze, and Tip's sapphire eyes sparkled in return, as did the amber eyes of Beau.

Now Loric held a hand out toward the Warrows and said in a voice all could hear, *"Alor Talarin e Dara Rael, vi estare Sir Tipperton Thistledown e Sir Beau Darby, Waerlinga en a Wilderland. Lona eio faenier ivo Dhruousdarda—"*

A collective intake of breath swept the chamber, some gasping *Dhruousdarda?* while others whispered *Lona?*

Lord Talarin's eyes widened and he looked at the Waerlinga and said, "This is so? Ye came alone through the Drearwood?"

Mutely, both Tip and Beau nodded.

Talarin's mouth turned up in a grudging smile and he slowly shook his head. "Ye are either brave or desperate or fools or all three."

Tip grinned back. "Well, sir, I don't know about brave, but fools no doubt we were and indeed desperate at times."

Talarin laughed and spread his arms wide to the throng. *"Ealle hál va Waerlinga, Fors avor!"*

"Hál!" the throng roared, and they turned smiling faces toward the buccen.

Beau tugged on Loric's sleeve. "What did he say?"

Loric smiled. "All hail these Waerlinga, Fortune favored."

"Oh. Well, then." The center of attention, Beau shuffled his feet in embarrassment.

Now Lady Rael leaned forward. "And what news do ye bring, Sir Tipperton, Sir Beau? Encouraging, I hope."

Tip shook his head. "Nay, Lady, 'tis not. From all the signs that we have seen—loose bands of Foul Folk moving 'cross the Wilderland, Kingsmen slain, a balefire on Beacontor, and a great Horde on the march—wide war has come unto Mithgar to the woe of all. Yet by whom and against whom I cannot say, though Beau has a flag which may tell."

Beau slipped the banner out from under his jerkin and held it up for all to see—a circle of fire on black.

Talarin reached out and took the flag and stared down at it

as he held it draped over both hands, the circle of fire showing. A fell look came over his face. "Modru," he growled, "against High King Blaine."

But Rael shook her head. "Nay, *chieran*, I think not. Oh, indeed, as we suspected, Modru casts his forces 'gainst Blaine, yet behind it all I ween we see Gyphon's hand."

"Gyphon?" blurted Beau. "Do you really mean Gyphon?"

Rael canted her head.

"B-but Gyphon is a god. What would he have to gain?"

Rael sighed. "The whole of creation, wee one. Crushing dominion o'er all."

"Oh, my," breathed Beau, turning a stricken face to Tip. "Oh, my."

13

How will a war on Mithgar give Gyphon dominion over all of creation?" asked Tipperton. "And this Modru—just who or what is he?"

Talarin sat back down. " 'Tis a long tale, Sir Tipperton, Sir Beau, and one best told after ye have had a chance to wash away all travel stains and to take a meal. We sup in four candlemarks. Join us and we will speak of these things afterward. Too, ye can tell us a tale of how ye twain came to pass through Dhruousdarda, through the Drearwood."

"Four candlemarks?" said Beau. "Oh, my, that would be enough time for a full bath—that is, if you have hot water and a bathing room."

Rael laughed, her voice a silver trill. "Oh, yes, Sir Beau, a bath indeed we can furnish, though I'm afraid you'll have to provide thine own fresh clothing, for we have nought sized to fit thee or Sir Tipperton."

Beau's face fell. "Um, I'm afraid we'll just have to put these back on, m'Lady. All our goods were lost in Drearwood when— But here, I get ahead of myself. That tale'll have to wait until we've cleaned up a bit . . . scraped some of the dirt off, so to speak."

Rael's brow wrinkled, but then she smiled, saying, "Alor Loric, if thou wilt show our guests the way . . ."

Loric bowed and murmured, "Aye, crystal seer."

Loric turned and started across the wooden floor, Tip and Beau in his wake. Behind, Dara Rael called out in Sylva to the gathering, and just as the buccen and their Lian escort exited from the hall, Tip looked back to see her whispering urgently to Elfmaidens gathered 'round, while at the same time eyeing the departing trio.

Followed by the Warrows, their breath blowing white in the frigid mountain air, Loric crossed the snow to another long, low building, smoke from chimneys rising into the sky. Stepping inside and past another door, the Warrows found themselves in a warm bathing chamber, where copper tubs filled with water asteam sat on iron plates laid over a raised hearth below which ruddy embers glowed. And Loric and the buccen doffed their garments—gritty clothes which they had worn for weeks without respite—and hung them on hooks, all but their socks, which they draped over their boots. Loric shared out towels from a shelf, along with scrub cloths and soap mildly scented with the fragrance of meadow bluebells. They each eased into the large tubs—Tip and Beau in one, Loric in another—and the water came up to the wee buccen's chins, though only up to Loric's chest.

"Oh, Lor'," groaned Beau, "but this feels wonderful. It seems a lifetime since I've truly been warm."

Tip nodded, adding, "And another lifetime since I've been clean."

Leaning back, Tip and Beau luxuriated in the water, quiescent, not speaking at all, lolling as the grime and sweat of trek and flight and fear and hiding soaked away. Loric, too, slid down into his steaming bath and lazed, for he had been long on patrol.

After a goodly while, Loric said, "A candlemark or so, and they'll be expecting us."

Both Tip and Beau were awakened from a drowse by Loric's words, and they yawned and stretched, and Beau looked at his hands and fingers and said, "Lor', but I'm as wrinkled as a raisin."

Tip looked at his own crinkled hands and laughed, and both buccen ducked completely under, then stood and took up cloths and soap and began liberally lathering themselves. Tip was in the middle of scrubbing his hair when the door opened and an Elfmaiden came into the chamber and—

"Hoy, now," sputtered Beau, dropping down into the water. "I say, you should knock or give warning or something." Tip remained standing, for his eyes were closed against the soap slathering down from his locks.

The dark-haired Elfmaiden laughed aloud as she stepped to their clothes, and at this sound of femininity Tip gasped and splashed down and under, only to flounder up spluttering and wiping his eyes as he peered over the edge.

Loric grinned and canted his head and simply said, "Dara Elissan."

"Alor Loric," Elissan replied, plucking their clothes from the hooks and gracefully kneeling to take up their socks. Standing, she turned to leave.

"But, wait!" protested Beau. "We're going to need those."

Elissan looked down at the garments and wrinkled her nose in mild aversion. "Oh, I think not, wee one, at least not until they've been thoroughly boiled."

"But what'll we . . . ?" Beau's question went unanswered as she vanished out the door. He looked at Tip and shrugged, adding, "I suppose we can wrap ourselves up in towels to attend the banquet."

Tip slowly began lathering himself, and he glanced over at Loric. "I say, Loric, do your dammen—er, uh, do your Elf-maidens usually come barging in on bathers? I mean, I stood there naked as a newborn, and yet she, uh . . ." Tip's words stumbled to a halt, and he turned up his hands.

But Beau chimed in. "I think what Tip's trying to ask is, don't your kind have any manners of modesty?"

Loric barked a laugh. "When ye have lived as long as we, modesty at bathing and such is found for the most to be unnecessary. However, Elissan in her haste simply forgot that others share not this same—"

Loric's words were interrupted by a knock on the door, but

before any could answer, Rael and Elissan and three other Elf-maidens came sweeping in.

Once again Tip and Beau plopped down in their tub, though Loric, seated, nonchalantly canted his head, saying, *"Darai."*

"We have brought ye raiment," said Rael, turning to other of the Elfmaidens. Forward stepped a trio of Darai, each bearing folded garments. As one moved toward Loric, he murmured, *"Chier."*

Slender she was and had black hair and brown eyes. She kissed Loric and said, *"Chieran, ir aron soll."*

Loric nodded and grinned and said, *"Hai,"* and though he remained sitting in soapy water, he held his arms wide in display, adding, *"neh?"*

Now the Dara laughed, then turned and laid the folded clothes on a nearby bench.

The two Elfmaidens facing Tip and Beau smiled at the Waerlinga, both buccen peering over the edge of their tub, wrinkled fingers gripping the rim, water dripping and dribbling down their faces from fresh-washed hair.

"May I present Darai Seena and Jaith," said Loric, then added, "And she who kissed me is Dara Phais."

All three Elfmaidens curtseyed, and Tip and Beau both bobbed their heads and mumbled embarrassed hullos. Then dark-eyed Seena and redheaded Jaith held forth two folds of clothes, and Seena said, "These must needs do as garments." And Jaith added, "While those ye wore are laundered well." Then they, too, turned and lay the clothing on the bench.

Now Rael smiled at the Waerlinga. "I deem they will fit ye, for we all have a good eye. —Darai?"

Rael turned and glided from the room, followed by the others, including Elissan, who smiled at the Waerlinga and winked at Tip as she stepped from the chamber, leaving Tip blushing furiously, while Beau and Loric laughed.

Clean and warm at last and dressed in modified Elven tunics—their sleeves cut down and their waists gathered at the back to fit Waerlinga—Tip, in dark blue, and Beau, in pale yellow, sat with their feet dangling and swinging from Elven chairs, tall for the likes of the wee buccen. They were ensconced in a warm alcove with Talarin and Rael and Loric and Phais. Wrapped 'round the three walls of the retreat, a single muted tapestry hung, subtle colors seeming to move in the shifting light of the hearthfire, the hues and shades and tints depicting bowl-shaped slopes of an open grove wherein figures reclined to listen as a being in white held forth. The meal was long past, and the six had retired to these quarters, where Talarin served each a small cup of hammered silver filled with dark Vanchan wine. And as the night grew older, Tip and Beau related their tale—of the skirmish at the mill and the wounded Kingsman and his coin and request and warning ere he was foully slain, of the fire atop Beacontor following the capture and destruction of that signal post and its subsequent recapture, of the track of the Spawn into the Dellin Downs, of the finding of the flag and the muster at Twoforks and of Willoby and Harl's discovery of other slain Kingsmen, of the decision to bear the coin through Drearwood and east to Agron, and of the westward march of the Swarm and of the buccen's subsequent travails, ending with their capture by Vanidor's squad of march-ward Elves ". . . though perhaps rescue is a better term," said Tip, "for we were at the end of our string, and surely had the Spawn been lying in wait for us in that gulch, we would not now be here telling you this."

"Even had the Rûcks and such not been there at all," added Beau, "most likely we would have starved to death, out there on the ice, for we didn't know where Elvenkind lived, nor would we have ever found Arden Vale, for it is truly hidden. Loric and Vanidor and Arandar and the others saved our necks right enough, and in more ways than one."

Both of the buccen raised their drinks in salute to Loric, and he raised his chalice in return.

Talarin stood and took up the flask to refresh each of their cups, and Tipperton said, "Well, that's our story, and a sad one it is, what with us losing our ponies and goods and all, and nearly getting killed more times than I care to remember."

Talarin paused in his task and raised an eyebrow. "That ye survived at all is testament to your wiliness, for to come afoot through the whole of Drearwood in these times and without heavy escort is nigh miraculous."

"Adon must have had ye in His hand," said Rael.

"Indeed," replied Tipperton.

"Hoy, now," said Beau, "speaking of Adon, what's all this about Gyphon? Just who is this Modru, and why would he go against High King Blaine?"

All eyes turned to Talarin, but he in turn looked at Rael. "Chieran."

Rael took a deep breath. "I will answer thy last question first, and thy first question last, Sir Beau."

She paused as Talarin refilled her own cup, and Loric murmured, "Settle back, my wee friends, for the crystal seer's tale may be a long one."

Tip glanced from Loric to Rael in puzzlement, yet before he could say aught, Rael began.

"Modru is what some call a Black Mage—"

"Black Mage?" blurted Beau. "Sounds grim."

Rael nodded.

"Just what is a, um, Black Mage?" asked Tipperton.

"One who twists his arts toward evil ends," replied Rael. "One who seeks to gratify his own desires through any means, fair or foul. Perhaps the principal mark of a Black Mage is his complete disregard for the needs of others except as they serve his own pleasures and his lust for total dominion o'er all."

"Oh, my," said Beau.

"Are there many Black Mages?" asked Tip.

Rael canted her head. "Dara Arin once told me—"

"Dara Arin?" Tip interjected. "Lady Arin of the ballads? Lady Arin and Egil One-Eye and the quest of the Green Stone of Xian?"

Rael took a breath to answer, but Loric said, "Ah, wee ones, should ye continue to ask, mayhap it will be after the spring thaw ere the crystal seer can finish her tale."

Tip looked at Beau, and that buccan made a motion as if he were buttoning his lips together, and Tip turned to Rael and said, "Loric is right. Please do go on, and we will try to hold our questions for another time."

Rael smiled and looked at Tip. "Still I will answer thee: Dara Arin is indeed the Lady of the ballads, who, with others, quested after the green stone—the Dragonstone of dreadful portent. And during that quest she came upon knowledge that there are a number of Dark Mages upon Mithgar, though how many she knew not.

"Regardless, Modru is one of these, and he squats in his cold iron tower in Gron and seeks sway o'er the world, or so we do believe.

"In recent seasons, we deem, he has been gathering Foul Folk—the Spaunen pouring across the in-between, coming from the *Untargarda*, the iron tower being one of the principal crossing points 'tween Neddra and Mithgar, or so we think. Drearwood would seem to hold another crossing point, or so all the signs do say." Rael paused, for both Tip and Beau frowned in puzzlement.

"Ye have questions?"

Beau looked at Tip and then made a motion as if unbuttoning his lip. "This 'Untargarda,' these 'crossing points,' and this 'in-between,' Lady Rael—I know a bit of what you're talking about, but only a bit. Could you explain the whole of it?"

"Me, too, I'd like to know," said Tip. "My da told me some, but he didn't know much of what was called for, though he did say that Foul Folk came from Neddra below, and Elves from Adonar above, and Mages from who knows where, and Warrows should simply stay put and that was that."

Rael smiled and looked from Warrow to Warrow. "All right, my wee friends, this I will say: there are many Planes of existence, but the principal three are the *Hôhgarda*, the *Mittegarda*, and the *Untargarda*—the High Plane, the Middle Plane, and the Low Plane. And upon each of these Planes there are many worlds, though once again there are a principal three—Adonar, Mithgar, and Neddra."

Both Tip and Beau nodded, for this agreed with what they had been told.

"For the most, the Planes are separated from one another," continued Rael, "but there are crossing points where the Planes are congruent and one may go in between—in between worlds, that is—but only under certain conditions: the in-between points upon the separate worlds must be a fair match to one another, the better the match, the less difficult the crossing. Even so, there are certain times of the day when the crossings in between can be made easier still: to come from Adonar to Mithgar, dawn is best, for it is neither day nor night, but in between; and to go from Mithgar to Adonar, the crossing is best made at dusk, which again is neither day nor night, but in between; and it is said that to cross from Mithgar to Neddra, mid of day is best, for it is neither morning nor afternoon, but in between ... and to come from Neddra to Mithgar, mid of night is best. Yet there are still more things which ease the passage: crossing in fog, for it is neither air nor water, but in between; crossing along a seashore, for it is neither water nor land, but in between; at the brim of a woodland, for it is neither forest nor field, but in between.

"Still yet there is more, for to make such a crossing of the in-between, one must follow a ritual: and for Elvenkind it involves a stepping rite, on foot or by trained horse, neither a walk nor a dance, but in between; and a chant, which is neither talking nor singing, but in between; and because of the ritual of chant and step, the mind becomes lost in the rite, neither wholly conscious nor unconscious, but something in between.

"And this is why we call such passages where we go from one Plane to another, from one world to another, as traveling the 'in-between.' " Rael looked at Beau and then Tip, one brow raised.

"Lor'," breathed Beau.

And Tip added, "Lor' indeed. How did you ever come to discover such an arcane practice?"

Rael smiled, saying, " 'Tis said that Elwydd Herself taught Elvenkind."

"And you say that the Foul Folk are using such a ritual to cross into Mithgar from Neddra?"

"Aye, wee one, all the signs say they are swarming across the midnight in-between by droves—Ruch, Lok, Troll, Ghûlk on Hèlsteed, and more—at Modru's cold iron tower in Gron and mayhap in the Drearwood, too. He is gathering, has gathered, a great force of Spaunen to do his bidding. Too, it is rumored he woos Dragons to his cause, though I stress 'tis but a rumor."

"Dragons?" exclaimed Beau. "But I thought they mostly left folk alone."

Rael nodded. "All but the renegades—those who would not take the pledge."

"Ah," said Tip. "As told in the legend of Arin and Egil One-

Eye." The buccan frowned a moment in concentration, then chanted:

> *"All must aid when Dragons raid,*
> *And only the renegades do."*

And Phais intoned:

> *"Friend and foe, enmity must go,*
> *Or both the day will rue."*

Tip laughed and clapped his hands, saying, "Ah, Lady Phais, I see you know the *Ballad of Arin*, too."

"Indeed," said Phais, smiling. But then her smile vanished and she said, "Yet Dragons or no, suffice it to say that Modru has gathered Swarms of Spaunen unto himself and now makes war on High King Blaine."

"But what about Gyphon?" asked Beau. "How does He figure into this?"

Phais smiled grimly, and gestured at the walls. "That is why we have come unto this particular alcove, for the tapestry tells that tale."

"Huah," grunted Beau. "Tells the tale? All I see is someone in a dell who seems to be making a speech."

"Nay, Sir Beau," said Talarin. "Look closely."

Both Tip and Beau stood and stepped closer to the tapestry; then Beau clambered upon a bench and Tip upon a chair for a closer look still.

"Why," said Beau, "these aren't people at all, but instead are . . ." His voice faded as he shook his head in puzzlement, and he turned toward Talarin. "I say, what are these?"

"Beings of . . . light?" suggested Tipperton, reaching out to gently touch subtle colors of the silken weaving.

Beau swung back 'round and peered at the figure where Tip's fingers rested, and then at the others. "I say, Tip, they *do* look as if they're shafts of light . . . or some such."

Puzzled, Beau turned once more to Talarin. "But I thought that the gods would look like, uh . . ."

"Like us?" asked Talarin. "In the form of Lian and Waerlinga and Human and other such?"

Beau shrugged.

Talarin smiled and shook his head. "In spite of what some preach, 'tis the greatest of conceits for any peoples to believe they are created in the image of gods."

Tip again ran his fingers lightly across the tapestry. "And these beings of light are the gods?"

Talarin canted his head, and beside Loric, Phais said, "Indeed, Sir Tipperton. 'Tis as close as Lian artisans could come in recording the great debate 'tween Gyphon and Adon o'er the fate of the peoples of the worlds. What thou dost see as beings of light are our attempts to represent the gods: central and in silvery white is Adon, His daughter, golden Elwydd, at hand. On the wall opposite is Gyphon. Over there where thou dost stand, the pale blue figure is Garlon, next to coppery Raes, ruddy Fyrra is over here, as well as dusky Theonor. I will not name them all, but instead will merely say that this represents the time of the schism."

"These are truly the gods, then?" asked Beau, his gaze sweeping 'cross the tapestry.

Talarin and Rael and Loric glanced at one another, then all three looked toward Phais, and she said, "We name them gods, but Adon does not so style Himself. He says that there are those as far above Him as we are above the mayfly."

The buccen climbed down and resumed their seats. As he settled in, Tipperton frowned. "But if they are not gods, then what are they?"

Talarin sighed. "Given what Adon has said, we know not, Sir Tipperton. Only that they are very powerful."

"Bu-but," protested Beau, thunderstruck and staring at the tapestry. "I mean . . ." His words stumbled to a halt. He glanced at the ceiling then turned to Talarin. "Say, now, just who are these above Adon?"

Yet it was Rael who answered. "Adon says that even He is driven by the Fates. As to whether such beings as the Fates are in some manner incarnate, we cannot say. As to those who might be above the Fates, perhaps none are, though some say the Great Creator stands highest."

"Great Creator?"

"The source of all."

Tip's hand gestured outward, sweeping so as to include the

world. "But I thought Adon made Mithgar, and Elwydd His daughter created life hereupon."

Rael nodded. "We too believe as dost thou, Sir Tipperton: that Adon indeed created Mithgar, and Elwydd, His daughter, engendered life herein; we also believe Adon shaped Adonar, but on that High World He alone brought forth all life thereon, including Elvenkind."

"Just as Gyphon created Neddra and the life and folk therein, twisted such as they are," growled Loric.

Phais held up a hand, saying, "There are those of us who believe Adon and Elwydd and Gyphon and all the others did not bring the worlds and peoples and all else out of nothingness, but instead merely shaped and molded and forged these things out of that which the Great Creator provided."

Tip's eyes widened. "You mean like me whittling a whistle from wood I did not grow, or you weaving this tapestry from thread you did not spin?"

"Just so," agreed Phais.

Beau frowned, then appealed to Rael. "This Great Creator, just who is He? And if He creates all, then why does He create evil things? That's what I'd like to know."

Rael shook her head. "Thou dost ask that which is beyond my ken. Yet this I do believe: the Great Creator is He whose very spirit is in all things—living as well as not living—rocks, streams, trees, birds, animals, fish . . . all creatures of land and sea and air, and the land and sea and air itself, as well as the sun and moon and stars and light and darkness . . . *everything* . . . and ere ye ask, I deem His creations mayhap include Adon, Gyphon, and others whom we name gods. I believe that some gifted folk—mortal and immortal alike—can sense this spirit in their hearts and souls, while other individuals can see its aura in all things."

"Aura?" Beau looked at Rael and frowned. "Just what is this 'aura'?"

Rael smiled. "Some see it as a faint glow; others as an astral <fire>. It is but an outward sign of who the Great Creator is, an outward sign of what He does."

Again Beau frowned. "And some of what he does is create evil things?"

Rael nodded. "Indeed, Sir Beau, some of his creations are

malignant, whereas many are benign, yet most are neither good nor ill but merely exist, and their effect upon others is determined at times by chance and at other times by the intent of those who employ them for good or ill. Sir Beau, thou hast asked why the Great Creator begets evil things; heed me: I believe that He knows neither good nor evil but merely creation. It is up to those creations themselves—those who can— to freely choose which path to take: sinister or dextral.

"This is, of course, what I believe. There are those who would dispute my claims, saying that all is foreordained, and this the Great Creator knows, and that none has a choice at all.

"Others believe as does Phais, that He creates some things, while others with the power to do so use His creations to shape still other things from them.

"And then there are those who say that there is no Great Creator whatsoever, and that all is ruled by laws which we do not now apprehend but which are nonetheless true, laws which govern even Adon and Elwydd and Gyphon and all else as well."

Rael fell silent, and both Tip and Beau sighed and shook their heads in bafflement. But then Tip held out a hand toward Phais. "I believe as you do, Lady Phais, that we can make things from that which Adon and Elwydd provided. Whether they themselves in turn used the creations of the Great Creator to make Adonar and Mithgar and the peoples thereupon, well, that I cannot say. Just as I cannot say that Gyphon made Neddra and the peoples therein." Now Tip turned to Rael. "Yet I also believe in something you said, Lady Rael: there is a force, a spirit, a power in everything, be it a rock, a tree, a stream, or aught else, for although I don't actually see it, I believe I sense it, and if these things I feel are evidence of a Great Creator, then He does indeed exist."

Rael looked at Tipperton and nodded in agreement, and once again Talarin took up the wine flask and replenished all silver cups with the dark Vanchan drink, saying to the buccen, "We have ranged far afield from our original intent. Is there aught else ye would ask?"

Beau looked at Tip, then turned to Phais. "Lady, you did say something about a debate and a schism."

Phais sipped from her cup, then nodded. "Indeed, for 'twas the debate which resulted in some folk being free and others being bound."

"Free and bound?" asked Tipperton. "Say, now, what was this debate all about?"

Phais gestured at the tapestry. "Long past in Adonar there was a great disputation. At question was the gods' interference in the lives of the lesser folk, of mortals and immortals alike. The two mightiest gods—Adon and Gyphon—quarreled bitterly, with Adon holding that the gods would destroy those whom they would control, and Gyphon contending that it is the right of gods to do as they will. Adon spoke eloquently, saying that gods should give free choice unto all created beings—for were they not folk in their own right which only the Fates should sway?—whereas sly-tongued Gyphon, His voice dripping honey, argued forcefully for absolute dominion in all things—for were not these worlds and inferior beings shaped by the gods' own hands for purposes only they knew? Some of the gods sided with Gyphon—Brell, Naxon, Ordo, and mayhap one or two more—but most allied themselves with Adon."

Phais paused, and Talarin said, "And that is why, my dear Waerlinga, Adonar and Mithgar are free, whereas Neddra is not, for Neddra and its peoples are creations of Gyphon, and his will holds dominion o'er all, whereas Adonar and Mithgar are the works of Adon and Elwydd."

"Forget not Vadaria, Alor Talarin," said Phais, "for it, too, is a shaping of Elwydd."

"Vadaria?" asked Beau.

"The world whence come the Mages," replied Phais. "Or did before the destruction of Rwn." As the buccen's eyes went wide, Phais added, "As Dara Rael has said, there are many Planes of existence and many worlds therein—from the world of the Hidden Ones, shaped by Elwydd but now abandoned by those folk, to the Dragonworld of Kelgor, shaped by . . . we know not whom . . . mayhap by the Great Creator Himself. Yet I stray from the gods' debate. . . ." Phais turned to Rael.

Rael turned up a hand. "The pith of the debate was that Adon argued for the right of all peoples to freely choose the paths they would follow, whereas Gyphon spoke for the domination and control of those He named 'inferior beings.' "

Beau now stood and stepped to a different portion of the tapestry and climbed upon a chair, and Tipperton said, "I take it then that these Black Mages side with Gyphon, for as you have said, they seek dominion, control, power over others."

All the Lian nodded in agreement, and Loric said, "They have become allies of Gyphon, yet should Gyphon Himself gain the upper hand, he will utterly dominate them as well, much to their everlasting sorrow, though they believe it not."

Beau, standing on the seat, peered at the figure representing Gyphon. "Why, He isn't a pure single color at all, but instead shimmers like oil on water."

"Aye," responded Talarin. " 'Tis because He is the Great Deceiver, showing a given person or people whatever face need be until He has them in His grasp. Then and only then will His true nature show, and it is monstrous."

Hurriedly, Beau drew back from the tapestry, clambering down and resuming his chair.

"And this Modru in Gron, the Black Mage fighting against High King Blaine, he's been deceived by Gyphon?" asked Tip.

Talarin nodded, saying, "Beguiled, seduced, though he, like all the others, knows it not."

Beau frowned. "Say, now, let's get back to Tip's original question: what does all this have to do with Gyphon gaining total dominion over all of creation?"

Rael sighed. "With the destruction of Rwn, which held the only known crossing to Vadaria, the world of the Mages is sundered from Mithgar. The world of the Hidden Ones is abandoned by them, though some foulness remains behind. And although the passage to Kelgor remains open, it is said that Dragons will not be dominated by even the gods themselves, albeit Dara Arin believed and still believes the Dragonstone, ere it went down with Rwn, was one token of power which would give mastery o'er even them.

"It is said the gods themselves draw power from the very Planes. Hence, the one who controls two of the three primary Planes reigns over all. Adon is Master of the High and Middle Planes, and therefore is Master of all. Yet Gyphon rules the Low Plane, and Neddra therein. Thus, should Gyphon gain dominance o'er one of the two remaining principal worlds of either the Mittegarda or the Hôhgarda—gain dominance o'er Mithgar or Adonar—then He will displace Adon, to the woe of all existence."

"Well," said Beau, "why doesn't Adon stop Him? —Stop Gyphon, I mean."

Rael turned up a hand. "Adon intervenes not in the lives or destinies of any, not even in the life of Gyphon, evil as He is."

Silence filled the alcove, none saying aught for a while. At last Tipperton looked at Rael and said, "And Modru is Gyphon's acolyte, His chief lieutenant in Mithgar?"

Rael nodded.

Tip took a deep breath and blew it out. "And so, if Modru defeats High King Blaine . . ."

A look of profound distress fell across Dara Rael's features. "Then Gyphon rules all, wee one. Then Gyphon rules all."

14

*P*ale dawn light filtered in through windows as a soft tapping sounded on the chamber door. Clambering down from the lofty Elven bed and wrapping himself in a blanket, Beau tiptoed through the seeping light and across the cold wooden floor, hissing a wordless complaint with each chill step. Unlatching the door, he opened the portal to find Loric and Phais on the threshold, freshly laundered clothing in hand.

"Oooum," Beau yawned and stood back out of the way and motioned the Elves inside.

"Time to break fast, my friends," said Loric, moving across to the bed and holding a bundle out to Tipperton, that buccan sitting up and rubbing his eyes, "after which we will find ye suitable quarters, a place to stay until the season turns."

Tip reached out and took the clothing, saying, "Oh, Loric, do you mean for us to remain in Arden Vale until spring?"

"Indeed," replied Loric, catching up the bedside lantern to light it.

Beau, footing his way back across the cold floor, said, "Say, now, that's a while off, and if we're to deliver this coin anytime soon, we need to get cracking."

Phais closed the door after and followed Beau as a yellow glow filled the room, banishing the dimness. "Ye cannot go in this season, my friends, for winter bars the way."

Beau groaned. "I just *knew* it would be blocked in the winter." He clambered onto the bed beside Tip and under the remaining cover, flopping and flapping the one he had used for wrap in a futile attempt to spread overtop all.

"Thou art right, wee one," said Phais, handing Beau's clothing to him. "The city of Dendor lies far beyond the Grimwall, and the most direct and swiftest way through the chain is now barricaded with snow."

Beau, sorting through his bundle and mumbling to himself, said, "Dendor in Aven, that's where Agron lives."

Tip pulled his jerkin over his head. "And the straight way east is now blocked and we'll have to wait till spring?"

Loric nodded. "After the thaw, when the road through Crestan Pass is clear."

"Say, now," said Beau, "the thaw, that's what—two, three months off? Isn't there another way? Slower, perhaps, but passable? I mean, the Kingsman who was delivering the coin, well, wouldn't he have known about this Crestan Pass, it being blocked and all?"

Loric shrugged and looked at Phais, and she said, " 'Twould seem so. Yet mayhap he was riding south for Gûnarring Gap, to circle 'round and then north."

Tip glanced at Beau. "If we had our ponies, we could go that way."

Beau nodded, his lips pursed in regret.

"But we do not," continued Tipperton, now struggling to slip into his breeks under the cover.

Seeing his plight, Phais smiled and then deliberately turned her back to the bed. And both buccen threw off the blankets and quickly began to dress, Beau saying, "Well then, bucco, I suppose we'll just have to walk, though it'll take us awhile to reach Dendor. Oh, my aching feet."

Tip, pulling on his socks, said, "I suppose you are right, Beau. But by the time we get there, the import of the coin may have little or no meaning."

"Be not distressed, wee ones," said Loric, "for Alor Talarin has heard thy tale and knows of the need to deliver the token in a timely manner. Even so, he cannot perform miracles; he cannot banish the ice and snow standing across thy way. Still, knowing Talarin, he will find means to aid ye."

Both buccen hopped down from the bed and sat on the floor to pull on their boots. Phais turned back 'round and said, "After breaking our fast, we'll look at the maps and decide what to do, for I deem that waiting for the thaw and riding directly east will prove to be more expedient than traveling far south through Gûnnar and all the way northward again."

Fully dressed, the buccen caught up their quilted jackets and followed Loric and Phais to another long, low building, where they found Elvenkind at meal. Taking up trenchers and spoons and knives and a cup, they moved through a serving line and received biscuits and butter and a flagon of milk and bowls of porridge sprinkled with pine nuts. They took places at a long table, both Tip and Beau kneeling on the bench rather than sitting, for the table was sized for Elvenkind rather than Waerlinga. Loric passed an earthenware jug of milk to pour over the porridge, along with a small crock of honey to sweeten the meal. Too, Phais filled their cups with hearty tea, adding milk and honey to the drink.

They ate for a while in silence, but then Tipperton looked across at Loric and said, "Tell me this: thrice yesternight you named Lady Rael crystal seer. Why so?"

Loric remained silent for a moment, and Tip thought he wasn't going to answer, but at last he said, "Dara Rael is a rarity among Lian: she can at times divine things to come."

"Oh," replied Tip. "Like Lady Arin? They said she had wild magic and could see the future in flames."

Loric nodded, adding, "Aye, Dara Arin was indeed a flame seer, though it was the Mages themselves who named her talent 'wild magic.'"

"And Lady Rael has this same kind of wild magic?"

Loric pursed his lips, then said, "Mayhap. But instead of flames, Dara Rael divines her auguries using a crystal as her focus."

"Huah," grunted Beau. "It must be a rather dull life when you already know what's going to happen each day."

Phais laughed. "Nay, Sir Beau. Dara Rael does not know the everyday future. Instead she catches rare glimpses of portentous events, or occasionally speaks a rede, and not even she knows at times what they may foreordain."

"Oh, my," said Beau, now disappointed. "I mean, it would have been nice to know how our mission will turn out."

Phais sighed. "Would that it were so for all, for then mayhap we could take certain steps to thwart Modru."

"According to Delon's 'Lay of Arin and Egil One-Eye,' they took steps to prevent a foreseen disaster," said Tipperton.

At a puzzled frown from Loric, Tip continued: "What I am leading to is that if Lady Rael has foreseen anything of what is to come, then like Arin and her band, we could take steps to turn aside disaster."

Loric shook his head. "Not even Arin Flameseer could tell to what end her venture would lead. Whether or no she averted calamity, none knows."

"Even after all this time?"

"Even so."

"Say," said Beau, "if she had gotten together with Lady Rael, perhaps together they could have ciphered it out."

"But they *did* meet, Sir Beau," said Loric.

"They did?" exclaimed Tipperton.

"Aye," said Loric. "In Darda Galion. An ill-starred day, that, for 'twas when the Nine were felled."

"Yet well fated, too, for 'twas the same day Dara Rael and Alor Talarin pledged their troth," added Phais.

"Oh, my," said Beau. "Sorrow and joy mixed."

"Indeed," said Phais, "as is oft the case."

Tip took a deep breath and expelled it, and they finished their meal in silence.

Talarin peered down at the map lying open on the table. At hand, both Tipperton and Beau stood on chairs and gazed at the map as well.

Beau glanced up at Talarin. "So the southern route is three hundred leagues and some longer? I say, that's a bit over nine hundred miles, eh?"

Talarin nodded, adding, "Mayhap e'en a thousand." Then he looked across at Phais. "Thou art right, Dara. To wait for the thaw and travel directly east proves swifter than to ride south now through the remainder of winter and then angle northerly for Aven."

"Not if we use enough remounts," said Loric.

Talarin shook his head. "Given the state of Modru's gathering, we have none to spare, I fear, for war will be upon us soon."

Tipperton made a negating gesture. "Look, even if you could spare the horses, we couldn't use them; they're altogether too big for the likes of us. I mean, simply hoisting a saddle up on one would be a chore, the great, tall things they are."

"We could stand on stumps," said Beau.

Tip grinned. "Oh, right. And I suppose we'd have to camp only where stumps are, eh? That or chop down a tree each night."

"Perhaps we could carry a ladder," suggested Beau.

Tip laughed, then sobered. "I'm sorry, Beau, but I was envisioning one of us on a ladder leaned against the horse, and him shifting 'round to see what this fool was about, and then fool and ladder splatting to the ground. No, my friend, stumps, slopes, rocks, ladders—Warrows learned long past that ponies are for the likes of us."

Talarin turned to the buccen. "None of us knows the import of the coin ye intend to convey, yet if that slain band of Kingsmen were taking it unto Agron, it must bear some weight. Hence, this will I do: when the season permits, I will send ye forth on swift horses with an escort." Now Talarin looked across the table at Loric and Phais. "I am of a mind to ask ye twain to accompany the Waerlinga unto Dendor."

Loric glanced briefly at Phais and then asked Talarin, "E'en in these troubled times, Alor, with Modru at Arden's door?"

"Even so," replied Talarin.

At these words both Loric and Phais canted their heads, and Phais said, "It has been awhile since Alor Loric and I rode together in common cause 'gainst the Rûptish foe."

A grim look came over Talarin's face. "As did we all." Then he looked at the buccen. "Will ye accept our aid?"

Relief crossed both Tip and Beau's faces, and Tip said, "Oh, yes." He turned to Loric and Phais and grinned.

"Four horses," said Loric. "One for Phais, one for me, and two to hale the Waerlinga after, along with our supplies."

Beau glanced at Tip and sighed. "Until we can get some good ponies, I suppose we'll just have to get used to being hauled by Elves across the 'scape on the back of great beasts. Tethered tagalongs, that's what we are."

Phais laughed and Loric smiled. Talarin, grinning, said, "Even so, my friends, 'tis better to—" Of a sudden he paused, holding up a hand for silence, his head cocked as if listening.

Tip frowned, wondering just what—

taa-raa

—there sounded the distant belling of a bugle echoing from the stone canyon walls of Arden Vale and down through the evergreen trees.

Again the bugle sounded.

" 'Tis from the north entry and urgent," said Loric.

Talarin nodded, stepping across the chamber and taking up a sword and buckling it on. He looked at the Warrows. "If ye have weaponry, best fetch it now."

Tip's eyes widened and he turned to Loric and Phais, but they were gone, the door to the chamber swinging shut behind. "Come on, Beau," he said, springing for the door, "my bow and your sling are back in the room."

Beau groaned but followed on Tipperton's heels.

Out they darted and across the snow to the building housing the guest quarters, as somewhere in the distance a bugle sounded stridently.

Swiftly Tipperton strung his bow and strapped the quiver of arrows to his thigh. Beau rummaged through his pack. "Barn rats, Tip, I can't find my—! Oh. Here it is. Now bullets, bullets, where in the world—? Ah." Taking up the pouch, Beau swung 'round just in time to see Tip vanish through the door. "Hoy! Wait for me!"

Still the bugle sounded.

Beau caught up with Tipperton, that buccan with an arrow nocked and looking about for suitable cover. At hand, Elves, some girted with swords, others bearing spears or bows or long-knives or other such, took places all 'round, their stations seeming at random yet anything but.

Talarin strode by. "Sir Tipperton, take stance by that tree

yon. Sir Beau, there by the boulder where thy sling will do best."

"Ha," muttered Beau as he ran to the rock, "perhaps if we are attacked by a tree . . ."

Again the bugle sounded, and now they could hear the pounding of a horse. Moments later a rider on a black horse flashed into view, emerging from the pines.

Tip looked hard at the rider—golden hair flying, harnessed sword across his back, a long-knife girted to his thigh, a bugle in his hand. Now Tip stepped away from his cover and called to Beau, "It's Vanidor."

"Vanidor? But what's he doing up here?"

Tip shrugged and moved toward Talarin, who had stepped into the open before the gathering hall.

The hard-driven horse thundered across the clearing, snow flying from hooves. Haled up short, the steed skidded to a halt next to Talarin, the rider dismounting at one and the same time.

"Vanidor," called Beau, grinning and stepping toward the Elf, who glanced with weary eyes briefly at the Waerling, his brow creasing in puzzlement. But then Talarin embraced the Elf, saying, "Alor Gildor."

"*Athir*," replied the Elf, returning the embrace, then stepping back. "*Vi didron iyr velles.*"

Talarin glanced down at the Waerlinga, and then said in the common tongue, "Ill news, Gildor?"

Now Gildor, haggard, his face drawn, distress lurking deep within his eyes, replied, "Aye, Father, ill news indeed, for Modru sends *Draedani* through Kregyn to join his marching Hordes."

Talarin blanched, and nearby Elves moaned in fear.

15

Ashen-faced, Talarin turned and made his way back toward the chart room. Gildor gave his horse over to a Lian and then followed after. Unmarked, Tipperton and Beau tagged along in their wake, while other Lian—male and female alike—gathered in small groups and spoke with one another in hushed voices.

It was only after Gildor had doffed his trumpet and sword and grey-green Elven cloak that he and Talarin noted the presence of the buccen, so distracted were they.

"Alor Gildor," said Talarin, "may I present Sir Tipperton Thistledown and Sir Beau Darby. Sir Tipperton, Sir Beau, this is my *arran*—my son—Gildor."

Gildor canted his head, and the Warrows bowed in return.

"We thought you were Vanidor," said Beau, "for you look just like him."

"He is my *dwa*—my twin," replied Gildor, "and oft we are taken as one for the other." Then his eyes widened. "Yet if ye saw him, ye must have been nigh the marge of Dhruousdarda."

"We were," said Tip. "Vanidor and his band saved us from being slaughtered therein."

Talarin cleared his throat and then gestured to the map yet lying on the table. "These Draedani, Gildor, where didst thou—"

Gildor stabbed a finger down to the chart. "Here, Athir, at the southern end of Kregyn."

Tip clambered up on a chair, Beau likewise, and they looked at where Gildor's finger rested. The map showed a gap through the mountains where the chain of the Rigga joined the Grimwalls, the pass running between the wedge of Gron to the north and the Drearwood in Rhone to the south.

"We were on patrol," continued Gildor, "keeping account of the Hordes marching through. Yet a Swarm came and a great unease settled upon us as we drew back to hide among the crags. The fear grew as more Spaunen came marching, but then there was a great gap. And of a sudden, terror struck. Even so we managed to hold our ground and observe as three of the *mandraki* came forth. And then it was we knew what caused the dread, for Draedani walked among the Rûpt.

"After they were well away, then more Spaunen came marching, for they cannot withstand their own allies.

"I left Flandrena in command and rode to give warning."

Talarin shook his head. "Three. Three Draedani. Ai, dark is this day." Then he took a deep breath and said, "We must make immediate plans for this calamity, for should they discover the hidden northern entry or the one under the falls, we will need to evacuate Arden Vale."

"Aye, Athir," agreed Gildor. "Flandrena has orders to keep track of the Draedani, though from a safe distance, to make certain that if they turn toward the Vale, we will have fair warning. Duorn rides south along the bluff to the stands of the other patrols, for they must needs be forewarned as well."

"Say," said Beau, "just what are these, uh, Draedani, and why are they such, such—"

"Such terrors," said Tip, completing Beau's thought, for it was his own as well.

"Mayhap ye know them by another name—Gargoni or Gargons in the common tongue," said Talarin.

Both buccen shook their heads.

Talarin sighed. "They are creatures of Neddra, and some believe they are a breed of demon."

"Demons," said Tip, "now those I've heard of, though not by any of the names said here."

"You called them a breed; are you saying that this is but one kind of demon?" asked Beau.

Talarin held out a negating hand. "Nay, I am not, though some believe they are but one among many. I simply do not know. Yet whatever they are, they are terrible."

Beau turned up a hand. "Wull, just what is it they do?"

Gildor drew in a breath and said, "They are fearcasters, striking terror in the hearts of all. Few can remain steadfast in their mere presence, and none can withstand their gaze."

"Oh, my," breathed Beau, his eyes wide.

"Can't they be killed?" asked Tip. "I mean, you have a sword and a long-knife. Why not simply hack them down?"

Gildor shook his head. "Didst thou not hear me, wee one: none can withstand their gaze." Then Gildor's eye looked upon his sword lying on the table, and his hand touched the long-knife at his side. "Oh, aye, could I bring either Bale or Bane to bear upon one, mayhap these blades would deal a deadly blow. Yet it will never be, for I cannot now and hope I never need face such terror as these creatures cast."

"Wull, I'd stab him from behind, then," said Beau.

"Or slay him from afar," added Tip, raising up his bow.

"Ye know not what ye propose," said Talarin, "for these creatures, demon or no, freeze the very blood." Then he looked across at his son. " 'Tis dreadful news thou dost bring, Arran, and I will call the council immediately. Yet thou art spent and I would have thee well rested. Go unto thine *ythir* and thy *jaian*, for they would both see thee, and thence unto thy rest, for thou hast been in the presence of an enemy dire. I will speak to thee this eve and say what has been decided and what is yet to be done, and thou canst bear the word back unto thy patrol, and send word unto the others as well."

Gildor bowed, and then took up cloak, trump, and sword and stepped out the door.

Talarin turned to the Waerlinga. "I pray to Adon that the Draedani discover not this vale, for should they do so, then ye and the mission ye follow are like to go aglimmer, for we will be fleeing before them."

Tip took a deep breath and looked at Beau, but neither buccan said aught.

"Tell me, Loric," said Tipperton, "just what are all the foe we face?"

Loric cocked his head and raised a brow.

"What I mean is," added Tip, "name the allies of Modru and tell us what they are like, how they fight. I mean, here we are in the thick of things, or will be soon it seems, and neither Beau nor I know a pittance of what we should about any of the enemy. I mean, we didn't even know about these Draedani, these Gargons, until today. Yet the more we know, the better our chances of winning through whatever is to come."

Sitting on the bench beside Tip, Beau vigorously nodded in agreement.

Loric steepled his fingers and glanced at Phais, then turned to the Warrows. " 'Tis wise ye ask, for indeed the more ye know of thine enemies, the more ye can fend. As to the foe, there are these we know of:

"The Ruch—what ye name Rûck—is the most numerous. Small they are, though a hand or three taller than ye. They are skinny-armed and bandy-legged and dark in appearance, with bat-wing ears and viper eyes and wide-mouthed with pointed teeth set wide. Cudgels and hammers and other smashing weapons are their wont, for they have little battle skills, though some use bows and black-shafted arrows. What battle skills they lack they more than make up for by swarming over and whelming a foe by sheer weight of numbers alone.

"The Lok is next, that which ye name Hlôk. Like the Ruch he appears, yet with straight legs and arms, and taller as well—as tall as an Elf or a Human. Yet unlike the Ruch, the Lok is skilled in battle, preferring edged weaponry, such as tulwars and scimitars. Yet both they and the Ruch use other weapons as well—whips, knives, flails, scythes, strangling cords, and more—the Loka with greater skill."

Tip and Beau nodded, for this agreed with what they had been told about Rûcks and Hlôks. Too, they had seen both of these kind lying dead in Tipperton's mill yard and had even placed them on pyres.

"Next in numbers are the Ghûlka, what ye name Ghûls and

some name them the corpse-folk. These ye have seen in the depths of Dhruousdarda, and a dire foe are these man-sized beings. Dead white they are and bloodless, or so it would seem, for the corpse-foe are nigh unkillable in common battle, taking dreadful wounds without effect; even so they may be slain by wood through the heart, by beheading and dismemberment, and by fire, as well as special weapons, such as Bale and Bane, the blades Alor Gildor bears. Barbed spears they use, cruel as their own cruel hearts. Hèlsteeds they ride, horselike but hairless and scaled, with cloven hooves and snakelike tails, and they are trained to kill—so 'ware these slayers, too, their trampling and slashing of teeth as well as the lash of their tails.

"And speaking of dark animals, there are the Vulgs, Gyphon's hounds. Black as night and large as a pony. Their bite is poisonous, a venom which gwynthyme will dispel if ye survive their rending."

"They were after us in Drearwood," said Tip, "but we gave them the slip. Is it true they hunt mainly by sight?"

Loric nodded. "Yet ye were fortunate, for ye left little scent on the ice."

"I interrupted, Loric. Please go on."

Loric glanced at Phais, then continued: "Next among the Foul Folk come the Trolls—Ogrus ye name them. Scaled and dunnish tan or pale green they are, and huge—ten or twelve feet tall—and with a stonelike hide which makes them most difficult to bring down in battle, though a well-placed stroke will slay them—in the eye, or ear, or the soft of the mouth—whatever will pierce the brain. Otherwise, they may be slain by a fall from a great height or a massive rock dropped from above. And it is said that they cannot swim a stroke and so will plummet to the bottom and drown. The sole of the foot seems tender as well, for caltrops will turn them aside. Their numbers are few, yet not many are needed, for they are strong beyond belief and with great warbars they smash aside foes as if they were but mere stalks of straws."

"Oh, my," said Beau. "They sound the worst."

"Nay, my friend," said Phais, "there are more dreadful things by far."

"The Draedani?" said Tip.

"Aye, the Draedani."

"What weaponry do they use?" asked Tip.

"What do they look like?" added Beau. "Have you ever seen one?"

"Nay," said Phais, "and I hope I never do. Even so, still I can describe them. Eight feet tall they are, grey and stonelike, scaled as is a serpent but walking upright on two legs, a malevolent evil parody of Human or Elf. As to their weapons, some say they can sense intruders in their domain, and this very act inspires dread . . . as does the mere presence of one. And their direct gaze benumbs victims with fear, a terror so strong that one so transfixed cannot make any move whatsoever. The Gargoni hands are taloned, and their lizardlike mouth is filled with long, glittering fangs, and victims caught in their gazes are rended asunder by tooth and claw alone."

"Oh, my," said Beau, looking at Tip, "it seems you can't even run away."

"Aye," said Loric, "not if ye are captured in his gaze. 'Tis this very power of dreadful fear casting and transfixion which causes some to name them a spawn of demonkind."

"Then surely these are the worst foes of all," said Tip.

Phais shook her head. "Nay, wee one. For there are those who say the Fire-Drakes are worse, and yet others who name creatures of the deep more potent still. Yet I deem the worst foes of all are those whose behests they follow."

Beau raised an eyebrow. "And they are . . . ?"

"The Black Mages."

"Modru," breathed Beau.

But Tip, wide-eyed, held up a hand and said, "Oh, wait, there is a worse foe still."

Loric turned to the Waerling. "And that is . . . ?"

"You told me yourself yesternight," said Tip. "It is Gyphon Himself, for He rules them all."

16

I say," declared Beau, "right nice quarters, eh? . . . though the furnishings are somewhat overlarge."

Tip nodded abstractly as he stood at the window and looked outward across the snow running downslope through scattered pines to fetch up against the brink of the Tumble River, called *Virfla* by the Elves.

"And look, Tip, we have two beds," continued Beau, "though as big as they are, one would serve, with you at one end and me at the other."

"Umn," grunted Tip, not turning to see, his mind elsewhere.

While Tipperton brooded at the window, Beau went about the cottage, opening drawers, looking in cupboards, peering up at shelves, looking under counters, and commenting on whatever he found: cooking utensils, blankets and linens, washcloths and towels and lye soap and a tub for laundry as well as tallow soap for baths, a fireplace with cooking irons and a cauldron, a well-stocked pantry, an indoor pump and buckets and a washstand with a porcelain basin and pitcher, chairs, tables, a writing desk equipped with parchment and quills and inkpots and other such. Beau glanced out the back door, to see a stock of firewood nearby and a privy house across a short expanse of snow.

"Well," said Beau, coming at last to stand beside Tip, "it seems we have everything we need for living while we wait for the thaw."

Tip sighed. "I wonder if we're doing the right thing by waiting, Beau. Look, we don't know what may happen between now and then, and should these Gargon things invade this vale . . . well, you heard Talarin—we'd be on the run to who knows where. Perhaps it would be better if we simply set out southerly now."

"But Tip, even if we did leave today or tomorrow, who knows what we'd encounter? I mean, there's like to be Vulgs and Gargons and other Spawn all along the way, no matter which path we choose. At least here among the Elves we're safe for now. And by waiting for the thaw we'll be exposed much less time to whatever dangers lie before us . . . and as Phais and Talarin said, we'll still get to Agron sooner by the direct route than the longer roundabout way."

Again Tipperton sighed. "I know you're right, Beau, just as are they. Even so . . ." Tip's words trailed off into silence.

"Even so, you'd rather be doing something instead of hanging about doing nothing, eh?" said Beau. "Well, me too. And what I plan on doing is talking to Elven healers and seeing just what I can learn."

Tip looked up at his friend. "I suppose I could hone my skills with a bow. And you know, bucco, you could use some practice with that sling of yours."

Beau groaned and nodded reluctantly. "I guess you're right, Tip. I mean, back in Drearwood I was right dreadful at casting stones. And even though I'd rather heal than kill, if it comes down to it . . . well, I suppose I could hit 'em in the head with a rock."

Loric had gone back on march-ward, but Phais gladly arranged for the Waerlinga to sharpen their skills, providing Tip with an Elven-made bow—to replace his split one—along with additional arrows, and Beau with an Elven-made sling and more bullets.

"Oh, my, this is a beauty," said Tip, caressing the polished yew and bone laminate. "But I cannot accept such a gift. It needs to remain with its maker."

Phais laughed. "Nay, wee one, I'll not take it back. 'Tis the first time in seasons uncounted I have come across someone who can use it, for it is entirely too small for me now, this thing of my infancy. And its maker, my sire, will be delighted that it once again finds a use."

"Your da made this?"

"Aye, back on Adonar, when I was but a child."

Tip shook his head. "Wull, when this is all over—this war— I'll give it back to you so that your own children can use it, that is, should you have any."

Phais smiled. "Loric and I have talked of returning to Adonar to have a child when conditions among Elvenkind permit."

Beau looked up from his new sling. "When conditions permit?"

Phais looked at Beau for a long while, saying nothing. But at last she said, "Aye, Sir Beau. When conditions permit," and then she said no more, and Beau did not pry.

Over the next several weeks and under the Dara's gentle eye, they practiced long and hard at casting missiles with their newfound weapons—Tipperton's arrows flying true, *thunk*ing into the bull's-eye more often than not at ranges near and far, and Beau's facility at flinging bullets improving rapidly too, as hand and arm and aim became one with the sling. The Dara as well trained them in the skills of climbing, with rock-nail and jam and snap-ring and silken rope—skills in rappelling or moving 'cross stone faces, skills anchoring one another and paying out or taking up line, and skills at free-climbing too, relying on nought but legs and arms and fingers and toes. Upon the sheer stone of Arden's walls they climbed, upon the sides of lofty crags, down through crevices and up through cracks, backs braced hard against one side, feet against the opposite. Up to the very top of the western wall she took them, there where the stone was flat and more than a quarter mile wide. And the first time there they went to the far edge:

"Take care, wee ones, and stay low, using rock and lone trees for cover, for I would not have us silhouetted stark against the sky."

"Oh, my," breathed Beau, lying on his stomach and peering beyond the brim, looking to where a snarl of dark forest tangled out to the horizon westerly and to north and south as well. "That's Drearwood, eh?"

"Indeed it is," replied Phais.

"It's a wonder we ever made it through," said Tip, the edge of his gloved hand cupped against his forehead, shading his eyes. "Where is Kregyn Pass, the one the Gargons came through?"

"North," said Phais, pointing. "There where the hills rise up, though the pass itself cannot be seen from here."

Tip peered northward.

" 'Tis named Grûwen by men," added Phais.

"Oh," exclaimed Tip. "I've heard of it by that name, though just where . . ."

"There's an ancient song," said Phais, "of Geela guardians, singers of death."

"Ah, yes," replied Tip. "I say, is the tale true?"

Phais shrugged.

"I can't seem to find the Crossland Road," said Beau, peering southward.

" 'Tis beyond the horizon, Sir Beau," said Phais, "fifteen leagues, or thereabout."

Now Tip's gaze swept north and south along the capstone of the bluff. "I thought that there were warders up here on the wall, yet I see none."

Phais laughed. "They watch in secret, Sir Tip; it would not do to be seen. Yet they are here, I assure thee."

"Wull," said Beau, gesturing at Drearwood, "even though I know that Foul Folk are in there, I don't see how anything could be spotted down in that monstrous knot."

"The eye becomes accustomed to it," murmured Phais, "and movement within plucks at thy gaze."

Tip looked long and hard, then finally said, "I just hope no movement comes this way, at least until we're gone from Arden Vale." A stricken look flashed over Tipperton's features, and he turned to the Dara. "Oh, my, I didn't mean that how it sounded, Lady Phais. I did not mean to sound . . ." Tip struggled for the proper word.

"Selfish?" volunteered Beau.

Guilt momentarily flickered across Tip's face.

"Cowardly?" added Beau.

Anger replaced guilt. "No, Beau, not cowardly. It's just that I don't want anything to stop or delay us from delivering the coin."

The Dara smiled in understanding and gestured toward Arden Vale. "Thou didst not wish to sound unconcerned over the fate of those herein."

Tip nodded. "I am concerned, Lady. But I don't think there's one bloody thing I can do about it. Yet to take the Kingsman's token to Agron, well, that's something I can accomplish, given that nothing bars the way." He glanced easterly at the snow-laden Grimwalls rising up in the distance. "I wish the be-damned thaw would hurry and get here."

"Hoy!" called Beau. "Movement."

Phais turned. "Where?"

"Down there, down where the stream enters the wood."

Hearts pounding, long they looked, seeing nothing but dark snarls. "It's gone," said Beau at last, resignation in his voice, "if ever it was there."

During these same weeks, Rael, hearing of Tipperton's interest in legend and song, gathered the buccan under wing and began teaching him bardic lore. They spent many a candle-mark sitting before Rael's fire, she and Jaith singing songs and telling tales and teaching the wee buccan how to strum a lute, though it was a bit overlarge for the Waerling and his fingers didn't seem to fit.

Too, each night of these bardic doings, Rael would take up a small iron container and loose its tiny clasp and open its hinged top and remove a crystal from a square of black silk. Pellucid it was, the crystal, five inches down its length and six-sided, each end blunt-pointed with six facets. And the Dara would peer into its depths, seeking a clue as to Tipperton and Beau's fate. Yet nought came of her gazings, and she would at last sigh and say, "Though 'tis charged with moonlight to see the future, nought do the facets reveal," and she would lay it aside.

Meanwhile, Phais introduced Beau to brown-haired, brown-eyed Aris, an herbalist. And she took him to her cottage with its trays of various soils stacked here and there and waiting for the spring, and to the attached drying shed, aromatic in its presence. And they spoke of nostrums and poultices and medicks, of simples and teas and tisanes, of mints and flowers and oils, of harvesting and drying, of stripping and pressing, of dicing and grinding, of cooking and storing and other preparation, and of growing and foraging as well, she sharing her lore, he sharing the knowledge contained in his red-bound book.

"Lor', Tip," said Beau after one of his meetings, "she knows *everything*!"

Tip looked up from the lute he was trying in vain to chord. "Did you tell her of your plan to treat the plague?"

"That I did, and she said it might improve things, mixing silverroot and gwynthyme. She hadn't tried it, you see, and she and I both hope we never need to."

"Well then, Beau, she doesn't know it all."

Beau shrugged. "Perhaps she doesn't know everything, but she knows a deal more than I do, that's for certain."

Tip again attempted to set his fingers to the chord. Frowning over the strings, he said, "Given the ageless lives of Elves, I suspect that she's simply had more time to learn. —By the bye, did she give you any of that mint? Gwynthyme, was it?"

Beau sighed. "She offered, but I declined. I mean, with all that's going on in Drearwood—the Spawn and Gargons and other such, Vulgs among them—I said it'd have more use here than in some trial of mine which may never come."

Plang! Tip strummed a discordant sound. "Oh, bother," he growled.

Not only did the Warrows spend their time sharpening old skills and learning new, but they also were put to work in the Elvenholt, for as the buccen quickly learned, all shared in the labor of the vale, even Talarin, even Rael. In this case, Tip and Beau joined with others working in the stables, feeding horses and mucking out stalls and rubbing tallow into tack.

During this time they watched as more and more Elven patrols left the strongholt to scout deep into Drearwood or, acting upon the information gained, watched as mounted Lian warbands left the stables and rode away on raids into that great tangle of woods, often returning with bloodied swords and empty quivers and wounded of their own.

And at these times Beau would be called upon to tend injured Lian, though mostly he watched and learned as skilled Elven healers cleansed and bound wounds and stitched cuts and treated hurts.

And Tip would grind his teeth in frustration and practice all the harder with his bow, for Lord Talarin would not allow him to go on the Elven raids; nor had the time yet come for Tip and Beau to set forth to deliver the coin.

February had gone, and March slowly trod toward the coming of spring. During the second week of that raw month, Rael and Elissan and Seena came to the cote of the Waerlinga, and they bore with them clothing sized to fit the buccen: breeks, jerkins, tunics, stockings, vests, underclothing, and more. Among the garments were silken vestments, finely embroidered with Elven runes.

"I say," said Beau, holding up his russet silken robe, "these are splendid."

Tip held up one of lavender. "What are they for?"

Rael smiled. "In a sevenday and some comes the first of the cycle of the seasons, and we would have ye join us in celebration. E'en in troubled times such as these, three days we rejoice, three days of banquet, the midmost of which is the turn."

"Oh, I love parties," said Beau enthusiastically.

"Of needs ye must work," said Jaith, "for e'en in this 'tis share and share alike."

Tip nodded. "Gladly," he replied, then glanced at his lute in the corner. "Will there be music?"

Seena nodded. "That and dance."

"Then sign us up," said Beau, smiling broadly. "When do we work and when do we play, and what would you have us do?"

"Ye may take labor on the first night with me," said darkhaired Elissan. "On nights two and three we shall play." She smiled at Beau and winked at Tipperton, and still Tip blushed, for he yet recalled the night she had stepped into the bathing room and he standing there in the tub, blinded with soap and all unclothed.

Over the next week and some, as the days fled and the new moon slowly grew, the grim air of war was alleviated somewhat by knowledge of the coming celebration. Too, a warm wind blew up from the south, and much of the snow thawed in the deep-notched glen, though it clung stubbornly to the heights of the Grimwall. Even so, all took the melt within the vale as a sign of the spring to come. Finally, the three days of banquet came, and on the first of these days, Tip and Beau were assigned the kitchen task of running and fetching, while others tended the fires, and yet others prepared fish and game and vegetables, while still others cooked. A full third of the Elves were in some manner preparing the celebration for the others to enjoy. On the morrow and the next, another third and a third after would do the same, and those who worked this eve would celebrate in turn.

At last the sun set, with the waxing half-moon in the sky. And Elvenkind gathered in the great hall. And with great pomp and formality, the dishes of food were paraded about the hall for all to see, trenchers laden with venison and trout and goose and leg of lamb, with creamed parsnips and peas, brown beans, and breads and sweet breads and honey and jellies and jams . . . and more. And now with the cooking done, Tip and Beau along with several others were assigned the task of keeping the wine and mead and pure mountain water flowing from pitcher to chalice, and it seemed as if every Elf, Dara and Alor alike, called on the buccen to serve, for Waerlinga in their smallness and tipped ears and tilted eyes and bright smiles are much like the children of Elvenkind, and it had been long since any Elfchild had been seen. And so, thither and yon scurried the Warrows, bearing silver ewers of bloodred wine and filling the cups of soft-gazing Lian, some with tears in their eyes.

But finally the meal was over, and now commenced singing and dancing and the playing of harp and flute and lute and drum . . . and the epic telling of tales, though these sagas were spoken in Sylva. If it had not been for Elissan's whispered translations, neither Tip nor Beau would have understood a word of aught said, even though their hearts pounded in response to the wide-rolling words.

On this night Jaith sang a song so heartrending that all in the hall wept, even the Warrows, though they knew not a single word sung.

At last the celebration ended, and Tip and Beau helped with the cleaning, and dawn stood in the eastern sky when they fell into bed at last.

On the second night of celebration, Tip and Beau dressed in their raiment, silken vestments o'er all. Yet as they made ready, there came a tap on the cottage door, and Phais stood outside. "I am to escort ye to the clearing, for this is the eve of the day when light and dark exactly balance one another, and there the celebration begins."

Tip and Beau were led through the pines, and they could see a glowing spectrum of candlelit paper lanterns hanging from branches ahead. They came to a snow-covered meadow, red and blue and yellow and green lambency in trees ringing 'round. All Elves were present, those who could be spared, for some yet stood march-ward on the bounds of the vale, and others watched over Dhruousdarda to the west and Kregyn Pass to the north. Yet this night Loric and Arandar were present as were both Gildor and Vanidor—the two so like one another that only someone who had known them a long while might be able to tell which was which.

Dark-haired Elissan stood at one of the twin's side, while redheaded Jaith stood at the other's.

As Phais escorted Tip and Beau into the gathering, Loric came and offered his arm to the Dara, and together they accompanied the Waerlinga to a central point, where stood Talarin and Rael between two standards planted firmly—they bore the sigil of Arden Vale: green tree on grey field, the Lone Eld Tree standing in twilight.

Talarin glanced up at the gibbous moon nearing fullness. "Well and good, ye are here, and we would have ye join our observance of this special day, for spring strides onto the land and winter fades."

"What would you have us do?" asked Tipperton.

Rael smiled. "Pace with us our ritual."

"Bu-but," stammered Beau, "we don't know your rite."

Now Talarin stepped forward and held out a hand to each. "Just do as I do," he said, smiling.

Taking a hand of each Waerling, Talarin nodded to Rael. And she held up her hands and all in the clearing fell silent as all moved to a starting place, silks and satins rustling, leathers brushing in the quiet, Darai and Alori opposite one another, Darai facing north, Alori facing south. When movement ceased, Rael began to sing, or perhaps to chant, for it was something of each, and in this she was joined bit by bit by all Darai there.

Now Talarin took up the chant, or perhaps it was a song, and he too was joined by the Alori, each linking in seemingly at random, yet it was anything but.

And in the argent light of the silvery moon shining down on white snow, Darai and Alori began stepping out the turning of the seasons.

Singing, chanting, and pacing slowly pacing, they began a ritual reaching back through the ages. And enveloped by moonlight and melody and harmony and descant and counterpoint and feet soft in the silvery white, the Elves trod solemnly, gravely . . . yet their hearts were full of joy.

Step . . . pause . . . shift . . . pause . . . turn . . . pause . . . step.

Slowly, slowly, move and pause. Voices rising. Voices falling. Liquid notes from the dawn of time. Harmony. Euphony. Step . . . pause . . . step. Rael turning. Talarin turning. Darai passing. Alori pausing. Counterpoint. Descant. Step . . . pause . . . step . . .

And down among the shifting Lian and treading at Talarin's side, Tip and Beau were lost in the ritual . . . step . . . pause . . . step.

When the rite at last came to an end—voices dwindling, song diminishing, movement slowing, till all was silent and still—Darai and Alori once again stood in their beginning places: females facing north, males facing south. The motif of the pattern they had paced had not been random but had had a specific design, had had a specific purpose, and the same was true of the song, yet as to the overall design, as to the hidden intent, neither Tip nor Beau could say.

Yet they were exhilarated.

Now Talarin called for all to retire to the great hall, for food and drink and dance and song and story awaited them all. And amid song and laughter, to the hall they went.

Tip and Beau were given places of honor at the table just to the right of Talarin and Rael's dais, and once again the food was paraded 'round the hall, to the applause of all.

This night there was succulent wild boar, and duck and pheasant, and brook trout, and breads with honey and jellies and jams, and vegetables galore, and an assortment of nuts along with sweetmeats of crystallized fruit.

Mead flowed and wine and water and this night a ginger beer.

And Tip and Beau stuffed themselves as if they would never eat again.

And when the meal was done and the tables cleared—all but the drinking cups and pitchers of water and wine and ale—once again there were songs and singing, once again there were timbrels and strings and wind, and once again there were sagas spoken and chanted—and this night 'twas a ginger-haired, strapping Dara named Aleen, wearing leathers and bearing weapons, who whispered translations unto the buccen.

It was in the middle of "The Saga of Tugor and the Serpent's Eye" that the door swung wide and a bespattered Elf strode into the hall. Compact he was with dark hair and dark eyes, and a sword rode across his back.

The hall fell silent as his hard stride fell upon the wooden floor.

"Alor," said Talarin, standing at the Elf's approach, " 'Tis not often one of the Dylvana graces this hall."

"I hight Eloran of Darda Erynian, yet I am come from Adonar these past four days."

"Adonar? Then thou hast ridden the in-between."

"Aye, the difficult crossing at the circle of stone."

Talarin raised an eyebrow. "Yet thou hast come here instead of riding unto thy Darda."

"I am sent on a mission, Alor Talarin, to bring thee tidings: Adon has sundered the way from Neddra to Mithgar."

A collective gasp rippled throughout the chamber, and Beau looked at Tip wide-eyed. "What does this mean?"

Robust Aleen sitting next to them clenched a fist and growled, "It means Adon has taken up the challenge and Gyphon's invasion will cease."

17

Amid the astonished murmur among the Elves, wide-eyed, Tip asked, "How can he do that?"

Aleen looked at him. "Do what, wee one?"

"Sunder the way between."

"He is Adon," pronounced Aleen, as if that were enough.

Beau nodded and turned to Tip. "She's right, you know."

Tip frowned and shook his head. "But, I mean, what—how—what power—?"

Tip's unformed question fell unanswered as Talarin called for silence. Once again the Lord of the Hidden Vale turned to Eloran, but it was Rael who asked, "Is there more, Alor Eloran?"

"Aye," replied the Dylvana. "I am also come recently from High King Blaine: Modru of Gron has started a wide war."

Again a murmur swept through the assembled Elves, this one low and angry, for Eloran's words were from the High King himself and at last directly confirmed what had only been presumed true till now. Yet the undertone quickly subsided as Eloran continued: "A Horde of Foul Folk has cast down High King Blaine's garrison at Challerain Keep—"

"Oh, my," exclaimed Beau as shock rippled across the gathering.

"—and King Blaine and his small company now fight in retreat, hoping for others to join in the combat. Ere the garrison fell, the High King lit the balefires himself, and they call for an alliance of Men, Elves, Dwarves, and Mages to oppose this great threat."

Once more whispered comments purled throughout the hall, but Beau turned to Tip and querulously said, "Hoy, now, he's left us completely out. I mean, what about Warrowkind? Does the King not know we exist?"

"Ha!" barked Aleen. "He also left unnamed many others, my friend: the Hidden Ones, Utruni, Children of the Sea, Phaels, and more. Yet fear not, for although ye and they are not named, still all are Free Folk and will count in the end."

Talarin held up a hand to quell the unrest, and slowly the murmur died. "Eloran, I would see thee in my chambers. But first thou dost need rest, refreshment, and meal." Talarin motioned to Vanidor, then turned again to Eloran. "In eight candlemarks, neh?"

As Vanidor stepped to the Dylvana's side, Eloran canted his head forward in agreement, and then followed Vanidor from the hall.

Talarin called to the gathering: " 'Tis nought we did not already presuppose; Modru, Gyphon's chief agent, has begun a war for dominion o'er Mithgar. Yet Adon stands with the Free Folk, and we shall prevail. Let us on this turn of the season pledge our hearts unto His cause." Talarin raised his chalice, and all stood and held their cups aloft. "For Adon and Mithgar," he cried.

And as one voice came the collective response, *For Adon and Mithgar*, Tipperton and Beau joining in.

Now Talarin signaled the harper, and the harp rang out a stirring song, the notes belling across the gathering to kindle hearts aflame. Tone and voice, melody and lyric, voices rose up in accompaniment, Lian unified in harmony. In Sylva they sang, and neither of the two buccen understood a word, yet following Aleen's hurried whispers they sang along as well:

[In Lianion, the First Land, in Adonar so fair . . .]

And when the song came to an end, with a great shout all raised their cups and quaffed the contents down, and then without a further word, Lian began filing from the hall.

Tip and Beau turned to go, but Rael whispered to Lord Talarin and he in turn called unto them. And when they stepped unto the dais, he said, "As representatives of thy folk, I would have thee join me in my chambers, for we may have much to discuss and I would have ye advise me."

Taken aback, Tip glanced at Beau to find that buccan as astounded as he. Tipperton turned once again unto Talarin and said, "Well, sir, I cannot say we speak for all our folk, yet we would be honored to serve you in any way we can."

"Indeed, yes," said Beau, nodding vigorously.

Talarin smiled. "In eight candlemarks, then, come unto my quarters."

". . . not only the Foul Folk but perhaps the Lakh of Hyree and the Rovers of Kistan as well," said Faeon.

"Thou art right, my jaian," said Vanidor, taking a sip of tea.

They sat in a parlor in Talarin's quarters—Talarin, Rael, Faeon, Vanidor, Gildor, Eloran, Tip, and Beau.

Tip looked up at Faeon. "I don't understand."

"The Kistanians and Hyrinians—they are under the sway of Black Mages, acolytes of Gyphon," said Faeon. She turned to Rael. "Is it not so, Ythir?"

"Aye, 'tis true," replied Rael, "or so Aravan tells."

"Aravan?" asked Beau.

"One of the Lian," said Rael. "He sailed the seas when Rwn was yet an isle."

"Oh." Beau nodded and looked at Tipperton, who sadly shook his head, for both buccen knew of the destruction of that place. After all, it was a cataclysm marking the end of the First Era and the start of the Second.

"Aye, for thousands of seasons Aravan traveled the world, sailing the seas in his splendid ship, the *Eroean*. But when Rwn fell, Aravan left the sea behind. And though the destruction was Durlok's doing—Durlok, a Black Mage and votary of Gyphon—Aravan deemed that Gyphon Himself had had a hand in the devastation, though I understand Gyphon humbled Himself before Adon and declared He had nought to do with such—'twas a renegade acolyte, he claimed."

Tip held out his cup and Gildor refreshed the buccan's tea. As Tip added sweet honey, he asked, "What has this to do with the Hyrinians or the Kistanians?"

"Aravan tells that these two nations worship Gyphon in their temples and towers," replied Rael. "And so, aught concerning a war 'tween Gyphon and Adon will involve them as well."

"Hmm," mused Beau. "So you think they're in this fight, eh?"

All eyes turned to Eloran. He shrugged and set aside his cup, then said, "Most likely, wee one. Most likely. Though when I left Adonar we had no word on whether or no they were engaged or even on the move."

"Say now," said Tip, "just where is this, uh, in-between crossing you made in coming here?"

Eloran glanced at Talarin and, at a nod from the Alor, said, "Four days south of here lies the circle of stones . . . in Lianion, the land thou doth name Rell."

"Lianion?" Tip turned to Rael. "Isn't Lianion what we sang about tonight? Lianion, the first land? I thought that was on the High Plane, in Adonar to be precise."

Rael smiled. "Aye. Lianion is indeed in Adonar. Yet when first we came unto Mithgar, we made the crossing at the circle of stones, and the realm we came into was called Lianion as well, for it was the first land we trod upon in this world. 'Twas only later it became known as Rell."

Tip nodded and then turned back to the Dylvana. "Tell me, Lord Eloran, did you see any Foul Folk on your four-day journey through Rell?"

"Movement in the distance at times," replied the Elf. "Yet whether or no 'twas Foul Folk, I cannot say, for my mission unto Arden Vale was urgent, and I did not turn aside to investigate."

Tip sighed and glanced at Beau, as if to say, We should have gone south and 'round.

But Beau gave a slight shake of his head, wordlessly replying [No, bucco; wait till the thaw].

"When dost thou plan on returning, Eloran?" asked Talarin.

"Mayhap tomorrow."

Rael shook her head. "Nay, Eloran. Rest instead. Tarry a day or so." The Dara took up the small iron container lying on the table at hand and opened the clasp. "I feel that something looms. What, I cannot say." Carefully she unwrapped the crystal from its black silk as all remained silent. Deeply she looked into the pellucid stone, and no one moved, and Beau's mouth gaped circular and wide in bated anticipation. Long moments passed, but at last she sighed and looked up and shook her head. "Nothing," she murmured, and pent breaths were released.

Talarin reached out and touched her hand, then turned to Eloran. "Dara Rael is right: thou shouldst tarry awhile and rest, for alert eyes are needed in these times."

Eloran nodded. "A day or so," he replied. "But then I must go. First to the circle of stones, and thence across Adonar unto the oaken ring, where I will ride the in-between and back unto Mithgar."

"Ah, the Weiunwood," said Gildor. "Well do I like that shaggy forest."

"There's an in-between crossing in the Weiunwood?" asked Beau, his eyes wide.

"Aye," affirmed Eloran.

"Oh, my. Then you had better watch out where you ride, for I have foraged there and some of that wood is, um, 'closed.'"

Tipperton looked at Beau. "Closed?"

Beau nodded. "Places with an eerie feel, and you enter at your peril."

Eloran smiled. "Indeed, wee one, for in those places dwell the Hidden Ones, and they do make it so, and not all who set foot therein e'er come out again. The oak ring itself is within a place what thou dost name 'closed.'"

"And you plan on going there, to this oak ring?"

"Aye," agreed Eloran. "There I'll emerge. Yet fear not for me, for Elvenkind has permission to travel within."

Beau's mouth formed a silent <Oh>.

Eloran turned to Talarin. "And from the ring I will ride to join King Blaine, wherever he may be found."

Talarin looked up from the floor. "When you reach him, say

this unto the High King: Arden will rally to the cause and oppose Modru at every turn. Warn him as well that Draedani walk among the Foul Folk."

Eloran blanched. "Gargoni?"

Talarin gestured and Gildor replied. "Aye. Three of the Mandraki came through Kregyn a moon past. Amid a Horde they marched, though wide was the berth given. South into Dhruousdarda they went, yet thence we know not where."

"I say," said Tip, "what with all this talk of crossing from Mithgar to Adonar and back again . . . could we ride down to this circle of stones and cross the in-between and then ride somewhere in Adonar and cross back over to Mithgar, to Aven? I mean, that way for the most part we could avoid any foe who might stand in our path."

Talarin looked at Rael, but she was gazing dejectedly at her crystal. It was Faeon who answered: "Ye both would need to know the ritual, the learning of which is no easy thing."

"Especially to cross at the circle," added Eloran.

"Huah," grunted Beau. "And just how long does it take to learn this ritual?"

Faeon turned up a hand. "Some master the rite in as short as a year, while others never learn."

"Wull, how do so many Foul Folk get across, then? I mean, are they all smart enough to learn the rite? If so, then surely we're as smart as they."

Faeon sighed. " 'Tis said they are aided by Gyphon."

Tipperton frowned. "Couldn't you just carry us across on your horses? I mean, we could simply ride on your laps . . . or behind your saddles."

Faeon shook her head. "Nay, Sir Tipperton. Thy mind, heart, soul, spirit, and body must be attuned to make the crossing."

"But I don't understand," said Tip. "What about the horses? How do they get across? Surely they don't know the ritual; surely they are not attuned. Does Adon help them?"

Gildor cleared his throat. "One of the Mageborn once told me whatever was embraced within the aura of the chanter would be borne across."

"You mean like clothes and weapons and such?" asked Beau.

Gildor nodded. "Those and more. —And as Sir Tipperton has pointed out, horses . . . as well as other animals."

"Well then, we've come full circle," said Tipperton. "If horses can be taken across, why not me and Beau?"

With both hands Gildor gestured at his own body. "Heed, the aura of a lesser animal can be enveloped in the aura of the chanter, and thence borne across. Yet thine aura cannot be embraced within mine own."

"Why not?"

"The aura of a living person is too strong to be girdled, my friend. Though at times I have thought were a chanter to bear someone who stands at the door of death, then mayhap could be done, for then I think the aura of the dying one would be weak enough to be held within that of the chanter. But given one who lies not at death's doorway, then it cannot be done. And that leaves only objects and lesser animals which a chanter can take between."

Tip sounded a dejected "Oh."

Vanidor turned up a hand, then said, "I would add but one thing my dwa has said, and it is this: a well-trained animal seems to attune itself unto the master. Hence, master and animal, they mesh and unify into one, and this eases the crossing. As to whether a raging wild animal can be taken between, that I cannot say, for I have not tried, nor do I know of any who has."

"Lor', Tip," breathed Beau, "if we were dumb beasts tamed or even rocks, then we could go."

"If we were dumb beasts tamed or even rocks," replied Tip, touching high up on his silken jerkin under which rested the coin, "we wouldn't have this mission in the first pla—" Suddenly Tip's voice jerked to a halt, and then he turned to Eloran. "I say, Lord Eloran, did the High King say anything of a mission to Agron to deliver a coin? This coin?" Quickly Tip pulled the pewter disk from under his collar and looped the thong over his head and handed the token to the Dylvana.

Eloran studied the token, then handed it back, saying, "Nay, he did not. Yet times were chaotic, and we were hard pressed, and I was not privy to all."

Tip sighed and slipped the thong back over his head.

"Say this, then, to the High King," said Talarin. "The

Kingsmen bearing the plain coin are slain, yet these worthy Waerlinga will deliver the token unto Agron. We shall see that it is done. But if there is a message the King sent with the token as well, we know it not."

Eloran frowned in puzzlement and started to speak. Yet ere he could say aught, Rael groaned, and all eyes turned to the Dara to find her gaze locked vacantly upon the glittering crystal lying on black silk in her lap. Tip started to rise but Vanidor motioned him down, while Beau looked about as if seeking his medical bag, saying, "She nee—" but Faeon shushed him to quietness. And then Rael's voice chanted out in plainsong:

> *"Jes a at an thas nid mahr*
> *Ut cwenz a fyra an rok,*
> *Als Vyir raifant avel ulsan*
> *E iul peraefiral."*

Then with a sighing moan Rael swooned, slumping back in her chair.

18

"*B*ut what does it mean?" asked Tip.

Rael, her hand slightly trembling, took another sip of bracing tea. Pale she was and weary, yet in spite of Beau's suggestion she refused to retire.

But it was Faeon who responded to Tipperton's question. "Ythir at times upon peering in her crystal speaks arcane redes. This is one of those times. Yet we cannot know if the message she uttered is meant for one at hand or someone afar. Neither do we know whether the words relate to the past, the present, or the future."

Tip shook his head. "No, Lady Faeon. What I meant was, what did she say? We don't speak your tongue, but for a word or two."

"And these weren't any words we know," added Beau, yet standing by to chafe Rael's wrists again if it seemed needed.

"Yes, *Ayan*, I too would like to know what I said," murmured Rael, taking another sip of strong tea.

"Oh," said Faeon. She drew a deep breath and then repeated:

> *"Jes a at an thas nid mahr*
> *Ut cwenz a fyra an rok,*

Als Vyir raifant avel ulsan
E iul peraefiral."

Rael's eyes widened, and she pondered a moment, while Tip and Beau looked from her to her daughter and back.

"Well?" said Tip.

Rael turned her gaze toward the buccan and said, "A bard would translate it thus:

"Seek the aid of those not men
To quench the fires of war,
Else Evil triumphant will ascend
And rule forevermore."

"Oh, my," exclaimed Beau.

"Indeed," said Eloran. "Dara, 'tis true thou dost not know for whom this rede is intended?"

Rael shook her head. "As Faeon has said, it could be one at hand or another afar."

Tip frowned. "What does it mean, 'not men'? Who are the 'not men'?"

Rael shrugged. "That I cannot say. Mayhap it means not Human, or not male, or not people altogether."

Beau's eyes flew wide. "Not people? You mean, um, like plants—trees and such? Or say animals? Horses, birds, whatever?"

Again Rael shrugged.

Tipperton shook his head. "No offense, Lady Rael, but what good is a rede if no one knows what it means?"

Rael turned up her hands. "Would that I could wholly master this gift, yet redes come at their own beck, and not at the behest of another. And their import is obscure until someone somewhere divines their true intent. As to when if ever someone will divine this rede's true meaning, I know not." Rael paused to take another sip of tea, then continued: "This rede may be for one of us in this very chamber, or mayhap more than one—Alori Eloran, Talarin, Gildor, or Vanidor, or Dara Faeon, or Sir Beau, or thyself, Sir Tipperton, or even me. Then again, it may have nought to do with anyone herein, or even anyone without. It may have significance in a time gone by or one yet to come. I cannot say. But heed, my belief is that it is meant for this age, for someone of this time. For we are faced with a peril dire: war now stirs across the land, driven by an evil who may rule forevermore can we not find a way to win."

Beau drew in a gasping breath, then managed to say with a shudder, "Oh, my."

With the pall of certain war now hanging o'er the vale and the High King in retreat, the celebration the next evening, the third and final day of the equinox, was subdued, the ballads of the Elven singers generally morose or dire, though occasionally one would sing of heroic deeds done. Still, for the most part quiet converse filled the hall rather than song and gay chatter, and only now and again would someone take up harp or lute, timbrel or flute.

Tip and Beau sat at a table with Eloran, Aleen, Gildor, Phais, Jaith, and Vanidor. And only Eloran seemed to relish the food, for he had been long on the trail. For the most part the others ate little and drank little and talked hardly at all, muteness filling the void.

Finally, to break the silence, Tip said, "Tell me, Eloran, just how does one go about finding one of these crossing points to go in-between."

The Dylvana set aside his joint of beef and quaffed a hearty draft of wine. He wiped his lips with the back of his hand and looked at the buccan and said, "Elwydd Herself pointed the way to the circle of stones, or so it is said. As to the others, in my experience 'tis by happenstance we find them. We must look for places congruent from Plane to Plane, places resembling one another."

As Eloran took up a chunk of bread, Tip said, "And this stone circle . . . ?"

"It is set atop a hillock, Sir Tipperton, where the rivers Firth and Hâth join one another."

"A difficult crossing, I heard you say."

"Aye, 'tis that, for although the circles themselves in Mithgar and Adonar reflect one another, the 'scape nearby is contrary—there being but one matching river in Adonar at that site. Even so, the crossing from Mithgar unto Adonar will be easier than the crossing opposite."

"Oh, why's that?"

"I will be going home, Sir Tipperton."

"Home?"

"To Adonar. 'Tis said—and I've found it to be true—that going to where one's blood calls, that is the easy path. Going opposite is harder. Why? I cannot say."

Eloran looked about the table to see if others might know why, but all the Lian shrugged, for they knew not, either, though Vanidor cleared his throat and said, "Aye, 'tis true. Even Humans themselves find it so when they come back to Mithgar."

Beau looked up, startled. "Humans cross the in-between?"

"Aye," replied Vanidor. "Any who master the rites can do so. And all find it easier to go where their blood calls."

"Even the Rûcks and such, I suppose," said Tip glumly. "Everyone but us, that is."

Beau sighed. "I just wish they would all go home."

They sat in silence for a while, and then Tip said, "I say, perhaps the Rûcks can't go home on their own."

Jaith looked across and raised an eyebrow.

"I mean," said Tip, "perhaps they are like horses and such, and need to be in another's aura."

Phais shook her head. "I think not, Sir Tipperton, for then they would be nought but dumb beasts."

Tip grinned. "And who's to say they're not?"

Gildor barked a laugh and all the others smiled, the first good humor they'd had that night.

Just after the cold dawning of an overcast day on the twenty-sixth of March, Eloran and Aleen prepared to set out for the circle of stones, Eloran to return to King Blaine and bear Talarin's pledges as well as his warning of the presence of the Draedani within Modru's ranks. Aleen was to accompany him, for in the few days Eloran had been in the Vale, robust Aleen had taken him as her lover, she a half head taller, but he diminished in no way by her statuesque size. Yet she was not going merely because she and he were lovers; nay, Talarin would have an emissary at King Blaine's side, not only to represent Arden Vale, but to give tactical advice; Aleen was well trained in the arts of war—the conduct of battles her special forte.

Tipperton, Beau, Phais, and Rael all stood at hand, and a chill breeze blew at their backs.

Talarin stepped to Aleen's side. "Though I would have thee at hand in the coming conflict, Dara, High King Blaine can use thy knowledge and arm as well. Too, I would have him know that Arden stands at his side, and thou art the champion I send."

Aleen touched the hilt of the sword at her waist and canted her head forward. "Well will I represent thee, my Alor."

Canting his head in return, Talarin acknowledged her pledge, and then he turned to Eloran.

"A better warrior thou couldst not ask," said Talarin to the Dylvana, nodding toward Aleen, the Dara now astride her horse. "None more fit to fight at thy side or to watch thy back."

Eloran grinned and nodded, then mounted, casting a salute to Talarin and the others near.

"Ward each other well," said Talarin, stepping back.

Eloran glanced at Aleen, and at a nod, they spurred away across the clearing, clots of earth flying from racing hooves.

"May Fortune's smiling face be ever turned your way," cried Tipperton after them, but in that same moment they disappeared among the trees, and if they heard him, he could not say.

As Tip and Beau trudged toward their cottage, Tip sighed and said, "I just wish it were us who were setting out."

Beau looked up at the distant white crests of the Grimwall, and then down at the Virfla at hand, the river running swift with snowmelt. "Don't worry, bucco. Phais said we'd be riding over Crestan Pass within five weeks or so. I mean, look, spring has come, and the thaw can't be far behind."

As if to put a lie to his words, snow began falling down.

March came at last to an end, and then April plodded by, though the month itself was marked by birds returning with the spring, and still the buccen practiced at weaponry and mucked out stalls and watched as warbands came and went. Too, Tip yet attended Rael and Jaith and listened to them sing and tell tales, while he attempted on his own to master the lute with little if any progress. On the other hand, Beau spent time with Aris learning herb lore and other such, and he recorded all in a companion journal to his red-bound book. And Beau continued to help with the healing of Lian who had taken wounds. In addition, both Tip and Beau attended strategic meetings called by Talarin and his planners, as all tried to decide how best to aid King Blaine and oppose Modru. In these meetings neither Tip nor Beau proved to be of significant aid, for they were not trained in the arts of war. Even so, Talarin insisted that they be there, for they alone in Arden Vale could represent their kind.

In mid April, word came from the east march-ward that a Horde was on the move. South it tramped, down through Rhone, heading it seemed for Rhone Ford to cross over into Rell—into Lianion of Old. Talarin dispatched scouts—Flandrena and Varion—to follow at a safe distance until the Horde's destination became clear and, if necessary, to skirt 'round the Horde and warn those ahead.

In the last week of April, Loric returned from the marches, he and Phais to prepare for the journey unto Aven, for they yet were to escort Tip and Beau unto that distant land. And together with the Waerlinga, they selected and set aside whatever supplies they were likely to need.

As they worked, Phais said, "The Baeron should have Crestan Pass cleared by the first week in May."

Beau looked up from the jerky he was bundling. "Baeron?"

"Aye, the woodsmen of the Argon vales. Though mostly they live in Darda Erynian and Darda Stor. They also keep clear the pass, and charge tolls for doing so."

"Um, where is Darda Erynian and Darda Stor?" asked Tip, Beau nodding vigorously that he would like to know as well.

"Oh, ye have seen them on Alor Talarin's maps: in the common tongue, one goes by the name Blackwood or Greenhall, and the other by the name Greatwood."

"Oh, yes," said Tipperton, remembering the sketch of

Tessa's map as well as those Talarin had in his war room. "Along the eastern side of the Argon, stretching from the Rimmen Mountains all the way down to Pellar."

But Beau remembered only vaguely where lay these two woods; even so, he did recall a rumor: "I say, isn't one of these woods haunted? I seem to recollect Tessa saying so, though which one it is, I can't bring to mind."

Phais laughed. "If either is haunted, wee one, then 'twould be news unto me. Mayhap she speaks of Darda Erynian, for Hidden Ones dwell therein."

"Hidden Ones? Oh, my. Then perhaps it is 'closed,' like places in the Weiunwood."

For three days they hemmed and hawed over things needed for the long journey, Loric saying, "If war has come unto the towns along the way, we'll be hard-pressed to resupply should the need arise. Even so, we cannot take more than it is wise for two packhorses to bear—ye twain, spare clothing, bedding, grain for the steeds, food for ourselves, and the wherewithal to prepare it."

"Can't we live off the land?" asked Beau. "I mean, Tip here is a splendid archer, and I can sling a fair rock."

"If we would get to Aven soon, 'tis better that we carry our food, for need we hunt or fish or forage, 'twill slow our journey markedly."

But even as they prepared, a swift-running horse bearing a Lian messenger came galloping into the stead. And within a candlemark, Alor Talarin called the Waerlinga and Phais and Loric to the Elven war room.

Alor Talarin's face held a stony look as they entered, and Gildor, Vanidor, and Rael were at hand, their faces hard as well. Too, there stood flaxen-haired Inarion, one of Talarin's chief planners. Mud-spattered, the messenger was at the table as well, his dark hair plastered down by sweat. A map showing part of the Grimwall Mountains lay open on the table.

As the Waerlinga took their places, Talarin gestured to the messenger and said, "Duorn brings ill news."

Talarin turned to the Elf. Duorn cleared his throat and stabbed a finger down to the map at a place in the mountains no more than ten leagues from Arden Vale. Tip's heart fell when he saw where Duorn's finger landed, and his worst fears were confirmed when Duorn gritted, "Crestan Pass has fallen into the hands of Modru. One of his Hordes now occupies those heights and stands across the way."

"Hold on, now," protested Beau. "We're supposed to go through that pass." He turned to Tip, to find that buccan grinding his teeth in frustration.

"I know, wee one. I know." Talarin closed his hand into a fist, gripping so hard his knuckles shone white.

"But we've waited all this time," said Tip, "and now the way is shut? We've got to get through there somehow, else our plans are all for nought."

Rael's soft voice sounded. "It cannot be, Sir Tipperton, Sir Beau. As opposed to Dhruousdarda, ye cannot hope to pass through a Horde athwart the way, for unlike gnarled trees and scattered Foul Folk, in Crestan thousands stand alert and across the only path. We must needs make other plans."

Tipperton groaned yet otherwise remained silent, but Beau slammed his fist to the table and gritted, "Damn the Rûpt! Damn the Rûpt! Damn, damn, damn."

Phais turned the map about so that the Warrows could clearly see it, and she said, "We shall have to go a different way."

"The next pass south crosses the slopes of Coron Mountain," said Vanidor, "just north of Aevor." His finger touched the map along the mountain chain some fifty leagues south of Crestan Pass.

"Over Drimmen-deeve," said Gildor, nodding. "I have been that way."

Tipperton, mastering his frustration, said, "Drimmen-deeve? Isn't that the Dwarvenholt under the Quadran?"

"Aye," said Loric.

"But wait," said Beau. "A Horde marched south from Drear-wood two weeks back. What if they've captured this pass over the mountains, too?"

Tipperton looked up at Gildor as the Elf stroked his chin. Then he touched the map, a finger tracing a route through the chain. "Then mayhap, Sir Beau, Sir Tip, the Drimma will allow ye passage through their deeves, from west to east, debouching here on the Falanith slopes."

"You mean for us to go under the mountain?" asked Beau, looking at the map. "Why, it must be thirty, forty miles that way under all that stone. Just thinking about it gives me the blue willies."

Gildor nodded. "Aye. 'Tis all of that and mayhap more, for once on a trade mission I traveled that way—under the stone, as thou dost say. And I would hope never to have to travel that way again, for as thou hast said, it gives one pause."

"Blue willies," muttered Beau, staring at the chart. "Blue willies indeed."

Tip shook his head. "Beau is right about the Horde that marched south. What if they're across our way, not necessarily in the pass over the Quadran, but elsewhere?"

"We can avoid them, Sir Tipperton, if they are in the open," said Loric, "for Elven eyes are keen. 'Tis only in the straits where they are like to trap us."

"The passes," said Tip bitterly.

"Aye, the passes," agreed Loric.

"All right then, what other ways are there? I mean, other than Crestan and the pass at the Quadran and the way under."

"Gûnarring Gap," said Vanidor, pointing even farther south. "Through Gûnar Slot to Gûnarring Gap."

Tip groaned. "But that's even farther, another three, four hundred miles."

"And what if the slot is under Modru's control?" asked Beau. "What then?"

"Ralo Pass," answered Talarin.

"How about we go north instead?" asked Tip. "Isn't there a pass through the Grimwalls to the north?"

"The only one we can easily reach is Kregyn," replied Phais. "And the Rûpt march through that from Gron. Too, I would not care to ride into Modru's very realm, 'cept were it to take war unto him. Nay, on a mission such as this, Kregyn is not the way to go."

"We could circle 'round Drearwood and go up through Rian," said Beau. "No, wait . . . Rian itself is under attack by the Foul Folk. I mean, Challerain Keep has fallen and all. Barn rats! That won't work."

"Drat!" agreed Tipperton. "It seems no matter where we turn, Modru bars the way."

"Not necessarily," said Inarion, speaking at last, "for even though one of his Swarms has gone south, we are not certain he bars all the ways through. Surely one or more will be open."

Tipperton looked up at Talarin. "What say you, Lord Talarin?"

Talarin stood a long while looking at the chart, but at last he said, "Alor Inarion is right." Talarin's finger touched down to the map and traced a course. "South through Rell seems the least of the evil choices ye face. Can ye not pass 'cross Coron Mountain—a mountain some name Stormhelm—then try the way under, through the holt of Drimmen-deeve. If it, too, is blocked"—his finger moved southward—"then there is Gûnar Slot and the Gûnarring Gap beyond. If the Slot is closed"—again his finger moved, sliding westerly this time—"then Ralo Pass may be open. If that way is barred, then mayhap ye can go farther downchain to where Trellinath meets Gothon"—now Talarin's hand moved to the border between the two, more than a thousand miles west of the pass into Gûnar—"for I seem to recall there is a way through the mountains nigh here, leading into Tugal. Beyond that I cannot say, for if the choices come to such, only ye four will be able to weigh what needs at that time to be done."

With every one of Talarin's words, Tip's spirits fell, for each of the subsequent choices given seemed to be pushing them farther and farther away from Dendor in Aven, where King Agron ruled. Sighing, Tip touched his breast where the token rested and wondered if his vow to a dying Kingsman would ever be fulfilled.

Two days later, sunrise found Tip and Beau and Phais and Loric in the stables, saddling two horses and lading two others with provisions and a smattering of gear. Soon all was ready, and Phais and Loric each took the reins of two steeds and began leading them from the mews, Tip and Beau following. But even as they did so, they met Aris and Rael and Jaith coming down the passage within, and each bore a small bundle, yet what each held lay concealed within enwrapping cloth.

The three Darai stepped aside to let Phais and Loric and the four steeds pass. Then they beckoned the Waerlinga unto them.

The buccen stepped forward to say their farewells.

"I will miss our days together, Sir Tipperton," said Jaith, "for 'twas a joy to play and sing for thee, as well as to tell thee legendary tales."

Tip smiled. "I just wish I could have learned the lute, my Lady, to play along as you sang."

Jaith laughed. "Fear not, my friend, for thou wilt one day learn. And speaking of lutes, I have for thee a parting gift." Smiling, Jaith unwrapped her bundle and presented Tipperton with a lute small enough to fit his hands.

Made of light and dark wood it was—blond clasped in ebony—and had silver frets and six silver strings tuned by black wooden pegs set in the head. A grey baldric embellished with a green tree looped from the neck piece to a small peg at the base of the body. "Oh," breathed Tipperton, taking the lute and handling it as if it were a precious fragile thing. And he fingered a chord and strummed the argent strands, and concordant tones sounded pure and silver.

He looked up at Jaith, tears standing in his eyes. "Oh, Lady Jaith, I cannot take this where I am going, for it is entirely too precious. You keep it till I return." And he thrust it toward her.

"Nonsense, Sir Tipperton," responded Jaith, refusing. "Bards as thyself oft travel the world, and neither heat, cold, storm, wind, nor wave, neither fair weather nor foul, stay them from their ramble . . . as neither do peril nor peace. Into hazard thou dost now go, yet song must go with thee as well."

"But I have nothing to carry it in to protect it from the weather."

Rael smiled and said, "Fear not, Sir Tipperton, for we have thought of all." And she presented to Tipperton a dark velvet bag and one of brown leather as well, saying, "These will keep thy instrument safe from the elements."

Tipperton reached out and took the bags, each inscribed identically with Elven runes— دصخیتمفسـهاف دخفقتحدهڧ — one sewn by hand in silver thread, the other branded in gold. And each was affixed with a carrying strap which could be set wide to slip 'round a shoulder or short to carry by hand. As well, there were thongs attached for tying onto saddles or racks.

Tipperton started to slip the lute into the velvet bag, but then stopped and looked at Jaith. "Do I need loosen the lute strings? I mean, where I go, there will be rain, heat, morning dew—"

Jaith held out a hand to stop his words. "Nay, Sir Tipperton. 'Tis Elven made, and will not warp. I saw to it myself. Too, the strings should last forever, for silver is mingled with starsilver."

"You made the lute?"

Jaith nodded, adding, "And drew and wrapped the strings."

Again tears welled in Tip's eyes, but he swiped at his eyes with his sleeve and then gently slipped the lute into the velvet bag and pulled the drawstring secure and then in turn slid that bag into the leather one and cinched the thong at the opening tight and wrapped it 'round the neck and knotted it. As he did so, he asked, "What say the runes, my Lady?"

"Why, 'tis thy name, Tipperton Thistledown, scribed in Sylva."

Tipperton grinned, then adjusted the buckle and slung the strap 'cross his shoulder and chest, and settled the lute at his back.

Now Aris stepped to Beau's side. "Much have I enjoyed our talks, my friend, and much I have learned from thy red-bound book and from thy lore as well."

"Not one whit as much as I," replied Beau. "Ignorant was I when I came into this glen, and ignorant am I still, yet much less so, thanks to you, my Lady. I just wish that I could stay here longer, then maybe I'd know even more. But Modru has seen to that, eh? For now I must go."

Aris nodded solemnly. "And where thou goest is into peril, and I would have ye take this to have at hand should the need arise." And she unwrapped the cloth she held and took from it a small silver case and gave it over to Beau.

His eyes wide, Beau slipped the catch and opened the case; inside he found pressed leaves of a golden mint. "Gwynthyme!" he breathed, then looked up at Aris. "Oh, but you will have more need of this than I, what with Vulgs in Drearwood nearby."

Aris shook her head. "Vulgs might lie along thy path as well, Sir Beau, and shouldst thou or thy companions be bitten, then this will counter the venom. Thou knowest the way of its use. Husband it well, for 'tis but six doses in all."

Carefully he closed the silver box and slipped it into the left breast pocket of his jacket, saying, "I thank you for this gift, my Lady, more precious by far than gold. Close to my heart will I keep it ever to remind me of you." Then he made a sweeping bow to Aris, and she smiled in return.

Then did Rael step forward again, and this time she presented the Waerlinga with hooded cloaks sized to fit them—an elusive dun brown on one side, a shadowy grey-green on the other. Dark metal clasps were affixed at the collars. "Now that ye go into peril, wear these well. Choose which side to mantle inward and which to mantle out depending upon the surround, and hard-pressed will be eyes to see ye, whether they belong to friend or foe."

Oohing and Ahhing and turning the grey-green side out, the buccen donned the garments, Tipperton setting aside his lute to do so.

Twirling about, Beau said, "Well then, how do I look?"

"Like a wee Alor, my Lord," replied Jaith, and then she and the other Darai burst into gay laughter, Tip and Beau joining in.

But then Beau sobered and looked at Tip and said, "But we have nothing to give in return."

"That ye go against Modru is enough," said Rael.

"Speaking of going against Modru," said Beau, glancing at the open stable doors and the sunshine beyond, "it looks as if the time has come."

Catching up his lute and shouldering it, Tip said, "If we're ever to deliver this coin . . ."

They turned to go, yet Rael stayed them with her hand, and kneeling, she kissed them both, then said, "Though we know not what they mean, remember the words of the rede: seek the aid of those not men."

"Lady Rael, surely your words are not meant for us," protested Tip, "but for Eloran instead. He is the one riding to the High King's side, not us. All we have to fulfill is my promise to a Kingsman dead."

Rael stood and looked down at the two Waerlinga. "Nevertheless, Sir Tipperton, Sir Beau, ye both were present when those words were said."

"Yes," agreed Beau, "we were there. But so were others:

Eloran, Gildor, Vanidor, Faeon, and Talarin . . . and yourself, of course, Lady Rael. I agree with Tip: surely those words were meant for someone other than us, for we're nothing but a couple of country bumpkins and totally inconsequential."

"Nay, Sir Beau, inconsequential thou art not," said Rael.

Jaith cleared her throat. "When thou dost get a chance, Sir Tipperton, tell Sir Beau thy sire's tale of the curious fly and the sleeping giant."

Tip laughed. "That I will, Lady Jaith. That I will."

Rael smiled, then looked down the passageway and said, "Loric and Phais, they await ye without."

Tip took a deep breath and looked at Beau, and together they started down the corridor leading from the mews, the three Darai coming after.

And they found outside a gathering of Lian, come to see them off, for they had made many friends in the eleven weeks following their capture by the march-ward at the edge of Drear-wood. Too, resembling as they did Elven children, many had come to see them embark on this mission dire, for their hearts would not let them do otherwise. And when the Waerlinga, resplendent in their Elven cloaks, stepped out from the stables and into the bright sunshine of spring, many gasped and turned aside, tears springing to their eyes, for it was as if precious young of their own were setting forth on a mission which would put them athwart harm's way.

Now Talarin stepped before them, his gaze somber but clear. And he said in a voice all could hear, "Fare ye well, my friends, fare ye well. And may the hand of Adon shelter ye from all harm."

Then he embraced Loric and Phais, and knelt and embraced each of the Waerlinga and kissed them as well, whispering to each, "Take care, my wee one. Take care."

Now other Elves came unto the four, and many knelt and kissed the buccen, some weeping openly as they did so. And Tip found tears on his own cheeks as well, yet whether they were his or those of the Lian, he could not say.

Last to come unto the buccen were Jaith and Aris and finally dark-haired Elissan. And when Elissan kissed them both, she turned to Tipperton and forced a smile and said,

"When next thou doth take a bath, keep thine eyes open; else thou mayest once again have thy splendor revealed."

Tip blushed and even though both were weeping, they managed to laugh through their tears.

And then the buccen were lifted up to the backs of the packhorses, where amid the cargo they straddled fleece-covered frames built especially for them, with stirrups on short straps for their feet.

Mounted on their own steeds, Loric and Phais turned to the buccen tethered behind. "Art thou ready?" asked Phais.

Tip nodded, and Beau said, "As ready as I ever will be."

But then Tip called out, "For Adon and Mithgar!"

And all the Elves lifted their voices in return: *"For Adon and Mithgar!"*

And then Loric and Phais spurred their horses, and across the clearing they galloped, packhorses and buccen trailing after, with Beau on the one behind Loric, and Tip on the one after Phais.

And all the Elves, some yet weeping, stood and watched as the foursome rode away, to reach the edge of the clearing and pass into the trees beyond . . .

. . . and then they were gone.

And only the sound of the spring-swollen Virfla broke the quiet of the vale.

19

*S*outhward among the soft pines of Arden Vale rode Loric and Phais, with Tip and Beau on packhorses trailing after, a high stone rampart to their right and a river engorged on the left, the swift-running Virfla singing its rushing song of flow. A crispness filled the air, and bright sunlight filtered through green boughs to stipple the soft loam of the valley floor with shimmering flecks and dots and streaks of glowing lambency. And in the distance a lark sang. Now and again they crossed meadows burgeoning with blossoms of blue spiderwort and white twisted stalk and pale yellow bells and other such early spring flowers, the meads abuzz with queen bumblebees harvesting the nectar rare.

They rode at a trot and a canter and a walk, Phais and Loric varying the gait to not overtire the steeds. And now and again all would dismount and give their own legs a stretch. Occasionally they would stop altogether, to relieve themselves or to water the steeds, or merely to pause and rest. But always they mounted up again and rode ever southward.

"Lor', but it's good to finally be underway," said Beau, at one of these stops.

But Tip shook his head, saying, "Had we known of the Horde in the pass, we could have gone long ago and be ten weeks farther down the road."

"Hindsight oft gives perfect vision," said Phais.

"What?" asked Tip.

"Hindsight oft gives perfect vision," repeated Phais. "Not only do we seldom foresee the full consequences of actions taken, but we are just as blind as to what will occur as a result of actions delayed. It is only after we have chosen a course and followed it as far as we can that we see some of the outcomes of our choice . . . though perhaps not all, for many a consequence may yet lie beyond our sight in morrows yet to be, e'en mayhap some so far in the future none will remember just what choice or choices caused it to occur. Regardless, in this instance, all we can say is had we known then what hindsight now reveals, indeed we would have been on our way weeks past. But we did not, and so we waited . . . and circumstances changed . . . and now we follow a different course, one which has unseen outcomes yet to occur."

Tipperton sighed. "You're right, and I know it. Even so, still I wish I had, wish that we had, started ten weeks ago."

" 'Tis in the past and lost," said Phais, "and thou must set it aside. What passes now and what lies ahead should be thy chief concern."

Before Tip could respond, Loric took up the reins of his steed and said, "Let us press on."

And so they mounted once more and resumed the southward journey through the wooded vale, occasionally taking unto the high stone pathways now that the river was in flood.

Altogether they covered some thirty miles before stopping that eve to camp on high ground above the flow.

Loric and Phais tended the steeds, tethering them to a tree-strung rope and removing saddles and harness and cargo and racks, and then giving them a small bit of grain while they curried any knots from their hair. And Tip and Beau cleared a space on the ground and gathered stones into a ring and built a small fire to brew tea to go with a light evening meal. And they spread bedrolls on the ground nigh the blaze.

And as the kettle came to a boil, Loric said, "Though I deem it safe in Arden Vale, once we are gone from it we will need keep a watch, and we might as well start now." He held out a hand in which he grasped four pine needles trimmed to four different lengths. "Short draw wards first, long draw guards last, the others in between."

But Phais shook her head, saying, "Nay, Loric; though Waerlinga see well by moon and stars, Elven eyes see even better. Thou and I shouldst stand the midwatches, while our two friends take first and last."

Loric touched his own temple. "Thou art right, Dara, I had forgotten."

"Oh," said Beau, disappointed. "But I say, let's draw straws anyway just to see what would have happened."

Loric glanced over at Phais, and when she shrugged, he held out the trimmed needles. And when they compared, Tip had the first watch, Beau the last, and Phais followed Loric in between.

"Ah," said Loric, grinning, "Sense and Fortune agree."

That eve, as Tip and Beau took a trip to the river to draw fresh water for the morrow, "Coo," said Beau, squatting by the run, the flux chill with high-mountain snowmelt. "Something that Phais said, well, I just never thought of it that way."

"Never thought what way of what?" asked Tip.

"That the choices we make now may have consequences so far in the future that none then will know the cause of it all."

"Like what?"

"Oh, I dunno," replied Beau, scratching his head. "Oh wait, here's one: how did your da meet your dam?"

A soft look came over Tipperton's face. "He said that once when he was delivering a load of flour, he saw her pass by in a wagon, and was so smitten by her that the next time he was in Stonehill he asked after her, and met her, and events went their natural way."

"Well, then, what if your da had chosen to deliver the flour a different day? Perhaps, bucco, you wouldn't have been born, we wouldn't have met, and there'd be no one to deliver the coin to King Agron, and the whole course of the war would have been changed because of it. So, it's because of your da's choice to deliver flour that day, and your dam's choice to be riding in the wagon, that the entire war will be won."

"Oh, I do hope you're right, Beau. —About the war being won, that is."

A silence fell between them as they filled water skins. But then Beau said, "Oh. Here's another one. And this one is about a choice even further back—one made two thousand or so years ago. Imagine this: what if Lord Talarin and Lady Rael had never decided to settle Arden Vale way back when they did. Wull then, we wouldn't have been rescued those two thousand years later by Vanidor and Loric and such. And that means we wouldn't get to deliver the coin, and who knows what would have happened then?"

Tip's eyes widened, then narrowed, and he said, "Listen, bucco, we *still* haven't delivered the bloody coin. What if we never do?"

"Oh, Tip, don't say such things." And the wee buccan looked over his shoulder, as if attempting to see dark fate lurking in the shadows behind.

"Or how about this one?" said Beau to Tip at breakfast the next morn. "When Gyphon and Adon had their debate long past, who then could have known the consequences? I mean, here we are involved in a struggle, one that may be a direct result of that quarrel."

Phais looked up from her tea. "Indeed, I never thought then that the disputation, though bitter, would lead to the darkness which followed."

Tip's eyes flew wide, but ere he could say aught, Beau asked, "Darkness? You mean the war, eh?"

"That and more," replied Phais. "For Gyphon not only ruled the Low Plane, He also seduced others on other Planes unto His unworthy cause, and these became Black Mages and rovers and ravers—any who were won over to His precept that the strong shall take whatever they wish to gratify their desires, regardless of the consequences to those they take from."

Phais fell silent, but Tip said, "Lady, did I hear you right, that you never thought then that the disputation, though bitter, would lead to the darkness which followed?"

Phais nodded.

"But then, I mean," stammered Tip, "that is, by putting it

that way, it makes you sound as if you were there. I mean, there during the debate itself."

Phais smiled gently. "I was there, wee one. Indeed, I was there."

Now Beau's mouth fell open. "In the glade with the gods? Oh, my. Oh, oh, my."

"Then you actually witnessed what we saw depicted on the tapestry in Talarin's hall?"

Phais turned up her hands and said, "The artisans who wove it did so from my description."

"Oh, my," said Beau again.

Tip took a long pull on his mug of tea. "I see what you mean by unforeseen consequences arising from things long past."

"Are they really beings of light?" blurted Beau. "The gods, I mean?"

Phais turned to the buccan. "That is how they seemed to me, Sir Beau, as beings of light; yet 'tis said that each one sees them differently."

"Oh, my," said Beau, his eyes wide and gazing at Phais as if she were somehow touched by the gods themselves.

Phais laughed and stood. " 'Tis time we were on our way."

That morning as they rode southward through the vale, with Tip practicing on his lute and Beau, as soon as he had recovered from his astonishment, prattling about unforeseen consequences of even the simplest acts, and he kept up a running chatter with Tipperton:

"I mean, I could jump up a coney and it run into the jaws of a fox and the fox not raid a henhouse and the farmer sell the nonstolen hen to a sailor who would take it across the sea to Jûng or another one of those faraway places, where it lays eggs which are sold to a peddler who in turn sells them to a royal cook, who prepares them wrong and as a result a king or emperor or some such dies, and then the realm falls into ruin . . . all because I kicked up a coney one day."

After perhaps the hundredth example—where a sneeze in the Boskydells resulted in the total destruction of the moon—Tipperton stopped chording his lute and said, "Oh, Beau, I just remembered: Jaith told me to tell you my da's tale of the curious fly and the sleeping giant."

"That's right, she did," said Beau. "Though I don't remember why."

"Well, bucco, it was right after you had declared we were country bumpkins and totally inconsequential."

Beau shook his head. "Haven't you been listening to me, Tip? I mean, I don't believe that anymore. Look, if a sneeze in the Bosky can destroy the moo—"

"Yes, yes," interrupted Tip. "But I'll tell you the tale regardless." And before Beau could object, Tip began:

"It seemed there was this curious fly, and a very clever fly at that, who wanted to travel the world and see all it could see in the time allotted to its short life. Well, one day it came across the greatest fortress it had ever seen. Huge it was, with solid stone walls hundreds of feet high and set on a sheer-sided headland above the rolling waves of a sea. Formidable it was, this mighty bastion, and it belonged to a great giant, and none had ever conquered it, though several fools had tried, for 'twas rumored that there was a great hoard within.

"Now on this spring day when the fly flew by, the windows were open wide, for the giant's wife was airing the bedchambers to clear out the winter just past. 'Well, as long as they're open,' says the fly to itself, 'I think I'll see what's within, for I've certainly never been to such a large and fine and invincible fortress in all my life.' And so the fly, curious as ever, flew through the window and in.

"Inside the fortress were many fine chambers and even one laden with gold, for the rumors were true, you see. And the fly coursed throughout the whole of the fortification, its jewellike eyes sparkling with wonder at all the greatness revealed. But in the kitchen the fly came across the greatest apple pie it had ever hoped to see, and it settled down for a meal.

"Long did it eat, filling its tiny belly, for it had been awhile since the fly had supped on such fine repast, its last splendid meal a days-old dead rat gloriously rotting in the sun.

"As you may suspect, with its stomach full near to bursting, the fly became drowsy. And so, up behind the warm chimney it flew to settle down for a nap.

"Some time later it seems, the fly awoke, eager to see the

rest of the world. 'I'll fly up the chimney,' it said to itself, but a fire yet burned in the stove. 'Not to worry,' said the fly, 'I'll just go out the way I came in.' And so it flew back to the bed-chamber window, but lo, the sash had been slammed to, for the giant's wife had aired out the entire stronghold and every window and door was now shut tight.

"'Oh, woe is me,' said the fly to itself. 'Now I will never get to see the other great wonders of the world.'

"But then it espied the monstrous giant himself, taking an afternoon nap on the bed.

"Now this particular fly, although of small stature and seemingly insignificant, was a very clever fly, and so it devised a scheme to escape from this unbreachable bastion.

"Down it flew to the sleeping monster and landed on the giant's immense face, where it began licking and daubing spittle on the behemoth's left cheek, right at the rim of the eye.

"*Slap!* went the giant against his own face, but the fly evaded the blow. And once again the fly settled to the giant's left cheek and daubed oozing spittle again.

"*Slap!* The giant struck another open-handed smack, once more missing, though this time the blow nearly succeeded. The fly's plan, you see, was not without risk, yet it was desperate to escape.

"*Slap!* struck the giant, and *Slap!* again, and *Slap!* and *Slap!* and *Slap!* each time coming closer and closer. Yet the fly was wily and persistent.

"By now the giant was fully awake and totally enraged, and he bellowed at the tiny fly, his voice a thunderous boom. And he leaped out from his bed and, raving, began pursuing the pest about the bedchamber and swinging his great fists.

"This was just what the fly wanted, for the monster was trying to kill it. And so the fly lit on the wall nigh the window, and *Boom!* the maddened giant smashed his fist against the masonry, but the fly was not there, having just barely escaped the mighty and devastating stroke.

"Well, the wall collapsed from the horrendous blow, and great cracks shattered throughout the entire fortress, and the whole of it crumbled into the sea, carrying the giant and his wife and a vast treasure under the billows below.

"But as the shattered bastion fell, the fly itself flew away, completely free at last, its only regret was that the great apple pie had been swallowed by the waves as well.

"And so you see, Beau, as my da used to tell me when I was but a wee child, though at times it might be risky, even the most insignificant, inconsequential one can bring down the mightiest of all, given a clever enough plan."

Beau laughed and then said, "Yar, but for the mighty to fall, there needn't even be a plan. I mean, like the Boskydell sneeze that destroyed the moon, there was no plan involved, just an inevitable chain of connected events. And speaking of unforeseen outcomes, I've thought of another, Tip . . ."

And on they rode through the vale, Tip trying to master a song on his lute, and Beau prating of exceedingly dire consequences of ostensibly innocent acts.

In midafternoon they came to a place where the river curved 'round a bend. And as they passed beyond the shoulder of the stone palisade looming to their right, in the distance ahead they could see the Lone Eld Tree towering into the sky. Too, the distant rumble of Arden Falls sounded within the vale, white mist roiling up into the sunlight shining aslant through the high stone gap of the embracing walls.

Under the branches of the soaring giant they stopped for a bite to eat, and spoke with Alaria, captain of the South Ardenward, to give her what tidings they held and to hear of any news in return.

"Aye, the pass itself is held by the Spaunen, and corpse-foe on Hèlsteeds patrol the road—"

"Road?" asked Tip.

"Aye, the Old Way down through Rell."

Beau turned to Phais. "Isn't that the road we were to follow?"

Glumly Phais nodded. "It means we must instead ride cross the open wold, avoiding the Ghûlka altogether."

Tip sighed and shook his head. "Our best-laid plans gone askew once again."

Loric made a negating gesture. "'Tis but a minor inconvenience."

Phais turned to Alaria. "What knowest thou of the Horde gone south from Dhruousdarda?"

Alaria shrugged. "Nought. And although Flandrena and Varion came through in the mid of April to follow the march and give warning at need, neither have returned."

"Did you see Eloran and Aleen?" asked Beau.

"Aye. Late March they passed on their way south, riding to the ring of stones."

Beau nodded and said, "That puts them well ahead of either the Horde going south out of Drearwood or the Ghûls patrolling the road."

Tip growled and said, "Would that we had gone when they did. Then we'd be well past those dangers too." Then he glanced across at Phais and held out a hand. "I know. I know. Hindsight and perfect vision and all."

Loric looked at Captain Alaria. "Is there aught else, Dara?"

Alaria shook her head, but then said, "Vulgs have been heard howling in the Grimwall up nigh the pass. Take care, for they may patrol the road as well."

"Oh, my," breathed Beau, his hand involuntarily touching the breast pocket which held the silver case of golden mint.

Bellowing greatly, the spring-swollen Virfla roared out through the high gap and thundered into the churn below, and behind the falls rode the four, the slant of the hidden rock road awash with water running down the stone slope. Yet the horses were sure-footed, and nought went amiss, though when they reached the concealing crags beyond, steed and rider all were adrip with water, drenched by the swirling mist.

Among tall upjuts of soaring rock they wended to the base of the rampart to enter among screening pines, and within this wood they rode southerly, the sound of the cataract diminishing behind.

Less than a mile south, the Tumble River curved away westward, yet the four did not follow its course but bore on southerly, to pass over the Crossland Road winding upward into the Grimwalls. This route, too, they ignored as they rode on south and into the wolds of Rell.

With his Elven-made bone-and-wood bow now at hand and his quiver of arrows strapped to his thigh, Tip looked leftward to the east, where loomed the towering Grimwall, blood-red in the afternoon sun, a stony barrier 'tween him and his goal.

And he looked rightward toward the west, where, just beyond the horizon and unseen, dreadful Drearwood lay, a place he hoped never to set foot in again. And he looked rearward, to the north, where silvery Arden Falls plunged over the high linn and down, the vale beyond the swirling mist a safe haven, yet he was leaving it behind. And lastly he looked to the south, across distant folds of land, toward . . . toward . . . who knew what? Toward an unknown future, was all. And he gripped his bow and a shiver shook him in silence, though he knew not why.

Beau, too, seemed stricken to muteness, for he prattled of consequences no more.

20

*S*outh they rode through the folds of the land, faring another ten miles beyond the Crossland Road before setting camp in a meager copse. And as before, while Phais and Loric took care of the horses, Tip and Beau made camp, though on this night they set no fire, for the thicket was too sparse to shield the light it would cast.

Loric and Phais fed the animals an amount of grain from their replenished supplies, for ere the foursome had left the encampment under the Lone Eld Tree, Alaria had insisted upon replacing the small amount of grain the horses had taken when coming down through the vale. In addition to the grain, she had replenished the meager amount of provender the four had consumed as well, adding even more dried fruit and vegetables, tea, jerky, and mian—food of the Elven wayfarer.

During his watch Tip stood at the edge of the thicket, peering through the twilight and to the south, his jewel-eyed vision probing the growing dark. The moon in its last quarter had set long past, and the glimmering stars were yet to fully emerge. Even so, the Grimwall loomed dark against the gloaming, the chain but some twenty miles away. But Tip's mind was elsewhere, and not dwelling upon mountains to the east or Drearwood to the west, or Arden Vale northward and behind. Instead his thoughts lay southward, where unknown events waited.

Phais came and stood beside him, and for a long while neither spoke, but at last Tip said, "Is it true, Lady, that all things are somehow linked?"

Phais looked down at the Waerling. "What wouldst thou say?"

"Well, part of yesterday and all day today, Beau has concocted the wildest tales concerning how a seemingly insignificant event in one time and place can cause great havoc in another. Oh, he started out mildly enough, where accidental meetings ultimately result in marriages and families, and that I can readily see. And then he spoke of how a puff on a dandelion could provoke an avalanche on a distant mountain. And the chains linking the first event to the last kept getting longer and longer, where a minor initial cause eventually resulted in a major catastrophe—such as bees gathering nectar among meadow flowers giving rise to a great storm half a world away, or a simple sneeze resulting in the total destruction of the moon." Tip looked up at Phais, silhouetted against the darkening lavender sky. "But you know, each of the links in those long chains of his seemed reasonable. I mean, like the puff and the avalanche: Beau presupposed someone plucking a tufted dandelion and blowing the seeds into the air, where they are caught up by a gentle zephyr, and the zephyr in turn swirling up into the sky, where a stronger wind whirls away one of those seeds and bears it far over land and sea and over land again to a distant mountaintop, where that wind-borne seed finally lodges 'gainst a pebble on the high slopes, where months later a foraging mouse comes across the seed and takes it up and in the process dislodges the pebble, which causes the avalanche which destroys the town below and all the people therein. Who knows what might result from this catastrophe? . . . a catastrophe that never would have been had someone somewhere not months ago puffed on a tufted dandelion a thousand miles away.

"And so I ask you again, Phais, are all things linked? If so, then how can any of us do even the slightest of things for fear of causing ruin?"

Tip fell silent and Phais stood looking at the emerging stars—more to the east, where the sky was darkest, than in the still glowing west. Then she took a deep breath and gazed down at the wee buccan. "Thou hast asked if all things are linked, to which I say, indeed." Tip groaned, but Phais did not pause. "If not directly then, as thou hast said, through chains long and short. But e'en were there no chain whatsoever, still would all things be conjoined, or so I believe, for ultimately do not all things spring from a common source: the Great Creator Himself?

"Yet though all things are connected, events here or there need not result in disaster; good can result as well as ill. Too, events occur which seem to lead to nothing at all.

"Hear this: had the dandelion seed instead been one of flax carried aloft not by the wind but rather by a bird, and had it fallen on fertile ground far away, and years later had people discovered the resulting field, then they could create fine linen and linseed oil and their lives would be better for it.

"And so dost thou see that events here can bring benefit there?"

"Yes," said Tip, "I can see that."

"Then think on this: some events are driven by erratic chance, while others are deliberate. We do not control those which are haphazard, but we do have a say over choices we intentionally make. Those are the ones I bid thee to consider, for choices made are much like stones cast in a vast pond, the resulting ripples moving outward in an ever widening circle, causing echoes in all they touch.

"Yet as the ripples widen, their effect diminishes the farther they travel."

"Yes," said Tip, "but it is also true that the greater the stone, the greater the waves created, no matter the distance."

Phais nodded. "Indeed, thou art right. Each event is a stone cast in the water—some large, some small, some nearby, some distant—and the resulting waves and wavelets cross and recross in complex patterns—strengthening here, weakening there, diminishing with distance. Sometimes even the weakest of waves, no matter how far they have traveled, come together to spark an event which will ultimately lead to great harm—a dandelion seed, a wee mouse, a small dislodged stone, and rocks balanced precariously on the slopes of a mountain above a village. At other times strong waves in places, no matter how close, completely annul one another—tyrant slaying tyrant, where neither survive to crush the conquered. Yet for the most part we cannot know how deliberate choices will eventually interact with one another or how chance events will come into play, for there are too many, the pattern too complex, to have certainty in the outcome.

"Adding here, subtracting there, the intermingled ripples and echoes and patterns can lead to peace and plenty or to famine and war, to lofty joys or deep frustrations, to amiable comfort or petty worry, to gentle convenience or feeble bother, to a fleeting smile or a momentary frown, or can result in ends which have little or no lasting effects one way or the other, for the pebble cast into the water was too small, or the wave too diminished by distance."

Tip growled. "You mean, Lady Phais, that no matter how well intentioned our choices, the outcome may be unexpectedly bad?"

Phais smiled. "Or mayhap unexpectedly benevolent."

Again Tipperton groaned, saying, "Well, if we can't tell, why choose at all?"

"Because we must," replied Phais, "else evil will triumph through our inactions."

They stood a moment in brooding silence, and then Phais added, "This I will say, Sir Tipperton: mayhap in the majority of choices one cannot predict with any certainty whether a given decision will result in great good or great ill, or in lesser good or ill, or become so insubstantial that the effects vanish altogether.

"This does not diminish in any way the truth that all things are related, for it is in the nature of the Great Creator to make them so—some forged with links virtually unbreakable; others with links tenuous at best.

"And so, my friend, whether by choice or by chance, events can lead to good or ill . . . or perhaps to nothing at all.

"As to those we choose, we can only hope the choices we make are worthy and do not lead toward ill. But for those events which overtake us—be they random or driven by the choice of another—it is how we respond to them which may help determine the nature and degree of what will come about in the end."

Phais fell silent, and Tip stood long without speaking, but at last he said, "To what ends, I wonder, will our choices bring us?"

"That, my wee one, I cannot say."

After a while, Phais returned to the camp, leaving Tip in the dark alone.

Although Elves pay little heed to the passage of time, of days and weeks and even months, seeming to note only the passing of the seasons, still they know at all times where stands the Sun, Moon, and stars. And at the appropriate time Tipperton was relieved in his watch by Loric.

Loric in turn was relieved by Phais, and she in turn awakened Beau for his stand at ward.

"Huah," said Beau as he and Tip tied thongs 'round the bedrolls, "ripples and waves crossing and recrossing, I never thought of it that way."

Beau tied another knot, then added: "Modru has dropped a vast boulder in the water, and a frightful wave rolls outward. We can only hope it doesn't drown the world."

Three more days they bore southward, riding parallel to and fifteen or so miles west of the Old Way, a north-south trade route running down the western side of the Grimwall Mountains. The land they passed through was rough, high moor with sparse trees and barren thickets and lone giants, many now setting forth new green leaves in the crisp spring air. In the folds of the land grew brush and brambles, and here and there winter snow yet lingered down in the shaded recesses 'neath ledges. Yet the route they followed was rugged, and slowly across the upland they went, bearing ever southward, and only occasionally did they see signs of animal life: birds on the wing afar, heading for more bountiful realms; an occasional hare; and once a distant fox. But for the most the harsh land was meager of game of any kind.

Five days past they had left the Elvenholt in the northernmost reaches of Arden Vale, some forty leagues behind. Although they had covered nearly sixty miles the first two days after setting forth, they were now moving only twenty or so miles a day out on the open wold, for the land was hard and they would not press their steeds beyond the pace they could sustain in the long days to come.

The seventh day on the open wold, they turned at last toward the Old Way—a road Alaria had said was patrolled by Foul Folk—for a westward spur of the Grimwall Mountains stood out across the route, and they would have to gamble on passing unseen along the road through a wide gap in the low chain ahead.

Tip and Beau readied their weapons and scanned the countryside, for they were come to a dangerous pass, and if Ghûlen patrols or Rûcks and such roamed it, the way would be filled with risk. Yet with sharp Elven eyes to guide them, likely any movement would be seen by Lian ere the reverse occurred, though if the Foul Folk lay in ambush . . .

Southward they went, through rising hill country, another ten miles before coming to the Old Way where it first entered the wide gap. No enemy did they see, though the way seemed churned by many feet tramping.

"A Horde," said Loric, remounting.

"The one from Dhruousdarda," said Phais. She turned in her saddle. "Keep a sharp eye, Sir Tipperton, Sir Beau, for somewhere ahead lies a Swarm."

Into the gap they went, eyes alert, nerves taut, Tip's heart beating rapidly. He looked at Beau to find that Warrow nervously loading and unloading his sling. They rode another two leagues, and the land began to fall, the close hills spreading out, while the route they followed swung southeastward, rounding the side chain and heading for the Quadran through rising hill country.

"Well, my friends," said Loric, "it appears there was no trap, and mayhap the danger is past, for the land opens up and we can leave this abandoned road once more." Then he turned to Phais. "Even so, we must return to this route ere we come to Quadran Pass, for from it rises the single road which lies across that col."

Phais nodded, then said, "Let us pray that the Horde has not captured that way as well."

Southeasterly they rode, another five miles or so, but evening drew nigh, and so out of sight in the shelter of a hollow they set their nightfall camp.

"Another day's ride should see us to the foot of Quadran Pass," said Loric. "And then the following day we'll ride up the Quadran Road and over."

"Can we make it all the way across in one day?" asked Tip, remembering Talarin's maps. "I mean, it's forty or fifty miles, isn't it?"

Loric shook his head. "Nay. Thou art thinking of the way under, for Gildor says the winding way he went passes 'neath Aevor Mountain to the south and Coron in the north. The way over is shorter, for it crosses the col between those same two peaks. Even so, it will press the horses to go up and back down in one day, yet we can relieve them by walking much of the way, and by going lesser distances in the following days."

"Then where? I mean, after we get across."

"After that we must cross the Argon River, and to do so we have two choices: six or seven days east and south lies the ferry at Olorin Isle; ten or eleven days northward lies Landover Road Ford."

Phais shook her head. "Not north, Alor Loric, for not only does that way lie alongside the Grimwall, where Spaunen dwell, but since Crestan Pass is held by the Foul Folk, mayhap they hold the ford as well; recall, but twenty leagues lie between the two. Rather would I cross at Olorin, for it is more likely to be free, standing as it does nigh the marges of Darda Galion."

Now it was Loric who shook his head. "But the ford itself lies on the marge of Darda Erynian and is not likely to be in the hands of the foe. And didst thou forget, Dara, our other choice, the ferry, is plied by Rivermen."

"Nay, Alor, I did not forget."

Beau looked up from his mian. "Rivermen?"

"Aye," replied Loric.

"I mean, is it bad that Rivermen ply a ferry?"

Loric shrugged. "Mayhap, for apast the Rivermen on Great Isle acted as guardians of the Argon, and for this protection they exacted tolls from merchants who plied the flowing tradeway. Yet the Rivermen turned to piracy—some say at the behest of Gyphon or one of His acolytes—slaying the merchants and looting the cargo, making it appear to be boating accidents in the rocky straits of the Race, a dangerous narrows downriver. To give truth to this lie, much of the wreckage and cargo would be set adrift, to be salvaged by their ferrymen kindred on Olorin Isle, a goodly way below the Race. The woodsmen of the Argon Vales, the Baeron, discovered the piracy of those on Great Isle and banded together and destroyed their fortress, slaying many of the pirates, perhaps all, though some may have escaped.

"Yet far downstream the Rivermen on Olorin Isle claimed innocence, saying that they knew nothing of what their kindred did upriver, and maintaining that whatever flotsam and jetsam was salvaged from the wrecks in the narrows, the ferrymen came by it honestly. Nought could be proved otherwise.

"Even so, after the destruction of the fortress upriver, and the subsequent loss of drifting salvage, many of the Rivermen on Olorin Isle went to live elsewhere. Only a few families remained behind to ply the ferry."

"And you think they were guilty," declared Beau, "—all the Rivermen, I mean."

"Aye," replied Loric.

"Well then, why did they go unpunished?"

"Suspicion alone is not proof."

Tip turned to Phais. "And yet you want us to go by the ferry?"

Phais nodded. "Those events are long past, and the Rivermen alive today are not those who committed the acts."

"That notwithstanding, Dara," said Loric, "back then they were Gyphon's puppets, or so I do believe. And in these dire times Rivermen may be His puppets still."

Phais turned up her hands. "Nevertheless, Alor Loric, the ferry seems safer than riding alongside the Grimwall all the way north to Landover Road Ford, even though the ford itself may be free of the foe."

Loric frowned in thought, then grinned and said, "Aye, it does at that."

Beau expelled a great breath. "Well, I'm glad *that's* settled. Tomorrow we go to the foot of Quadran Pass. The next day we cross over and, following that, make for the ferry."

Twilight turned to night, and Tip walked up to the rim of the hollow to stand his turn at watch. Yet upon reaching there he immediately spun about and ran down again, hissing, "Loric, Phais, Beau—fire in the Grimwall."

To the rim they all rushed, and far to the east and on the slopes of a great mountain, a long ribbon of fire shone, twisting its way up the stone.

Loric groaned and Beau asked, "What is it? A forest aflame? What?"

Phais sighed. "Nay, Sir Beau. I ween 'tis instead the missing Horde."

"The Horde?"

"Aye, for 'tis campfires and torchlight we see. They are encamped along the Quadran Road."

"But couldn't it be the Dwarves instead?" protested Tip, grasping at straws. "I mean, after all, it is the Quadran, and Dwarves dwell below."

Loric shook his head. "Nay. Were it the Drimma of Drimmen-deeve, then 'twould not be torches we see, but Drimmen lanterns instead."

"I don't understand."

"Their lanterns illume with a blue-green glow," said Phais. "Yet among the brighter lights of the campfires we see on yon slopes of Coron Mountain are minor glints—the ruddy light of brands, favored by the Foul Folk."

"Oh, no," groaned Tip. "This means we have to go farther south."

"Not necessarily," said Beau. "I mean, they could merely be crossing over."

"The light moves not," growled Loric.

"Well, crossing over on the morrow, then."

"Nay, Sir Beau," said Phais. "I agree with Loric. They are encamped. Too, if they intended to cross over, then they would have done so long past, for they left Dhruousdarda in mid April and now it is mid May. I agree with Sir Tipperton; south we must go."

"To Gûnar Slot?" asked Beau.

"Nay, not that pass but to the Dusk Door instead, and seek permission from the Drimma to go the way under."

Now both Tip and Beau groaned.

To the east and south they rode, faring across the open moors. And as they went the land began to rise, for they were bordering upon the foothills of the Grimwall. Four candle-marks they rode, and then four more, heading for the distant vale that would in turn lead them to the western entrance into Drimmen-deeve.

And they rode at a goodly clip, yet at a varying gait, for they must needs husband the strength of the steeds, for the entrance to the vale of Dusk Door lay some fifteen or twenty leagues southeastward—forty-five to sixty miles away—or so Loric said.

"More than one day altogether," groaned Tip.

"Aye," replied Loric. "We must camp tonight."

"I just hope no Vulgs are about," muttered Beau to himself, his hand touching the pocket holding the silver container of gwynthyme.

Through the hills they wended, ever bearing southeastward, and the land grew rougher as they went, and now and again they could glimpse Quadran Road wending upward over the pass, and although the Warrows could but vaguely make out movement thereon, both Loric and Phais with their keener sight assured them that it was indeed a Horde. And onward the foursome rode.

"I say," piped up Beau as through a slot in the foothills he again glimpsed the Quadran Road, "isn't this bringing us closer to the Rûcks and such?"

"Aye, it is," responded Loric. "Nevertheless, 'tis the quickest way to our goal."

"Fear not, Sir Beau," said Phais. "The Horde is well in the pass, and we are reasonably away from its flanks."

"Adon, but I hope she's right," muttered Beau, as they turned among great rounded stones and skirted thickets and rode along the faces of low-walled sheer bluffs.

But at last, as the day drew to an end, they came into a set of low rounded hills, the slopes thick with silver birch trees.

"Here we camp," said Loric, and set camp they did.

That night, again the torchlight blazed, though now it was closer, much closer.

"Oh, my," exclaimed Beau, "it looks as if we are on their very doorstep. How far away would you judge they are?"

Loric pointed. "That way, two miles by your measure, is the place where the Quadran Road splits off from the Old Way to ascend into the pass above. Mayhap the fringe of the Horde encamps there."

Beau swallowed. "Lor', I don't think I'm going to sleep well at all."

The next morning, bleary-eyed, Tip and Beau were rolling the blankets when Phais hissed, "Be quiet."

Tip looked up at her, and she stood attentively, listening. Yet Tip heard nothing, and he glanced across at Beau, who shrugged his shoulders and shook his head, that buccan too at a loss.

"The battle has begun," said Phais, Loric nodding in agreement. And then they resumed saddling the steeds and lading gear on the packhorses.

Hearing nothing but the faint rustling of birch leaves, again Tip looked at Beau, and received another shrug.

They returned to their tasks.

Out from the birches they rode, and high up in Quadran Pass, they could see a place on the road where it seemed a struggle was taking place. But neither Beau nor Tip could tell which side was which, or even whom the Foul Folk were fighting, though Loric and Phais said 'twas Drimma.

"How can you tell?" asked Beau.

"I can see them well," said Phais.

"Well then, how can we tell who is who? —Tip and me, I mean."

Phais frowned, but Loric said, "Do ye see one side is darker than the other?"

"Unh," grunted Beau, but Tip said, "Oh, yes, now that you mention it, one side *is* darker—the side on the higher ground."

"They are the Drimma, dressed in their black-iron chain."

"Oh, I see."

No sound came to the buccen from the battle on the mountain, the distance lending the illusion of two vast armies confined to a narrow road, and where they met they battled in eerie silence. Yet both Loric and Phais seemed to hear the conflict.

"Lor'," whispered Beau to Tip, "are their ears that much better than ours?"

"It would seem so," murmured Tipperton.

"I agree as well," said Loric from his place ahead.

Both buccen's eyes flew wide.

South they rode, away from the conflict, now aiming for a vale some fifteen miles removed, a valley that would lead them to the western door into Drimmen-deeve.

Yet neither Tip nor Beau could keep their gazes away from the combat up in the pass. And so they rode, twisting about, ever peering hindward.

After a while Beau said, "Oh, look! I think the Dwarves are winning."

And indeed it seemed that the darker force had pressed the Horde down the mountain somewhat.

Onward they rode another mile, but then Tip said, "What's that in the sky?"

Beau turned and looked back. "Where?"

"Up there, way back along the Grimwalls, one-two-three-four-five, no, six peaks back. Um, moving this way, I think. See it? A silvery speck."

The horses stopped.

"No, I don't see it," growled Beau, nettled. "Six peaks, you say? Counting from where?"

Before Tip could answer, Phais gasped, "Adon, is it true?"

Tip turned to see both Loric and Phais looking back as well, their features pale with shock.

"Six peaks from where?" demanded Beau.

"Is what true?" asked Tip, startled by the grim looks on the faces of the Lian.

"Counting from where?" gritted Beau.

Tip turned to see Beau angrily glaring at him. "Up there, Beau," Tip said, pointing. "See it? Oh, my, it's only five peaks away now, and getting bigger."

Beau gazed up toward where Tip pointed. "Oh, yes," he said at last. "Why, it seems to be a . . . a silver bird."

"Nay," came Loric's voice. "No bird is that, but a Dragon instead."

Dragon! both buccen gasped simultaneously.

"Settle down, my friends," said Loric. "The Drake is yet far away."

And so the buccen relaxed somewhat and watched as the great beast flew along the Grimwall peaks.

"Skail?" asked Phais. "Or is it Sleeth instead?"

"I know not," replied Loric, "for neither one have I seen before."

"I have seen each," said Phais. "They are much alike. And renegades both, I add."

"Renegades?" asked Beau, glancing at Tip.

"Those who did not take the pledge at Black Mountain," said Tip. "Don't you remember us talking about it back at Arden Vale? 'The Ballad of Arin,' the Dragonstone, and all."

"Oh, yes," said Beau. "Now I recall."

"Why is a Dragon in these parts, I wonder?" asked Tip.

Still they watched as the Drake drew onward, ever nearing, growing larger with every beat of its wings, while in Quadran Pass a mighty battle raged, the Dwarves driving the Horde hindward, pressing them down the ribbon of road.

"I say," said Beau, glancing about nervously, "with the Dragon nearing, shouldn't we get out of sight?"

Loric looked at Phais, and she said, "The Waerling is right, for Drakes have a taste for horse meat."

"To say nothing of tasty Warrows," muttered Tip.

Loric scanned the countryside, then pointed at a thicket a furlong or so away. "In there," he said, and spurred his steed, Phais doing likewise, the pack animals coming after.

Safely ensconced among the trees, they all dismounted and tethered the horses and walked to the edge of the copse.

Still the battle raged, and still the Dragon drew closer, now but three peaks away from the conflict.

" 'Tis Skail of the Barrens," said Phais at last.

"How can you tell?" asked Beau.

Phais sighed. "I see him well."

"You must have the eyes of an eagle," said Tip.

"Not quite," replied the Dara, smiling.

"As thou hast said, Sir Beau," murmured Loric, "the Drimma indeed are winning."

Tip shifted his gaze from the Drake to the battle in the pass. The black-iron-armored Dwarves had driven the Swarm even farther downslope.

Now Skail was but two peaks away from the conflict.

"Look! Look!" cried Beau. "The Swarm flees!"

Downward fled the Horde in silence, or so it seemed, Dwarves racing after.

Skail was one peak away.

Of a sudden Phais cocked her head as if listening. "Horns. Rûptish horns blow. Mayhap a hundred or more. 'Twas the signal to flee, though the sound is but now reaching us."

Loric nodded, though neither Tip nor Beau heard aught.

Now the great Dragon swung outward, westward, away from the peaks of the chain. Out he flew and out.

Still the Dwarves pursued the fleeing Spawn.

Now Skail wheeled on his great leathery pinions, turning toward Quadran Pass and swooping low, following along the road upward.

Still the Horde fled.

Yet the Dwarves stopped, for they had seen the gleaming Drake rushing through the air.

Flame gouted from Skail, washing over Rûpt.

Tipperton shouted, "He fights for the Dwar—" but his voice chopped shut as Skail's flame spewed across the Dwarves as well, and they turned and fled upward, burning with Dragonfire.

Now Skail had passed beyond the Dwarven ranks, and up he soared and up, upward into the crystal air above the peaks of the Quadran, where once again he wheeled in the sky, turning on his vast wings. And then down he plunged, aiming for the gap.

And in that moment the vast roar of gushing Dragonflame reached the thicket, for it was far enough away from the conflict that sound lagged well behind sight.

And even the Warrows heard the mighty bellow of fire mingled with a Dragonshout of triumph.

Back down hurtled Skail, and once again Dragonfire ravaged, burning not only Dwarves but raking over fleeing Spaunen as well.

Still the Dwarves fled upward, those in the lead to disappear from sight of the foursome, their vision blocked by a flank of Aevor, the mountain just south of Coron.

Once more Skail wheeled, and again came the delayed roar of his bellowing flame and his trumpet of exultation.

Again and again he ravaged the Dwarves, raining fire down upon them, his strikes affecting the Spawn less and less the higher the Dwarves fled.

And still the Dwarves ran fleeing, those that were not dead and burning.

Finally the foursome could see the Dwarves no more, for all had passed from their sight beyond the intervening shoulder. Yet still the Dragon flew and stooped and vomited more terrible fire.

Pass after pass he made, flame and glee roaring.

But at last he made a pass and no flame spewed, and then he settled on the very summit of Coron Mountain, and bellowed in elation over what he had done.

"Dragons attacking warring armies," said Beau. "What does it mean?"

"He is a renegade," said Tip, as if that were enough.

"Nay, wee one," said Phais. "I deem it much worse than a mere renegade harassing victims."

"Oh, how so?"

"I fear the rumors are true: that Modru has somehow wooed Dragons unto his cause."

"But he burned Rûcks, too," protested Beau.

"Modru cares not if he loses Spaunen," gritted Loric. "They are nought but fodder for his cause."

Phais nodded in agreement, then added, "Ye can see Skail does not now attack the Swarm. His mission was to slay Drimma, and slay them he did, until they were all dead or had escaped back through their high mountain door. The fact that Rûpt were burnt as well is merely a trivial consequence of war to Modru."

"Remember the trumps? 'Twas a trap," said Loric, "for at signal the Spaunen did flee downward, drawing Dwarves after, when Skail came winging nigh."

Beau nodded, and Tip said, "If it's true that Modru has Dragons at his beck, then it's no small pebble he's dropped in the pond, is it now?"

Phais nodded grimly. "Indeed, Sir Tip, indeed."

Beau sighed, then said, "Well, pebble or no, what are we going to do now? I mean, given our horses and all, we can't very well set out for the Dusk Door with Skail up there shouting in glee."

Loric turned up his hands, and Phais said, "Thou art right, Sir Beau. We have no choice but to wait."

It was midafternoon when Skail stopped his triumphant bellowing and took to wing, flying away northward, back the way he had come.

Untethering the steeds, Loric said grimly, "I deem we must now strike for the Old Way and make a run for it if we are to reach the Dusk Door into Drimmen-deeve ere dark."

"What about the Rûcks and such?" asked Beau. "I mean, isn't the road dangerous?"

"Mayhap, yet where we now ride the land is rough, and reaching our goal will be slow going."

Tip looked to Phais, and she said, "The Foul Folk are licking their wounds. I think they will not be coming this way."

Loric nodded in agreement, and so they turned and deliberately pressed toward the road, riding through the ruptured land. Within four candlemarks they found the way, yet when they did, it too had been churned by many feet.

"They seem to be going both ways on this road," said Loric, kneeling, "north as well as south."

"I say that we ride the road regardless," said Tip, "for the sooner we are within Drimmen-deeve, the sooner we are safe from marauding Drakes."

Loric remounted and looked at Phais, and she shrugged. And so southward they rode at a swift pace, the horses cantering over trodden ground. Yet the sun sank low in the sky as evening drew near, for much time had been lost to Skail.

They reached the entrance to the vale of the Dusk Door just as the gloaming fell.

As they came to the mouth of that long valley, suddenly Phais threw up a hand and reined to a halt, Loric stopping as well.

"What is it?" asked Tipperton.

But even as the question flew from his lips, his gaze followed the line of Loric's outstretched arm. And there in the distance down the high-walled glen ruddy firelight gleamed.

21

*I*n the deepening twilight Tip heard the soft footfalls of a nearing steed. With his heart pounding, he readied his bow and peered out through a gap in a jumble of boulders where the four had taken cover. He could glimpse a dark figure moving up through the trees and toward their hiding place.

" 'Tis Loric," hissed Phais from better vantage.

Relief washed over the buccan, and he relaxed the pressure upon his bow string and waited.

Loric reached the rocks and dismounted and led his horse inward as Phais, Tip, and Beau stepped out to meet him.

"Aye, 'tis the Rûpt down the vale," he growled. "I followed their tracks a short way, and they continue on toward the Dusk Door."

"If they have this west way blocked," said Phais, "likely they stand at the Dawn Gate as well."

"Dawn Gate?" asked Beau.

"The eastern door above Falanith."

"Oh, you mean the way out of Drimmen-deeve. —On the other side."

"Aye, it would be the way out, could we get in by this door."

Tip groaned. "Dusk Door, Dawn Gate, Drimmen-deeve, Quadran Pass: what does it matter? They're all blocked. Even if we could get into the Dwarvenholt, from what you say we'd be trapped."

"Speaking of being trapped," said Beau, glancing nervously back in the direction of the valley, "don't you think we ought to get out of here? I mean, who knows what might be scouring the land 'round about? —Rûcks and such, I shouldn't wonder. —Perhaps Vulgs and other things as well."

"Thou art right, Sir Beau," said Loric. "We must press on."

Tip sighed. "Farther south, I suppose."

"Gûnar Slot," said Phais.

Loric grunted in agreement and said, "We'll ride awhile in the night, then camp."

The Elves boosted the Waerlinga up onto the packhorses and then mounted, and away from the boulders and trees they spurred and down the Old Way, Tip and Beau trailing after, leaving the Spawn-blocked Valley of the Door behind.

They rode another five miles ere making camp in a hillside thicket somewhat above the road. Once again they set no fire, for still they were too close to the foe.

After his turn at watch, Tipperton tossed and turned, fretting over the delay. But at last, under wheeling stars overhead, he drifted off.

No sooner, it seemed, had he gone to sleep than he awakened to Phais with her finger across his lips.

"Mph." He tried to speak—

"Hush, Sir Tip," she breathed. "Danger this way comes."

"Where?"

"Along the road."

Starlight alone illumined the night, for the moon had set with the sun. Even so, as Tip got to his feet and took up his bow and arrows, he could see Loric and Beau moving toward the horses.

"We needs must keep the steeds calm," whispered Phais, "for should they call out a challenge . . ."

Quickly all four stepped to the animals and stood stroking

them, Tip and Beau reaching up to do so, the Lian now and again whispering soothing words in Sylva.

And Tip listened for the enemy, yet heard nought until—

Finally, to the north he could detect a faint patter, growing louder, until it became the slap of heavy boots jog-trotting through the night along the Old Way. And mingled in with the thudding of feet, he could hear a faint jingle of . . . of armor. Now and again there came a snarl of language, and a cracking, as of a whip. Moments later in the starlight, a jostling band of Rûpt trotted darkly into view, coming from the north, heading to the south.

Still the Elves and buccen and horses stood silently as the Spaunen loped along the road below, moving near and past and onward into the night beyond, and slowly the sounds faded in the distance.

"*Vash!*" cursed Phais. "They are on the road ahead, mayhap to set ward on Gûnar Gap."

"Oh, no," groaned Tip. "Does this mean we have to ride even farther out of our way. —To Ralo Pass?"

"Not if we go 'round them ere they reach the gap," said Loric. He turned to Phais. "In less than a league the road swings in a drawn-out arc from north to southwesterly, striking for the ford o'er the River Hâth. If the Spaunen follow the long flexure of the road, we can cut the bow straight across and mayhap gain the ford ere they do. I say we ride at first light and make directly o'er the wold for the ford."

"Why wait for first light?" asked Beau. "I mean, can't we go now?"

"Nay, Sir Beau," replied Phais. "The land of the wold is too rough, too hazardous, for the horses to cross in the night. E'en could we go now, still we may not be able to outpace the Rûpt, for ravines and bluffs may bar swift progress. Still, Alor Loric's plan is sound and gives us the best chance to reach the gap ere they do."

"How far is Hâth Ford?" asked Tip.

"As flies the raven, ten leagues or so," replied Loric, "though should we encounter barriers, 'twill be more."

"And how far by the road?"

"Mayhap another two leagues."

"And how soon is first light?"

"Ten candlemarks."

Tip frowned in contemplation, but Beau said, "Oh, my, this will be close, eh?"

Loric nodded. "Should the Spaunen delay—to camp or rest ere reaching the ford—then we should be across and gone ere they arrive."

"Then let us hope that Foul Folk legs grow weary and need long rest," said Beau.

They saddled and laded the horses, then fed each of the animals a ration of grain and broke their own fast while waiting for dawn to come creeping o'er the Grimwall. And while they waited, a chill wind sprang up from the west.

Across the high land they fared, pushing as swift as they dared, the wold rugged, then smooth by turns, with rolling hills interrupted by gulches and bluffs and rough stretches of jagged rock. Now and again the direct way would be barred by dense growths of furze and whin and gorse, and Beau would fret and Tip would fume as they were forced east or west and 'round. At times they would come to deep ravines, where they would dismount and lead the horses down and across and out, could they find a way; occasionally they would need ride the rim to locate suitable crossings, and always Tip wondered if they were ahead or behind the Foul Folk on the road. At other times the wold ran in long undulant stretches of loamy soil bearing a soft green sward with scatters of ling, and here they would canter at a goodly clip. Yet they could not run at this pace overlong, for e'en were the land friendly, still they had some thirty miles to go altogether, a long ride for horses they would spare. And so they varied the pace, now and then dismounting to walk or to stop for short rests, though neither Tip nor Beau did aught but pace while waiting to set out again.

But even though they occasionally paused in their journey, the sun did not, its inexorable passage influenced not a whit by the fates of those below.

Weapons in hand, they crept to the brow of the hill, crawling bellydown the last few feet, where they lay in the late afternoon sun and peered intently at the scanty woods alongside the River Hâth. To their left the Old Way crossed over the land and down the bank to where the water ran wide, the river yet flowing swift with spring melt from high snow in the distant Grimwall. The road itself was empty, though less than a mile to the north it swung out of sight 'round the flank of a hill.

Long they looked, peering into the ever lengthening shadows as sundown drew nigh.

"I don't see a thing," hissed Beau at last.

"Neither do I," murmured Tip. He turned to Phais. "What do your eagle eyes see?"

"Trees, shadows, a river," murmured Phais, "and nought of Foul Folk. E'en so, it seems unnaturally still, for no birds wing nigh, nor do animals chitter and scurry among the leaves. Too, only in places can I see past the trees at hand and to the far bank beyond." She glanced at Loric. "What sayest thou, chier?"

Loric turned his head to the others and took in all three with his gaze. "There is but one way we will know, and that is to cross over now, ere the sun sets, for if it comes to combat I would not have the Waerlinga's sight and battle skills hampered even one jot by darkness."

At these words, Tip's heart leapt into his throat, and he heard Beau gasp. Tip took a deep breath and then blew it out. "Then we'd better get cracking," he said, looking at the sun now lipping the horizon, the strength in his voice belying the knot in the pit of his stomach.

They slid back from the brow of the hill and then, stooping, made their way down to where they could stand without being seen by anyone nigh the ford. As they reached the horses, Loric said to Phais, "What wouldst thou have, chier? Ride at a gallop or a walk?"

Her brow wrinkled. "At a gallop we chance riding full-speed into an ambush. At a walk, any lying in wait will have longer to prepare."

She looked at Tip.

"The sooner in, the sooner out," said the buccan.

She looked at Beau.

He shrugged.

She turned to Loric and grinned. "As Sir Tipperton has said, the sooner in, the sooner out."

Loric grinned back. "At a gallop, then."

The Lian boosted the Waerlinga onto the packhorses, Phais saying, "Make ready, for even though we saw nought, still there may be Rûpt ahead, especially on the far bank where we could not see."

Tip nocked an arrow to string, and Beau loaded his sling with a leaden shot. As Phais turned to mount her steed, Beau said, "I just wish I had practiced at casting from horseback," to which Tip responded, "Who knew, Beau? Who knew?"

Loric mounted and said to Phais, "Chieran?"

Phais smiled at him, her eyes glistering. *"Vi chier ir, Loric."*

"E vi chier ir," he replied tenderly.

Phais looked ahead and drew her sword, saying, "When we round the cant of the hill . . ." Then with a light touch of her heels, she urged her horse to a walk. Loric, his own sword in hand, moved forward as well. And riding on packhorses trailing, the buccen followed after.

Around the foot of the hill they went, four horses, two warriors, two Warrows, and when they reached the place where Hâth Ford came into view, Phais and Loric spurred the horses to a gallop, the tethered animals running fleetly after.

Now they came to the road, the ford but a furlong ahead, the road itself running a short way to enter among the bordering trees and down to the swift-flowing water.

Along the hard-packed course galloped the horses, then into the long afternoon shadows cast by the verging woods, and within ten running strides the steeds splashed into the chill rush of the ford, their forward pace slowed by the deepening water, the current hock high on the coursers.

And from somewhere behind there sounded a distant bugle blat, a Rûptish horn blowing—

—Tip gasped and his hands involuntarily clenched, and he nearly lost his grip on the arrow nocked to his bow string. But then relief swept over him. *They are behind us! We've beaten them to the—*

—the blat to be answered by a loud horn blare ahead.

And still the horses lunged through the shallows, while on the opposite bank dark forms rose up among the enshadowed trees on each side of the road.

"Down!" cried Phais, leaning low against the neck of her

steed and spurring the horse forward as black-shafted arrows whined through the air.

And from the back of the following packhorses, Tipperton took aim at one of the figures and let fly, reaching down for another arrow even as the one just loosed hissed over the water and into the—

Somewhere someone screamed, yet not from vicinity where Tip had aimed, but he heard Beau cry out in Twyll: *"Blût vor blût!"*

And once again Tip aimed, loosing just as an arrow sissed past his ear; yet whether or not his own shaft sped true he knew not, for he was busy nocking another arrow to string, even as someone among the foe shrieked in agony.

Out from the water and up the far bank now plunged the horses, and howling dark forms rushed into the road ahead. *Rûcks and such,* Tip could now see, and he aimed and loosed again.

"Deyj ut a Rûpt!" cried Loric, raising his sword on high as his steed with Beau after thundered toward the Foul Folk barring the way.

Over the thin line of Spaunen they hammered, first Loric, then Phais, with Beau and Tip coming after, Rûcks scattering aside or shrieking in death as hooves smashed them down and under, with Hlôks swinging tulwars at the four, Loric and Phais answering with Elven steel as they flashed past and away, black-shafted arrows sissing after.

Yet within twenty running strides, of a sudden, Beau's horse collapsed, pitching to the roadway, hurling Beau tumbling ahead and snapping the long tether tied to Loric's rear saddle cantle.

"Beau!" cried Tip as he galloped past. Then, "Phais! Loric!"

Behind, Foul Folk howled and rushed toward the fallen steed as Beau floundered to his feet, disoriented.

Loric wrenched on his reins, the steed squealing in pain as it jolted to a skidding halt and turned and leaped forward, running toward the downed buccan and the oncoming Spaunen beyond.

Now Phais turned her own mount, Tip's horse running to a halt behind. Then she, too, spurred toward the felled Waerling.

Beau looked wildly 'round, then laded his sling and let fly, the missile crashing through the skull of the lead Hlôk, though he was yet a hundred feet away, and the Spawn pitched backward, dead ere hitting the ground.

Black-shafted arrows flew in response, sissing through the air.

"Sir Beau!" cried Loric, thundering toward the buccan. Beau looked back, then ran to the felled horse and with his dagger he cut something loose from the cargo.

Tip let fly with another arrow, and this one he saw strike one of the Rûcken archers in the neck, the dark creature to gasp and gargle and clutch his throat as he fell.

More arrows flew, and Loric grunted in pain, yet he leaned down low in his saddle and held out an arm. And amid flying arrows Beau stood upright, his rescued medical satchel in his left hand, his right hand held high, Loric to catch him by the wrist, jerking him up and away from the road and across the horse's withers, shafts hissing all 'round.

Now Loric turned his steed, and Phais, still approaching, slowed and turned as well, while Tip loosed another shaft at the Spaunen coming on still.

Yet now the steeds raced away, and within a furlong left the Foul Folk behind, while in the distance beyond the ford they had just crossed a Rûptish bugle blatted.

22

As Beau wound bandages 'round Loric's rib cage, the buccan said, "Another handbreadth to the left, my foolish Lord Loric, and we'd be setting fire to your funeral bier . . . although I must say I am grateful you saved me. Even so, your action put our mission in jeopardy. I mean, Tip is the one carrying the coin, not me, and he's the one you've got to get to King Agron. And to do that you shouldn't be taking such risks."

In the flickering light of the small sheltered fire, Loric glanced at Phais. She smiled and said, "List not to his chiding, chier, for I would not have thee abandon our companions. E'en so, I also do not desire thy Death Rede."

"Death Rede?" asked Beau as he took up a knife and cut a split in the cloth preparatory to binding it off. "Sounds ominous."

Loric looked up at Phais and, at her nod, said, " 'Tis a . . . gift given to Elven folk, by Adon or Elwydd, we think: a gift of . . . leave-taking."

Beau tied a knot, then frowned at Loric. "I don't understand. I mean, the only rede I know of is the one Lady Rael said. Goodness, hers is not a Death Rede, is it?"

Loric sighed. "Nay, hers is a rede of advice, of counsel, whereas a Death Rede is like unto a final message—a sending of feelings, visions, words, more—imparted to a loved one, no matter the distance, no matter the Plane, when death o'ertakes one of Elvenkind."

"Oh, my," said Beau, his eyes flying wide. "Sounds more like a curse than a gift."

"Nay, my friend, 'tis no curse," said Loric, "but a final touching of souls."

Blinking back sudden tears, Phais drew in a tremulous breath and turned and walked toward the edge of the woods.

Shaking his head, Beau tied a final knot and stepped back. "There. All done. We'll look at it again in a day or two. Now drink that gwynthyme tea, for we know not if the arrow was poisoned, Rûcks being such as they are."

Loric did not respond, but instead looked toward retreating Phais.

Beau waved a hand in front of Loric's eyes. "Did you hear me, Lord Loric?"

Loric frowned and looked at the Waerling and shook his head. "Nay, Sir Beau. My thoughts were elsewhere."

"I said, drink that gwynthyme tea, for we know not if the arrow was poisoned, Rûcks being such as they are."

Loric nodded and took up the cup of still warm tea and sipped slowly.

As Beau washed and dried his hands, he added, "My Aunt Rose always said that Rûcks and such are born without any heart, and that's why they are so sneaky and underhanded and cruel and wicked and . . . and well, she had a thousand names to call them, none of them good."

"Thine Aunt Rose was a wise Waerling, Sir Beau," said Loric. "The Foul Folk are born without compassion or conscience. Gyphon deliberately made them that way."

"But why would he make them such? Such uncaring things, I mean."

"It was a testament to his own nature: that the strong should take from the weak, the powerful from the vulnerable, the wicked from the innocent."

"Oh, my, how appalling." Beau put away needle and gut and bandage cloth and medicks and then buckled his medical bag shut. "By the bye, speaking of the Foul Folk, d'y' think they'll come at us this night?"

Loric shrugged, then winced from the pain of it. "Nay. The band we saw marching has traveled far and likely will not come after. And the ones we rode past at the ford are yet licking their wounds. They will think twice ere coming after, for mayhap as many as a dozen of their own lie dead in our wake—"

"A dozen!" Beau's eyes flew wide.

"Aye, or so I do believe: some by thy sling, some by Sir Tipperton's bow, some under the hooves of the horses, and two or three felled by Elven blade."

"Oh, my," said Beau, looking at his hands as if expecting to see them dripping with blood.

With the crescent moon just setting, Phais made her way to where Tipperton, on watch, sat on a fallen tree.

He looked up. "How is Loric?"

Phais took in a deep breath. "Sir Beau has stitched his wound and treated it with a poultice enhanced with a bit of the gwynthyme tea to counter any poison. Loric will be in some pain for a span, yet it will pass as he heals."

"Good," said Tip, exhaling in relief. "I was worried."

"As was I," replied the Dara.

They looked out over the land for a while without speaking, but at last Tip said, "I think my heart has finally stopped racing."

Phais turned and took a place beside the buccan.

"Lor', but it was scary," added Tip, comforted by her presence, "though at the time I don't think I even noticed. I mean, it wasn't till afterwards, after we got free of the mess, that I had time to realize just how close a thing it had been."

"That is the way of it, Sir Tipperton. Fear before, fear after, but only action and reaction during."

Tip's eyes widened. "You were afraid as well?"

Phais smiled. "Aye, just as wert thou: before and after, but not during."

They sat together in silence, peering back along the road in the direction of the ford, some fifteen miles arear. At last Tip sighed. "Back in my youngling days I used to play at being a warrior: rescuing dammen and slaying foul creatures and all. But now I don't have the slightest inclination to do so. Why, I loosed five arrows in all, or so I think, yet I can't really remember if *any* found the mark, though I seem to recall one or two striking true."

Phais smiled. "I am put in mind of my first battle, when I, too, could not remember the number pricked."

"Oh?"

"Aye. 'Twas after the Felling of the Nine. For seasons I was advisor unto High King Bleys. When word came of the slaughter of the Eld Trees, I was enraged, yet at the time there was a Kistanian blockade to deal with in the Avagon Sea. When they had been defeated, I asked leave to join the Lian of Darda Galion in teaching the Rûpt a lesson. King Bleys and a platoon of Kingsguards rode with me. We fared unto the Grimwall north of Drimmen-deeve, for that was where the retribution was at that time. We joined up with Coron Aldor's warband, and just afterward the company came to a stronghold of Spaunen, and we confronted their leader, their *cham*, and showed him the remains of the despoilers. Foolishly, he decided to fight. Afterward they told me that I had slain twelve with my bow, yet I remember but one or two."

"You were too busy nocking and aiming and loosing, right?"

"Exactly so, Sir Tipperton. I was too busy to see. I have since learned 'tis common to disremember much in the rage of battle."

Tip took up his bow and appeared to examine it in the starlight. But then he shuddered. "I do remember the one I hit in the throat. But none of the others, Lady Phais. None of the others."

Phais reached out and briefly hugged the Waerling unto her.

Again a quietness fell between the two, and somewhere an owl hooted, to be answered by another afar.

" 'Twas there I met Alor Loric," said Phais at last.

"There? In battle?"

"In the Company of Retribution."

"Company of Retri—? Oh, you mean in the Elven company going after the Rûpt."

"When I first met him, I knew I loved him. Yet he was with another."

"With another," Tipperton echoed, but he asked no question.

Even so, Phais answered. "Ilora was her name . . . at the time a Bard like thee. The common ground between the twain faded, and so they went separate ways: she to follow her heart to the bell ringers in the temples of the distant east; he to learn about horses on the Steppes of Jord.

" 'Twas after his time in Jord, five hundred summers past, he came unto Arden Vale, where we met again. Then did he find that our two hearts beat as one, though I knew it all along."

Tip sighed. "I wish I could find the one of my heart."

"Mayhap thou wilt, Sir Tipperton. Mayhap thou wilt."

They sat awhile longer, listening for the owls, but the raptors had fallen silent and only the soft-stirring air and the chirrup of springtime crickets was heard. At last Phais said, "Thy watch has come to an end, Sir Tipperton. 'Tis time thou wert abed."

Tip sighed and stood, and started away, only to have Phais call after him: "Know this, my friend: of the five arrows thou didst loose, I but saw the flight of three, and of those three, all hit the mark."

Just after dawn Tip was awakened by a drizzling mist, and as the day grew, so did the rain, and so did the wind. Huddled under their cloaks, Beau behind Tip on the lone packhorse, through the strengthening downpour they rode into the vast cleft known as Gûnar Slot, cutting through the Grimwall Mountains, connecting the land of Rell to the realm of Gûnar. Here it was that the Grimwall Mountains changed course: running away westerly on one side of the Slot, curving to the north on the other.

And all that day into the teeth of the storm they rode through the great rift, ranging in breadth from seven miles at its narrowest to seventeen at its widest. And the walls of the mountains to either side rose sheer, as if cloven by a great axe. Trees lined the floor for many miles, though now and again long stretches of barren stone frowned at the riders from one side or the other or both. The road they followed, the Gap

Road, would run for nearly seventy-five miles through the Gûnar Slot ere debouching into Gûnar, and so, a third of the way through, the four camped well off the road and within a stand of woods in the great notch that night.

And still the rain fell.

And still the wind blew, channelled up the cleft by high stone to either side.

Loric built a lean-to as Phais tended the horses, but the scant shelter did little to ward away swirling showers from the blowing rain.

It rained the next day as well, though not steadily. Even so, at times water poured from the skies, while at other times only a glum overcast greeted the eye.

"Lor', but I wish we had ponies," said Beau during one of the lulls in the rain.

"Or even another horse," said Tip. "Oh, not that I mind riding with you, Beau, but should the Foul Folk jump us again, well, I'll just hamper your slinging."

"We'll hamper each other, bucco," said Beau. "And you're right, another horse would do. Too bad the one I was riding took one of those black arrows."

"Oh, is that what happened?"

"Yar. The arrow went in right behind the shoulder."

"Heart shot, he was?"

Beau nodded. "Looks that way. Must have been struck just as we broke through the line. I think he ran another twenty strides or so before he collapsed, though to tell the truth, I was too busy loading and slinging to know."

"You, too? Oh, Beau, so was I—loading and loosing, that is. And I don't know how many I hit—Phais says that it's common not to know—but I seem to recall one or two."

Beau expelled a breath. "I remember the Hlôk I slew at the last. Loric says altogether we killed perhaps a dozen, and from what he said, I think it was mostly your arrows and my bullets that did the job."

"Adon," breathed Tip. "Quite a bloody pair, we two, eh?"

"Oh, Tip, don't say that."

With these words chill rain began falling from the grey skies above.

*   *   *

That eve they camped among thickset trees well off the road.

"Another day should see us out of this slot," said Loric as he shared out jerky and mian.

"Is there a town somewhere near after that?" asked Beau. "I'd like to sleep in a bed, if you please, and have a warm bath."

"Aye. Stede lies a league or so beyond. 'Tis but a hamlet now, yet once was a town of import when trade flowed into and out of Rell."

"Yes, but will they have an inn?"

Loric smiled. "Mayhap, wee one. Mayhap."

"If not," added Phais, "then surely one of the villagers will put us up."

"Well, I'd like an ale, myself," said Tip. "After a bath and before a bed."

"I am hoping we can replace the horse," said Loric. "And take on some additional supplies. We lost much when the steed was slain."

"Yes, yes, a horse, but after the bath and the ale and the bed, if you don't mind," said Beau.

Once again the skies opened up and rain came tumbling down.

All the next day it continued to mizzle, fine mist blowing through the slot.

"Lor'," said Beau, "even if we don't get a bed and a bath and an ale, just to get out of this drizzle will be enough."

"Aye," agreed Tip, "I'll be glad to simply get before a fire."

"With hot tea," added Beau.

"And soup," appended Tip.

"Or stew," amended Beau.

"Anything warm," said Tip as the chill wet wind swirled 'round.

"Lor'," breathed Beau. "What happened?"

Afoot, they stood looking at charred ruins in the glum light of the dismal late day, the hamlet entirely destroyed, the blackened wood sodden with three days of rain, ashes washed to slag. Only here and there did stone chimneys stand, though some stood broken, as if deliberately shattered, and still others lay scattered across the ground.

The horses snorted as if something foul filled their nostrils, and Loric and Phais spoke words to soothe them.

Loric squatted on the wet ground and took up a burnt split of wood and smelled it and plucked a bit of char and rubbed blackness 'tween thumb and forefinger. He looked at Phais and shrugged, saying, "I cannot say when this misfortune befell, for the rain has washed away the day of the burning."

Leading the skittish horses through the damp air, on into the ruins they fared afoot.

"Hoy, what's this?" called Tip, and he stepped to one of the fallen chimneys and picked up a broken arrow shaft. Black it was and fletched with ebon feathers, wet and mud caked. "Maggot-folk," he declared, stepping back and handing it over to Beau, that buccan to look at it briefly before passing it on to Phais.

"Aye," said the Dara, " 'tis one from the Rûpt."

Even though they could see no foe across the leveled town, still they readied their weapons, and then on they went, Phais going wide to the right, Loric wide to the left, and Tip and Beau in between.

Soon they came to the end of the wrack, and Loric joined the buccen.

Beau looked up at the Elf and said, "Well, one thing for certain, even if the maggot-folk did this, the villagers must have got away."

Tip cocked an eyebrow. "How so?"

"No corpses, Tip."

"Perhaps any who were killed are buried, Beau. By those who escaped. That or they burnt up in the fires."

Loric shook his head. " 'Tis said that horseflesh is not the only provender favored by the Rûpt."

Beau's eyes flew wide. "Surely you don't mean—"

"Over here," called Phais from the lip of a small ravine, her horse shying back.

And there in the shadows they found the dead—hacked, smashed, pierced with black arrows—men, women, children, babies, thirty-seven in all, bloated in death, some with great chunks of flesh torn away, as if eaten by animals. A faint miasma of rot drifted on the rain-washed air.

Beau turned away trembling, but Tip stood looking down, his face twisted in rage. "They're not even armed," he gritted.

"It matters not to the Rûpt," said Phais.

"It looks as if they were herded here and then slain."

Loric nodded. "Aye, as lambs to slaughter."

"How long?" asked Tip.

Phais stepped before Beau and knelt. "How long, wee one?"

Beau swallowed, then turned and faced the carnage and after a while said, "From their condition, two weeks or thereabouts, or so I would gauge."

Phais canted her head in concurrence. "I agree."

"Does that mean there's a Horde somewhere in Gûnar?" asked Tip.

Loric turned up his hands. "Mayhap. Mayhap not. This could have been committed by a small band of ravers rather than a full Horde. Yet whoever did so may no longer be in Gûnar at all."

Beau shuddered. "All this slaughter by a small band of ravers?"

"Look and see," said Phais. "A third are old men and women. A third are but children or babes. The remainder are all who could have put up a fight—how effectively, I cannot say—yet they number no more than ten or twelve in all."

Beau nodded numbly.

Loric glanced at the waning sun. "We must make camp."

"Not here," said Beau. "Please."

"Nay, we will press on some way from this place of death."

"What about the dead?" asked Tip. "Shouldn't we bury them or place them on a pyre?"

Phais shook her head. "War yields little time for such, Sir Tipperton. We have no dry wood to give them proper burning, and burial would take many days."

Tip nodded sharply once, then turned away, saying, "Let's go."

"But I didn't want to look."

Tip nodded. "I know, Beau. Neither did I. But even though it's terrible, I think she's just trying to get us to look at war straight on—to look at sights such as that one back there without flinching—so we don't fall apart at the wrong moment."

"Nevertheless, it was hideous, Tip. The babies . . . the babies . . ."

Tears spilled down Beau's cheeks as the horses pressed on through the gloaming, but Tip's own eyes were filled with rage.

Over the next days, down through Gûnar they passed, following along the Gap Road, camping far from it at night, for mayhap Foul Folk went that way as well, though they saw none.

Gûnar itself was a land embraced on the east and south by two long, arcing spurs of the Grimwall, reaching out like enfolding arms ringing the land 'round to hug it tight against the main range all along the northwesterly bound. This encircling reach was named the Gûnarring, and in the southeasterly quadrant where these two spurs met stood the Gûnarring Gap, a passage through the mountains and into the land of Valon. It was through this wide defile that the four hoped to escape through the Grimwall barrier and turn northeasterly to head toward the city of Dendor in Aven afar.

And so along the Gap Road they fared, a full two hundred miles down through the land of Gûnar on a southerly course, passing across plains and among occasional stands of trees as the deepening spring days grew longer.

On the eighth night after leaving the ruins of Stede, as they made camp Loric said, "Somewhere not far ahead lies the hamlet of Annory, at the joining of the Gap Road and the one named Ralo. If the town yet stands, there we will resupply and gain another steed. Yet I would not have us ride into the village without first making certain it is safe. Hence, we will reconnoiter ere faring within."

"Reconnoiter?" asked Beau.

Tip looked up from the small smokeless fire he had built. "He means scout it out, Beau. And, Loric, I should be the one to do so."

Loric frowned, but Tip plunged on. "None can move as silently as Warrows. We're small, and that makes it easy for us to hide in the most scant of cover. Besides, just being a tag-along is beginning to wear thin."

Loric shook his head. "Tagalong thou art not, Sir Tipperton. Even so—"

"Even so," interjected Phais, "Sir Tipperton is correct. Ever have the wee folk made some of the best scouts."

Tip's eyes flew wide. "We have?" he blurted. Then, recovering, "Indeed, we have," he said more confidently.

Phais laughed aloud, then shook her head. "I was so told by Aravan, who occasionally took Waerlinga on his voyages to act as scouts."

Beau frowned in puzzlement. "A scout at sea?"

Again Phais laughed. "Nay, wee one, but aland instead, for Aravan's voyages were to places of adventure. And in these sites of peril he said the Waerlinga made the best of scouts—silent, small, clever, and, when properly trained, quite fierce in a fight."

"There you have it, Alor Loric," said Tip. "And Lady Phais agrees. Besides, if I don't do something, I'm going to go entirely 'round the bend."

Now Loric laughed and held up two hands in submission. "Well, wee one, we must not have thee go mad."

Beau cleared his throat. "Wull, if you're—"

"No, Beau," interrupted Tip. "One has a better chance of going undetected than two. Besides, we can't risk losing you and your medical skills should aught go wrong."

Beau glanced at Phais. "He is right, Sir Beau."

Beau frowned and shook his head, yet remained quiet.

The next day they rode another twenty miles ere making their way off the road and into the surrounding forest, jumping up a herd of deer which ran scattering among the trees. "Lor'," said Beau, "but if we'd only been ready, perhaps we could have supped on venison tonight."

"Mayhap in Annory we'll find an inn where venison is served," replied Tip.

"I can only hope," said Beau as onward they pressed.

There was yet a goodly amount of daylight left as they passed among the trees, but Annory lay at the far edge of the woods, and so they continued forward. Yet ere the sun had fallen another three hands, they came to the final reach of the timber.

As they dismounted, Loric said, "We are nigh the splicing of the two roads; the village lies to the west less than a third of a league. Here we will wait until sunset, Sir Tipperton, for within four candlemarks after, the moon will rise nigh full and shed her silver light the better for thine eyes to see by."

And so they waited: Tipperton sighting down his arrow shafts, inspecting for trueness and finding them straight; Beau fretting and sorting through his medical bag, then asking to examine Loric's wound, now some twelve days on the mend; Phais sitting quietly and sharpening her steel; and Loric standing watch.

At last the sun set.

Tipperton gave over the coin on its thong to Beau, saying, "Should aught happen to me, see that this makes it to Agron."

Beau tried to refuse the token, but Tipperton prevailed.

And in the twilight Tip took up his Elven-made bow and began making his way among the trees and to the west . . . and was soon lost to the sight of the others.

The moon rose, nearly full and bright.

"Lor'," gritted Beau, stopping his pacing, "how long has it been? Twelve candlemarks? Fourteen? Sixteen? Something is wrong. Tip should be back by now."

"He has been gone nigh ten candlemarks, Sir Beau," said Loric. "See Elwydd's light?"

Beau looked aslant at the moon and sighed, for the argent orb had traveled less than a hand up the sky. "All right. So it's been ten candlemarks. Surely he should have returned."

Phais glanced at Beau through the moonshadows and said, "Another two candlemarks and we shall go and see. Ere then thou shouldst rest, else the trench made by thy pacing will be too deep for escape."

"My tren—? Oh."

Beau plopped down on a log, but within moments was back on his feet pacing again.

His back to the remnants of a shattered stone wall, Tipperton crouched within an arching, tumble-down mass of climbing-rose vines, the thorny tangle yet clinging to the base of the ruin an arm's length to his left, the buccan motionless and scarcely daring to breathe as guttural voices neared, harsh laughter ringing. What they said he could not tell, for it was in a tongue he knew not. Yet he had heard words such as this before: in Drearwood, among the maggot-folk.

The village of Annory itself had been burnt, just as had been Stede. Yet Tip had caught sight of a campfire amid the ruins, and he had crept close to see if it warmed friend or foe.

Foe. Definitely foe. And now you're in a fine pickle, bucco.

With his heart hammering, Tip gripped his bow, arrow nocked to string, and still the voices came onward.

"I can't stand it any longer," said Beau. "We've got to do something."

"Another candlemark, my friend," said Phais. "Then we'll see."

Footsteps crunched through debris on the opposite side of the broken wall, moving nigh, now passing, and now scuffing away. His heart yet racing, Tip breathed a sigh of relief, then moved past thorns to a gap in the stonework and cautiously peered 'round.

Count 'em, bucco: one, two, three . . .

Phais stood and unsheathed her sword. Loric, too, uncovered his blade.

Beau looked up.

" 'Tis time," she said.

The buccan sprang to his feet, his sling already laden with a bullet. And together they moved silently away, the horses left tethered behind.

Tip sensed he was not alone before he heard or saw aught, and he slid back behind the arching jumble of vines, thorns snagging at his Elven cloak but unable to find any purchase. He scanned past tumbled rock and char and at last saw a stir within the moonshadows as a dark figure—nay, as *several* dark figures—four or five altogether, each the size of a Hlôk—slipped among the burned timbers and ash and rubble and toward the campfire. Tip shrank even farther into the bramble and cast his cloak hood over his head and pulled the garment tightly 'round himself. *All right, bucco, let's hope that everything you've heard about Elven cloaks deceiving the eye is true.*

Even as Tip sought concealment, as if at silent signal the figures spread apart, but still they came onward. And Tip's heart leapt into his throat, for one of them moved directly toward his imperiled hiding place, moonlight dully glinting off wicked edges of a double-bitted broad-headed axe.

"Hsst!" breathed Loric, pausing among the trees. "Rûptish voices to the fore—"

Of a sudden the stillness was broken by howls torn from bellowing throats.

"Tip!" cried Beau, springing forward, running heedlessly ahead. "They've discovered Tip!"

23

"*Châkka shok! Châkka cor!*" thundered the dark figure as it sprang forward from the concealing moonshadows and on past the wall where Tipperton hid. Startled, Tip nearly loosed the arrow he had aimed square at the being's heart, but even by then it was too late—

"*Châkka shok! Châkka cor!*" bellowed the other four figures rushing at the shocked maggot-folk gathered 'round the fire.

—and Tip pushed through the thorns to the wide gap in the tumbled-down stone in time to see—

Bloody axes driven by broad-shouldered, bearded folk nearly the size of men riving through shrieking Rûcks trying to flee and Hlôks scrambling up with tulwars in hand to fight desperately.

—*Dwarves! They're Dwarves!* Although Tip had never before seen a Dwarf, there was no doubt whatsoever in his mind.

But they're outnumbered nineteen to five! Even as the thought crossed his awareness, a Hlôk sprang at the back of one of the savagely cleaving Dwarves. Without conscious thought Tip loosed his first arrow, the shaft sissing past the riving Dwarf to slam into the left eye of the Hlôk, the Spawn pitching backward and falling dead ere he could deliver the blow.

"*Blût vor blût!*" shrilled Tipperton in ancient Twyll as he nocked another arrow and loosed, this time felling a back-stabbing Rûck.

But the Dwarves were ferocious in their devastation, axes shearing through muscle and gut and sinew and bone alike, tissue and blood and viscera flying wide, limbs and necks and even torsos hacked entirely through with but a single blow. Fully more than half the foe had been felled by these cleaving blades.

Squealing in fear, the surviving Spawn turned to flee, running in panic toward the woods just as a tiny figure bearing a sling burst forth from the trees.

"*For Tipperton!*" he shrieked, and whipped his arm about, a leaden bullet flying through the moonlight to strike the foremost foe in the head, and the Spawn crashed to the ground, tumbling down as if he'd been hit by a sledge.

And as the slingster reloaded, two sword-bearing Elves lunged out from the shadowy forest, dire steel glinting with the promise of death.

Even as the Elves leapt forward, *Aiee!* screamed the Rûpt and turned aside, but then—*Châkka shok! Châkka cor!*—the Dwarves were among them again, severing, riving, slaughtering.

In blood and gore the battle ended, and nineteen scattered Spawn lay dead: three by arrow, two by sling, two by Elven blade, and twelve by Dwarven axe.

"Nevertheless," said Phais, " 'twas a foolish thing to do."

"But I thought they'd got Tip," replied Beau, applying salve to the cut on a black-haired Dwarf's upper arm.

"Even so," countered Phais, "to cast thine own life heedlessly to the winds without knowing the number and makeup of the foe is to court disaster. Had Tipperton merely been captive, then thine action could have led to his demise rather than to his rescue."

"She's right, bucco, and you know it," said Tip. "Were I dead or captive or completely free—as was the case—you could have been killed running out of the woods like that and challenging the whole lot of them."

The Dwarf cleared his throat, then grated, "Had they slain you, healer, still your honor would have been intact. Like you, I find skulking about in the shadows untasty. Even so, there are times when it is necessary."

Beau ripped a strip of linen from the bandage roll. "Oh, Raggi, I don't mind skulking about. I mean, who better than a Warrow at skulking, eh? But in this case, if I had a thought at all, it was that Tip needed help." Beau turned to Tipperton. "Look, I know the point you're making, and you and Phais and everyone else who's likely to talk to me about this, well, you all are right . . . yet let me ask you: can you honestly say you'd have done any differently?"

Tip's sapphirine eyes flew wide, and he looked at his friend. Finally he said, "I don't know, Beau, since it didn't happen that way. Perhaps the only difference would have been that I would have come charging out with bow and arrow rather than with bullet and sling."

"Well, then, shut your gob," said Beau, turning again toward the Dwarf, who rocked back and roared in laughter, then glanced over to a companion and said, *De tak au cho va Waeran at cha te og hauk va lok mak au va Grg, ut ven tak dek ba luk der gur.*

Now the other Dwarf roared in laughter.

"What did you say?" asked Beau, wrapping muslin about the arm.

"I simply told Bolki what your comrades had said to you, and then I told him your reply."

Only two of the Dwarves had taken cuts in battle—Raggi and Bolki—and finding that Beau was a healer, the captain of the Dwarves, Ralk, had ordered them to follow Beau back to where the horses were tethered. And so Tip and Phais and Beau set out with the wounded, while Loric went with Ralk and Vekk and Born to fetch their ponies.

Upon reaching the encampment, at Beau's direction Phais had built a small sheltered fire and placed a kettle above, and Beau had fetched his medical bag and set about patching up the Dwarves. With tepid water from the kettle, he had thoroughly cleansed their wounds, then stitched the cuts closed: a leg wound on Bolki—who didn't speak Common, but only Châkur, the Dwarven tongue—and a slash high on the arm of Raggi. Then he had applied a salve to each and bandaged them in linen, Bolki first, Raggi now.

Even as he wound the cloth 'round Raggi's arm, Loric stepped from among the enshadowed trees and into the camp, Dwarves leading ponies coming after.

Beau looked up at the Elf and said, "I know, I know, it was stupid, but we've already covered that ground."

As Loric frowned and canted his head in puzzlement, Raggi burst out in laughter again, turning to Bolki and rattling off a string of Châkur, Bolki to laugh as well.

Through the silvery moonlight streaming down among the trees, Tip looked closely at the five Dwarves. But for their heights—ranging from four foot seven to five foot two—and their clothing and hair color, they all seemed much the same to Tip. *Come on, now, bucco, that's like Big Folk saying all Warrows look alike just because we're small.*

Even so, to Tipperton's eye all the Dwarves were broad-shouldered, half again as wide as Loric, and they all bore double-bitted war axes, the oaken hafts with soft brass strips embedded along their lengths to catch at any foe's blade so it could be twisted aside, and at the axe head the helve was tipped with a cruel iron beak made for stabbing through armor. Each of the Dwarves wore a dark cloak, earthen-colored—brown, deep russet, dark grey—yet under their cloaks they all wore black-iron chainmail shirts, matching the black-iron of their plain helms. They were dressed in leather breeks and boots, and under their armor they wore quilted shirts made of a silken cloth.

As to their features, they all seemed fierce of face, hair down to their shoulders, some braided, others loose. Their beards whether braided or not were forked and reached down to the mid of their chests. As Tip had noted, each had hair of a different color: Raggi's black to go with his black eyes; Bolki's a honey brown, and he had hazel eyes; Vekk had brown hair, too, but darker than Bolki's; Born's hair looked to be ginger; and Ralk's hair was a dark auburn shot through with grey. As to the eye colors of these latter three, Tip did not know, for after the Elves and Warrows had made themselves known to the Dwarves back at the ruins of Annory, Loric had gone off with that trio, and Tip was just now seeing them in a placid setting, where the dregs of battle and dead maggot-folk did not catch at the heart and the eye.

Ralk looked at the fire and said, "It would not do for us to be caught as were the Grg. Even so"—he reached into a saddle-bag and withdrew a packet—"ere you quench the flames, we could all use a good mug of tea."

Loric grinned and reached for the packet, and Ralk said, "Vekk and Born and I will stand ward." He turned to the other two Dwarves and hefted his axe and grunted, *"Trekant."*

They set off in three different directions.

Tip stood and stepped to the ponies and began unloading them. Phais joined him, and soon they were rubbing down the animals with twisted sheaves of grass.

"A mission to Aven."

"Aye," replied Loric, nodding to Ralk.

"Ooo," said Beau, "that reminds me . . ." Fishing under his collar, Beau removed the thong with its pewter token from 'round his neck and gave it over to Tip. Tip took the disk and sighed, then slipped the leather cord over his head and tucked the coin 'neath his jerkin.

Over the rim of his cup, Ralk's gaze followed this exchange. He set his cup to the ground. "Your mission you may keep to yourselves, but as to what you have seen and heard, bear you any news?"

Loric glanced at Phais, and she said, "Modru of Gron has begun a war to conquer all of Mithgar."

"Modru," growled Ralk. "Aye, that we knew." He gestured for Phais to continue.

"Challerain Keep has fallen and High King Blaine calls for all Free Folk to join together to overthrow the Rûpt."

As Ralk nodded, "He left out the Warrows," muttered Beau.

Phais glanced at the buccan, and then looked back at Ralk. "Borne by Eloran, news has come from the High Plane: the way from Neddra to Mithgar has been sundered."

Ralk's eyes flew wide.

Loric said, "Adon did so to stop the invasion of the Rûpt, or so the herald said."

Ralk clenched a fist. "Good," he gritted, then added, "though it has come late."

Beau looked at him. "Not too late, I hope."

Ralk frowned. "That I cannot say." He turned his gaze once again to Phais.

"Crestan Pass is held by one of Modru's Hordes, and the way is barred."

"Ah, then that is why you have come this way to reach Aven. Yet there is the pass over the Quadran—"

"Quadran Pass is blocked, for Drimmen-deeve is under attack by the Foul Folk," said Phais, "and it seems that Modru has made an ally of at least one Dragon, for Skail of the Barrens did come and war with fire against the Drimma."

Ralk gasped in dismay. "Kraggen-cor under attack, and by Drakes?"

"By a Horde and a Drake," confirmed Loric.

"*Kruk!*" exploded Raggi, sitting nearby. The Dwarf leapt to his feet and began stalking back and forth, rage on his face.

"*Ka ta det?*" asked Bolki, looking in surprise at Raggi, and Raggi stopped pacing long enough to step to Bolki and speak in a low voice . . . and Bolki gasped in dismay.

"Gûnar Slot is occupied by a small force of Rûpt, though we did slay a few as we broke through the ring of their guard.

"At this end of the slot the village of Stede has been destroyed . . . much the same as Annory."

"I say," said Beau, "could it be that the same maggot-folk who destroyed Stede also destroyed Annory? If so, well then, we've avenged those we saw lying dead in that ravine."

"That I do not know, wee one," said Phais, then she looked at Ralk.

Ralk shrugged.

Phais took a sip of her tea, then said, "But for the detail, that is the news we hold. Hast thou any question, then ask it, for on the morrow we leave for Gûnarring Gap and beyond."

Ralk held up a hand, palm out. "No you will not, Lady Phais."

As Tip took in a deep breath, fearing what was to come, Phais raised an eyebrow. "Why so?" asked the Dara.

"Because, Lady, that way, too, is held by the foe."

24

*L*oric slammed clenched fist into palm. "*Vash!* Modru blocks the ways so that the High King cannot unify his forces and bring them to bear."

Phais frowned. "The gap, it is wide; mayhap we can steal through in the night."

Ralk threw up a hand of negation, saying, "Nay, Lady, a full Horde holds the gap, and worse yet, they have a Ghath among their ranks."

Loric and Phais drew air in between clenched teeth.

"What is it?" asked Beau. "This Ghath thing, I mean."

"A Draedan," gritted Loric.

"A Gargon," growled Ralk.

"Oh, my," breathed Beau, turning to Tip. "One of those fearcasters."

Tip groaned and looked up at Phais. "If we are to deliver the coin, we've got to find a way 'round. Does it mean we must ride back across Gûnar and up to Ralo Pass? Cross over if it's not blocked? Ride another thousand miles west looking for a way into Tugal?" Tip jumped to his feet. "Is this the way it is always to be, that we are driven south and west when we want north and east?"

Ralk looked at Tip. "Tell me, Waeran, is the delivery of this coin important?"

Tip took a deep breath and let it out. "I don't know. It seemed so to the Kingsman who bore it. Before he died at my mill he gave me the charge to see that it was carried to King Agron."

Ralk cocked an appraising eyebrow. "You are a miller, eh?"

Surprised by the question, Tip nodded, then plopped back down.

"A good and honorable craft," said Ralk. His gaze swept over all of them, then he turned to Raggi. *"Raggi, da skal vad dek gein va Chucah."*

Raggi's eyes flew wide. *"Det ta a Châkka na."*

"Ne va net."

Raggi bowed his head. *"Ma da taka."*

Now Ralk turned to Tipperton and the others. "There is a way to go across the Grimwall, a way known to few who are not of the Châkka, yet Raggi will show you the way. But should you choose this path, you cannot take your horses, for only ponies are small enough to go through, and even then it is a squeeze."

Phais looked at the ponies and then the horses. "We will trade ye our three horses for three of thy ponies."

Ralk blanched and pushed out his hands, as if warding a blow. "Nay, we cannot, will not. Were we merely to use your steeds as pack animals or as dray horses to draw a wagon, then yes, we would trade and trade gladly. But we have no ponies to spare, and those we do have are needed to bear us throughout much of Gûnar, and horses we *will not* ride."

Phais shook her head. "I do not understand."

Ralk leaned forward. "We are sent by Okar, DelfLord of the Red Hills, to scout out the strength of the enemy within Gûnar, for there will come a time when Châkka will attack this Horde standing in the gap."

"In spite of the Gargon?" asked Tip.

Ralk nodded. "Okar has sent for a Mage. It is said that they know of ways to deal with the fearcasters.

"In the meanwhile we are to ride the land at their back and

see if they hold more forces arears. And that, Lady Phais, is why we need our mounts, for we must cover much ground in the coming days, then ride back unto the Red Hills with news of what we find."

Phais shook her head in puzzlement. "But thy mission would go swifter from the back of a horse."

Ralk shook his head. "Hear me, Lady Phais, in the name of Durek, no Châk will *ever* ride a horse."

Tip looked 'round to see Raggi nodding in agreement and whispering translations to Bolki, that Dwarf nodding as well; and Tip had no doubt that Vekk and Born would concur if asked, though for the moment those two stood at distant guard.

"Why not?" asked Beau, but Ralk merely looked at him and did not reply.

"Then thou art saying that if we use this secret way, we must walk across a reach of Valon." Phais's words were a statement and not a question.

"Aye," confirmed Ralk. "That I am. Unless of course you can find mounts in Valon to ride. Yet I fear that most of that land is abandoned, for a Ghath stands at the western door, and who knows what strides within the margins of that realm?"

Phais looked at Loric and Tip and Beau, then said, "Even walking we can reach Darda Galion ere we could go the longer way around, assuming that way is not enemy-held as well."

"Darda Galion?" Beau frowned.

"To get fresh steeds from our kindred," explained Loric.

"But wait," protested Tip. "What if the Horde has moved on?"

Ralk cocked an eyebrow.

"I mean," continued Tip, "if they've pulled out, say to attack someplace south—"

"Pendwyr," murmured Loric.

"Yes, such as Caer Pendwyr," agreed Tip, "well then, we'd be taking a long walk for nought."

"Tip's right," said Beau. "We must make certain that the gap is still held."

Ralk shrugged. "They were still there yester."

Tipperton's face fell. "Oh."

"Nevertheless," said Loric, "Sir Tipperton's advice is well

taken. We should see that what was true yester still holds true on the morrow."

Phais nodded, then turned to Ralk. "Given that the gap is yet held, we will accept thine offer to lead us a different way, for we have little choice elsewise."

"Aye," grunted Ralk, "your choices are spare. Even so, I must have your word to keep the way of this path most private."

"Wouldst thou accept a pledge unto Elwydd?"

"Indeed."

"Then in the name of Adon's daughter, Elwydd, I do so swear."

Now Ralk looked at Loric, and he repeated the oath . . . as did Tipperton and Beau.

In the early morn, Raggi slowed the pace, for they were nearing Gûnarring Gap, a choke point in times of peril, for here the Ralo and Gap and Reach and Pendwyr roads all merged to feed through the breach. Wide left of the combined Ralo and Gap roads they fared, wide to the north a mile or more, riding in furze and whin and pine and out of sight from the road, to remain unseen by any foe who might happen along that way.

Wide they rode in the gorse, and even wider now, for as they neared they could see trails of smoke wafting upward from the direction of the pass, as if many fires burned.

And Tipperton found his heart hammering and his stomach clenched in apprehension. And he looked at Beau to find that buccan, too, ill at ease, unsettled.

" 'Tis the Gargon, wee one," said Phais. "We all feel the pulse of his dread."

Now Raggi shushed them with a finger to his lips and guided them all to the backside of a hill that would overlook the passage through, where they dismounted and made their way through deep heather and a scattered growth of scrub pine and up to the crest, moving the last few feet in a crouch, all of their breathing quick with anxiety.

They lay on their stomachs and peered at the slot afar, and Tip's heart clenched and Beau groaned, for thousands of tents and campfires and animals penned in corrals filled a gap stirring with folk. And here and there black flags flew, bearing red rings of fire. In the center stood a lone black tent, a broad space all 'round, and with his heart hammering Tip knew without asking that therein resided the Ghath.

Phais sighed and turned to Raggi. "Lead on to thy hidden path, Raggi, for Modru yet holds the way."

Northeasterly they fared for three days, an arm of the Gûnarring looming on their right, its dark jagged peaks stabbing upward into the crisp, clean air. Yet spring was full upon the land, here in the last week of May, and in the lengthening days fragrant blossoms flowered, grasses grew, and late buds unfurled on awakened trees to join foliage green and splendid. And water seemed to run everywhere, down from the slopes of the Gûnarring, pellucid bournes bearing pure drink outward to quench the thirst of the foothills and the plains beyond. And animals scurried upon the slopes, some burrowing, others freezing in alarm as the riders fared past, hoping in their stillness to remain unseen. And birds sang in the meadows and the trees and upon the high rock above, mating, nesting, engendering life. And nowhere in this eternal cycle of renewal was any acknowledgement of the vast war that had come.

Nigh sundown of the third day, Raggi turned easterly, and they followed him in through the hills and to a high aspen grove on the slopes of the Gûnarring, where they made camp amid the trembling leaves.

"Thou canst take our steeds back unto thy comrades and use them as pack animals," said Phais, "for I would not abandon them unto the wilds."

"Even so, Lady Phais," replied Raggi, pausing in the sharpening of his axe, "when my squad comes this way again, we cannot take the horses through."

"Mayhap in thy scouting thou wilt find someone with need," said Phais, turning now to Loric. "Hast thou aught to suggest, chier?"

Loric frowned, then said, "Nigh the Alnawood lies a barony, at least 'twas so long past—in the time of Fallon the Fox, ere the destruction of Rwn. Mayhap it still exists."

"Fallon the Fox, the trickster Bard?" asked Tipperton.

"Aye."

"Why, there must be a hundred songs about him, and many of his sire and dam."

Loric nodded but did not speak.

"Delon the Bard and Ferai the Ferret and Fallon the Fox their son. And now I discover they lived in the Alnawood right here in Gûnar. Oh, but I would like to go there, and go there now." Tipperton looked at his lute, but did not take it up. He sighed and then rubbed his fingers across his cheeks, and they came away wet. "Oh, Loric, is this the way it always is in war? That we are driven to choices we'd rather not make? Impelled down dark paths by circumstances not of our choosing?"

Loric took a deep breath, then said, "Most of life's roads have unknown ends, yet in war more of the ways are perilous. That we are driven down these dark and deadly paths instead of choosing a brighter lane is a tyranny of war, an affliction forced upon us by the foe."

Raggi spit on his whetstone, then took it again to his axe blade. "The sooner they are dead," he growled, "the sooner we can return to paths of our own choosing."

"This is the way," said Raggi, pointing at the stony path leading up into the enshadowed Gûnarring steeps. "The horses cannot go farther."

It was early morn, with the sun yet to rise above the peaks though dawn was well past. Raggi had had them prepare their backpacks, and then he'd led them to the far edge of the aspen grove, and now they looked upon the narrow way before them.

"We call it the Walkover," said Raggi, "though in Châkur its name is *va Chuka*. Twenty miles it extends, twisting and turning, and near the top you will find a long, low, constricting tunnel. Even were the path not narrow, this corridor would still bar horses. *Cha!* well-fed ponies at times find it difficult to squeeze through."

Beau looked up the way, then shifted his shoulders to settle the pack he carried. He glanced at the others and said, "The day isn't growing any shorter, and the sooner started the sooner done, as my Aunt Rose would say."

"Thine Aunt Rose had the right of it," said Phais. She turned to Raggi. "I thank thee, my friend, for thou hast guided us well. Would that we could fare onward together, but thou hast thine own mission to follow just as we have ours. May Elwydd light thy way."

At this benediction Raggi's face broke into a smile, and he replied, "And may the hand of Adon shield you all."

"Bye, Raggi. Take care of that cut like I told you," said Beau. Then he turned and started up the way.

"Take care, little Waeran," said Raggi after him.

"Fare you well," said Tip, and hitched his lute strap into a better position.

"And you as well," replied Raggi as Tip set off after Beau.

"Châkka shok, Châkka cor, Raggi," said Loric, adding, *"ko ka ska."*

At these words Raggi's eyes flew wide, for few other than the Châkka knew the Dwarven tongue, and yet here was an Elf who had just spoken to him in Châkur.

Loric cast Raggi a grin and a salute as the Dwarf stood mute, and then Loric turned to catch the Waerlinga.

"May thine axe remain sharp, my friend," said Phais, last, starting to turn.

"My Lady, should our paths cross again, it will be an honor to serve you and yours," replied Raggi.

Phais turned back and without a word kissed him on the cheek, then set off after the others.

With gnarled fingers Raggi touched his cheek where she had kissed him, and his eyes glistered as he called after, "Can it be done, I'll find a home for the horses."

With Loric leading and Phais following, they walked up the slope to the first twist along the narrow way, and Loric paused and looked back. Raggi yet stood at the edge of the aspens, watching. All waved, and with two hands Raggi raised his axe overhead. Then Loric and the others passed 'round the bend and out from Raggi's view.

With a sigh he turned and stepped in among the trees, and all about him the aspen leaves trembled in the shadows of early morn.

All that morning they wended upward along the slender path, the way steep at times and at other times relatively flat and rarely sloping down. But always it was narrow, strait, stone rising up about them or falling away sheer. Here and there tenacious grasses and scrub pines and mosses clung to crevices in the rock, and now and then they would see a cascade of flowers clinging to the lichen-spotted stone. The air became crisper the higher they went, and from time to time they came to places where ice yet clung stubbornly to enshadowed clefts.

"My, my," said Beau at a particular stretch, "no wonder horses can't come, and it's a marvel that ponies do."

Tip nodded in agreement. "I'm of a mind that even the Dwarves must have to sidle along, given the breadth of their shoulders."

And still they twisted and turned and gained ever upward, pausing now and then to set down their packs and rest their weary legs.

"Ungh," groaned Beau at one of the stops, "I'll be sore on the morrow, you can stake your life on that."

"I'd rather not, Beau," replied Tip. "I mean, just going on this little sojourn of ours to Aven, well, we've already staked our lives quite nicely, and I don't care to add something as trivial as sore legs to the wager."

"Oh, don't say that, Tip."

They sat in silence for a moment or more, and then Beau said, "Lor', but I also could use a week or two in a comfortable inn. This walking about and living on jerky and mian and sleeping on the ground isn't for me. And I wouldn't mind a good barrel of beer, too."

Tip nodded, saying, "Perhaps we'll find an inn in Valon."

Loric shook his head. "I would not count on it, my friends, for did not Ralk say that mayhap the foe strides across that realm?"

"Oh, I don't even want to think about that," said Beau. "Let's talk about something else."

Silence again fell among them, but finally Phais said, "Tell me, chier, what didst thou say unto Raggi in the Drimmen tongue?"

Loric turned up a hand. " 'Châkka shok, Châkka cor, ko ka ska.' In Common, that translates as 'Dwarven axes, Dwarven might, come what may.' "

"You speak the Dwarven tongue?" asked Tip, his eyes wide.

Loric grinned. "Aye. Châkur. I learned it long past from a Dwarf named Kelek. We were stranded for three summers on an island in the Bright Sea. He taught me Châkur; I taught him Sylva."

"You'll have to tell me that tale sometime," said Tip.

"One day, Sir Tipperton, but not now, for although we tarry, the sun does not, and we must press on."

Along with the others Tip sighed and stood, lifting his pack and settling it into place, then slinging his lute as well. But before they set out he said, "Alor Loric and Dara Phais, we've known each other a goodly while and I have a formal request to make."

Both Lian looked at him questioningly, for seldom did he address them by their titles.

"It's just this: you insist on calling us 'Sir Tipperton' and 'Sir Beau.' Well, I've had enough of it. And though Beau's a splendid healer, I'm just a plain miller, so from now on I'd rather you drop the 'sir' and simply call me Tip or Tipperton"—he glanced at Beau and found him nodding vigorously—"and perhaps call him Beau. But if you do insist on some kind of formality, then please save it for very special occasions"—Tip gestured about—"and living on dirt and eating rations isn't what I'd call special."

Phais looked at Loric and, at his nod, turned to the Waerlinga. "Agreed, Sir—agreed, Tipperton; agreed, Beau. Mayhap in court we will speak of ye as Sirs, but thou dost speak true in that living on dirt and eating field rations certainly is not special."

Beau laughed, then said, "Not special unless 'specially bad' qualifies."

Grinning all, and with Loric leading and Phais trailing, they set off upslope once again.

"Lor'," said Beau, his voice sounding hollow in the darkness of the narrow way, "Raggi was right. A fat pony couldn't make it. Why, I can reach out and touch both sides."

Though the Warrows walked upright, in the lead Loric stooped low as he made his way through the natural rock tunnel. Bringing up the rear, Phais did the same.

"Huah," grunted Tip. "Not only a fat pony but a tall one as well—neither could make it through . . . and as I said before, given their shoulders the Dwarves would have to walk sideways."

They rounded a turn and ahead an arch of light showed they had come to the end, and shortly they emerged into the sunlight.

"Two furlongs, I make it," said Loric, ere any could ask.

"Why don't the Dwarves enlarge it?" asked Beau. "I mean, with their skill at carving mountains—"

"Because," interjected Tip, "were it made wider, it likely would become a well-known route. This way the Dwarves keep it hidden. Besides, if they were being pursued, here just one Dwarf could hold off an army of foe."

"Oh," said Beau, enlightened, as on down the slope they fared, the path now heading down the opposite side, though crags and bluffs and massifs stood in the way of Valon.

As the day grew toward evening and they took up the trek again, Beau's eyes widened. "I say, Tip, I just thought of something."

Tip looked at Beau, a question in his eyes.

"Just this," said Beau. "Dwarves are not men."

Tip frowned. "And . . . ?"

"Don't you see: *'Seek the aid of those not men,'* she said, did Rael, *'to quench the fires of war.'* Well, we were aided by the Dwarves—Dwarves who are not men. Perhaps their aid will mean the quenching of the fires of war."

Now Tip's own eyes widened at the thought. "But Beau, that assumes the rede she spoke was meant for us, and I don't see how that can be."

"I don't see how it can be, either, bucco, but let's keep it in mind just in case. Remember, a small event in one place can cause great catastrophe in another; all things are somehow connected, you know."

Tip shook his head but made no reply as onward they pressed down the way.

Down they strode and down, and came to a place where at last they could see out across the land ahead, out where a vast grassy plain swept to the horizon and beyond. Yet Tip gasped in dismay, for in the far distance a pall of black smoke curled into the afternoon sky.

Upon Valon burned War.

25

*T*hey reached the eastern foot of the Walkover just as the
waning half-moon rose, shining her argent light aglance across
the tall grass of Valon.

"We'll camp here among the concealing crags, then set out
on the morrow," said Loric, unbuckling his backpack.

"But what about the smoke we saw, the fire out there on
the plains?" asked Beau. "I mean, shouldn't we go see if
anyone needs our help?"

Loric glanced at Phais, then shook his head. "I deem we
look upon another Stede, another Annory, Sir— Beau. 'Twas
entirely too late when first we espied the burning."

Tip nodded glumly. "Besides, it's another good twenty or so
miles to the site, and even if we went straightaway without
any rest, still we wouldn't get there till late in the morning,
perhaps at the noontide."

"Oh, my," said Beau dejectedly. "I was hoping it was
closer . . . in miles as well as time. But to walk all night and
not get there till noon, well, to tell the truth, I don't think I
can go on without a bit of a lull. I mean, it isn't every day that

I've gone climbing with a pack on my back up over the Gûnar-ring and down again."

" 'Tis more or less on our path, Beau," said Phais, "and so the morrow should bring us to what burns upon the plain. But for now thou art right: 'tis rest we need."

Tip set his pack to the ground and sighed in relief, then looked back at the Gûnarring. "Will it ever get any easier? This walking about, I mean."

Loric nodded "The farther we walk, the easier 'twill be, for our packs will fare lighter as the food dwindles. Our strength and endurance will grow as we cross the plains unto Darda Galion."

Beau groaned. "Oh, surely we aren't going to have to walk all the way to the Eldwood. I mean, there must be some place we can purchase horses . . . or ponies."

Kneeling at her backpack and untying the thongs on her bedroll, Phais sighed. "With war upon the land, who can say?"

Tip looked across at the Dara. "How soon will we reach the Eldwood if we go on foot all the way?"

Phais cocked an eyebrow at Loric. "If we tarry not," he replied, "a fortnight and some should see us there."

"A fortnight? fourteen days?"

"Aye. 'Tis nearly a hundred leagues."

"Three hundred miles?"

"Aye, three hundred miles, Tipperton. And can we walk seven leagues a day, then a fortnight 'twill be."

Tip groaned. "Twenty-one miles a day for fourteen days—oh, my aching feet."

Beau snorted and said, "Huah, Tip, compared to our slip-sliding on ice most of the way through Drearwood, this little jaunt to the Eldwood will be a lark. I mean, what could be better than walking on soft sod across a grassy plain? Besides, bucco, you've got to remember, given the choices we faced, this is the quickest way."

Tip cast his friend a skeptical eye, but did not respond as he groaned to his feet preparatory to standing the first short turn at watch.

Just after dawn they set out northeastward across the rolling plains of Valon, the prairie covered with tall grass as far as the eye could see. Though the grass itself came to midthigh on the Elves, it was chest high on the Warrows, and it rippled in long green waves, stirred by a morning breeze blowing down from the Gûnarring behind. Far across the rolling land, a thin smudge of smoke yet stained the sky, drifting up and eastward, driven by the breeze as well. And toward the unseen origin of this smear they trod.

"What if it is a town like Annory—burnt, destroyed—with a passle of maggot-folk camped therein?" asked Beau. "What'll we do, the four of us?"

Phais sighed. "Pass it by."

"You mean just leave them alone?" asked Tip.

Phais nodded. "Aye. Most likely they will be too many and we too few."

Tip growled. "But the Dwarves attacked nineteen foe, and they were only five."

Loric shook his head in resignation. "The Drimma are a fierce race, where honor stands well above prudence. Aye, they attacked nineteen head-on, with axes swinging, depending on surprise and brute force to quickly carry the day. Yet were we faced with the same odds, I would hope that we would use stealth and cunning and guile to accomplish the same ends. Yet heed: stealth and cunning and guile take time, and should we come across a large number of foe, would we soon accomplish this mission to Agron, then we must pass them by."

Tip frowned, and Phais, noting his look, said, "Tipperton, if we are to engage every foe 'tween here and Dendor in Aven, then I suspect it will be many a year ere we see Agron King."

"Even so," added Loric, " 'tis meet we gather knowledge of the foe along the way, and pass on such particulars to those who need to know."

"Somewhat like scouts?" asked Beau. "—I mean, as long as we don't stray too far from our mission to Agron in Aven, that is."

"Exactly so," replied Loric, smiling down at the buccan.

And across the plains of Valon they went, toward drifting smoke afar, while in the distant sky above, birds circled and spiraled down.

*   *   *

"*Ssst!*" hissed Loric just as they reached the crest of a rise. "*Down!*"

They dove into the grass. "What?" whispered Tip. "What is it?"

"Horses," breathed the Alor, unbuckling his pack and drawing his sword. Phais nodded in affirmation and pulled her blade as well and slipped free from her pack.

Beau, lying prone, put his ear to the ground. His eyes widened and he motioned for Tip to do the same. And Tip's own eyes widened as he heard the thudding of many hooves knelling within the soil. He raised his head slightly. "What if they're friends?" he asked.

"What if they're foes?" whispered Beau right after.

Phais said, "Friends we'll hail; foes we will not." Then she put her finger to her lips and signaled for quiet.

But Beau sucked in a deep breath and then hissed, "Oh, my, what if they're Ghûls on Hèlsteeds?"

Remaining hidden down within the rippling green, Tipperton wriggled free from his pack and set an arrow to string. Beau likewise shed his own pack and laded his sling.

Now even without an ear to the ground the buccen could hear the hammer of hooves, and Tipperton lifted up just enough to peer outward through swaying heads of grass.

From the north they came, rounding the flank of a low hill, a cavalcade of riders—men on horses, thirty or more—and running alongside were men afoot, twice as many as the riders, it seemed, and all bearing spears. Dark and swarthy were the riders and dressed in turbans and long, flowing robes, with curved swords slung loosely at their sides; the men afoot were even darker, nearly black, and wearing nought but short belted skirts 'round their waists, their feet shod in sandals, their long hair gathered and held behind by tortoise-shell clasps; and on their bodies a sheen of sweat glistened.

"Down," sissed Loric, pulling Tipperton low. " 'Tis the foe."

Through the swale below they ran, their breathing heavy, that of the horses and running men. Yet still they pounded on southward, and soon passed from sight in the long folds of the grassland.

Cautiously Loric raised up, first peering above the undulant green, and then rising to his knees, and finally standing.

He motioned the others up as well.

Tip got to his feet and looked southward. Nothing but long, rolling waves of green grass did he see. "What—who were they?"

"Men of Hyree," said Loric, "and men of Chabba."

"The ones on horses—?"

"Hyrinians," replied Loric.

"And those afoot—?"

"Chabbains."

"Hoy," said Beau, "there's something about the Chabbains I should remember, but just what, I can't bring to mind."

"Say, weren't they the ones who burned Gleeds?" asked Tip. "I think my da told me so." Tip looked to Phais for confirmation.

"Aye, back in the First Era," she said.

"But we're over two thousand years into the Second Era; what are they doing here now?" asked Beau.

Phais sighed. "Seeking vengeance for deeds done long past."

At the buccen's raised eyebrows, Phais continued: "Gleeds was the city of wood on the Argon, established there by the very first High King, Awain. Some sixty summers after, Chabba and Pellar did dispute certain trade routes with one another, and the Chabbains crossed the Avagon sea in ships and burnt the young city down. Yet the then High King's army did entrap the invaders and, but for a niggling few, slew them one and all, e'en though many had surrendered. Long have the Chabbains clutched hatred unto their breasts and sworn one day to avenge those who were slaughtered.

" 'Twas from the ruins of the city the High King did move the center of government unto Caer Pendwyr."

"That's right," said Beau. "I remember now. —The history, that is . . . not that I was there. But oh, my, that was long, long ago, and the Chabbains yet seek revenge?"

"Lor', Beau, but you're right," agreed Tip. He turned to Phais. "You say that was back in the First Era?"

Phais frowned. "Aye, near the very beginning: in King Rolun's time, the grandson of Awain. 'Twas Awain who established Gleeds, and Rolun who saw it burnt to the ground."

Tip shook his head. "Well, Beau, given that it was near the beginning of the First Era, that was some twelve thousand years ago." Tip looked up at Phais. "Are you telling us that the Chabbains have held a grudge all this time?"

"Not only for that slaughter, but for other defeats as well," replied Phais. "They venerate the ghosts of their kindred and carry hatreds on, believing that all dark deeds need avenging, whether done of late or long past. Else the ghosts will find no rest, no solace, and their wailing will inflict misery upon any kindred yet alive."

"Well, I must say—" began Beau, but then, "Oh, down! Down, I say!"

As the comrades ducked low in the grass, upon a far distant roll of land the cavalcade and runners hove into view. Quickly they topped it and passed beyond, yet running south, their pace not slackening a bit. And then they were gone from sight once more.

Phais turned to Loric. "They have a camp nigh."

Loric nodded in agreement.

"How do you know this?" asked Beau, peering about warily.

"They carried no supplies, wee one," replied Loric.

"Oh, my," said Beau, pointing to the fore, where in the near distance faint tendrils of smoke yet rose into the sky, "do you think that could be their camp?"

Loric frowned, and Phais said, "The pall we saw yestereve seemed not like that of campfires but rather of a burning thorp, and the birds are an ominous sign. Even so, we should go forth in caution."

As Loric shouldered his pack, he said, "Henceforth we must leave little trace of our passage, else we are fordone should they come across our trail and follow it to us."

"I say, couldn't we walk in their path?" asked Tipperton, pointing downslope to where the cavalcade had passed. "I mean, then our tracks would be lost in theirs."

"Aye, we could," said Loric. "Yet if this is a trail they often follow, I'd rather not be in their lane."

Not knowing what lay ahead, the foursome walked in silence awhile, keeping a span between themselves and the wide track beaten in the grass by the cavalcade. And where they stepped, they left no permanent wake, for Loric had shown the Waerlinga how to ease their feet among the tall stalks so that the blades sprang back upright. Even so, their passage was slowed considerably by the need to leave no trace.

And still they pressed toward the rising smudge just ahead of the circling, spiraling birds, dreading what they might find.

To break the somber mood, Beau asked, "This first High King Awain, what year did he come to power?"

"Why, in the Year One of the First Era," replied Phais.

Beau frowned and looked up at her.

" 'Twas with the coronation of the very first High King that the counting of Eras began," she added.

Beau's mouth made a silent O of enlightenment. "I always wondered how they got started."

Tip nodded. "Me too. I mean, the counting of Eras had to begin somewh—"

Suddenly Tip's words jerked to a halt, for they had come to a crest of a hill, and down in the plain below smoldered the ruins of a town. The town had been burned, buildings destroyed, and nought but charred timbers and scattered stones remained. Yet that was not the worst of it, for carnage littered the streets. Whatever had once been alive was now not. People—Humans—young, old, male, female, babes, ancients—all were dead. Horses, dogs, sheep, cattle, fowl—all had been slain as well.

Yet there was a stir among the dead, for gorcrows feasted and kites. Vultures stalked and drove away lesser birds, though there was more than enough for all. And midst squawks and graks and chortles, beaks tore at flesh and gobbets of raw meat dangled to disappear down ravenous gullets.

Beau burst into tears, and Tipperton turned and stared in the direction of the cavalcade, hatred burning in his gaze.

Phais took in a deep breath and sighed. "Come. There's nought we can do here."

And they passed beyond the place that now was no longer a town.

They found a rare stand of trees and set camp among them that eve, where they built a small fire and brewed tea.

"Lor'," said Beau, "but I think I'll never purge that sight from my mind."

"I don't ever want to forget what I've seen," gritted Tip. "They should pay for what they did, and if ever it is in my power to avenge those souls, then so shall I do."

"Thou dost sound as one of them, Tipperton," said Phais, "so like the Chabbains, I mean."

"Unh?" grunted Tip, startled.

"Retribution: it drives their lives. Gyphon and His agents see to it."

"Are you saying that evil deeds should go unpunished?"

"Nay, Tipperton. Yet thou must take care thou dost not fall into the same set of mind as they. Hatred must not drive thy life, else it will consume thy spirit, thy very soul."

"But what about those you slew because of the Felling of the Nine? Wasn't that retribution?"

Phais's eyes widened, and she glanced at Loric, and he said, "Aye, it was. There are times when just retribution need be extracted."

"Well then, I think this is one of those times."

Phais sighed and nodded in agreement, then said, "Nevertheless, Tipperton, let not hatred consume thee."

A silence fell upon the campsite, and remote stars wheeled in spangled heavens above.

At last Beau said, "Tip, if I get killed in this venture of ours, see to it that I get a proper burial. I mean"—he shuddered—"I don't want crows pecking out my eyes, kites rending my face, vultures tearing at my guts, all squabbling over my remains."

"Don't worry, bucco, you're not going to die," said Tip.

"But if I should . . ."

Tip threw an arm about his friend. "All right. I promise."

"Good," said Beau.

They sat in morose silence a moment more; then Beau looked up through the leaves at the stars and said, "If by chance I should die, think only this of me: that in some corner of a foreign field in a foreign land is a place that forever will be the Boskydells."

"Oh, Beau, don't say such a thing," said Tipperton. "I'm sure one day you'll be in your beloved Boskydells again."

Beau looked 'round at Tip and sighed. "We can only hope, Tip. We can only hope. —But, say, you're coming too, aren't you? To the Boskydells, that is. There's plenty of need for millers."

Tipperton glanced at his lute. "What about bards?"

"Them too, Tip. Them too."

The following morn they set out again northeasterly, aiming for the place where the River Nith plunged over the Great Escarpment and down into the Cauldron, some two hundred eighty miles away in all. Yet they had gone no more than a mile or so than they espied more tendrils of smoke rising into the sky ahead.

Beau gasped. "Oh, my, is it another burning town?"

"Nay, Beau, these are campfires," replied Loric. "But whether those of friend or foe, that I cannot say."

Cautiously they moved forward, though swinging wide to the left, for should it be foe they would need give wide berth and pass beyond.

" 'Tis foe," hissed Loric.

The camp lay nearly two miles away.

Even so, both Tip and Beau could see the site held men like those who had passed in yesterday's cavalcade.

"Three flags fly," said Phais, "—nay, four: Hyree, Chabba, Kistan, and Modru's ring of fire."

"We must gauge how many are encamped," said Loric. "And take word with us to Wood's-heart."

Beau looked up across at Loric. "Wood's-heart?"

"The Lian strongholt in Darda Galion," replied the Alor.

"But the encampment goes to the other side of the hill," said Tip.

Phais pointed off at a rise in the land. "I'll move around and count from there."

Tip glanced at the Dara. "I'll go with you."

Loric raised an eyebrow, but Phais nodded in agreement.

They spent nearly all day observing, as cavalcades came and went, and now and again in the far distance black smoke would rise into the sky.

"They're burning farmsteads," said Phais.

Tip made a fist and pounded the ground in rage.

* * *

When night fell, at a far distance they began slowly arcing 'round the large campsite, seeking to pass it by, for it held nearly two thousand men in all, or so they judged. Now and again they would crouch down in the grass, for returning raiders would pass nearby on their way back to camp.

The camp was yet in sight when dawn came.

"We must rest," said Phais, cocking an eye at Loric, then looking casually at the flagging Waerlinga.

And so they spent a second day hidden within the grass atop a long low mound, alternately keeping watch and dozing throughout the flight of the sun.

And this day, too, cavalcades came and went.

That night they finally got free from sight of the camp, and yet leaving no trace of their passage they walked most of the next day, too, before stopping in the afternoon.

They rested well that night and the following day resumed their northeastward trek.

"How far have we come these past days of edging through the grass?" asked Beau, slipping his feet carefully among the tall blades.

"Twelve leagues or so," said Loric, glancing at the sun.

Tip sighed. "That's only ten or twelve miles a day. At this rate it'll take us two or three fortnights to reach Darda Galion instead of just one."

"On the morrow we'll pick up the pace," said Loric, "for we are enough away from the campsites of the raiders and their cavalcades that the chances of them cutting our track is remote."

"I say," said Beau, "what we should have done is steal some horses from that camp."

Phais smiled. "Horses know not how to hide their tracks, Beau. Yet could we have taken two or three swift steeds, we would have raced them across these plains, tracks or no."

The next day they set out at a swift pace, no longer trying to hide their wake. Even so, the grass was hardy, and Loric judged that in less than a day it would spring back to fullness

and only a well-practiced eye would discern their passage—
". . . unlikely from the back of a moving steed."

Over the next several days they fared northeasterly, their progress slowed by the need to be vigilant and the need to hide, for often a cavalcade would be seen coursing afar, or at times a single horseman with two runners afoot crossing the plain, and the comrades would crouch down and watch, remaining still so as to keep from being seen.

And distant trails of smoke wreathed up into the sky.

And they came across another burned town, this but a small hamlet, and all things that had lived were slain. And they passed it by, pressing on toward the Great Escarpment and Darda Galion above.

"Why don't we rest by day and move by night," asked Tip at a stop, "when there's less chance of being seen?"

Phais looked at Loric and her mouth split into a great grin.

And so they fared at night thereafter.

And the dark of the moon came and went.

Yet the days were growing long and the nights short, and even though they made good progress under the stars, still when the sun came early and stayed late, their pauses between treks grew longer.

"We'll move through part of the day as well," said Loric. "Else as you once declared, Tipperton, it will take more than several fortnights to reach our goal."

And so in the days thereafter, they continued until mid-morn, and rested well through the heart of the day, and set out again in midafternoon.

"It looks like a burnt farmstead," said Beau.

Tip glanced at the sun, gauging it to be four hands from setting. "Our provisions are low," he said. "Let's go see can we find anything to take with us."

Down into the swale they went and past a destroyed corral, rounding the burnt hulk of a byre. Of a sudden Tip stopped, for there, bloated, maggots writhing just under the skin, lay the corpse of a woman, though the only way of knowing it was a female was by the clothing she wore. She was clutching the corpse of a child, bloated and infested too, skin swollen and ready to burst.

And the stench was unbearable.

Tipperton turned and vomited, and Beau sank to his knees in dismay, his eyes wide, his hands pressed to his mouth.

"Oh, Adon, what is it we see?" whispered Beau.

"Death," said Loric.

"War," amended Phais.

And soon they moved onward, striding into the grass again.

Rain fell down and down, and lightning stalked across the plains. And during the three days of the violent storm, little progress was made.

Streams became raging torrents, and often they would have to walk far ere they found a place to cross, and these dangerous to the Waerlinga as small as they were. Yet with Loric and Phais's help, across the roiling waters they went.

And when the skies finally cleared, they were far afield of their chosen path. Yet once again across the plains they went, now and then espying riding Hyrinians or running Chabbains or both and hiding whenever they did. And still they had to take wide detours to cross 'round waters yet wild.

And they ran out of food.

"We need to take a day to hunt, to forage, while we yet have the strength," said Loric. "Else we'll be too weak to reach our goal."

"On the morrow, then," said Phais, "we hunt."

The buccen strode back into the camp together.

"I feathered a fat marmot," said Tip, raising his bow in his left hand and the arrow-pierced burrower in his right.

"And I brought down a rabbit," said Beau, canting his head toward the long-legged, long-eared hare slung over his shoulder.

"Stealthy Waerlinga," said Loric, smiling at Phais, then turning back to the buccen. "We garnered nought from any of our snares."

"Even so," said Phais, "there are these." And she held up a bundle of wild leeks.

Loric looked at the fare. "With careful rationing, two days, I would say, then we must hunt again."

*   *   *

"Huah!" snorted Beau, pausing to look leftward as his companions strode on. "So that's the Great Escarpment, eh?"

In the far distance, low on the rim of the world and lit aslant by the rising sun, stood a long upjut of land, running from horizon to horizon west to east.

"Aye," replied Loric, striding past the buccan, " 'tis the Great Escarpment, her steeps well warded by Lian Guardians, for above stands Darda Galion."

Beau shook his head. "Well, it doesn't look so great to me," he said, trotting after the others.

"How far away is it?" asked Tipperton, trailing behind Phais.

"Some fourteen leagues," replied Loric.

"Fourteen leagues!" blurted Beau, catching up to Tipperton again. "Forty-two miles?"

"Aye."

"Hmm," mused Tipperton. "Then it must be rather tall."

"Aye. Two hundred fathoms in places, though east of the Argon it dwindles to the level of the land on which the Greatwood stands."

Beau shaded his eyes and peered again. "Two hundred fathoms, four hundred yards, twelve hundred feet: that's quite high. Hmm, perhaps it *is* rather great after all." He glanced at Loric. "When will we reach it?"

Loric pointed straight ahead northeasterly. "Vanil Falls and the Cauldron lie mayhap thirty leagues afar. Can we maintain a goodly pace, and given that we yet need a day or two along the way to hunt for food, mayhap we'll be there in a fiveday or seven."

Tipperton sighed and strode on.

The following day, Year's Long Day, they went another five miles before the sun set, and they continued walking under the stars and a gibbous waxing moon. Yet at the mid of night and by the argent light of the westering moon, Loric and Phais and Tip and Beau trod out the Elven rite of Summerday in the tall green grass of Valon.

Step . . . pause . . . shift . . . pause . . . glide . . . pause . . . step. Phais chanting, Loric singing, step . . . pause . . . step . . .

The moon had fallen considerably when they took up the trek again, and they walked until dawn and a bit after ere stopping for the day.

During the hunt the next day they brought down no game, Beau missing the only quarry seen, a ring-necked pheasant that had taken to wing at his very feet.

Yet Phais managed to find double handfuls of small root vegetables she named *nepe* but which both buccen knew as rutabaga, though these were wild and immature.

"Lor'," said Beau, taking another bite and making a sour face, "but I didn't think I'd be eating young raw turnips out here in the open plain. Regardless, this one meal a day isn't to my liking, for my stomach is touching my backbone, and so raw or not, wild or not, these'll do."

Tip, chewing, looked at his friend through watering eyes. "A bit tart, though, wouldn't you say?"

Loric laughed, then sobered. "We will have to hunt again, if not on the morrow, then certainly the day after."

Tip swallowed and looked at the Great Escarpment, yet some distance off to their left. "Are you certain that we're drawing closer to our goal, Loric? I mean, we seem to be getting no nearer."

Loric peered northeastward. "Another twenty or twenty-five leagues, my friend, will find us ascending the Long Stair next to Vanil Falls."

Beau took another bite of the pungent fleshy root, then said 'round the mouthful, "Well I for one will be glad to be shed of these plains, what with riders and runners about."

After resting throughout the long day, they took up the trek again in the eve and walked through the night. The following morn they made camp in a small grove.

"Lor', but I'm famished," said Beau, "and thinking of eating grass."

"We need to hunt and forage once more," said Loric. "Else we'll not have the strength for the climb when we do reach the Cauldron."

"But first we should rest," said Phais. "Then hunt."

They bedded down, all but the one on watch, and slept

through the heart of the day, but in midafternoon they set out in separate directions to forage: Beau with his sling, Tip with his bow, and Phais and Loric running the line of snares they had set while the Waerlinga had slumbered.

Tip found another set of burrows and settled down to watch, his back against a nearby mound, an arrow set to string. Yet worn as he was, he dozed in the afternoon light.

The sun had reached the horizon when a sound startled him awake, and he looked up to see—

"*Yaahhh!*" shouted the spear-bearing Chabbain, leaping at the Warrow, spear stabbing forward even as the shrieking buccan desperately rolled aside, his arrow lost to his grasp.

Shnk! the blade of the weapon knifed into the soil, only to be jerked free and plunged again at Tip.

But Tipperton had gained his feet, and he darted aside, the spear catching nought but Elven cloak, the cloth sliding across the blade and away.

"*Maut!*" sissed the Chabbain, whirling after the fleeing Warrow.

Tipperton ran toward the thicket, and *Thkk!* the spear flew past him to bury itself in the sod.

And all in one motion Tip stabbed to a halt and spun while snatching an arrow from his quiver and set it to string and drew and loosed, impaling the rushing Chabbain square through the heart, the dark man to tumble dead at the buccan's feet.

And Tipperton heard another shout and looked up to see a second Chabbain running at him with raised spear in hand, while a Hyrinian on horseback thundered after.

Calmly, Tip nocked a second arrow to string and loosed, and even as it flew, he set the third shaft to his bow.

"*Ungh!*" grunted the Chabbain, and looked in surprise at the feathered shaft that sprang full-blown from his chest even as he pitched to the ground.

Now the horseman hauled back on the reins, the animal squealing in pain as the rider sawed the steed about.

Sssss . . . Tipperton's third arrow whispered through the air to slam into the Hyrinian's side, the stricken man yawling in pain, yet spurring away.

With sword in hand, Loric burst forth from the woods behind the buccan, Phais on his heels, her weapon drawn as well, as Tipperton snatched another arrow from his quiver and whirled about, ready to slay whoever was coming at his back; yet when he saw it was Loric and Phais, he spun back toward the bolting rider and aimed and loosed, but this shaft flew beyond the fleeting Hyrinian, now distant and drawing away.

Loric ran past the Waerling and after the galloping steed, running as if to catch the racing horse now flying across the plain, clots of dirt and sod flinging up from its hooves. Yet the horse was too swift and Loric quickly fell behind, the Elf stopping after sprinting a hundred paces or so.

Tipperton was shaking when Phais came to his side, and suddenly the strength went out of the buccan's legs and he fell to his knees gasping.

"I couldn't—he almost—they nearly—"

"*Shhh, shhh,*" shushed Phais, kneeling beside Tip and drawing him to her.

Beau came running from the thicket, his sling in hand, and his face twisted into anguish when he saw Phais down on the ground holding Tip. "Oh, my. Oh, my," he groaned. Then: "I'll get my medical satchel," he called, and spun back toward their campsite.

But Phais called out, "No need, Sir Beau, for none here are wounded." Then she whispered, "Except perhaps in heart."

Beau turned and rushed to the Dara's side.

On the way back, Loric stopped at the distant slain Chabbain and rolled the corpse over. Then he walked past the huddle of Tip and Phais and Beau to the dead Chabbain nearby, and with a *thuck!* he pulled Tip's arrow free, wiping the shaft and blade clean of blood on the tall waving grass.

"I went to sleep. I went to sleep," whispered Tip, "and it nearly proved our undoing."

Arrow in hand, Loric came to stand at their side. Phais looked up at him. "We will have little time," said the Alor.

Phais glanced at the running horseman afar and nodded.

"Little time?" asked Beau.

Loric canted his head toward the distant Hyrinian. "He will bring others. We must run."

Tip drew in a shuddering breath. "It's all my fault—"

Phais clutched him hard by the shoulders. "Nay, Sir Tipperton. 'Tis not the fault of any here."

"But I fell aslee—"

"They were tracking us, I ween," growled Loric. He held out the arrow to Tip. "The other was broken when the Chabbain fell."

Tip took a deep breath and then exhaled, and reached out to accept the arrow. He stood and shoved the missile into his quiver and gazed at the fleeing Hyrinian, now disappearing beyond a distant roll in the land. "How far to safety?" he asked, looking at Loric.

Loric gazed at the Great Escarpment rising in the distant sky, the length of its face mostly enshadowed in the setting sun. "Ten leagues, mayhap fifteen."

"Then we'd better begin," said Tip, "for either way—thirty miles or forty-five—it's a deal to go."

"And on an empty stomach, too," groaned Beau.

Across the prairie they fled, not attempting to hide their tracks, for as Loric had said, "They know we are here and are certain to overtake us should we walk carefully. Instead, we'll choose haste over caution."

And so in the light of a flush full moon they alternately walked and trotted: five hundred paces of hard strides followed by five hundred at a run, over and again, five hundred and five hundred, throughout the short bright night, pausing but occasionally for brief rests, these especially for the flagging Warrows.

Just after dawn when they rested again, Tip said, "We're just slowing you down, Loric, Phais. You should go on ahead without—"

"Nonsense, Sir Tipperton," said Phais. "Fear not, for we have but a short way to go, for even now I can hear the roar of mighty Bellon."

Tip looked at her. "Again I bid you to drop the 'sir' and just call me Tip; that or Tipperton will do. I mean, after the way I let everyone down, I don't—"

Phais thrust a hand palm out toward Tip to shut off the flow of his words. "Aye, I will call thee Tip or Tipperton. 'Tis only in the stress of the moment I—"

"Riders!" called Loric, pointing.

All gazes followed the line of Loric's outstretched arm. On the distant horizon a band of riders topped a crest to disappear down in the grass again.

"How many?" asked Tip.

"A score and some," replied Loric.

"Let's go," said Beau, and once again they started northeast-ward, now running alongside the towering flank of the Great Escarpment.

And they trotted without pause, no longer alternating their pace with that of a walk.

And the breath of the Waerlinga grew harsh and labored.

While behind the riders drew on.

And now the four rounded a long, curving haunch of the escarpment, and in the distance before them they could see an enormous torrent pouring over the lip of the steep. Here it was that the mighty south-flowing Argon River fell a thousand feet into a churning basin below, for here did Bellon Falls plunge into the Cauldron. And the roar of the cataract thundered out-ward from the escarpment to shake the very air.

"How far?" gasped Beau.

"Two leagues or three," came Loric's panting answer.

"To the left," puffed Phais.

Now leftward from Bellon by perhaps as much as seven miles, both buccen could see a second falls, a silvery cascade of water plunging over the escarpment and down. It was Vanil Falls, where beyond a turn in the rim the east-flowing River Nith hurtled out from Darda Galion to plummet into the westernmost reach of the Cauldron.

Tip glanced back. In the near distance the Hyrinian riders flew over the grass at full gallop, and swords waved above their heads and their mouths were agape in howls, though Tip could not hear them above Bellon's roar.

"We'll never make it," gasped Tip. "Take the coin and go without us. We'll try to hold them here."

But Beau gritted, "Run!"

And run they did, as swift as they could . . .

. . . yet the horses were swifter still.

Another mile they ran, no more, and up a gentle rise.

And Loric stopped.

As did the others.

Panting, Loric drew his sword. "Here on this slope we will make our stand."

Gasping and with trembling hands, Tip set an arrow to string.

Likewise did Beau load his sling as Phais unsheathed her blade.

And twenty-four Hyrinian riders came thundering up the hill.

Tip took a deep breath and exhaled half . . .

And riders howled in triumph as they charged upward . . .

. . . and with eyes for nought else, Tip took aim . . .

. . . and Hyrinians leaned outward, making ready to hack and chop as they swept by . . .

. . . and Tip loosed . . .

And a sleet of arrows hissed downslope and slammed into the riders.

"Waugh!" burst out Tipperton as a dozen or more arrows pierced Hyrianian throats and eyes and hearts, and riders tumbled backwards to crash to the ground or to be stirrup-dragged as another sleet of arrows flew at those yet galloping forward. And free-running horses hammered past Tip and Beau and Loric and Phais, the four dodging this way and that to keep from being trampled, as yet another volley of arrows hissed past and into the foe.

And when the riderless horses had thundered by, Tip gaped at the arrow-slain Hyrinians and then in amazement at his bow and turned to the others . . .

. . . to see . . .

. . . hard-breathing, bow-bearing Elves striding over the crest. And among them one called out, "Well, Loric, it seems we arrived just in time."

26

Alor Galarun!" Loric sheathed his sword.

As some Lian went after the loose horses and other Lian moved down to make certain of the Hyrinians, Galarun grinned and clasped Loric's hand. He turned to Phais and embraced her, then stepped back and held her at arm's length. "Dara Phais, too many seasons have passed since thy beauty has graced these eyes."

"Alor Galarun," acknowledged Phais.

Dressed in an elusive grey-green, Galarun stood nearly six feet tall. His hair was dark brown, nearly black, and his clear eyes a deep shade of grey. And a smile seemed barely withheld from his generous mouth.

Now Galarun released Phais and glanced at the Waerlinga.

"Alor Galarun," said Phais, turning to the buccen, "may I present Sirs Tipperton Thistledown and Beau Darby, Waerlinga of the Wilderland."

Tip, yet shaken, looked up at Galarun and took a deep breath and blew it out, though he couldn't seem to utter any words; even so, he did cant his head in acknowledgement.

"Oh, my," said Beau, "but am I glad you and the others

came, else we would have been deaders for sure . . . though not without taking some of them down with us."

Galarun gestured up at the escarpment. "We saw ye running ere dawn, with horsemen coming after, following thy track by bright moonlight. I gathered these of the march-ward and we hastened down, hoping to arrive in time . . . as it haps we did."

"In the nick, thereof," said Phais. " 'Twas a close thing."

"Too close," said Tip, finding words at last as he passed trembling fingers across his brow. "Oh, don't take me wrong. We were in desperate need, and we thank you for saving us."

"Speaking of desperate need and of saving us," piped up Beau, "have you any food? I mean, every time I've been rescued by Elves, it seems I am starving. And at this very moment, I swear, my stomach is eating itself."

They rode Hyrinian horses the last five miles to come to where Vanil Falls plummeted into the Cauldron, the water furiously churning under the onslaught while rainbows shined in the mist. A grove of willows stood nearby on the banks of the thundering pool. By hand signals Galarun bade them to dismount, for all speech was lost in the roar.

With a few more gestures Galarun directed eight of the Lian to gather the horses and ride eastward, for they would take them to the outflow of the Cauldron, where they would signal others on the far banks and fare across the Argon on rafts and into the Greatwood beyond. Along with Tip and Beau and Loric and Phais, Galarun kept the remaining seven Lian of the march-ward with him, and he turned toward the escarpment at hand.

And as they started for the way up, Tip wondered why he and Beau and Phais and Loric didn't simply take some of the horses and cross the great river and continue on toward the city of Dendor in Aven, where King Agron sat.

Hold on now, bucco: we have no supplies for that long journey and frankly, you are too spent to go on without considerable rest—and the same is true of Beau. And what better place to recover than Wood's-heart, the Elven stronghölt in the Larkenwald above?

And so up a long and steep path switching back and forth they made their way toward the top of the escarpment, stopping often to rest, for they were climbing fully a thousand feet up to the high rim overhead, the way arduous and narrow and precipitous, the outer edge of the path plunging sheer, with no railing whatsoever, and both Tip and Beau stayed as far from the brink as they could, eight or ten feet at most—in places it narrowed down to three. And although elsewhere the Great Escarpment could be scaled by determined climbers, this was the Long Stair, an entry into Darda Galion above, and one of the few places where climbing gear was not needed at all, though Tip would have felt more secure were they all roped together.

The higher they went, the slower they fared, for the Warrows were weary beyond measure, having run throughout the previous night and a bit after dawn. And finally, in spite of their protests, Lian Guardians bore them pickaback the last hundred feet or so and into the march-ward camp beyond, where among the towering Eld Trees with soft grey twilight glowing though it was yet day, both Tip and Beau fell asleep, their wafers of mian but half eaten, their mugs of tea but half quaffed.

The buccen slept through the rest of the day and the whole of the night till dawn, but even with all this sleep, they were yet weary the next morn. Even so they were awakened at dayrise by the singing of Silverlarks, and then drawn from their beds by the smell of food, for it was the break of fast, and Lian Guardians prepared them eggs and bacon, toast and tea, and even laded out some cherry preserves.

It was the first hot meal they'd had for weeks on end, and Beau's eyes filled with tears at the sight of it. And they ate their fill and more.

"I'm stuffed," groaned Beau, even as he reached for another dab of preserves. "Maybe our stomachs have shrunk."

"I'll swear, Beau," said Tip, popping the last of his toast into his mouth, "I've never seen you look so slender. Why, you're practically a skeleton."

Beau shuddered and paused in slathering jam on toast. "Oh, don't say that, Tip. If I'm to be a skeleton, I'd rather not know it in advance." He resumed spreading the sweet preserve. "Oh,

I know someday I'll be nothing but bones, yet I hope it's years from now after a long and uneventful life."

Tip choked on his tea. When he recovered his breath—"Long and uneventful? It'll take many a year to make these days fade, my lad."

Beau grinned and nodded. "I should say so, bucco. Indeed so I would say."

Throughout the rest of this day they napped, waking long enough for meals and to relieve themselves. Waking as well to marvel over the towering trees all 'round.

Like the Lone Eld Tree these forest giants were, yet here they stood seemingly without number, with twilight galleries reaching inward to fade beyond sight among the massive boles. And like the Lone Eld Tree, these towered upward toward the sky, three hundred feet or more.

And high among the branches, silvery birds winged. These were the Silverlarks, the *Vani-lêrihha*, who lived by day in Mithgar and by night in Adonar, their singing and flight somehow allowing crossings of the in-between, flying unto Adonar at the eventide, returning to Mithgar on the dawn. It was from these argent birds that this mighty forest took one of its names: the Larkenwald.

"Aye, 'twas started by Vanidor Silverleaf long past, this forest, transplanted as seedlings," responded Galarun to a question by Beau at the evening meal. He paused and looked long at the enshadowed giants. "It reminds us of home," he said at last.

"Transplanted!" exclaimed Beau, his eyes wide with wonder as he peered all 'round. "Why, it must have taken forever. —Centuries at least."

"Millennia," corrected Galarun.

"Oh, my," breathed Beau.

Galarun smiled. "We had the time, wee one. We had the time."

Tip looked askance at the Elf. "You say it reminds you of home?"

At Galarun's nod, Tip continued: "Do you miss the High World?"

The Alor stroked his chin and then said, "At times. But it is a simple matter to return and renew ties." He glanced at Phais across the fire. She nodded. Galarun looked again at Tip. "You see, Sir Tipperton—"

"You don't need to call me 'sir.' Tip or Tipperton will do. And the same for Beau."

Galarun smiled and nodded. "Tip it is."

"I interrupted," said Tip.

Galarun turned up a hand. "What I was to say is that here in Darda Galion there is an in-between crossing unto Adonar, where we cross over at twilight and return upon the dawn."

Beau frowned, pondering.

"Dost thou have a question, Beau?" asked Galarun.

Beau took a deep breath. "I was just wondering why you are here. I mean, what brings you to Mithgar in the first place?"

Galarun laughed. "I assure thee, we are not invaders, though some would name us so—some of whom thou didst meet yester riding at thee up the slopes of a hill."

Flustered, Beau reddened. "Oh, my, I didn't think you were. —Invaders, I mean. I am simply curious as to why anyone would leave their own world to live upon another. I mean, I left the Bosky because I needed to find special herbs and other such, but you . . ."

"Ah, Beau, why does anyone leave anywhere of their own will if it is not to find something? Their heart's desire, adventure, peace, love, excitement, knowledge, or the like."

"But why here? Why from Adonar to Mithgar?"

Again Galarun threw back his head and laughed, his long hair free, his teeth flashing whitely in the firelight. "Ah, my friend, Adonar is . . . tamed: peaceful, placid . . . dull." Galarun threw his arms wide, as if to encompass all the world. "But Mithgar . . . Mithgar is yet wild, tempestuous, unkempt, savage, turbulent, exciting. We come here to feel . . . alive."

Beau shook his head. "Wull, at the moment, what with Modru's war and his Foul Folk and Kistanians and Hyrinians and Chabbains running amok, I'll take dull anytime."

The smile fled from Galarun's face. "In this case, Beau, thou art right, and gladly would I join thee in tedium."

*   *   *

As dawn came and the Silverlarks returned in a burst of wings and song, Tip said, "Hmph, even the birds know how to go in-between. I don't think it can be all that hard."

"You know, bucco," replied Beau, "after this is all over, the war I mean, we ought to learn just how it is done, just to see for ourselves."

Tip shook his head. "No, no, Beau. I think my da had the right of it: Warrows ought to stay put and that's that." Tip scratched under his jerkin. "Besides, I need a bath."

Tip asked one of the Lian, Hadron by name, where they might find some soap. "We're going to bathe in the River Nith," said Tip. "It's been awhile since we've been clean."

"When it rained three days out on the plain," added Beau, "though that washing was completely involuntary."

Hadron fished around in his gear and came up with a bar of mildly scented soap, its bouquet that of wildflowers. "Take care, wee ones, for the waters of the Nith are swift, and should ye get caught in her current, ye will be swept o'er the brim of Vanil and down her long silvery plume unto the Cauldron below."

"*Ooo*," crooned Tip, envisioning the fall and shuddering.

"Maybe we ought to take a rope and tie ourselves to a tree," said Beau.

Hadron laughed. "Nay, instead I will show ye unto a safe eddy."

Hadron left them at a shallow pool, its slow-turning water sheltered by a close-set row of boulders protecting bathers from the swift-running Nith beyond.

"I always wondered why the Elves came to Mithgar," said Beau, hearkening back to the conversation of the night before. "And now we know. —At least, that is, we know why Galarun came."

"Excitement," said Tip, lathering. "Hmph. It seems a rather improvident reason to come." He passed the soap to Beau.

"Oh, I dunno," said Beau. "I mean, given the endless lifetime of Elvenkind, spending forever in dullness would seem an unending bore, don't you think?"

"Hmm," mused Tip. "Perhaps you're right, Beau"—he reached for the soap. "Perhaps we just don't live long enough to see that peace and plenty becomes drab after a lengthy while."

"Oh, I dunno, Tip. It seems that after a good long while of boredom, one could take up games or a hobby or a project to bring some life to life."

Tip smiled, then his eyes widened. "I think you've hit upon it, Beau."

"Hit upon what?"

"Just this, bucco: perhaps Mithgar is not a hobby or games to the Elves, but a project instead."

"Project? What kind of project?"

Tip shook his head. "I don't know, Beau, but they do call themselves Guardians . . . guarding against what, I can't say."

"Perhaps it's against Modru," said Beau.

"Perhaps it's against Gyphon instead," replied Tip.

"Maybe it's against the rape of this world, no matter the cause," said Beau, "be it gods or acolytes or aught else."

Tip looked at Beau. "Even mankind?"

Beau nodded. "Even mankind. Everything's connected, you know."

They stood well back from the brim of the Great Escarpment and looked out over the plains of Valon a thousand feet below, their sight flying far, and here and there they could see faint trails of smoke rising into the sky.

"Lor'," said Beau. "Was it just two days past that we were rescued from the Hyrinians?"

Tipperton nodded in affirmation but did not otherwise reply.

"And it looks as if the war yet burns," added Beau.

"I think it'll burn for a long while, Beau," said Tip, turning to the left, where mighty Bellon Falls thundered down. And where the water left the Cauldron, the Argon River continued onward, curving away to the south in a vast arc, marking the eastern border of Valon. Beyond the river stood a mighty forest; oh, not one like the Larkenwald with its great tall eldwood trees, but a woodland of oak and pine, or maple and birch, and other common trees. Yet this forest was vast. It was the Greatwood, and therein dwelled the Baeron, tall men and strong, and tales told that some of these Baeron took on the shapes of Bears and Wolves.

But Tip wasn't thinking of these legends of old as he stared out across the world. Instead through his mind ran this morning's conversation about Elves and gods and acolytes and last of all of men.

Seek the aid of those not men to quench the fires of war, she said. Certainly the Elves are "not men," and they did save us. Ah, but her rede cannot pertain to us, to Beau and me. We are just a pair of unimportant Warrows caught up in a dreadful war.

"A silver penny for your thoughts," said Beau.

"Huh? Oh. Hmm. Nothing, Beau, nothing at all. Certainly nothing worth a silver."

Galarun clasped Loric's hand. "Say hello to my athir."

Loric nodded. "That I will," he replied.

Now Galarun turned to Phais and embraced her.

"Is there aught else thou wouldst have us convey?" asked Phais.

Galarun stepped back and frowned. "Nought more than that which ye have told us." He looked down at the Waerlinga, then knelt and gravely shook each buccan's hand. "Though I ween he would be proud to hear of our timely meeting."

"Oh, yes," said Tip. "We'll certainly tell your da how you saved our bacon."

Beau grinned and said, "And we'll tell him, too, how we savored *your* bacon the very next morn."

Galarun threw back his head and laughed, then sobered. "Fare ye well, my friends, and may the smiling face of Fortune be ever turned thy way, and may thy mission to Aven go swiftly. Ye'll find the boats at the Leaning Stone, and Hadron will see ye across."

Waving good-bye to the Elves of the march-ward at Vanil Falls, the four along with Hadron set off upstream, following the banks of the Nith.

Within a mile or so they came to a great stone, leaning like a monolithic block against the southern bank of the Nith. In the hollow under the rock, three Elven wherries were tethered, and they used one of these to cross to the opposite shore, Hadron and Loric and Phais all plying oars.

Now Hadron prepared to row back over alone, yet before he took to the swift-running water, they towed the Elven boat upstream a ways, so that the current itself would aid rather than hinder Hadron's return journey.

Then Hadron handed Beau a small block, scented of wild-flowers and enwrapped in waxed parchment, and it was a gift for the Waerlinga. " 'Tis soap, wee ones, yet take care to bathe in places of safety. I would not have ye swept away."

Tip laughed, and Beau hugged the Lian, and then with a "fare ye well" Hadron stepped into the wherry and plied oar to water and was borne away on the swift River Nith.

Through the Eldwood they strode, through the Land of the Silverlarks, the massive trees of Darda Galion towering all 'round. Soft and mossy loam carpeted the forest floor, with tiny flowers blossoming in the silvery twilight glimmering among the giant boles.

"It's like a fairyland," whispered Beau, "but right peculiar, too, what with the trees shedding dimness down. Look at how the light doesn't seem to change even though the sun rides up the sky. I think a body could lose track of the days, and months could pass without notice, for it doesn't seem that time steps into this place at all."

Tip nodded in agreement, yet otherwise did not reply, and on they strode, faring northwesterly, the swift River Nith purling off to their left, sometimes rushing near, other times dashing afar. And as they walked, now and again a roebuck or red hind would startle away, their hooves nigh soundless upon the soft land. Yet no other game did they see, though both Phais and Loric assured the buccen that the land was rich with life—in the streams and down on the forest floor and high in limbs above, though how one might take game from those towering heights, Phais did not say.

They paused in the twilight at the noontide to take a meal and a rest.

"How far did you say it is to Wood's-heart?" asked Beau.

"As the lark wings, thirty leagues and some," replied Loric. "Yet by foot, mayhap thirty-five."

"Huah"—Beau scratched his head—"a hundred fifteen miles."

"Five or six days at a comfortable pace we can hold throughout," said Tip, reflecting back on their journey across Valon.

"Aye," agreed Phais, "though had Galarun the horses to spare, 'twould have been swifter at need."

"Why didn't we bring some of those Hyrinian—?" began Beau, but then interrupted himself. "Oh, barn rats, but I'm a ninnyhead; the path was entirely too steep for horses."

"And too narrow in places," added Phais.

Tip stroked a chord on his lute and looked up. "Perhaps not even Durgan's fabled iron steed could have made it up that slender steep."

"Wull, if we hadn't been hauled pickaback, we wouldn't have made it either," said Beau.

Phais smiled. "Had ye not run nigh forty miles through the night, ye would have needed no aid."

"Had we not run," said Tip, strumming several more chords, "we wouldn't be here today." Then with a sigh, he packed his lute away. "Let's be off, for time does fly, though here in the Larkenwald, who can tell?"

Five days and a mid-morn later, on the second day of July, they passed through a ring of warders, and within a mile or so they came in among thatch-roofed dwellings. They had reached Wood's-heart, the Elven strongholt within Darda Galion. And everywhere they looked, Lian prepared for war.

27

And that was when Galarun and the march-ward saved us!" exclaimed Beau, but then he clapped a hand across his mouth and mumbled through his fingers: "Oops. Sorry, Loric, I didn't mean to interrupt."

Coron Eiron's grey eyes widened, and then he smiled in pleasure. "My arran was one of those who rescued you?"

"Your son? Galarun is your son?" blurted Beau, then slapped his hand back across his mouth.

Eiron grinned at the Waerling. "Aye, Galarun is my son."

By the light of the eventide lanterns, Tipperton looked at the Coron, and now the buccan saw the resemblance: Eiron's hair like Galarun's was brown, though not as deeply so, and his tilted grey eyes resembled that of his son's, yet were of a lighter shade. And Eiron was tall, five foot nine or ten, perhaps an inch or so less than Galarun.

"Then that must mean he's a prince," said Beau, unable to keep his mouth shut.

Eiron shook his head. "That I am Coron does not make it so, Sir Beau. Among Elvenkind we oft take up duties we will shed seasons hence. I am but recently Coron, and will lay the burden down some seasons from now—just when, I cannot say—and someone else will accept the duty."

Beau opened his mouth to ask another question, but closed it again when Tip, sitting beside him, kicked him under the table and whispered, "Later."

Now Eiron turned to Phais and Loric and slowly shook his head. "Ye bring woeful tidings: of Draedani and Drakes and Hordes run amok; of the fall of Challerain Keep and the unknown whereabouts of High King Blaine. We knew of the Swarms to the north and east, and of the men to the south— the Lakh of Hyree and the Rovers of Kistan as well as the Askars of Chabba—but the others, the Drakes and Draedani, 'tis ill news, indeed. Even so, we simply cannot let Modru reach out his iron fist and seize Mithgar, else Gyphon will rule all, to our woe everlasting."

"North and east?" blurted Tip. "You said north and east. There's Hordes east of here?"

Eiron nodded. "Aye, wee one. To the north, as you know, a Horde sets siege not only upon Crestan Pass but upon Drimmen-deeve as well." The Coron gestured toward the out-side, where the night was illuminated by the lanterns of Lian making ready to march. "Even now we prepare to ride to the aid of the Drimma. In two days we shall set forth to break the Rûptish hold upon the Dawn Gate."

"But what about to the east?" pressed Tip. "I mean, Aven lies to the east and north. Do Hordes bar that way as well?"

"The way to Aven? That I cannot say," replied Eiron, pushing the pewter token on its thong back across the table. "There are reports that Foul Folk stride across the marches of Riamon on the east of Darda Erynian."

Tip shook his head yet remained silent as he reached out to take up the small metal disk.

Eiron's glance swept over them all. "That ye may find the way to Dendor rife with Spaunen, that I do not doubt, yet the land is broad and if ye take care, they can at best only hinder thy mission."

"Do they enter Darda Erynian?" asked Phais.

Eiron frowned. "I think not, for therein dwell the Hidden Ones, and even a Swarm gives them wide berth . . . though with Draedani and Dragons to aid them, who can say? —Yet no word has come of any such."

"Well then," replied Phais, smiling at Tip and Beau, "we can at least make our way north through that woodland."

"But say," asked Beau, "isn't Darda Erynian—Blackwood, that is—um, closed? To outsiders, that is? Like parts of the Weiunwood? I mean, with us being outsiders and all, won't they—?"

Phais shook her head. "Nay, Beau, for though the Hidden Ones for the most remain apart from Elvenkind, still on occasion in the past we have come to their aid . . . and, I hasten to add, they've come to our aid as well."

"Dylvana more so than Lian," amended Loric, "yet Elves nonetheless."

Eiron raised an eyebrow. "Aravan, though, seems to have a special bond with the Hidden Ones."

Beau frowned. "Aravan, hmm . . ."

"The one with the Elvenship," said Tip.

"But no more," added Phais.

Beau brightened. "Oh, yes, now I remember the name."

"Regardless," said Tip, "they will let us make our way north through Darda Erynian, the Great Greenhall?"

At a nod from Phais, Tip smiled. "Well, at least it's a start."

"A start!" exclaimed Beau. "What do you call all this we've been doing so far? I mean, I thought we *started* when set out from Twoforks."

Tip now grinned at Beau. "Actually, it all started when a Kingsman gave me a coin."

Beau shook his head. "No, it really started with a debate between Adon and Gy—"

Tip raised his hands in surrender. "I know, I know, Beau, everything is connected. Next you'll be telling me that it started with a sneeze in the Boskydells."

Beau's chin shot out and he said, "And just who's to say it didn't?" And then he broke into a fit of giggles with Tip joining in, while Coron Eiron looked on in wilderment at these tittering Waerlinga, while outside goods were packed and blades were sharpened and armor was polished fine.

They stood at the brim of a wide pool in a small glade in the heart of the Larkenwald. Mist curled up from the clear surface in the dawntime air, and dusky twilight glowed from the Eld Trees all 'round.

"So this is a point of crossing," said Tip, his words a comment rather than a question.

"Aye," replied Phais, "an in-between, linking Mithgar and Adonar. The Eld Trees and the glade and pool make it so. See the mist: 'tis neither air nor water but an in-between, and always at dawn and dusk it rises. See the glade: in its smallness 'tis neither forest nor field but an in-between. And now see the dawn: neither night nor day but an in-between, as is dusk, and the in-between is somehow made easier by the light of the Eld Trees, here and in Adonar."

"There's Eld Trees on the other side in Adonar?" asked Beau.

"Aye, as is needed for a crossing point, there must be a fair match on each side, and between here and there it is nearly exact. Some say Vanidar Silverleaf made it so."

"The one who started this whole forest," said Tip.

Phais nodded, confirming his words. "It is told that three of the crossings are deliberately designed to be so: the one here, the one in Atala, and the stone ring in Lianion. As to the latter, mayhap Elwydd Herself made it so. It is said all other crossings are natural, such as the Oaken Ring in the Weiunwood."

Beau sighed. "If we had only known the rite, we could have crossed at the stone ring and come back across here and avoided all our delays and woes."

Phais nodded. "Aye, and if that were true and if we but knew of an in-between near Dendor . . . Ah, but we don't, and so we must needs take the perilous way."

The following day, armed and armored Lian—Alor and Dara alike—mounted fiery steeds and rode out from Wood's-heart, Coron Eiron at their head, all riding north for Drimmen-deeve to break the siege of the Horde. And though both Loric and Phais yearned to go with their kindred, still there was a pewter token to deliver in a land far away.

In spite of Tipperton's protests, Phais would not set out in the dark of the moon, but insisted upon waiting for it to come full, for the past eight weeks of riding and running and hiding and combat and living on the land had taken its toll on the

Waerlinga, and by waiting they would regain some of the stamina they had spent.

And a week and two days after the Lian had ridden forth, dispatches began coming from the siege at Drimmen-deeve, where the Elven forays into the Foul Folk lines became increasingly bloody.

And Death Redes came all unbidden to loved ones left behind, final messages somehow passed from love to love though no messengers arrived. And grief settled like a pall upon the forest entire, as if the trees themselves somehow knew of many deaths afar.

"Lord, oh lord," said Beau in hushed tones to Tipperton, "endless lives lost, lives they had just begun no matter their age."

Tip did not reply, but instead strummed his lute, while tears ran down his cheeks to fall glittering like diamonds upon the silver strings.

In the dawn of the twenty-second of July, as Silverlarks returned to sing sweetly overhead, Loric, Phais, Tip, and Beau all set out from Wood's-heart, the four once again mounted upon four horses, Loric and Phais riding in the lead, Tip and Beau upon packhorses drawn behind.

Due north they rode through the towering trees, aiming for a shallow ford across the Quadrill, some eight or nine leagues away. And enwrapped in the soft gloaming shadows down among the trees Beau fell adoze in his makeshift packsaddle, while Tipperton strummed his lute.

And thus they made their way through Darda Galion, a land of many rivers—the Rothro, the Quadrill, the Cellener, and the Nith, and all of their tributaries, their sparkling waters flowing down from the northern wold or from the nearby Grimwall Mountains to course easterly through the forest and issue at last into the broad rush of the mighty Argon. In all, the four companions would have to cross two of the great forest's primary rivers—the Rothro and the Quadrill—though they would splash through many of the lesser streams.

And as before, they rode at times, at other times walked, and occasionally paused to relieve themselves or to give the horses a drink in a stream or to feed the steeds a bit of grain.

And little was said on the journey, for the Eld Trees were hush, and to gravely disturb the quiet seemed at odds with the nature of these woods. And so Beau drowsed and Tip strummed softly, mastering notes and chords.

It was late in the day when they came at last unto the Quadrill, where they splashed into the crystal flow, pausing in the pellucid stream just below the eastern end of a mid-river isle to let the horses drink, while Silverlarks caroled their evensongs and flew, to vanish in midflight as well as midsong, the forest somehow bereft with their absence.

"We will camp just beyond the far bank," said Loric, Phais nodding in agreement.

Horses watered, they surged on across and up, and into the twilight beyond.

The next day they turned to the northeast, aiming for Olorin Isle, and in early morn they splashed through the Rothro, the river running down from the wold lying beyond the north marge of the Larkenwald.

"Ten leagues," answered Loric to Beau's question, "but we will not ride that far. Instead we'll spend the night with the march-ward and cross the Argon midday on the morrow."

And in the evening they came unto an Elven camp, where warders on these bounds of the Eldwood were eager for any news of the progress of the war. And even as Loric and Phais told what they knew, one of the listeners cried out in anguish dire and fell stunned unto her knees.

A Death Rede had come.

In a sudden burst of wings and song, Silverlarks heralded the dayrise, appearing from nowhere, from everywhere, from the between, as they crossed on the morn into Mithgar.

After break of fast, while Tip and Beau rolled blankets and gathered gear, Loric and Phais saddled the horses, then lashed the goods to cantles and pack frames.

Bidding farewell unto the warders, they made ready to depart, but ere they did so Beau stepped unto the rede-stricken Dara, she yet pale and grieving, and he hugged her and whispered something into her ear, then turned and let Loric lift him to his mount.

Tipperton did not ask him what he had said, and Beau didn't volunteer.

"Lor'," breathed Beau, "but what a river."

Out before them stretched the mighty Argon, its broad waters sparkling under the midday sun. Beyond midriver lay Olorin Isle, and at its northern end they could see smoke rising from a few sparse dwellings of the Rivermen. Down before the comrades a ferry dock jutted out into the river, and from the pier an overgrown path bore southward alongside the stream. They all dismounted and led the horses down to the jetty.

"Why, it must be more than a mile across," said Beau, yet marveling at the width of the river, as Loric haled on the pull-rope to ring the summoning bell.

After a while they could see the ferry, with four men rowing, leave an island pier; a mule stood in their midst. As the oared barge crossed the wide stretch, the river current carried the float southerly; it would land somewhat downstream below the dock.

"So these are the Rivermen, eh?" said Tip, staring over water at the rowing men, their backs to the near shore, though now and again they turned their faces 'round to gauge their progress. "The ones whose kith pirated from an island upstream?"

Phais nodded. "From their fortress on Great Isle—Vrana was its name, I've heard."

"Hmm," mused Beau, "from here they don't look like looters."

"Those who are seduced by the Evil One oft look fair," said Phais. "Yet recall, these on Olorin Isle claimed innocence, and nought could be shown otherwise."

"Besides," said Tip, "that was long past . . . some twenty-five hundred years."

"Maybe they're like the Chabbains," said Beau, "and hold their grudges long."

Still the ferry drifted southward.

"Should we ride along the path to meet it?" asked Tip.

Loric shook his head. "The mule will haul it here. Else on the journey back we could miss the island altogether."

Beau frowned. "Why are we going to the isle when it's the other side we want?"

" 'Tis the way of the Rivermen: one ferry to carry us to the isle, another from there to the far shore."

"A twofold toll?" asked Beau, grimacing.

"Grudge them not their double fare," said Phais, "for they are few and scrape for every silver penny, and without the twofold toll there would be no shuttle at all."

"Oh well, then . . ." said Beau, yet the frown did not leave his face.

Some time later, harnessed to the ferry, the mule came plodding along the pathway, one man leading the animal while the three other men fended with poles to keep the float from grounding against the shore. And when the men saw the Warrows they whispered among themselves of children of Elvenkind.

The barge landed nearly five miles downstream on the long shores of Olorin Isle, where the comrades offloaded and mounted up and rode along the tow path toward the northern point of the island, where the second ferry was docked on the eastern side.

The sun moved two hands across the sky ere they reached the north end and rode in among ramshackle cabins, collapsed and abandoned for the most part, though here and there stood an occupied dwelling. A few men and women and a child or two—all ill-clothed—watched as the four rode past, some to step from their cotes to do so. And they too looked wide-eyed at the buccen. And when the strangers were gone, they spoke briefly among themselves before resuming whatever tasks they had pursued ere the Elves and their children had come, some Rivermen to step back into their dwellings, others to resume a vigil for river flotsam, hoping for a wreck upstream.

When the four reached the east ferry and dismounted, once again four men and a mule were there to greet them. Loric paid the second fare and then he and Phais led the horses onto the barge, Tip and Beau coming after, the men and the mule already aboard.

This time the crossing was swifter, for from the eastern side of the island it was but a quarter mile to the eastern bank of the Argon, though the rowed ferry was carried some three miles downstream ere it arrived at the opposite shore.

* * *

They rode into the southernmost tip of Darda Erynian, a forest known to some as the Great Greenhall but to most as sinister Blackwood, for its reputation was dire. And Beau gazed all 'round, looking for Hidden Ones and finding nought as he wondered if the forest were "closed." East-northeast they fared the remainder of the day to come to the banks of the River Rissanin, where they made camp.

A light rain fell that night during Loric's watch, but the next morn dawned bright, though no Silverlarks came to sing them awake.

They followed along the west bank of the river, riding and walking and resting, their route carrying them northerly. And once again they camped in the woods, and the night was crisp and clear. And during Tipperton's watch he thought he could see from the corners of his eyes foxes skulking among the trees, but when he looked straight-on, only shadows seemed to be there.

The next day they continued following the banks of the Rissanin, and just ere midmorn they sighted in midriver the grey stone towers of Caer Lindor, her turrets aglint in the rising sun.

They had come to a fortress isle, a legacy of the Elven Wars of Succession, a relic of the elder days, when neither man nor Fey nor Dwarf nor Mage nor aught other bestrode the world of Mithgar, and only the Elves walked the land, and they yet filled with madness. But those days were long past and the Elves now sane, yet the huge, square fortress still remained. It was left as an outpost in event of future want, and until these troubled times had served as a waystation for travelers in need. Yet located where it was, on the border between the warded Blackwood to the north and the Greatwood to the south, seldom had many come this way, and they mostly Elves or Baeron, though now and again a venturesome soul or two would come trekking past. But now war bestrode the land, and a bastion once more it was.

And toward this looming strongholt Phais now led them all, aiming for the western end of a pontoon bridge crossing to the fortress isle.

At the entrance to the bridge there stood a picket at ward; he was the tallest Human either Tip or Beau had ever seen, nearly seven feet in all. Dressed in buckskins he was, and his face was bearded rust-brown, its color matching his hair. And swinging from his belt was a two-handed mace, though Tip thought in this huge man's grip, one hand would be enough. *Huah! He could probably hold this narrow bridge all by himself against a full Horde, if they could only come at him one at a time and had no missiles, that is.*

"Hál, Baeran," called Phais.

So that's a Baeran.

"Lady," rumbled the man, his amber gaze sweeping across the four.

Eyes of a Wolf . . . or a Bear.

"Who is commander here?"

"Lord Silverleaf, with Aravan as his second."

Tip's eyes flew wide. *Silverleaf and Aravan? Oh my, legends come to life.*

Phais looked back at Loric and smiled. "Vanidar is here, Aravan as well." She turned to the Baeran and gestured at the fortress entire. "Ye all are in safe hands."

Apparently satisfied that these visitors represented no threat, the Baeran stepped aside, and Phais spurred forward onto the bridge, drawing Tipperton's horse after, Loric and then Beau coming after.

Toward an enshadowed stone archway they rode, with great iron gates standing open. Atop the castellated walls with its merlons and crenels, Tip could glimpse warriors standing ward, peering down from the battlements to watch the strangers approach. But then Tip's eye was drawn downward toward the arch, where a tunnel led under the wall, and he could see the fangs of a raised portcullis within. Into his shadowy passage they went, horses' hooves aclatter on the cobbled pave, and overhead in the stone ceiling above, machicolations—murder holes—gaped darkly, and somewhere above stood vats of oil to pour burning down on any invader who had breached the gates. And high along each side of the passage were arrow slits, set to rain piercing death.

The corridor itself wrenched 'round a sharp corner and then another beyond, the turns set there to prevent the passage of heavy rams and other engines of siegecraft. And beyond the second turn another archway stood, daylight streaming inward.

Beneath another recessed portcullis they rode and past the
heavy panels of a second iron gate standing open, and thence
into the bailey beyond.

A massive stone building loomed before them, fully six
storeys high, with turrets and towers rising even higher.

The yard itself was abustle with activity and filled with
Baeron men and Elves working at tasks and moving to and fro:
some shoeing horses or repairing tack or cleaning stables,
others haling crates and sacks and such from standing wagons
and into the main building or one of the storage sheds, and still
others practicing at swords and spears and other weaponry.

But to Tipperton all of these sights and sounds faded to
insignificance when his wide gaze swept past the movement
and stir and across the bailey to alight on a leather-clad group
of archers flying arrows into dark silhouettes fastened to
shocks of hay.

Small and quick were these archers, and Warrows all.

28

Beau, look!"

Beau Darby looked where Tip was pointing. "Warrows!" he exclaimed. "Let's go meet them." And he jumped down from the packhorse and motioned for Tip to do the same.

Tip glanced at Phais. She smiled and inclined her head toward the archers. "Tipperton, why Waerlinga are here in Caer Lindor, I know not. Yet 'tis thy folk, and thou shouldst mingle among thy kindred."

Tip, his bow in hand and his quiver on his hip, scrambled down from the horse and followed the other buccan through the bustle of the yard.

But for his sire and a dim memory of his dam, Tip had never seen another Warrow until Beau had come to Twoforks. And now as he looked across the bailey here were—as his da would have said—a whole gaggle of jackanapes. And with his heart pounding, he followed Beau into the cluster, most watching as two flew arrows into the shadowy forms. And just as he came among them, a cheer rose up from the gathering as an arrow struck the dark wooden silhouette dead in its pinned-leaf heart.

Turning to Beau with Tip coming after—"Oh, hullo," said one of the Warrows, a dark-haired, blue-eyed young buccan of nearly the same age as Tip and Beau, twenty-two or -three at most. "I've not seen you two before. Are you newly come?"

Beau grinned. "Aye. We just rode in. But, say, I'm Beau Darby, and my friend here is Tipperton Thistledown. We're from"—a cheer drowned out Beau's words.

"From where?"

"Twoforks," repeated Beau. "Though the Boskydells is my true home."

"The Boskydells? Now there's a place I've heard of," replied the Warrow, "but Twoforks?" He shook his head. "And by the bye"—he touched the brim of the hat he wore—"I'm Winkton Bruk, but Wink'll do."

"Wink it is, then," said Beau, grinning.

In that moment the crowd cheered again and clapped in hearty approval. Someone had won.

Wink's eyes lit up as he saw Tipperton's bow. "I say, would either of you like to join our contest? Try your hand at besting our champion?"

Before Tip could respond, Beau glanced through the applauding crowd at the archers. "Not me. My weapon is the sling. But Tip here, he's the arrow caster, and a mighty fine one at that."

Wink smiled at Tip. "Would you give it a go?"

Tip felt his face flush, and he dipped his head and mumbled, "I'm just a—"

Wink held his arms on high. "A challenge, a challenge!" he cried out above the assembly.

"But I—" said Tip as nearby Warrows turned.

"A champion of Twoforks has come!" cried Wink.

More Warrows turned, puzzlement in their jewellike eyes. *Twoforks?*

"Um, wait. I don't—" began Tip, but Wink grabbed him by the wrist and towed him through the press.

As he did so, one of the archers stepped away from the shocks, leaving the contest winner behind, plucking arrows from the target, while two Warrows readied two fresh leaves to fasten in place.

"Here we go," said Wink, pulling reluctant Tip to the line.

There he abandoned Tip, leaving him all alone. Tip turned to step away, only to face some twenty-five or thirty Warrows watching.

In the crowd, Beau stuck his thumb up and called, "For Twoforks and the Bosky!"

A lusty, good-humored cheer greeted these words.

Tip sighed and lifted his bow in acknowledgement. The sight of the Elven-made weapon brought forth a hushed murmur of admiration from the assembled buccen.

Tip took an arrow from his quiver and was setting it to string when a lyrical voice behind asked, "Are you ready?"

Tip turned—

—and fumbled the arrow, the shaft to clatter upon the ground—

—as he looked into the amber-gold eyes of their champion—

—and his heart clenched—

—for she was a young damman, the first Tipperton had ever seen.

Dressed in brown leathers, she stood three inches shorter than Tipperton's own three feet four. Her hair was a rusty red-brown and held back by a leather band, and she smiled up at him, a twinkle in her amber eyes.

"I, uh—" Thunderstruck, Tipperton bent down to reclaim his arrow.

Laughing, her voice silvery, the damman set a shaft to her own string and let fly at the target, the arrow to strike dead in the leaf marking the heart.

"Your go," she said, stepping back from the line.

"My g—? Oh." With his fingers trembling and his heart hammering, Tipperton nocked the retrieved shaft. He then drew in a breath and let out half and pulled the bow taut and aimed. But his hands yet shook and he lowered his bow. *Get a grip, bucco. What if it were a real Rûck standing there instead of—?* Again he aimed, remembering the skirmish at Annory. He loosed the arrow to fly true and pierce the heart as well, his shaft embedded not a hairsbreadth from hers.

And the crowd roared in laughter.

Tip frowned.

"Um," said the damman, stepping to his side, "nice shot, but your target is over there."

A howl went up from the watching buccen.

Tip looked at the other shock, its silhouette pristine.

Four more arrows each they flew, all to strike the heart, the last four of Tip's in his own target, his first one in hers.

As they walked forward to retrieve the shafts, Wink trotted after to come to Tip's side and said, "Sorry, old chum, but you could have tied or even won had you not aimed at the wrong heart."

Beau, also striding alongside, looked at Tip, watching as his friend's gaze followed the damman. "Hmm," said Beau, "I think more than pinned-leaf hearts have been pierced here."

"Huh?" asked Tipperton. "Sorry, Beau, my mind was elsewhere. What did you say?"

"Oh, nothing," said Beau, turning to Wink and laying a finger alongside his nose and receiving a waggle of eyebrows in return.

Tip fetched his four arrows from the soft, corklike dark wood, and then screwed up his courage to the sticking point and stepped to the other shock. His heart hammering, his palms sweating, he said, "I'm Tipperton Thistledown."

She looked up at him with her golden eyes and smiled brightly and handed him his other arrow. "Rynna Fenrush, though most call me Ryn."

"Wren like the bird?"

Rynna laughed, and Tip couldn't but catch his breath from the sound of it. "No, no, Tipperton, it's r-y-n, though some claim otherwise—"

"As do I," said a voice from behind, and Tip turned to see a golden-haired Elf standing at hand. "Feisty she is and small and red-brown with a golden eye, and chatters sharply when angry, and if that does not describe a wren—"

"Oh, Silverleaf, you're nought but a great tease," declared Ryn, laughing, though Tip thought he could detect a fiery glint in her perfectly lovely eyes—

—and then he suddenly realized: "She called you Silverleaf!"

"Aye, in the common tongue I am Silverleaf; in Sylva, Vanidar; and in Darda Erynian some have another name for me in that lilting tongue of theirs."

As with all of immortal Elvenkind, Vanidar appeared to be no more than a lean-limbed youth, though his actual age had to be several millennia, for he had been Coron when the trees of the Eldwood forest were but seedlings, and now they were giants. He had golden hair cropped at the shoulder and tied back with a simple leather headband, as was the fashion among most Lian. He was clad in dark blue and wore a silver belt which held a long-knife. His feet were shod in soft leather dyed pale blue, and he stood perhaps five feet nine or ten. And even standing perfectly still, he seemed endowed with the grace of a cat.

"I'm Tipperton Thistledown," said Tip, bowing, "miller of Twoforks, though not of late."

Silverleaf smiled. "I know, and 'tis thee I came to find, for I would hear thy tale. But first"—he turned to Rynna—"wouldst thou see that these twain—Sir Tipperton and Sir Beau—are properly quartered, then fetch them unto the war room?"

"Gladly," replied Rynna, smiling at Tip, and once again his heart flopped.

Canting his head forward in acknowledgement, "In a candle-mark or so," said Silverleaf, and then turned back toward the caer.

"Where are your goods?" asked Rynna.

Tip looked at Beau, only to receive a shrug. "Um, I suppose at the stables," said Tip, swinging 'round and trying to locate them. "At least, that's where I assume Loric and Phais took the horses. Our goods were on them."

Rynna nodded and, linking her arm through Tipperton's, said, "Then that's where we'll go look." And she set off across the bailey, pulling Tip along, and he looked in wonder at her arm circling his . . . and tripped.

As they wound their way through the labyrinthine hallways of the caer, with its many twists and turns and shadowy corners and corridors, Tip, his bedroll and other belongings in hand, asked, "What are so many Warrows doing in Caer Lindor?"

Rynna made a low sound in her throat, and Tip thought it a growl. "The Rûcks and Hlôks and other such drove us here."

"Oh, my," said Beau.

"Oh, my, indeed," replied Rynna bitterly.

She came to a cross corridor and led them rightward. She

glanced at Tip and sighed. "We lived in Springwater, a village on the Rissanin up beyond Eryn Ford, up near the headwaters along the Rimmen Range."

"The mountains," said Tip, remembering the maps he had seen.

"Yes. North and east of here."

Tip groaned, and Beau said, "North and east, eh? That's the way to Aven, right?"

"Aven? Yes. Or rather it would be the way were a Horde not standing athwart. But Aven itself lies far beyond Springwater. Beyond Riamon, in fact."

"I'm sorry, Ryn," said Beau. "I interrupted."

Rynna shrugged. "There's not that much to tell, Beau. As I was saying, our village lies some fifty leagues upstream, up the River Rissanin . . . er, rather I should say, it used to lie up there, but no more: the Horde entirely destroyed it. We had small warning that they were coming, and less than half of us survived the initial onslaught." They came to another cross hall, where Rynna turned leftward. As they started down this way, she clenched a fist. "Those of us with weapon skills remained behind and fought, delaying the Foul Folk vanguard, leading them astray, while granthers and granddams and buccan and damman, some with younglings in their arms, made their way toward the safety of Darda Erynian, where the Dylvana and the Hidden Ones dwell."

Beau gulped but did not speak.

"After we had covered the flight of the others unto the safety of the forests, we turned upon the foe, raiding, ambushing, and taking down lone patrols. But in all they were too many for us, though we gave good account of ourselves."

Again Rynna sighed. "Yet no matter how well laid our plans, still there were casualties. Finally we—" Abruptly Rynna stopped before a hallway door. "Oh, here we are."

Rynna reached up and slipped the latchstring. "You can bunk in here," she said, pushing open the panel to reveal a small room, small for a Human or Elf, that is, but quite adequate for Warrows.

"These used to be Elven monks' cells, I am told," said Rynna, stepping inward, Tip and Beau following. "They worshipped someone called the Great Creator."

"We've heard of the Great Creator," said Tip. "—But go on with your tale."

"Oh, that. There's little more. When we were driven into the woods, we knew that we would need help in the destruction of the Horde, and so we came here. —Say, is that a lute?"

Tip nodded as he placed the instrument in its casings on one of the two bunks.

Rynna smiled at him. "I play a pennywhistle and I know quite a few tunes. Do you think we can make music together?"

Beau laughed and dropped his bedroll on a locker at the foot of his bunk.

"O-o-oh, yes," said Tip. "Though I don't know very many songs."

"I'll teach you some then . . . but later. For now we've got to get to the war room. Silverleaf awaits."

Silverleaf shook his head, then passed on the pewter token to the tall, black-haired Lian. "What dost thou think, Aravan? Canst thou sense any peril?"

Setting aside his crystal-bladed spear, Aravan took the disk and examined it, his sapphire-blue eyes full of curiosity. After a moment he shook his head. "Nay, Silverleaf, no peril do I sense." He frowned. "It seems nought more than a plain pewter coin minted with a hole in it, like many found throughout the world, though this has no stamp of the realm where it was struck. As to why Blaine would send such unto Agron . . ." Aravan shrugged and held out the token to a giant of a man, fully ten or twelve inches taller than Aravan's own considerable six-foot height. "Urel?"

Before the big man reached for the coin, he looked at Aravan. "Your stone?"

Aravan touched a small blue stone on a thong 'round his neck. "As I said, Urel, I sense no harm. Yet Tarquin's gift does not warn against all peril, and so as to the token I cannot say."

Somewhat assured, the brown-haired, brown-eyed Baeran took the coin. "I do not think that Blaine would send something of peril unto Agron. After all, they were fast friends when my father taught them the ways of the woods."

"The ways of the woods?" asked Beau.

"Aye. Kings oft send their children to the Baeron to learn the ways of the land and to learn to husband its wealth. 'Tis a manner of teaching young Princes of the keeping of the world."

Urel frowned at the pewter disk, then muttering, "Commander," he gave it over to Rynna, who held out her hand, tiny when compared to the Baeran's.

"Commander?" said Beau, looking at Rynna.

"Aye," replied Silverleaf. "Ryn leads the Waerlinga on our raiding forays."

"And better scouts we could not ask," added Aravan.

Beau's gaze flew wide, but Ryn looked up from the coin at Tip and closed one eye in a wink.

And Tipperton blushed and looked away, looked at Urel, and the big man rumbled, "If I were you, wee one, I would have a Mage examine that coin at first chance."

Now it was Tip's eyes that widened, and he glanced from Urel to the token. "Mage?"

Urel nodded, and glanced at Aravan's amulet and then at Aravan's spear, with its dark crystal and the long black shaft, the weapon nearly eight feet overall in length. "It could hold some kind of charm."

"Charm? M-magic? —Oh, Rynna, perhaps you ought not to handle it." Tip reached out.

She laughed her silvery laugh and tossed the disk and thong in the air and caught it. Then she sobered when she saw how serious he was. "Oh, Tipperton, I don't think it carries peril. I mean, you've told us your tale, and it seems you've borne it many a day without coming to harm."

Tip frowned. "I don't know about that, Ryn. I mean, we, Beau and I, well, ever since we got hold of this coin, we've nearly been killed a goodly number of times."

"Say," piped up Beau, "you don't think it *attracts* peril to the holder, do you now?"

Ryn frowned at the token, then smiled. "Oh, I think not, for you've also met up with many a good friend as well—those in Arden Vale and Darda Galion and elsewhere—Loric, Phais, Silverleaf, Aravan, Urel, the Dwarves in Annory, and many others"—she looked at Tipperton with her golden eyes— "me . . ."

At her gaze, Tip felt his heart leap.

*   *   *

"Lor', Beau, but she's the most beautiful damman I've ever seen."

"Bucco, she's the *only* damman you've ever seen."

Tip frowned, but then his smile beamed forth again. "You're forgetting my dam."

"I thought you told me you could but barely remember her."

"Well, I did," snapped Tip. "I mean, that's right. Yet I just wanted to, to—"

"You just wanted to show my words false, eh?" said Beau, grinning. "Well, here's what I'll concede: she's one of *two* female Warrows you've seen. Yet even with all your vast experience, bucco, I will tell you this about Rynna: I've never seen a damman in the Bosky more comely, and that's saying some. And she can really shoot an arrow."

"Oh, but that's not all, Beau. She's witty and clever and has got a temper and—"

A soft tap came on the door.

Tip opened it to find Ryn standing with a tin whistle in hand, her amber-gold eyes aglitter. "Take up your lute, Tipperton. We'll go to the battlements after we eat and play a tune or two."

Of the songs Rynna taught him that night, the second was a simple but sad tune: "The Waiting Maiden."

And when they had played it through several times, Tipperton gaining in mastery, Rynna asked, "Um, Tipperton, do you have anyone waiting for you back home?"

Tip frowned over the silver frets and set his fingers to play the most difficult chord in the tune. "Unh-uh," he muttered, yet concentrating on barring and placement. "No one." Then he struck the chord, followed quickly by a fingered progression, and silver notes cascaded forth as Rynna laughed gaily. When the last of the notes faded to silence, he looked up smiling to find Rynna smiling back.

"Now let me teach you a more lively tune," she said, picking up her pennywhistle, "and I'll teach you the words as well."

And so they played and sang, as a gibbous moon rode among

clouds across slashes of starry sky, while warders atop the battlements paced their rounds and smiled.

Over the next seven days, as they waited for reports on the location of the eastward Horde, although Beau met the remaining Springwater Warrows—buccen all, but for Ryn—and many of the Baeron and Elves, he saw little of Loric and Phais, off in their privacy. He saw little of Tipperton, too, and when he *did* espy the buccan, Rynna was ever at his side, those two walking about as if they were alone in a bubble, Tipperton meeting other buccen and Lian and men, yet seeming to have time only for the damman, and she seeming to have eyes only for him.

"Canoodling," Beau muttered, grinning as he watched them stroll by, oblivious to all others, the buccan using a word his Aunt Rose had taught him—"Canoodling, indeed"—yet Beau had seen how thunderstruck Tip was, not that she wasn't stricken likewise. Even so, they both had sworn missions to fulfill: Tip to deliver a small pewter coin; Rynna to command the Warrows on their frequent forays, as became all too apparent—

—For on the eve of that seventh day in Caer Lindor, word came that Foul Folk roamed along this side of the Argon, somewhere above Olorin Isle. And hastily a warband was assembled by Silverleaf, of Elves and men and Waerlinga, Rynna in command of the scouts.

And they rode out in the night, heading westward through Darda Erynian—Warrows upon ponies, Elves and men upon horses, Silverleaf in the lead, his bow of white horn in hand. And Tip stood on the battlements above and watched by the glimmering light of the stars as Ryn rode out from the caer and across the bridge and into the woods beyond, she looking back over her shoulder and up, letting her pony find the way.

And the next day Tipperton paced the battlements, and stood on the weapons shelf and peered out through a crenel, the buccan looking ever westward, seeking to see some sign of their return, seeking to see that Rynna and the others were all right.

"But they'll be gone for days," said Beau, standing on the banquette walk just below. "They said so before they left."

"I know," snapped Tipperton. Then more softly, "I know."

"And we've got to think about our own mission, bucco," added Beau. "After all, we've been here a week."

Tipperton, his face pale and stricken, turned and peered down at his friend. "Oh, Beau, I can't leave without knowing she's safe."

"But Loric and Phais say they've worked out the best way to go 'round the Horde in the east, and we'll be leaving soon."

Tip's shoulders slumped. "I know," he whispered. "I know."

Brushing his sleeve across his eyes, Tip turned back to peer out through the crenel, and Beau clambered up beside him and threw an arm across his friend's shoulders, and together they stood and looked westward, peering out and down into the forest reaching to the horizon and beyond, seeking movement, seeing none.

Three days passed, with no word, and at the late-day meal on the third of these days, Phais said, "We must go forth on morrow morn or the one after and no later, for the knowledge we have concerning the whereabouts of the Horde grows older each day we delay, and even now they may be on the move . . . or not."

Tipperton felt as if he'd been struck a blow in the stomach. "But, Dara, Rynna has not returned."

"And she may not," rumbled a bleak-eyed Baeran sitting at their table, his voice bitter, his arm bound and in a sling, a wound taken some days past during a raid eastward. "My wife did not."

With stricken eyes Tip looked at the man. "Ach, I'm sorry, Waldan," said the Baeran, shaking his head. "I did not think before I spoke."

His vision swimming, Tip looked away toward one of the doors of the great common room.

Phais reached out and placed her hand over the buccan's. " 'Tis ever so in war that friends and lovers are parted. Yet thou hast a sworn mission to fulfill, just as does she."

"I know," said Tip, his voice near breaking, his tears barely held in check. "But I . . . I just wanted to see her one last time.

I wanted to tell her . . . I wanted to tell her . . ." Tip could not finish his words.

"She knows, wee one," whispered Phais. "She knows."

That night, in deference to Tipperton, they decided to wait one more day in Caer Lindor, but come what may, they would set out the morning after. And so Tip spent the night atop the battlements, peering through starlight in vain, and just ere dawn the warders found him asleep at his west-facing crenel.

Wan and bleary, Tip picked at his breakfast, while Beau softly chided him about needing food and rest. Yet even though Beau was concerned for his friend, still his own appetite held strong. "Y' never know when we'll be without food again, bucco," he said. " 'Sides, we'll be on rations starting tomorrow and today's the last of the good cooking for a while."

Tip nodded listlessly and continued to pick at his food.

Unable to eat, he had just set aside his knife when a distant bugle sounded, to be answered by one atop the bastion walls.

"They're here," said Beau, but Tip was already running for the door.

Out from the caer and across the bailey he ran, Beau coming after, a rasher of bacon in hand along with a chunk of bread. Up the ramp darted Tip, up to the banquette above, where he leaped upon the weapons shelf and looked out through a crenel.

Tip peered westerly, the rising sun at his back, yet he saw no movement along the River Rissanin nor within the entwined foliage of the woodland below. And he waited, his heart hammering.

Beau clambered up beside him, and in that moment a slow-moving cavalcade emerged from the forest. They watched as more and more horses came out from among the trees, and for each one ridden there came another horse being led while dragging a travois behind.

"I'd better go, Tip," said Beau, "they've got wounded."

Tip nodded, not speaking, and Beau clambered down. Just as the buccan reached the ramp to the bailey below, Tip turned. "Beau, send someone to fetch me if, if—"

"I know," said Beau, nodding, and then he was down and gone.

Tipperton faced west again. Still the horses came out from among the trees.

Ponies. No ponies. Where are the ponies? Where are the Warrows? Where is my Rynna?

Finally, as the first of the cavalcade came onto the pontoon bridge, no more horses with riders or wounded emerged from the forest behind.

His heart thudding in the pit of his stomach, Tip waited until the last of the horses clopped onto the bridge, and then he sprang to the banquette and darted down the ramp and into the bailey below.

". . . were there, all right," Tipperton overheard as he came in among the wounded. "We engaged them two mornings back and drove them hindward to their boats and rafts," continued the speaker, a Baeran, a bloody bandage on his arm and another wrapped 'round his head. "But they fought fiercely, as you can see"—healers squatted beside the wounded, gauging the damage, applying unguents and herbal poultices and bandages, Beau enwrapping a fresh binding on a wounded Lian—"and some in our warband were slain."

Tip's heart lurched and he felt as if he could not breathe.

"What of Vanidar and the others?" asked Aravan, who had remained behind in command.

"Last I saw, Silverleaf and the Waldana were racing downstream along the bank and feathering them with arrows, though many a black shaft flew back at them. Those of the warband without bows and slings rode alongside covering the flanks just in case there were more aland, or to be on hand if those on the river turned ashore."

"And the dead?"

The Baeran gestured to where several of the travois had been unfastened and lay off to the side, the bodies thereon covered with blankets. "We brought back those we could, though if Silverleaf and the others take wounds, there's likely to be more."

Again Tip's heart flopped and, trembling, he stepped toward the dead.

Only one of those slain was the size of a Warrow, and with his breath coming harsh and gasping, Tipperton slowly raised the corner of the blanket to see, and he fell to his knees weeping, weeping in relief, for it was not Rynna, but Winkton Bruk instead.

She's safe, oh Adon, she's safe.

And then guilt flooded Tipperton's very soul.

Oh, my. Oh, my. How can I rejoice when Wink lies here dead; how can I be glad that it's Wink instead of her?

With tears running down his cheeks, Tip reached out with his fingers and smoothed back Winkton's dark hair.

I'm so sorry, so very sorry, Wink.

And he covered Winkton's face with the blanket once more and then stood. And he looked about, not only feeling guilty but also feeling utterly useless, for he knew nought but the most rudimentary of healing skills, and they needed more here. And his eyes sought the sight of Rynna—

Yet she is not here, not here, but out there somewhere still, black-shafted arrows seeking her heart. Oh, my Rynna, be safe.

Tip trudged to a ramp and up to stand vigil once more.

The sun had climbed to the zenith when another horn sounded from the forest, and Elves and men on horses and Warrows on ponies came plodding forth, some drawing travois behind, and on some of these drawn litters, blanket-covered bodies rode.

His heart thudding in fear, Tip sought sign of his loved one as each pony, as each horse, plodded forth from among the trees. Yet she did not appear and did not appear, and tears sprang to his eyes, to be shaken away, for he would see.

And then Silverleaf on his black came forth from the woodland, and none came after. And Tip cried out in despair, but in that same moment a morose Rynna rode forth from beside Silverleaf; her pony had been concealed by the larger mount.

"Rynna!" shrieked Tipperton. "Rynna, up here!"

And she looked up to see Tip waving madly.

With a wild whoop Rynna spurred her pony, her little steed to gallop across the bridge, Tipperton to dash down from above.

Tip reached the bailey at the same time Rynna did, and she

haled her mount to a skidding halt, seeming to stop and dismount at one and the same time.

And Tip caught her up and swung her about, and kissed her soundly, she kissing him just as fervently in return.

"Oh, my buccaran," she gasped, tears running down her cheeks, "I thought you would be gone."

"And I thought you wounded or worse," said Tip, his own eyes welling with joy. Then he gasped. "Buccaran. You called me your buccaran. Oh, my dammia, how did you know I loved you?"

She looked at him, her amber-gold eyes wide. "I've known it from the first moment I saw you. Did you not know it in return?"

While the Baeron bore their four slain kindred south into the Greatwood to lay them beneath leafy bowers, the Elves and Warrows built a great pyre at the edge of Darda Erynian for the remaining five dead: three Warrows and two Elves—a Lian and a Dylvana.

As they did so, Beau turned to Tip and said, "Lor', Tip, Warrows. Warrows killed in this war." And he burst into tears, Tipperton weeping as well. And Rynna took them both in her embrace, and the three stood together and cried.

And as the flames soared and the dead burned and the Warrows wept, Silverleaf and Aravan lifted their sweet voices and sang all the souls into the sky, while deep in the Greatwood, the Baeron stood in grim silence.

Evening fell, and in the twilight Rynna and Tip stood on the battlements and peered out at the forest and down at the river below, and as the darkness deepened they watched as stars came creeping into the moonless night.

"Isn't it strange," said Rynna, peering down at the glimmers in the water below.

"What?"

"The river."

"How so?"

"The water continually flows and flows and yet it is always there; it is always the same, yet every moment it is new."

"As is our love, dear heart, as is our love."

* * *

Bone-weary—Tipperton from lack of sleep and worry, Rynna from lack of sleep and battle—after a late supper, together they walked toward her quarters.

"We leave on the dawn," said Tip.

"I know," replied Ryn.

They came to her door.

"Stay awhile," she said.

A time later and at the request of Silverleaf, Beau went looking for Tip to have the buccan come and choose a pony.

Beau walked to Rynna's door.

He softly knocked.

No answer.

He knocked again.

No answer still.

Perhaps they're not in, bucco. Then again perhaps they are. Of course, they may be up on the battlements watching the stars and canoodling, for surely if they were in, either Ryn or Tip would answer.

Softly Beau opened the door. Tip and Ryn, fully clothed, were lying on her bed sound asleep spoonwise, Tip with his arm about her.

Softly Beau closed the door. *I'll just pick out his pony myself.*

Sometime in the middle of the night, Tip awakened to find Rynna lying beside him and studying his face by the light of the stars seeping in through the high window.

She was unclothed.

Tipperton sat up, and without speaking she knelt on the bed beside him and gently unlaced his shirt.

And though neither had any experience, they made sweet and tender love and fell asleep once more in one another's arms.

Stay.

I cannot. I have a promise to fulfill to a dead Kingsman.

Come with me.

I cannot, for I have my own pledge to carry out, an oath taken when Springwater was destroyed.

Wait for me.

Wait for me.

I will, my buccaran.

I will, O dammia mine.

And they made sweet, gentle love again.

Dawn came.

Horses and ponies were saddled and mules laden with gear and fare—grain for the animals, and rations for Lian and Waerlinga.

And Rynna gave over the gift of three red-fletched arrows to Tipperton, arrows with a woven collar of scarlet bark at the head.

As Tip accepted them he asked, "What are these?"

"Signal arrows," replied Rynna. "Light them and loose them into the sky. They make a bright crimson flare and leave a burning streak in the air behind. You never know when you may need one."

"Oh, Ryn, I have nothing to give you in exchange."

"You've given me yourself and that is enough. Just promise me you'll return."

"I will come when the coin is delivered," said Tipperton, placing the arrows in his quiver.

Rynna nodded and tried to smile brightly.

Tipperton took up his lute and tied it to the rear cantle and then stepped back from the pony and looked it over. All seemed ready. Then he turned to Rynna and embraced her. "Stay safe, my dammia," he whispered, his voice husky.

"Take care, my buccaran," she whispered back.

Tip glanced at Loric, and at a nod, they began walking the steeds across the bailey and toward the gate, Phais leading, Loric next, then Beau, with Tip and Rynna coming last.

Through the jinking passage under the wall they went, the animal hooves aclatter upon the stone way, Tipperton dreading what was to come.

"She was right, you know," said Tip above the clack and chatter and echo of shod hooves.

"Who was right?" asked Rynna.

"Phais. She said that war sunders friend from friend and lover from lover, and although I always believed it was so, never did I think it would happen to me."

Rynna sighed and nodded, but said nothing in return.

Somewhere above a horn sounded, its clarion call ringing down through the murder holes.

Ryn raised an eyebrow and glanced at Tip and took an arrow from the quiver at her hip. " 'Tis an alert, though not a battle cry."

Hastily, Tip retrieved his Elven bow from its saddle scabbard and set one of his own arrows to string, while Beau laded his sling.

They came out from under the wall and onto the pontoon bridge. Both Tipperton and Rynna scanned the edge of the woods lying a distance beyond the opposite bank, but Beau said, "Oh, look," and pointed downriver.

A number of small boats laden with men and plied by oars came rowing upstream.

"What is it?" asked Tipperton, turning to Ryn.

"I don't know, but we'd better be ready for whatever comes."

Loric and Phais began backing the steeds toward the fortress walls, the mules protesting yet grudgingly moving hindward, balking now and then. "Back," called Phais. "Take shelter, for we know not what this portends."

But in that very moment in one of the boats a man stood and held up his empty hands and cried out: "Safe haven! Safe haven!"

"I don't like this one bit, Ryn. These are Rivermen."

Rynna looked at Tip and whispered back, "Are we to deny them shelter just because of something their ancestors did long past?"

"But Rivermen were adherents of Gyphon once, and who's to say they haven't fallen back on those evil ways?"

"Are the sins of the ancestors to be visited upon the descendants?"

"Oh, Ryn, it's just that I don't want to leave you in any danger."

"Tipperton, O my Tipperton, in times such as this no place is safe."

Even as Tipperton and Rynna whispered back and forth, while the bulk of the Rivermen remained outside, their leaders negotiated with Silverleaf and Aravan, and on the walls above, Waerlinga stood with arrows nocked and ready, yet with bow-strings undrawn.

At last Silverleaf signed that all was well, and arrows were placed back in quivers and bows unstrung.

Phais and Loric came to Tip and Beau and Ryn. "Vanidar has granted them temporary sanctuary. Aravan is to go with a warband to Olorin Isle to see if their tale rings true, and if nec-essary across the river to Darda Galion beyond to discover what the march-ward has seen. In this mission as in all others, Rynna, he will need scouts."

Rynna nodded, then asked, "What tale do they tell, these Rivermen?"

"That Foul Folk came downstream and plundered and raided and slew, and these Rivermen were all who escaped with their lives."

Rynna sighed. "Foul Folk, eh? Perhaps some of those we chased down the Argon."

"I thought you slew them all," said Tip.

"So did I, yet it may be that some escaped, or perhaps some went downstream before we came upon the others."

"Regardless," said Phais, glancing up at the midmorning sun and then at Tip and Beau, " 'tis time we were on our way."

"With the Rivermen here?" protested Tip.

Phais glanced at Rynna and nodded grimly. "This fortress is in good hands."

"Well, I don't like it one bit," said Tip.

"Nevertheless . . ."

Now Rynna turned to Tip. "We'll be fine, my love. Besides, you said it yourself, that ever in war friends and lovers are parted, as we are about to be. Yet the sooner started, the sooner you'll return to me." She took a deep breath, as if to ready her-self for a blow, and then said, "Now be on your way."

Tip looked at her, his eyes wide and mingled with anguish and concern. But at last he nodded.

And so, once again the four companions along with Rynna

led their horses and mules and ponies under the wall and onto the pontoon bridge, this time gaining the far bank.

And Ryn hugged Beau and kissed him on the cheek and whispered for him to watch after her Tipperton, and he whispered back that he would.

And then she turned to Tip, and they embraced and kissed one another.

And while they held each other this one last time, Loric and Phais and Beau all mounted and rode to the edge of the woods, where they stopped and waited.

"I love you, Rynna Fenrush."

"And I love you, my buccaran."

Tipperton sighed and released his dammia, and she reluctantly let him go. He mounted his pony and then leaned down and kissed her once more. "Take care, my love. Take care."

She stepped away, tears in her eyes, and with a choked farewell he spurred after the others and into the woods beyond. When she could see him no more, she turned and, weeping, trudged across the wooden bridge and into Caer Lindor, while on the banks Rivermen unladed their craft and carried their goods within.

29

North they rode away from Caer Lindor, Tip morose, Loric and Phais delighting in the green of Darda Erynian, Beau timorously looking this way and that, for not only was this Darda Erynian—Greenhall Forest—this was also Blackwood, where Hidden Ones are said to dwell, and everyone knew that Hidden Ones were . . . were . . . well, they just were. And if you went into their "closed places," then you most likely would never be seen alive again, or so Aunt Rose had always said when speaking of those places in the Weiunwood.

"Birds and wild things," she would say, "deer, hare, foxes, voles, and other such, things that fly, run, crawl, slither—even snakes—for them to live in those places or just to wander through, well, that's all right. But for folk to intrude—" Here Aunt Rose would always shudder, and Beau's eyes would fly wide, trying to imagine the horrible fate of any who would be so foolish.

And now here he was, riding right through the heart of their domain. And he twitched and started at every movement, every sound, some imagined, some not, and looked all 'round, trying to see, trying to see, well, he just didn't know quite what, but trying to see regardless.

But as it had been when they had crossed through that southernmost corner of Blackwood, going from the ferry landing to the fortress of Caer Lindor, Beau saw nought except perhaps flickers of movement at the corners of his eyes, yet when he looked straight-on, it seemed nothing was there but shadows coiling 'round the feet of the trees.

"It gives me the shivers, it does."

Tip roused a bit. "What? What did you say?"

"I said, Tip, it gives me the shivers." Beau gestured all 'round.

"These woods?"

"Yar."

Tip sighed and nodded, but said nothing more, as they rode onward through the sun-dappled green galleries of the forest, with its birds flitting from limb to limb and voles rustling through leaves, and hares bounding away as the horses and mules and ponies approached.

All that day they rode northerly, their track paralleling the waters of the Rissanin, Tip's gaze turning ever and again toward the river flowing in the opposite direction, southerly and away. *Toward my Rynna.*

Now and again Loric or Phais would turn sharply—left at times, rightward at others—to ride 'round a section of woods . . . sometimes a stand of trees—oaks, birch, maple, pine, and the like—other times they would bypass an open sward, a pool or stream, a rocky outcrop, or other such, as if deliberately avoiding these places.

Tip paid no heed, but Beau knew, indeed, Beau knew . . . or so he thought.

"We will make for Bircehyll," Phais said during one of their frequent pauses.

"Bircehyll?" asked Beau.

"Aye. 'Tis where Coron Ruar will be, or so I think."

"Another Coron?"

"Aye. Of the Dylvana."

"What some call the wood Elves," added Loric, "for they are more reclusive than we Lian, seldom venturing forth from their Dardas."

"Lady Arin ventured forth," said Tip, momentarily emerging from his gloom.

Beau frowned, trying to remember.

"The Dragonstone," said Tip.

"Oh, yes," said Beau, enlightened. "She was a Dylvana, eh?"

"Indeed," said Phais, glancing into the nosebag of her horse. "Ah, the grain is gone."

Sighing, Tip stepped to his pony. Its feed was gone as well, and so he unsnapped the bag and slipped it in among the gear as Loric and Phais and Beau did likewise.

They rode another league or so and then set camp for the night. And during his watch by the light of the fire Tip softly played his lute, remembering . . . remembering.

And as he played, wild animals, it seemed, came to listen, or so it appeared, for among the trees eyes could be seen glowing, casting back the flame.

"I had the strangest dream, Tip."

"Oh?"

"I dreamt I was awakened in the night by someone speaking in a strange tongue, and saw Phais conversing with a small shadow, while nearby stood a fox."

"Mmm. That *is* strange. Was there any more?"

"No." Beau *chrk*ed his tongue, and his pony picked up the pace a bit, for he and Tip had lagged too far behind the riders ahead. "I must have dreamt I went back to sleep," called Beau over his shoulder.

Tip shrugged, then *chrk*ed his tongue as well.

Ahead, both Phais and Loric looked at one another and smiled.

In camp that night they heard foxes barking somewhere off in the woods, the high-pitched yips seeming to come from all quarters.

Progress was slow through the forest, for unlike Darda Galion with its mossy underfooting and wide-set trees, here the undergrowth was thick and in places the trees seemed to crowd 'round, as if trying to bar the way. Yet now and again they would come to an open glade, or field, or glen—and if they did not detour around it, they would kick the horses and ponies into a swift trot and ride across, the mules protesting at this unseemly gait, yet unable to do aught but follow after, drawn on the tethers tied to the rear cantles of Phais's and Loric's saddles.

But in one of these open places—a large field covered entirely with mounds, each some eight or ten feet high and twice as wide at the base, each hillock covered with a straw-like yellowish grass, or what seemed to be grass—Phais cautioned the Waerlinga to follow directly behind, and with the animals moving at a walk, she and Loric carefully threaded among the knolls, the buccen coming after.

Of a sudden, "Oh my," hissed Beau, calling back to Tipperton. "One of them moved, Tip. I swear one of them moved."

"One of the mounds?"

"Yes yes, one of the mounds. That one over there."

Tip looked where Beau pointed. As far as Tip was concerned, the mound looked insignificantly different from all the others, with nothing in particular to single it out.

"It turned a bit and, I vow, it seemed to, um, squat somewhat."

Tip started to speak, but Beau snapped, "And don't tell me I'm imagining things."

Tipperton closed his mouth and carefully followed in Beau's tracks, while Beau in turn carefully followed Phais and her pack mule, the buccan nervously twitching this way and that in his saddle, as if trying to look all directions at once.

That night again they heard foxes nearby, and when Tipperton played, eyes shined at him from the dark.

The following day, even though a grey overcast covered the sky, Tip awakened in a better humor, as if resigned that it would be awhile before he saw his Rynna again.

And during breakfast he said to Beau: "Just so she's safe, that's all I want, and I can't think of a safer place than Caer Lindor."

As they resumed their journey northward, down through the trees the rain began falling, leaves catching water in mid plummet but then shedding it down adrip. And although the earth drank it thirstily, still rivulets and streamlets ran under-foot and -hoof. And as the day grew, so did the rain as it fell down and down. Streams rose, their woodland courses running to the brim, some overflowing the banks, and birds sat grumpy and wet among the branches above and now and again shook away water or preened in vain.

Through it all the comrades continued northward, cloaks wrapped 'round tightly, warding off the wetness, though hair and faces were drenched.

Yet though it rained, still among the trees along their flanks did silent shadows run.

That night the rain continued to fall, and the four had no campfire to ward away the wetness, for no dry wood could be found. Even so, Loric erected a pair of lean-tos and they escaped the worst of it.

By the following morning the rain had stopped, but the forest remained adrip, and as they pushed through the heavily laden branches, rider and horse and mule and pony became thoroughly soaked.

Turbulent streams raced across the way, shallow for the most part, and here the animals had little trouble crossing. Yet they came to a wide forest tributary of the Rissanin and had to fare upstream several miles to find a shallow enough ford.

That night again they set a fireless camp, for the wood was drenched, and when Tip played his lute, if there were watchers and listeners, he saw no gleam of eyes.

In midafternoon of the eighth day after setting out from Caer Lindor, the four came in among what seemed a boundless stand of silver birch, the close-set white trunks marching off before them, with no end in sight.

" 'Tis a forest within a forest," said Phais, "and here Dyl-vana dwell."

"Oh," said Tip. "Is this Bircehyll? The place where we'll see Coron . . . Coron . . . ?"

"Ruar," said Loric. "Coron Ruar. And we'll see him if he is at court. But to answer your other question, Bircehyll itself lies a distance ahead, another two leagues or so."

With serrated green leaves rustling overhead and burbling rivulets flowing below, they rode into the silver birch weald, the trees all around glowing brightly in the afternoon sun, the bark of the clusters lucent in the radiance.

"Lor'," said Beau, "I thought the twilight of Darda Galion was magical, but this light all about is magical, too."

Tip nodded. "It seems safe, doesn't it?"

Beau's mouth dropped open. "Hoy now, but you're right. Not at all like"—Beau looked back over his shoulder—"like Blackwood behind."

"I think it's the light," said Tip. "After all, we're still in Blackwood."

"Oh no we're not. Phais said it herself: a forest in a forest, that's what it is, and I'll thank you to not tell me otherwise."

Tip laughed and turned to fetch his lute, and soon a lively tune sprang from the argent strings as they rode among silver birch.

The day waned as they rode onward, and before them the land began to rise. "Bircehyll," said Loric, pointing at the gentle slope, and up the incline they fared. And as the sun sank below the horizon and twilight crept upon the land, they came in among white-stone, thatch-roofed cottages, dwellings much the same as those in Arden Vale as well as those in Wood's-heart, and these were lighted with lanterns, glowing yellow as evening fell. Dylvana paused in whatever tasks they were doing, Darai and Alori watching as on upward rode the four, and the comrades could see that here, too, just as in Darda Galion, just as in Arden Vale, Elves were preparing to set out on some campaign, for they polished armor and sharpened blades and checked riding tack and gear.

"Why is it," Beau asked, "that every time we come to an Elvenholt, they seem to be on the verge of riding to battle? Do we bring this down on their heads? If so, then I suggest next time we pass them entirely by."

Loric smiled and said, "The war is wide, my friend. The war is very wide."

On upward they pressed, and now Tip could see that the crest of the hill was bare of dwellings, and the clusters of silver birch trees thereon were sparse and widely spaced.

Loric did not ride across the crown of the mound but circled 'round instead.

At last on the north side of the hill they came to the Coron Hall, this too a thatch-roofed building, long and low and wide.

Coron Ruar at a slender five foot three stood an inch shorter than Phais. His hair was dark brown, as were his eyes, and the clothes he wore were dark brown as well.

He slid the coin back across to Tipperton. " 'Tis quite the tale ye tell, yet I know nought of what this token means." As Tip retrieved the coin, Ruar turned to Phais. "Aye, we knew that Draedani walk among the Hordes, though not the fact that Skail of the Barrens and mayhap other renegade Drakes have sided with Modru. 'Tis ill news indeed. Yet heed, this I do know: thy chances of winning through to Aven are enhanced if ye ride with us."

"Join thy forces?" asked Phais.

"Aye, for we will soon hie north, where the Baeron muster, and thence into Riamon to help break the siege on Mineholt North."

"Mineholt North?" asked Beau.

Loric glanced across at the buccan. " 'Tis a Drimmenholt within the Rimmen Mountains nigh Dael."

"Another Dwarvenholt under siege?" asked Tip. "Like Drimmen-deeve?"

"Aye," said Ruar.

Tip frowned. "What is it about Dwarvenholts that Modru sets siege upon them?"

"The Drimma are mighty fighters," replied Ruar, "and should they win free, they will cause great destruction among Modru's Swarms. Hence, his Hordes set siege, for 'tis easier to do battle 'gainst someone trapped than to defend 'gainst them loose."

Beau's eyes flew wide. "I say, perhaps it's not to keep the Dwarves trapped inside but to keep people out; I mean, after all, Dwarvenholts are said to be the only places safe from Dragons."

Tip looked at his friend in surprise. "Goodness, Beau, but you're right. With Dragons at Modru's beck, the last thing he wants are havens from their flames."

Both Tip and Beau turned to Ruar, but the Dylvana Coron

held up a hand. "Ye may be right, my friends, yet still the Drimma need aid."

Phais cleared her throat. "When dost thou plan on marching?"

"Within a fortnight."

Tip shook his head and sighed. "Two weeks? Another two weeks delayed?"

"Aye," replied Ruar. "Yet by delaying two weeks and riding with us thy chances of reaching Dendor increase many fold."

Tip looked at Beau, and that buccan said, "It's taken us a half year just to get this far, Tip. Whatever the meaning of that coin, whatever message Blaine has sent to Agron . . . well, I just don't think two weeks one way or another will make matters better or worse. Besides, it's as Ruar says, by riding with him, our chances in fact will improve. Perhaps the two-week delay will save time overall."

Tip looked at Phais. She shrugged and said, "Stand now or go, only in hindsight will our vision clear. As thou dost know, each decision represents a turning point, and each action taken as a result, or delayed or not taken at all, these are the stones cast in the waters. How the waves will ripple outward to act 'gainst others, only time will tell."

"Yes, indeed," said Beau, nodding. "All things are connected." He turned to Tip. "Another thing, bucco: given what happened to us when we crossed Drearwood all alone, I now think I'd much rather go into peril surrounded by an army than not."

Tip sighed and reluctantly agreed.

And so the buccen waited and watched as the Dylvana of Bircehyll prepared not only for a campaign to lift the siege of Mineholt North, but also prepared for a prolonged war.

On the morning of the third day in the Elvenholt, as the Warrows sat at breakfast Beau said, "I wonder how they'll get supplies? —The army, I mean."

"Hmm, by wagons or some such, I should think," said Tip, sopping up egg yolk with a chunk of bread.

Beau looked about the common hall where Dylvana ate, and then down at the food on his plate. "You know, Tip, back in Arden Vale, Aris told me that in summer they take the sheep

up into the mountain vales, while the cattle stay down lower
. . . and the chickens and pigs and such, well, their coops and
wallows and pens are never moved, though for the sake of
breathing, they are kept a ways north of the Elvenholt. And we
saw the fields where they raised the grain and other crops . . .
their orchards too. But sitting here in the middle of a forest,
I'm wondering: just where in this place, or in Darda Galion,
for that matter, where do they raise their foodstuff? —That
is, the grain, vegetables, fruit. Where do they graze their herds?
—Assuming of course that they have herds. For that matter,
where do they grind their grain? Where are their mills? And do
they have tanneries? And—?"

Tip held up a hand to staunch Beau's words. "Whoa, bucco.
Look. I don't know where they keep gardens and fields and
herds and other such, but surely they must have them somewhere, right? I mean, else they'd starve."

Again Beau looked at his plate. "Righto, they must, else
we'd be hungry too." And he scooped up a spoonful of eggs and
shoveled it into his mouth.

At a table next to the buccen, an Elven warrior stood. As he
carried his trencher past the Waerlinga, he paused and said, "In
scattered glens throughout the darda."

"Mmhnh?" asked Beau, his mouth full.

"That's where the herds are, the grain fields, the gardens. As
for orchards . . . fruit trees are spread throughout."

Tip looked up at the warrior. "And the mills?"

The Elf smiled. "Where else?"

"Along a stream here and there," answered Tip, grinning
back.

The Dylvana nodded, then moved onward.

Tip turned to Beau. "Satisfied?"

The summit of the hill was kept free of dwellings and there
it was that Dylvana went to meditate, or so the buccen had
been told. And after breaking their fast, the two of them wandered up above the Coron Hall and in among the silver birch
clusters sprinkled across the grassy crest. The morning was
cool, and widely scattered clouds drifted through the sky
above.

Beau flopped down in the grass and lay on his back looking upward. Tip sat nearby, leaning against a tree.

"I always liked watching the clouds above," said Beau, "and to find whatever forms I could in their shapes: fish, people, trees, birds, Dragons, and other such."

Tip nodded but did not speak.

"My Aunt Rose used to say that in the daytime the clouds were one thing, but at night they were quite another, and when I was but a nipper she would at times lift me from my bed and take me out to see. And in autumn and winter, when the wind howled and the moonlit clouds scudded above, she would tell me that it was the Wind Wolves chasing cloud deer across the sky.

"Even now when I hear the wind at night, I think of my Aunt Rose and the desperate race above."

Beau fell silent, and they sat long moments without speaking. But finally Beau said, "Oh, that one looks like the head of a pony. I didn't see it at first; it's upside down."

Tip looked up, but the birch tree leaves stood in the way.

Beau glanced at Tip, then pointed skyward. "Over the— Hoy now, what's all this?" Beau sat up and looked about, his face twisted into a puzzled frown.

"What is it?" asked Tip, peering about as well yet seeing nothing untoward.

Beau shook his head in dismissal. "I thought I heard something." He flopped back down, and immediately sat up. "There it is agai— No wait, it's gone."

Then he turned and looked at the grass, and carefully put his ear to the ground. "Oh, my, Tip, listen. It sounds like your mill."

Frowning, Tipperton crawled to Beau's side and put his ear to the ground as well.

The earth groaned, but not as though great cogs and wheels turned within. Instead it was as if huge stones somehow had a voice, or as if the very ground mourned.

Tip looked at Beau in amazement. "What in the world?"

Somewhere downslope foxes barked.

Tip looked 'round, seeing nothing unusual, then put his ear back to the ground.

Still the earth groaned.

Again foxes barked.

Both buccen sat up.

"I say, Tip. Does it seem to you that these woods are full of foxes? I mean, we heard them all about as we came northward, and—"

"Look," said Tip, pointing. Downslope, Ruar ran from the Coron Hall and leapt astride a horse. He went racing down and away.

"I wonder what that's all about?" said Beau, looking at Tip in puzzlement.

"I don't know, Beau, but perhaps we'd ought to go down and see."

Tip stood, but Beau said, "Just a moment," and placed his ear against the earth once more. "It's still going on," he said, then stood as well.

They waited in the Coron Hall for what seemed a long while, and then Loric, Phais, and Ruar stepped within.

"I say," called Beau, but abruptly stopped, for Phais was weeping, and both Loric's and Ruar's aspects were grim.

Tip sucked air in between his teeth, and he stood and walked toward the three, Beau at his heels.

"What is it?" asked Tip as Beau took Phais by the hand. "What's wrong?"

Ruar looked at him, then said, "Caer Lindor has fallen."

"Oh, my," said Beau.

"Fallen?" asked Tip. "How do you know this?"

Ruar looked at Loric, and at his nod the Coron turned to the buccen. "*Eio Wa Suk* passed word to the *Pyska*."

"Eio wa suk—?"

"Groaning Stones and Fox Riders," said Loric. "They are some of the Hidden Ones, the Fey."

"Groaning?" Beau looked at Tip. "The ground. That was what we heard. Groaning Stones. And the foxes barking—"

Tip flung out a hand to stop Beau's words. "But Caer Lindor: what happened?"

"They were betrayed in the night, and—"

"The Rivermen!" spat Tip.

"Aye. They opened the gates and—"

"Wait!" cried Tip. "What matters is, is . . ." Tip choked to a halt.

"Only a few survived," said Ruar, "a handful of Baeron and Lian, Silverleaf among them, though he suffered terrible wounds."

"What about the Warrows. What about . . ." Again Tip could not finish his query, yet his heart plummeted when he saw the tears now running down Ruar's face.

The Dylvana shook his head. "I'm so sorry, my friend, but all Wee Folk in Caer Lindor died fighting valiantly."

Tip felt as if he'd been struck a deadly blow. "N-no, not all the Warrows. Not Rynna."

Ruar placed a hand on Tip's shoulder. "All, Tipperton. All are slain."

Ruar caught the buccan as he collapsed.

30

*K*ill them all." The words wrenched out of Tipperton, anguish and rage distorting the buccan's features as tears spilled down his face. "We've got to kill them all."

"What?" said Beau, his own eyes welling in grief. "Kill who?"

"All the Rûcks, Hlôks, all the Foul Folk, all the Rivermen, the Hyrinians, Chabbains, Kistani, Modru, Gyphon, all of them."

"But Tip—"

"No, Beau," sobbed Tipperton, wiping his nose on his sleeve, "no buts. We'll just go kill them, kill them all."

Phais knelt by the weeping Waerling and embraced him. He tried to push her away, yet she held him in spite of his resistance. And suddenly he clung to her and sobbed as if his world had come to an end. "Weep, my friend, weep," she whispered, stroking his hair.

Pulling his wits together, Beau wiped his eyes with the heels of his hands. He looked at Ruar. "How—? When did this happen?"

"Down the Rissanin they came sneaking, did the Horde, along the border 'tween the Greatwood and Darda Erynian, to eliminate this thorn in their side. And last night Caer Lindor was betrayed, sentries slain by traitors inside, by Rivermen, and the west gate flung wide unto the Horde massed and hidden among the bordering trees of the Greatwood. Into the bailey they rushed and swarmed up to the battlements, seizing nearly all before the defenders mustered. Valiantly they fought, yet they were o'erwhelmed, and so Silverleaf led the battle to the east gate, for the Horde yet swarmed inward through the west. With a handful he held it until those who were not already slain could escape, their numbers but few. Silverleaf was among the last to leave, and he bears the wounds to show it, or so the Groaning Stones relay. The Horde did not pursue, but instead stood on the walls and jeered, and even now Trolls ply hammers and mauls and rams to destroy the battlements from within. Caer Lindor will be a ruin ere another day has passed."

"And the Warrows?"

Ruar shook his head. "All were slain in the taking of the gate to win free."

Silence fell but for Tipperton's soft weeping. Yet at last Beau drew in a great shuddering breath. "Does this mean our plans are changed? That we'll be marching south instead of north? That we'll engage the Horde at Caer Lindor instead of the Swarm besieging Mineholt North?"

"Nay, Beau," replied Ruar. "Our mission is north and east, and—"

"No," gritted Tipperton, choking back his sobs and pushing free of Phais. "We should go south, not north, and throw these vile ones down."

Ruar shook his head. "Nay, Tipperton, for the Horde has bitten off more than it can chew. The Hidden Ones are enraged that the Foul Folk have encroached upon the Greatwood and stand on the borders of Darda Erynian, and even now the muster is underway: Fox Riders, Living Mounds, Groaning Stones, Vred Tres, Sprygt, Tomté, Ände—Fey and Peri of all kind. Modru will rue the day he sent Foul Folk into their domain."

With fire in his eye, Tipperton looked up at the Coron. "Then I would go with them and slay these killers."

Ruar shook his head. "Thou hast a promise to fulfill."

Crying "To Neddra with this worthless coin!" Tipperton jerked the thong at his neck, snapping the leather in two, and threw token and all across the chamber, the coin to strike the wall and land with a faint *ching*. "I will avenge my Rynna."

His eyes wide, Beau stepped toward the coin as Phais said, "Thou must not take on the mantle of the Foul Folk, Tipperton, and become as one of them, with nought but hatred filling thy heart."

"But I want them dead," gritted Tip.

Loric squatted and looked at Tip level in the eye. "The Fey will see that just retribution is extracted."

As Beau took up the coin and broken strand, Tip stared back at Loric but said nought.

Loric took Tip by the shoulders. "This will I say: seldom do the Hidden Ones rise up as one, yet when they do, nothing can stay their hand within the margins of their domain."

"Then why don't they march on Modru?"

Loric shook his head and released the buccan. "Given their history, given the wrongs done to them in the past, they would avoid all contact with outsiders, avoid acting upon aught that does not directly overstep the boundaries they have set."

Beau retied the broken leather and bore thong and coin back across the room and held it out to Tipperton.

Tip struck at the offering but missed, for Beau twitched it aside.

Again Beau held it forth.

Tip pushed it away, saying, "Oh, Beau, can't you see that this has changed everything?"

Beau shook his head. "No it hasn't, Tip, not one whit."

Tip looked at him, anguish filling his gaze, and he turned up his hands in silent query.

Beau peered down at the coin and then back at Tipperton. "Let me ask you this, Tip: if it were you who had fallen instead of Rynna, would you expect her to abandon her command, to abandon her post, to set aside her sworn mission, and come to avenge your death?"

"But I didn't die," cried Tipperton.

"No you didn't, Tip, but she did, and that's a cruel fact. But this is a fact, too: she would expect no less of you than you would expect of her. She had a mission she kept to the end; you have a mission yet to fulfill. What would she ask of you?"

Again Beau held out the coin.

Tip looked down at the floor and then directly into Beau's eyes, sapphire meeting amber.

Again Beau said, "What would she ask of you?"

With a sob Tip reached out and took the coin. He looked at it long moments; then drawing a deep breath, he turned to Ruar. "I will fulfill my promise to a dead Kingsman, Coron Ruar, yet hear me: on this mission to Mineholt North, I would be a scout, and when it comes to battle, I would ride among the warriors and take as much revenge upon the Foul Folk as battle will allow."

Ruar raised an eyebrow. "I have heard it said that Waerlinga make the best of scouts."

Tipperton knelt upon one knee and held out the coin and thong to Ruar. "Then accept my service, Coron of the Dylvana."

The Coron took the offering and slipped it over the Waerling's bowed head. "Rise, Sir Tipperton, for so do I accept thy terms and count thee as scout and warrior among mine host."

With single-minded intensity, Tip began fletching arrows to fit his draw, and he urged Beau to go to the Elven forge and cast lead bullets for his sling. But Beau had pledged to Ruar his healing skills for the mission to Mineholt North, and the buccan spent his days foraging for herbs and roots and leaves of mint and whatever else he could find that he could strip and peel and dry and grind to stock his medical supplies.

And whenever Beau went afield he was accompanied by Alor Melor, a slender Dylvana, some five foot two in height, with russet-colored hair and amber eyes. As Beau had said to Ruar, "I don't fancy being out there in the woods all alone with the Hidden Ones about. I mean, even though you say they are to be trusted, still, if one of them didn't get the word that Beau Darby was a friend, well then, Beau Darby just might come up among the missing."

Ruar had laughed but nevertheless had called to Melor and asked him to accompany Beau on the buccan's jaunts into the woods.

Melor himself was a healer, though he did carry a spear and seemed quite adept in its use, for when Beau had asked Melor to show him the way of such a weapon, Melor had demonstrated:

" 'Tis known as one of the great weapons," said Melor, flourishing the spear. "Thou canst stab with it—*hai!*—or use its blade as a cutting weapon—*uwah!*—nigh as well as a sword, though I must admit it has a long helve for such. Too, thou canst wield it in place of a quarterstaff—*an e da!*—or as a lance ahorse—*cha!* Lastly, thou canst cast it at a foe"—Melor hurled the weapon and spitted a shock of hay—"yet I would not advise flinging any weapon away except if no other choice presents itself."

"Huah," exclaimed Beau, "here all along I thought a spear was for throwing and little else."

"Nay, my friend"—Melor drew the spear from the hay and brushed stray stems from the blade—"that is the last of its uses."

Together Melor and Beau ranged far and wide across the glades and among the trees, and down in the fens as well. And Beau soon had his medicks well stocked, for Melor was an excellent herbalist and guide.

Tipperton, on the other hand, when he wasn't fletching, spent candlemarks at the target field, honing his already superb skill into one even the Elves admired.

And in the evenings he attended meetings held just for the scouts—poring over maps and listening to detailed descriptions of nearly every inch of the terrain 'tween here and there.

As days eked past, Tip's woe turned inward, and his eyes held an anguish deep . . . yet there, too, burned a simmering fire of rage. During the days he managed to set aside his heartache and devote his attention to preparing for war. Yet at night, at night, and alone in his bed, did grief in the darkness come sit at his side and fill the world entire.

At last, a fortnight and a day after the four had come to Bircehyll, Tip and Beau, Phais and Loric, along with the Elven host, they all set forth in a long cavalcade, astride horses—but for two ponies—with pack animals and spare mounts drawn behind.

They were heading for a rendezvous point some hundred miles away as the raven flies—longer by the route they would take—and ten days from now the Baeron were scheduled to come. As to the place they would meet, it was a clearing along the Landover Road, a principal east-west tradeway, anchored at one end at the high point of Crestan Pass in the Grimwalls and threading eastward through Darda Erynian and Riamon and Garia and Aralan and onward to lands far beyond.

And so, north they rode up through the heart of Darda Erynian, the cavalcade moving slowly among the thickset trees.

"I say," murmured Beau as they fared 'round the perimeter of an open glade, "did you notice, Tip, no shadows flickering out along our flanks?"

"Shadows?"

"Yar. When we first rode through these woods to Caer Lindor and then on to Bircehyll, it seemed that just beyond the corners of my vision there were flickers of movement, but each time I tried to see what was what, all I saw were shadows."

"Hmm. Perhaps that's all it was: shadows . . . shifting shadows."

Beau shook his head. "Me, I think it was Hidden Ones dogging our passage."

"And they're not doing it now?"

"Nar. They're all gone down south to deal with the Horde."

At this reminder Tip's eyes brimmed, and he and Beau rode onward another league or so in silence. But then out of the clear blue Beau added, "That, or they don't think we need watching, what with a whole Elven army at our beck."

"What are you saying, Beau: that the Hidden Ones were protecting us before?"

"Wull, from what Phais and Loric and Ruar have said, perhaps they are a bit more friendly than I thought." Beau threw up a quick hand of denial. "Oh, not that I think they're to be taken lightly—oh, no, I still believe they're as dangerous as can be—but with Phais and Loric along and showing no concern over the fact that we were in Blackwood, mayhap th— Oh, my goodness, I just remembered."

"What?"

"My dream. The one where Phais was talking to a shadow as a red fox stood by. Perhaps it wasn't a dream after all."

Tip rode onward, considering, yet ere he came to any conclusions, word was passed back chain that Ruar would have the remaining scouts up front to receive their assignments, and all thoughts of Hidden Ones flew from the buccan's mind as he spurred his pony forward.

Tipperton was paired with a scout named Vail, and together they rode out on the left flank, the buccan following the Dylvana, for she knew how to avoid the dwelling places of the Hidden Ones.

"We would not want to disturb them," said Vail, smiling, a sparkle in her dark blue eyes.

At four foot six, Vail was the tiniest Elf Tipperton had yet seen, though she towered over him by just short of a full four hands, fourteen inches in all. She was dressed in varying shades of green, including the dark leather band that held her black hair back from her face. Her feet were shod in soft boots, their leather also dyed a deep green. Like Tip, her weapon of choice was a bow, though a long-knife was girted at her waist.

Together, Tip on his gelded brown pony, Vail on a black and white palfrey mare, they roamed the woodlands out of sight of the main host.

Now and again Vail would stop and lean over to look at tracks, at times dismounting. In these places Tipperton would dismount as well, and together they would examine the spoor.

"Hast thou hunted a bit?" asked Vail as they examined a rather large track pressed into the soft earth.

"Coneys mostly," said Tip, "and marmots, though now and again I'd try for a pheasant or two."

Vail nodded, then pointed at the print. "This is a bear's track, likely black and likely a female if full grown, for were it younger, 'twould not be placed so firmly. Too, 'tis fresh— within this day—the edges mark it so. And see the spacing of this print from the next and the one after? It was walking cautiously. Mayhap a boar bear was nearby. And see this turned-up leaf. . . ?"

And thus did Tipperton's education in tracking begin, and in the next days Vail took every opportunity to instruct him, including the tracking of the scouts preceding them on the fore left flank of the host.

In early morn some seven days after leaving Bircehyll, the cavalcade reached the clearing along the south side of Landover Road, a field commonly used as an overnight respite by merchant caravans passing through Darda Erynian. Yet even though the merchants used this ground, they did not stay overlong, for crowding 'round was Blackwood, a place of dire repute. Elsewhere along this route caravans camped on the road itself until they were free of this sinister place.

Yet when the Elven host arrived, a hundred or so wains were drawn up in the mead. And standing by were the wagoners: huge men and great strapping women, Baeron all, most of the males nearly seven feet tall, the females a hand or so shorter.

"Lor', but look at those monsters," said Beau.

"Monsters?" asked Melor.

Beau pointed. "Have you ever seen any so big?"

Off to one side and confined in simple rope pens were the large, powerful draft horses used to pull the wains, the dark brown animals fully eighteen hands high, each having white, feathered hair on its fetlocks.

Melor laughed. "Ah, Beau, at first I thought you meant the Baeron."

Beau grinned and said, "Well, they're mighty big, too." Then added, "I say, let's go see what's in the wagons." And leading the Elf, the buccan headed off into the rows of wains of the caravan, hence did not see Tipperton and Vail as they came into the clearing and dismounted.

After signaling for Dylvana pickets to take up ward, and seeing to the encampment of his host, Ruar sought out the Baeron leader and was directed to a redheaded woman named

Bwen, who simply towered over the Coron. Together they called a small council of Baeron and Dylvana.

And Tipperton watched from a distance as the group conferred. After a while and much discussion, Ruar turned and spoke to Eilor, leader of the Dylvana scouts. And Eilor rose to his feet and stepped from the circle, his eye seeking and finding. In all he called four outriders together: Tipperton, Vail, Elon, and Lyra.

"Many of the Baeron are battling foe in the Grimwall, yet sundry of the clans will join us to break the siege at Mineholt North. There are yet three days ere the Baeron are due, time enough with remounts to ride the length of the Landover Road east and west to the margins of Darda Erynian and look for aught untoward. Vail, Tipperton, ye shall ride west unto the Rimmen Road Ford; with Tipperton's light weight, I deem four horses in all should suffice. Elon, Lyra, run east to the Landover Gape at the Rimmen Ring; thy goal lies more distant, yet we will ride that way when the remainder of the Baeron arrive, hence we will meet ye along the way; even so, I ask that ye twain take three remounts each should ye need a swift return ere then. All of ye, take care as ye approach these ends, for they are each just beyond the bounds of the darda, hence not subject to the protection of the Hidden Ones. —Be there aught ye would ask?"

Vail looked at Tipperton and he shook his head, and both Elon and Lyra merely shrugged, and so they moved toward the herd of spare mounts to choose the horses they would take.

"Is there enough time for me to find Beau?" asked Tip, trotting at Vail's side.

"A candlemark or so."

Tip scanned about. "I think I saw him at one of the wagons, somewhere over there."

"Go then. I'll meet thee at the road."

Tipperton turned on his heel and hurried toward the parked wains. Yet there were a hundred or so of the vehicles, and though Tip swiftly ranged among the rows he didn't see Beau. Yet just as he was about to give up—

"Hiyo, Tip," came a call.

Beau stood in the back of one of the covered wagons, this a hospital wain, Melor at his side.

"Isn't it grand, Tip?" said Beau, gesturing toward the interior of the wagon. "They've herbs and simples and all, and medicks I've never seen."

As Tip trotted to the wagon, he reached for the thong about his neck. "Beau, I'm off to the west, scouting, and I'd feel better if you'd keep the coin . . . just in case."

Beau took a deep breath and blew it out, then reached down for the token. As Tip handed it over, Beau said, "Listen, bucco, I really don't think the coin any safer with me than with you. In fact, I'd feel better if you kept it 'round your own neck, for with it reminding you there's a mission to do, well, I think it more likely you'll be less rash."

"Oh, Beau—"

"Don't give me that 'Oh, Beau' look. I'll keep it this time, but once we're underway from this place and toward Mineholt North, it's yours and yours alone to give over to Agron, and that's that."

Tip turned up both hands, then said, "Thanks, Beau." And without another word trotted off toward the road.

Fretting, Beau watched him go, then turned to Melor. "D'y' suppose he'll be more likely to take care of himself if he thinks he's the one who *has* to deliver the coin?"

Just as Tip reached the road, so too came the three Elven scouts, and within moments they set forth, Elon and Lyra riding east, Vail and Tipperton running west, she upon her own light and easy-gaited horse, the buccan upon one of the three remounts tethered behind.

In midafternoon Vail and Tip reached the edge of Darda Erynian some forty-three miles away, and here the Dara stopped to change mounts once again. As both she and the buccan took a moment to stretch their legs, Vail said, "For the next six leagues we must be wary, for now we leave the protection of Darda Erynian."

"What about the ford itself?" asked Tip. "I've heard it might be held by the Rûpt."

Vail turned up a hand. "Not likely, Tipperton. —Oh, they did try, yet the Baeron drove them from it." Vail pointed westward. " 'Tis Crestan Pass the Foul Folk command."

Tip peered across the open land lying ahead. Far to the west and rearing up beyond the horizon he could see the snow-capped tips of the distant Grimwall Mountains, the chain reaching away to north and south. The Rimmen Road itself ran westerly toward this range. "That's where Crestan Pass is," said the buccan, his eye seeking but failing to find the place where road and mountain met, his words a statement rather than a query, for he had studied the war maps long and hard. Tip sighed. "To think: it's but a ride of a day or three from Arden Vale up the Crossland Road to the peak of the col where the Landover Road begins . . . up there at the top of Crestan Pass." Again Tip sighed. "Oh, my, but I've come so far to reach a place so close to where I started."

Vail shrugged.

Tip laughed bitterly and, at Vail's raised eyebrow, said, "Is it often the case that much of life is spent running in great large circles?"

Vail smiled in empathy and said, "At times, Tipperton. At times."

They stood and peered westward a long moment more, and then mounted up and rode out into the open wold.

In late afternoon the trees bordering the Argon River came into view, and the Landover Road fell down a long and gentle slope toward the unseen flow ahead.

Vail slowed the horses and turned to Tipperton. "Be wary, my friend, and keep a sharp eye." As Tip set an arrow to string, Vail urged her horse onward, drawing the other three behind.

The sun was just sinking beyond the distant Grimwall as they neared the band of riverside trees, and Tip's heart leapt as a huge figure stepped out into the road . . . but then Tip calmed when Vail called out a greeting—"*Is breá an lá è!*"—and the buccan saw that it was another of these tall Baeron men.

"It is at that!" he called, and Vail kicked the horses into a trot.

As they sat on the east bank of the Argon, nigh where the road crossed the ford, Bren gestured toward the Grimwalls and said in his deep rumble, "We fight to free Crestan: Baeron on this side, the Elves of Arden Vale opposite, the Spawn trapped in between. Yet the winning goes slowly: they are deeply entrenched and have hurled us back several times."

"I hear the Foul Folk tried to hold this ford too," said Tipperton.

Bren's hand dropped to the mace at his side. "They did at that, but we hammered them free. 'Twas a shame to pollute the waters with their dark blood, though not a shame to kill Wrg."

A grim look came into Tipperton's eye. "I pity them not."

Vail looked long at the buccan, her expression unfathomable, and Tipperton became uncomfortable under her intense scrutiny. Finally she turned to Bren. "Hast thou aught word I should bear to my Coron?"

The big man took a deep breath. "Just this: from the tidings you bring and from what I know, I deem we fight this war in too many places. Modru controls all the choke points: Crestan Pass, the Black Hole, Gûnarring Gap, even the Straits of Kis—"

"I say," interrupted Tip, "where's this, um, Black Hole?"

" 'Tis Drimmen-deeve he speaks of, Tipperton."

"Oh."

"Drimmen-deeve to Elves," rumbled Bren, "and Kraggen-cor to the Dwarves, but to the Baeron and other men it is the Black Hole."

"I see," said the buccan. "But I interrupted."

Bren shrugged. "There's not that much to say. Just that those of us who can should come together and choose which of Modru's forces to crush, for he too is spread thin. And by fighting in one place at a time we could break through Crestan, or lift the siege on the Black Hole, or some such . . . allowing more and more of the allies of the High King to unite, and then when we've enough, we can go cast down Modru himself in Gron."

Vail nodded. " 'Tis a splendid strategy thou hast proposed, Bren, and when we leave on morrow morn I will indeed bear thy words unto my Coron."

Bren grunted in acknowledgement, and in that moment one of the Baeron called; stew and bread and tea were ready.

* * *

There was no moon in the night, yet Tipperton sat by a river with stars glimmering in its depths, and he watched the water flow by, ever there, ever new, ever the same, the buccan remembering ... remembering ... as tears spilled down and down.

31

It was late afternoon when Vail and Tipperton returned to the host, and together they sought out Alor Eilor and reported in, and together they bore the news to Coron Ruar.

"Well and good," said Ruar. " 'Tis meet the Baeron command the ford. Would that the Crestan Pass were free as well. Yet as to the strategy offered by Bren: there is much to recommend it. E'en so, there is also this: were the Free Folk to gather all forces and march upon Gron, much would be left vulnerable, and the Foul Folk free to bring destruction unto those thus exposed. Still, could we move swiftly, mayhap we could cast Modru down from his iron tower ere he could combine his Hordes to stay our hand."

Ruar peered at the ground. "Yet, 'twould not be easy, for the iron tower is a formidable fortress and Modru a powerful Mage. And not only does he command Foul Folk, 'tis said in the season of cold he has winter at his beck. If true, we would need many a powerful Mage at hand to counter such a foe.

"Still, the plan has merit, and I will think on it."

Eilor cleared his throat. "But first, my Coron, we must break the siege at Mineholt North."

Ruar looked up. "Aye, we must at that."

Tip sought out Beau and took back the coin, and the rest of the day they spent wandering about the encampment, gaping up at the huge draft horses of the Baeron, and they helped a wagoner feed one of them, marveling over the amount of food it took.

"A goodly measure of the cargo we bear is for the horses," said the Baeron, slapping one of the large animals on the flank. "Else we'd be hauling the freight ourselves."

Beau looked up at the towering man and horse and over at one of the massive wains. Then he grinned and said, "Well, it's not as if a pony would do."

The big man laughed, but Tip turned to Beau. "Speaking of ponies, bucco, it's time we fed and watered ours again."

They strolled to where their own animals were penned, and as they poured a ration of oats into nosebags, Beau looked at the little steeds and said, "I wonder just how they feel, here among the Elves' big horses and the even bigger horses over there?"

Now it was Tip who grinned. "No different from us, I should think, Beau. No different from us whatsoever."

Later that eve, Tipperton strummed on his lute, playing it for the first time since hearing of . . . of the fall of Caer Lindor.

A deep melancholy ran under the tunes.

The next morning, a day early, five hundred Baeron mounted upon huge horses came riding into the clearing. Their chieftain was Gara, a redheaded man, short for a Baeran, standing just six feet three. Yet there was an air of command about him, and he seemed not at all diminished by his taller kith.

Once again Ruar called a council, and Beau and Tip watched from afar, Tipperton picking out songs on his lute. And the sun walked up through the sky and over as the council went on. And the buccan fed the ponies and led them to water, and then watched from afar again, Tip once more lightly strumming doleful tunes. Finally Vail came. "We leave on the morrow, Tipperton, thou and I on the fore left flank. As for

thee, Beau, thou wilt ride among the healers' wains, or so
Melor did say."

Beau sighed and looked at Tip. "It seems as if we've seen
little of one another, especially these past few weeks, less and
less as the days go by."

"Oh, Beau, it's not as if we are parted. I mean, even on the
trail I'll see you in camp each night."

Vail shook her head. "Nay, Tipperton. Once we are underway, as scouts we'll oft be days on our own, searching, seeking,
probing for foe. And we will rendezvous daily with a message
rider and tell him what we have seen, and 'tis he who will bear
word back unto Eilor and thence to the war council. —Oh, we
will return at times, in haste when and if we find the enemy.
Yet for the most, we will be long on the track and short within
camp."

Tip looked at Beau and turned up his hands and shrugged,
and Beau returned a faint grin.

Tip glanced at his friend and then took up his lute, and a
lively tune sprang forth from the silver strings: it was "The
Merry Man of Boskledee," Beau's favorite.

And when the song came to an end, both Warrows laughed
in glee, Beau especially, for it was the first time in a long while
that merriment had touched his friend.

The next dawn found huge horses being led to wains and
harnessed and hitched to great wagon tongues, while Elves
saddled their own mounts and lashed goods to pack animals,
and big men cinched big saddles to big horses and tied bedrolls
behind. And down among the horses and Elves and Baeron,
two Warrows saddled two ponies and tied their goods after.

Finally all seemed ready and the wains pulled out in a long
line along the road, flanked on either side by men on horses. In
the fore, mounted Baeron and Elves waited, and farther out a
vanguard of Elves and horses stood.

Vail, a packhorse tied behind, signaled Tip, and he turned to
Beau. "Well, bucco, it looks as if we're about to start. I'll see
you when I can."

Beau nodded glumly but said nought, and Tip mounted his
pony. As Tipperton reined the animal 'round, Beau said, "Now
you take care, Tip. I mean, you've a coin to deliver, and I don't

want to see you here at one of the healers' wains." Beau's eyes flew wide. "Oh, my, I didn't mean that how it sounded. Of course you must come should you need patching. I just meant you ought to take care and not need any patching whatsoever."

"Don't worry about me, Beau. I have it on good authority that Warrows make the best scouts of all, right?" And with that he kicked heels to flank and the pony trotted away.

Beau mounted his own pony and rode to his assigned hospital wain.

Moments later from somewhere ahead a horn sounded, and with slaps of reins and *chrk*s of tongues and calls of *Hai!* and *Yah!* the wagon train began to roll.

For two days the caravan fared eastward, and nigh noon of the second day a rumor spread down the line that a pair of scouts had come racing west unto the column moving east along the road. It was Elon and Lyra come back from Landover Gape at the Rimmen Ring, or so the rumor said.

And near midtrain—"I don't like this not knowing," said Beau. "Buzz and tittle-tattle is all we hear, and as to the truth of it, there's none to be had hereabout."

Melor laughed. " 'Tis always so, wee one, that speculation flies on the wings of conjecture. Yet take heart, for are we to go into battle, truth will soon arrive."

"Battle? Who said anything about battle?"

"No one, my friend, no one at all, at least not that we've yet heard."

"See what I mean!" growled Beau.

" 'Tis the track of a catamount, Tipperton," said Vail at last. "Seldom do they come this far into the darda."

"Perhaps it was driven," said Tip, scanning the surround, seeing no movement other than birds flitting among the lattice of greenery above.

Vail nodded. "Indeed. Mayhap its haunts in the Rimmens have been overrun. When Lerren comes, we'll send word back to Eilor and Ruar."

Tipperton squatted and took another look at the impressions. The buccan had wondered why they were scouting within the northern reaches of Darda Erynian. After all, if it was protected not only by Hidden Ones but by the Baeron too, then it would seem fruitless to scout in such well-warded quarters. Yet with the finding of these tracks, perhaps he had an answer.

He looked at Vail. "How old would you make these? Five days? Six?"

"At least a sevenday, for when they were made the soil was yet wet, soft from rain—see how each print spreads?—and when last it stormed 'twas just ere we set out from Bircehyll. After these were laid the soil dried, binding hard the spoor."

Tipperton nodded, then stood and glanced through the rustling leaves at the sun passing overhead. "Shouldn't we be on our way? I mean, don't we have some distance to go to reach the rendezvous with Lerren?"

"Indeed," said Vail, standing as well. "Yet just as today, we will see him on the morning."

They mounted up and rode on eastward, wending among the trees.

In late afternoon Tipperton and Vail reached the clearing and rode up the hillside where to their surprise they could see two tethered horses: one bearing a saddle, the other with a modicum of goods lashed to a pack frame. As they did so, Alor Lerren stood up out of the tall grass and called, *"Hai roi, vi didron velles!"*

"Kal æ iyr?"

"Iyr."

"What did he say?" asked Tip.

"He brings news."

"For good or ill?"

"He said 'twas ill."

"Oh." Tip felt his heart plummet.

They reached Lerren and dismounted.

"What is this news thou dost bear, Alor Lerren?" asked Vail.

"Nigh noon, Lyra and Elon brought word: Spaunen raze Braeton."

Tipperton frowned. "Oh, my, another town—ill news indeed. This Braeton, it's just inside Rimmen Gape, isn't it?"

"Aye," replied Lerren.

"How many Rûpt?" asked Vail.

"Mayhap a thousand."

"Ah," said Vail, "a segment."

"Segment?" asked Tip.

"A tenth of a Horde," replied Lerren.

"Oh."

"Is there aught else?" asked Vail.

Lerren looked at the buccan. "Coron Ruar remembers the pledge he made unto Sir Tipperton, and he bids ye twain to return unto the main host and join the war council."

Vail raised an eyebrow and gestured eastward. "What of scouting this verge?"

Lerren frowned. " 'Tis my task now."

"And thy messenger?"

"Arylin . . . though each of us would rather ride in the vanguard."

Vail smiled. "If and when it comes to battle, thou wilt surely be called in from the flank."

Lerren shrugged, then asked, "Is there aught I should know of what ye have seen this day?"

Vail looked at Tip. "We saw the tracks of a catamount," said the buccan. "And perhaps now we know why it was driven from the Rimmens, given that maggot-folk are in the gape."

"Aye," agreed Lerren. "Mayhap they crept through its domain to come upon Braeton, and it fled to the safety of Darda Erynian." He glanced at Vail and then back to Tipperton. "Is there aught else?"

Tip shook his head, and Vail turned up a hand.

"Then ye had better be on thy way, else ye will be late to the council."

Both Tipperton and Vail mounted and with a "fare thee well" they rode down the hill and away, heading southerly for the Landover Road and the host and war. As Tipperton entered the forest again, he found his heart beating heavily within his chest.

As they rode into the evening campsite, Tipperton and Vail saw Coron Ruar's war council nigh the head of the camped train. They were gathered in a circle on a sward below the out-reaching limbs of an oak. Tip was surprised to see Beau sitting in Ruar's circle, Melor at his side. There, too, were Chieftain Gara and Wagonleader Bwen of the Baeron and two other Baeron men, along with several Dylvana, among them Eilor and Lyra and Elon. Phais and Loric attended the council as well.

Beau scooted aside and made room for Tipperton, and he and Vail sat.

Ruar nodded at the two in acknowledgement, then motioned toward one of the Baeron. "Thou wert saying, Durul . . . ?"

"Just this, Coron: as much as I would like to lay these Wrg by the heels, our mission is to lift the siege at Mineholt North. If we stop to fight every ragtag band of Foul Folk along the way, we'll be months longer getting there and less when we arrive."

Bwen snorted. When faces turned her way, she said, "And just how do you propose we *not* fight these Spawn?"

Durul raised a questioning eyebrow.

Bwen gestured westward along the road. "I've a hundred wains filled with food and weapons and grain for the steeds and medicks and other such. We cannot roll them across the peaks of the Rimmens, no matter how hard we try. Nay, if the wagon train is to accompany the host to Mineholt North, it's through the Rimmen Gape or not at all. Heed: if you would have me and my wagons, we'll have to fight our way through."

Durul blew out a breath in exasperation, but nodded in reluctant agreement.

Gara looked from Durul to Bwen and then 'round to all others in the ring. "Has any a suggestion as to how we can bypass the Wrg at Braeton?"

A sudden rage filled Tipperton's heart, and he jumped to his feet, his fists clenched. "Bypass them? I say we kill them all."

Beau reached up and tugged at Tip's pant leg, but the buccan was too furious to heed. "They're maggot-folk, responsible for untold deaths, not only at Braeton, but also at Stede and Annory and unnumbered places elsewhere: the Kingsmen at Twoforks, the Dylvana and Baeron and Warrows at Caer Lindor." His face twisted in anguish. "They killed my Rynna, and all of them deserve to die for it. All of them."

Coron Ruar held forth a hand, palm out, and his gesture

stopped Tipperton's words. And the buccan ground his teeth and plopped back down, yet the anger did not leave his face.

Now Ruar spoke, his words soft in the growing twilight. "Durul has a point in that our main endeavor is to lift the siege at Mineholt North and not to engage every foe along the way. Yet so too does Bwen, in that the wagons must go through Rimmen Gape. Too, e'en should we find a way to bypass them, I would not have Rûpt at our backs. And so it seems we have no choice but to engage the foe at Braeton, as Sir Tipperton desires. How to engage them such that we suffer the fewest losses becomes the problem before this council."

"Seek not to accomplish by brute force that which cunning and guile will achieve instead," said Phais.

"Eh?" said Gara, looking first to her and then to Ruar and then back to Phais again. "Why say you this thing?"

Slowly Phais smiled. "I say it, Chieftain Gara, for given the information brought by Lyra and Elon, I have the seed of a plan."

The council over, Tip and Beau walked toward the rope corral where their ponies were penned. And Beau stopped and turned to his friend, Tip stopping as well.

"I say, Tip, I don't know what's gotten into you, raging at Gara as you did. I mean—"

Tip threw up a hand. "You're right Beau. I was over the line, but something in me snapped. I mean, the thought of maggot-folk going unpunished, well . . ."

"I know, Tip. I know. With what they did to Rynna and Wink and the others . . . —But listen, are we the ones, or rather, are *you* the one, to set the scales to right? I mean, is it yours to gain vengeance for all?"

"Perhaps not for all, Beau, but for Rynna, yes: I am the one who will make them pay."

"Well then, tell me this, bucco: just how many will you have to kill before the balance is struck?"

A stricken looked came over Tipperton's features, and Beau turned and walked onward, saying, "Just as I thought."

"I was in the council, Tip, because Ruar said that healers would need to ride with the vanguard, and Melor was chosen to do so, and he chose me in turn. And we joined in on the planning."

"Oh, Beau, by riding in the vanguard, you'll be in the thick of things. I should think you'd be much safer if you stuck with the wagons instea—"

"And I suppose you aren't in any danger?" interrupted Beau. "I mean, out there nearly all alone, just you and Vail, out where the Rûcks and such can spring ambushes or run you down or what have you. At least I'll have an army surrounding me."

"Oh, Beau, let's not argue. I mean, we'll both be in the thick of it shortly. Just promise me two things: first is for you to keep safe, and second, if I should not make it through, find me and take the coin and deliver it to Agron, eh?"

"Oh, my, don't say that, Tip. I mean, we'll both make it through."

They curried in silence a moment longer, combs scritching through pony hair, then Beau added, "But if I *shouldn't* make it through, promise me you'll deliver the coin in the end. I mean, that's what we set out to do, and surely if we don't, well then, the whole trip is wasted."

Tip nodded, then held out a little finger and said, "I promise."

Beau hooked his own little finger through Tip's and said, "I promise, too."

In that moment up and down the line mess triangles rang. Tip put away the curry combs while Beau packed the nosebags, and then they snatched up their kits and set off for the nearest cook wagon, where a short line of big men shuffled forward, tin plates and cups and spoons in hand.

Beau sniffed the air, then turned to Tip. "Ah, beans and biscuits: my favorite."

Three days later in the afternoon light, Tipperton crept toward the southern marge of the thicket, Lyra trailing after, and even with her keen Elven hearing she could detect but a faint rustle as the buccan moved ahead, sounding no more than a minor stir of a handful of leaves in a gentle zephyr, if that. Finally he paused, and Lyra came up alongside him.

Out from the screen of the copse they peered and down a

gentle slope, and finally Tipperton pointed. In the near distance and partly concealed in the shadows of an outcropping lounged a Rûcken lookout.

"Dost thou see the signal horn?" breathed Lyra.

"From here I can't tell." Tip gestured leftward. "But if we move . . ."

Up and to the left they crept, and finally Tipperton stopped again.

"See the baldric?" asked Lyra. "Over his left shoulder."

Tipperton saw the leather strap, and now at the Rûck's hip he could see— "Yes, he has a horn."

"As expected," said Lyra.

Beyond the warder and far downslope, Tip could see the town of Braeton, or what remained of the town. And there, too, he could see a great stir of movement as Foul Folk yet looted and razed. But even though the destruction was great, they had not put the town to torch.

The two remained silent and motionless for long moments, and then Tip looked at the sentry once more and murmured, "It's as you and Elon said: he stands where he has good view of the road to the west as well as the town below."

Lyra nodded, then whispered, "Aye, 'tis the highest of the two high sentries along this western slope. There are two others who stand watch on the eastern approach, though they are of no moment."

"Where is the sentry Vail and Elon go after?"

Lyra pointed. "Downslope and left. There by the crag."

Tip peered long. At last he saw the lower sentry shift about. "And these are the two who can best see westward?"

"Aye."

They watched a moment more, then Lyra added, " 'Tis as we said in council: judging by placement of the sentries—these two as well as the others—they do not expect a force to emerge from north within the darda and advance south through these hills, for they fear those woods and would not come that way themselves. Instead they believe if any come from the darda it will be eastward along the road."

"Ah, I see. And so this warder and the one below scan the commonplace approach."

"Aye," replied Lyra, "as do the sentries on the far side of

town; they watch the road yon as well. Yet watching the road or not, the sentry below and his comrade just beyond will alert the others if we do nought but watch them watching, for after sunset the vanguard will arrive, and they will not come creeping on catspaws as did we, but on the hammer of iron-shod hooves instead."

They waited moments more, and the sun crept down and down, to finally slide below the horizon.

Twilight stole over the land 'neath a waxing half-moon.

Tip glanced at Lyra.

"Aye, 'tis time," she said. "Elon and Vail are surely in position now and await our signal." She set an arrow to her string, and hastily Tip did the same. "We will loose together," she murmured, "for 'tis unlikely both shall miss."

Tip nodded.

"Thou shalt count off, and we loose on three," Lyra added.

Again Tip nodded, and Lyra drew and aimed, Tip doing likewise.

And of a sudden he realized that he was to slay an unsuspecting foe—

—whereas before it had been kill or be killed—

—shoot him in the back—

—yet the Rûck below—

Come on, bucco, you can do this.

—didn't know.

Shakily Tipperton lowered his bow.

Lyra looked at him inquiringly, then lowered her own bow.

"He doesn't even know we are here," hissed Tip.

Lyra nodded and then whispered, "Think of all who have been slain by his ilk. Too, think of the folk in Braeton, for surely they lie dead. Think as well on those slain at Stede and Annory and at Caer Lindor betrayed: Baeron, Elves, Waerlinga, thine own Rynna and—"

Tipperton threw out a hand to stop her words, an echo of his own said but three days past. He gritted his teeth and raised his bow once again, as did Lyra after.

Inhale full, exhale half, aim . . .

"One . . . two . . . three—"

Th-thnn strummed two bowstrings, *ssss* . . . two arrows whispered through the air to *th-thnk!* into the Rûcken ward, cruel iron points punching in through back and out through chest, and with a grunt he toppled forward to lie in a sodden heap alongside the outcropping.

"Come now," said Lyra. "We must take him from that place and conceal the evidence of his slaying."

"But—"

"Nay, Tipperton. No buts, for I need the garments. Too, others may come to relieve him, and we would not have them sound an alarm."

And so, staying low, they scurried down the hill in the twilight and took up the slain warder, the Rûck's eyes wide in surprise, yet seeming to stare accusingly at Tipperton as he carried the dead sentry by the feet while Lyra carried him by the shoulders.

Back to the thicket they went, the Rûck's horn dangling from a leather strap and clanking and chinging against rocks as it dragged on the ground. They dropped the corpse in the woods, and then down to the outcropping they scuttled once more, this time to take up a scimitar and a half-full canteen and a small bag holding meat dark and stringy, and to kick soil over the small amount of blood spilled.

Lyra stepped to the shielded side of the outcrop and waved toward a hummock downslope and easterly. Then she and Tip scurried back to the woods.

Then, while Lyra went to retrieve her horse and Tip's pony from the back slope of the hill, Tip stood watch from the thicket, the dead Rûck at hand.

Tip refused to look at the corpse lying there, two arrows piercing its back.

When Lyra returned, horse and pony in tow, she tied them to nearby slender trees, then squatted beside the Rûck and grunting, straining—*thuc!*—she pulled one arrow completely through, and then—*thuc!*—the other. She handed Tipperton's to the buccan, the point and shaft and fletching slathered and dripping with dark grume.

Tipperton turned and grabbed the shaft of a sapling as vomit spewed from his mouth.

*   *   *

Sometime after full dark Lyra stood. *"Hist,"* she whispered.

Tipperton heard nothing and, peering outward, saw nothing. He shook his head. "What is it?"

"Someone comes."

Now Tip stood and strung arrow to bow.

But soft came a signal: a faint chirrup, and Vail came slipping among the saplings. " 'Tis done. Elon stands watch in place of the lower sentry."

"Well and good," said Lyra, getting to her feet. "I will return soon." She stepped to her horse and untied the reins and led it northwesterly through the thicket.

Vail turned to Tipperton. "Art thou secure, Tipperton?"

Tip nodded.

"Then I am off to rejoin Elon. Should come a change of guard, we should stop them. Yet if perchance a Rûpt comes here first, thou dost know what to do." At Tip's brief nod, Vail slipped away through the night.

The buccan sat in the edge of the thicket, peering by the light of a nearly half-moon at the sentry post and hoping he would not hesitate and his own aim would be true should Rücken relief come.

Finally he heard a faint jingle of armor and the sound of heavy hooves. And shortly Lyra came slipping through the thicket again, a huge man at her side along with a tiny form.

It was Durul—

—and Beau.

"I just came to see how you were doing, Tip."

"Me, I'm all right," said Tip. "But I say, what about the wagons?"

"Oh, they're on the move and should be in position well before dawn."

"Good."

And they all sat quietly as the night slipped by, while down in the town torchlight and campfires burned.

At length the moon set, and still no Rücken relief came.

Just ere dawn and ignoring the blood and grime, Lyra slipped into the Rûck warder's garb and took up the horn. Then she went to the sentry rock and waited.

Now Tipperton and Beau and Durul moved to where they could see the road as well as the town.

In the dimness below they could make out the bowed canvas tops of the wagon train standing in a long line athwart the road, fetching up nigh the flank of a hill in the north and running into a grassy mead on the south. And in full view in the southern sward stood several of the great draft horses, though not nearly as many as were needed to draw all of the wagons.

Durul turned. "I go to prepare."

"Me too," said Beau.

Tipperton nodded. "I'll be ready."

Durul smiled and looked down at the Waldana. "Keep free of our horses, for doubtless with but one great hoof they could squash either of your tiny steeds."

Beau shook his head. "Not likely, Durul, we're tiny but quick."

Durul slipped away into the thicket, heading back toward the waiting vanguard.

"You keep safe, bucco," said Tip.

"You too," said Beau, and then he followed Durul away.

And Tip waited as dawn brightened, the day edging toward sunrise.

And still the wagon train sat quietly with no stir of movement, as if all were yet asleep.

The rim of the sun broached the horizon.

Lyra in Ruchen garb stood and blew the horn, the blats slapping and echoing among the crags. And she clambered atop the rock and blew again, frantically leaping up and down, her arms flailing akimbo as she pointed down at the stationary wains.

Another sentry farther downslope took up the blaring call, a sentry also in Ruchen garb, yet he stood atop the rock where Vail and Elon had gone.

Down in the shadows of the vanquished town a stir quickened.

And Spawn took up cudgels and scimitars and tulwars.

Foul Folk rushed down through the town and out onto the road to see, and some who had espied the standing train ran back to a roadside building and in.

And from somewhere within the town another horn blew,

and Tip could see several of the Foul Folk stalk from the roadside building and mount waiting horses.

—Nay! Not horses, but Hèlsteeds instead!

Oh, no! It's some of those Ghûl things!

And Tip racked his mind for what he could remember of
them: *Nearly unkillable. Terrible foe. Wood through the heart
and beheading and fire.* He could remember no more as the
maggot-folk below scrambled into a ragged mass on the road.

Lyra hopped down from her post and came into the thicket
and quickly shucked the Ruchen garb, her nose wrinkled as
she did so. "I'll be chasing nits and lice and fleas for weeks can
I not get a bath."

Again the horn blew, and the segment boiled westward,
churning toward the waiting merchant train, where plunder
and spoils were theirs for the taking as well as great horses for
the eating.

"Come, Tipperton, 'tis time to ride." And Lyra and Tip leapt
astride their mounts and rode through the coppice and away.

As they emerged from the thicket, they saw two other
riders appear in the morning light and move toward them. And
again they heard the Rûptish horn blat in the distance below.
"Ah, it goes well," called Lyra to Vail and Elon, "just as Dara
Phais planned."

From behind a wagon Bwen watched as the Wrg came
seething down the Landover Road, cudgels and tulwars and
scimitars in hand, Hèlsteeds with Guula astride in the fore
with Rutcha and Drôkha coming after.

She touched the morning star hanging from her belt, then
took hold of a rope and called, *"Bheith ar fuirechas!"* and her
command was relayed down the line, not only in the Baeron
tongue but in Sylva as well.

Now the Rutchen horn blew again, and the segment spread
wide in a long line so as to swarm over all the wagons at once.

"Go maith!" she grunted under her breath and grinned, for
two days back Phais had guessed they would do just that. All
was going according to plan.

Once again the Wrg horn sounded, and with howls and
squalls of triumph and baying ululations, the segment charged
past the Hèlsteeds, past the Ghûls and their blowing horns,

tulwars and scimitars and cudgels raised to smash down stupid merchants.

"*Ullmhaigh, ullmhaig . . .*" Bwen called and gripped the rope all the tighter, "*fan, fan . . .*"

And the long line of Wrg hurtled closer and closer, Hêl-steeds in their midst . . .

"*Fan . . . fan . . .*"

Howling, shrieking, the Spawn were nearly on top of the train . . .

And the ground shook from the hammer of heavy hooves.

"*Anois!*" shrieked Bwen, hauling on a rope with all her strength. "*Anois! Anois!*"

And everywhere along the line Baeron haled on ropes, and canvas was pulled up and across the arched wagon bows to reveal the Dylvana archers, arrows nocked, bows drawn taut—

—Ssssss . . . a sleet of arrows sissed forth all up and down the line, whispering of death in their flight, the trace of their fatal sounds unheard in the cries of the charging foe and lost in the thunder of heavy hooves—

Waugh! cried a thousand Rûpt voices, their shouts of triumph turning to shrieks of fear as arrows slammed into their ranks, hundreds to tumble down, dead as they hit the ground.

Ssssss . . . hissed another hail of shafts, and more Spaunen fell as they tried to turn and flee—

—but then the column of heavy horses running four abreast smashed into and over and past fleeing foe as Baeron on their massive mounts thundered down the length of the ragged file of Spawn, limbs and ribs and spines and skulls smashing under thundering hooves and hammering maces and shearing blades and crushing morning stars, viscera and muscle and bone and brain bursting outward from the whelming blows of hoof and weapon alike—

And running alongside were two fleet ponies, with shrieking Warrows astride, arrows and sling bullets flying into the foe.

And racing after the heavy horse column came Dylvana on lighter mounts, swords reaving down those yet standing as the running steeds flew by.

And in the lead one of the massive horses crashed into and over a Hèlsteed; the Ghûl astride, quilled with arrows, was smashed under, and there came the sound of breaking bones.

Yet the corpse-white foe gained his feet, his barbed spear still in hand. And he stepped aside from the next galloping horse and, smiling a yellow-toothed grin, stabbed upward at the rider, the brutal spikes on the spear blade punching through the Baeran's stomach, knocking him back over the saddle cantle, driving the Ghûl hindward and wrenching the weapon from the corpse-foe's grasp.

Yet as the Ghûl stepped toward the felled man and took hold of the haft and stared down in malignant glee, there came a call—"*Cha!*"—and he looked up to see—

—Loric's blade flash as he thundered by—*Schlak!*—the face yet leering as the Ghûl's head flew through the air to land in the way and be crushed 'neath smashing hooves, the Ghûl's headless corpse yet holding the haft of the cruel barbed spear as it toppled sideways to fall under hammering hooves as well.

And when the thundering horses and two wee ponies and light Elven steeds had gone past and away—*Sssss . . .* —more Dylvana arrows sissed into the surviving Rûpt, most to punch through the backs of the fleeing foe.

And now, led by Bwen, Baeron raced from behind the wagons, their great long legs overhauling the Wrg, shorter Dylvana leaping o'er wagon sideboards and dashing after, some with long-knives in hand, others yet loosing arrows.

And running easterly fled two Hèlsteeds, arrow-quilled Ghûls astride.

Yet riding after came the heavy horses of the Baeron and two fleet ponies. But Dylvana horses were swifter still, and Phais, Loric, Ruar, Eilor, Elon, Lyra, and a host of others raced in grim silence after the fleeing Ghûlka, the Elves gaining with every stride, their keen blades glinting lethally in the morning sun.

Seeing that they could not catch the Guula, the Baeron turned the heavy horses and once again smashed over shrieking bands of the fleeing Rutcha and Drôkha.

There were not many survivors when the Baeron and Dylvana on foot caught the scattered remainder.

And then there were none.

Leading horse and pony back toward the train, Ruar and Tipperton passed among the slain foe—bodies smashed, intestines and viscera burst and strewn, dead eyes staring from those faces not crushed, brains leaking from shattered skulls, limbs broken, arrows through throats and hearts and abdomens, gaping slashes yawning wide—a thousand pierced and hacked and crushed and broken corpses.

Tipperton was numbed by the carnage, for the face of war was hideous.

"Thou didst say to kill them all, Sir Tipperton, and kill them all we did, and thou canst see what we have done—the wreaking of havoc upon the enemy.

"Yea, mayhap they deserved this end, yet one cannot be casual about such, for to be so is to be no different from them."

On they walked, their route bringing them at last to the hospital wains, where among the healers tending the wounded, Beau stitched a tulwar cut on the leg of a Baeran. Nearby lay three cloth-covered bodies: two of them large, as of Baeron; one of them smaller, as of a Dylvana.

Ruar dropped the reins of his horse and stepped to the corpses and lifted the sheets away from their faces. Tipperton gasped, for although he knew neither of the Baeron, the slain Dylvana was Lerren, the scout who had come into Darda Erynian bearing Ruar's summons for Tipperton and Vail to join the war council, the scout who had relieved them there.

Ruar turned to the buccan. "And this is the price we paid for killing them all."

Tipperton burst into tears.

32

While the Dylvana gathered wood and cut branches from nearby pines to build a pyre for slain Lerren, the Baeron took up their dead and rode northwesterly toward the fringes of Darda Erynian—the Great Greenhall—standing some three leagues away. Loric went with them, for as he had said, "Someone should be present to sing their souls into the sky."

But it was Vail who came to Tipperton and asked that he play his silver-stringed lute at the Dylvana death rites, and so he did as the flames rose up, tears streaming down his face. And a thousand Elven voices lifted in song out on the meadow that day . . .

. . . while in the quiet green folds of Darda Erynian there sang but a single one.

Passing the corpses of two beheaded Ghûls lying beside the road, their slain Hèlsteeds nearby, Coron Ruar and a contingent of Elves and Baeron and two Warrows rode into Braeton nigh midday. And they were appalled by what they found therein—the innocent dead, the mutilation, the wanton destruction and slaughter—the whole wreathed in a foetor of putrefaction.

Sickened, Tipperton looked up at Phais and declared, "This is ten times over what was done at Stede, at Annory."

At Tipperton's side, Beau peered 'round. "A city of the dead, that's what this is, a terrible city of the dead."

Phais nodded, then looked down at the buccen. "Ye will see more of the like or worse ere Modru is laid by the heels."

From down nigh the road a clarion called. Phais sighed. " 'Tis the signal to assemble."

They mounted their steeds and rode back down through the streets of the slain, joining with others answering Ruar's summons. And when all had gathered, the Coron said, "We ride back to the wains, for there is little we can do here."

"Can't we even bury them or burn them?" called Beau.

Ruar shook his head. "Nay, wee one, except for our own the dead must lie where they are felled until this war is done. Then mayhap kindred or others will come and see unto the slain."

Ruar turned to Bwen. "Is there aught, Wagonleader, thou canst use among these ruins?"

"Aye, there's some bales of bush clover we can take for the steeds; a bit of grain, too."

"Then do so."

"Are we no better than Rûcks and such to rob the dead?" whispered Beau to Tip aside.

"They have no use for it," sissed Tip back. "Besides, the maggot-folk are the cause of all this, not us."

Phais looked at the buccen. "Aye, Beau, Tipperton is right. Were we to slaughter merely for plunder, then would we be no better."

Beau frowned but held his tongue.

In midafternoon the Baeron came back from the woodland funeral, and they drove the remainder of the great horses with them, horses which had been corralled in Darda Erynian for safekeeping. And among those huge steeds were the lighter horses of the Elves, for their spare mounts had been corralled in the wood as well.

* * *

The next morning, with outriding scouts far in the lead, the vanguard and cavalcade and wagon train moved easterly through Rimmen Gape, leaving behind the field of slaughter, leaving behind the city of the dead, leaving behind two leaf-covered bowers in the fringes of the Great Greenhall and a circle of scorch in the mead.

And even as they rode, an Elven rider on swift steed and trailing three remounts overtook the train and the cavalcade and galloped past and away, riding in haste for the vanguard a mile or so ahead.

Tipperton, Beau, Vail, Melor, Loric, and Phais were in the rank following Ruar when the courier rode alongside the Coron's file, her horses lathered and blowing.

"The Hidden Ones, my Coron," she called, "they've driven the Horde from the ruins of Caer Lindor. The Swarm fled from Darda Erynian and Darda Stor in terror, and ere they won free of the dardas, fully half of the Spaunen were slain, ne'er to answer Modru's bugles again."

Ruar clenched a fist. "Well and good, Dara Cein. Is there aught else?"

"Nay, my Coron. Eio Wa Suk report no more."

"And Caer Lindor, it is in ruins?"

"Aye, my Coron, or so the Pyska who relayed the message say."

Ruar shook his head in regret as Cein added, "The caer betrayed is a mighty stronghold no more."

Phais turned to Tipperton and Beau. "Thy kith are avenged."

"The Hidden Ones, they should have killed them all, all the Spawn," said Tipperton, his face stormy.

"But fully five thousand lie dead, Tipperton."

"Nevertheless, these Hidden Ones, they should have pursued until all the maggot-folk were dead."

Phais looked at him as if to ask how many dead would it take to satisfy his thirst for revenge, but instead she held out a hand of negation and said, "The Hidden Ones will not go beyond the bounds of their dardas."

"On occasion one or two will," said Vail.

Phais nodded. "Aye, even a handful, but not the nation itself."

Ruar called to Cein, "Ride awhile with us, and this night we will relate all that has happened since we left, and thou canst bear word back unto Birchyll."

A look of disappointment fell over Cein's features, yet she said, "I was hoping to ride with thee into battle, my Coron. Yet, as thou wilt."

That night they camped at the far side of the gape, some twenty-five miles away.

And Ruar and Eilor called the scouts together and once again laid out the maps. And they were attended by Gara and Bwen as well. Another Baeran was there, too, a tall, dark-haired man. So too was Cein in attendance, to carry word back to those behind in Darda Erynian.

When all had settled in place, Ruar said, "We are at a point of choosing the route we follow from here. I have called ye all together so that scouts and war leaders alike will know." Ruar turned to the dark-haired Baeran. "Uryc has traveled within the Ring of Riamon, and so has come to give us his advice."

Eilor handed an arrow to Uryc, and the big man touched the point of the shaft to the map to illustrate: "Mineholt North is some forty leagues northerly along the Rimmen Range. Yet the land 'tween here and there is one of rolling foothills, broken at times by washouts and chasms and gullies. It will be difficult going for the wagons. If that's the way chosen, the task for the outriders will be to find the easiest route through."

Tipperton and Vail, because of their small stature, had been given places up front, and Tipperton looked up from one of his own sketches to the big map and then raised his hand.

At Uryc's nod Tip said, "Isn't there an easier way to go? A road or some such? I mean, I thought the Dwarves were crafters and traders, and it would seem unlikely they would isolate themselves without having a road."

Uryc grunted, and then touched the map with the arrow. "Aye, they are crafters and traders, yet the road they made leads east from the mineholt to Dael, and there another runs southerly to the Landover, where they go east and west to do their trading. Or from Dael they ride the flow of the Ironwater down through Bridgeton and Rhondor and past Hèl's Crucible and on to the Avagon Sea."

Tip glanced at the map and then thumbed through his own scout-book sheaves to a similar sketch. "Well, then, this road up to Dael and the one across, why not use them?"

Vail reached out and her finger traced a route over Tipperton's sketch. "To do so, Tipperton, we would ride east for thirty or thirty-five leagues thus, and then north another thirty or so, and finally back this way westerly thirty more. That's three sides of a square rather than one should we go straightly north instead."

Bwen cleared her throat and then said, "Even so, wee Tippy may be right and the road a deal better, for if there are ravines standing across our way, going the longer may be shorter overall."

Gara nodded. "Indeed there is that, but there is this too: likely the roads are watched, whereas by coming at them through the foothills we will come upon the foe unawares."

Bwen looked up at Uryc. "How rough is the land?"

The big man peered down at the map. "A deal. Yet it was in the higher land I ran my traps. Down lower it seems *bisiú*— better—yet I didn't travel it all."

Bwen canted her head, then turned to Gara. "Well, Chieftain, it seems it's a hundred and some miles over rough ground or three hundred and some by road. If the land is too ugly, we'll be all the later for it, but if fair, then all the better."

The discussion lasted many candlemarks longer, but finally the decision turned on the fact that they bore a greater risk of being spotted if they followed the roads, for would not Modru set his own patrols along these ways? Whereas overland, though a harder pull, they were more likely to reach their goal without alerting the Spawn.

When Tip carried his blankets to the campfire where Beau was bedded down and told him of the decision, Beau grunted and then said, "Goin' overland, eh, and not on a packed road? Well then, Tip, tell me this: with these great big wagons, heavy as they are, what'll it be like if it rains?"

*   *   *

For two days the wagon train rolled cross-country, the great horses drawing the heavy wains after, Dylvana and Baeron escort riding alongside and a rear guard following. Directly out front fared the cavalcade, and farther ahead by a mile or so rode the column of the vanguard, Elves and men alike, but for a lone Warrow: Beau on his pony down among the great horses. And ranging farther out still, by two leagues or three or more, fared the scouts, some to the fore, some aflank, some bringing up the rear. Tipperton and Vail now rode point.

As late afternoon drew down on the day, Beau turned to the Dylvana riding alongside. "I say, Melor, just how far do you judge we've come? I mean, I've been trying to track our progress by sighting on the cap of that mountain over there, and it seems not to have changed at all."

"The mountain moves not, for we but plod," replied the Elf. "A better measure of progress might be the number of steps thy little steed takes."

"Perhaps better, Melor, but it would be a measure dull beyond measure."

Melor laughed, then said, "Six leagues at most, my friend."

"Six leagues?"

"I gauge that to be the measure of how far we've rolled overland—seven by the end of this day."

"Seven leagues, twenty-one miles altogether. Let me see, at this rate we should reach Mineholt North in, um . . ."

"Twelve days of overland travel," said Melor, "two of which we've done, or will have done when we camp this eve."

Beau smiled. "Oh, well, then, that's not so bad now, is it?"

"Nay, wee one, 'tis not," replied Melor, then added: "Of course, that assumes the land remains friendly."

Far out front, ten miles or so, Tip stood on the lip of the ravine. "We can't take wagons through this."

"Aye, we cannot," said Vail, shading her eyes and peering easterly along the rim, "at least not here." She stepped to her horse. "Ride west, Tipperton, while I ride east; we'll look for a place to cross. Shouldst thou find one, turn and ride to me. I will do the same."

Tip nodded and mounted and kicked his heels into the pony's flanks.

Westerly he rode, away from Vail and up the rising land. In the near distance, the Rimmen Mountains jutted up, barring the way. "If we don't come to a place soon," Tip muttered to his pony, "the land will be entirely too steep, too rugged for the wagons to roll this way."

On he pressed and up, a mile and then another, the deep cleft to his right becoming narrower. Yet another mile beyond he came to a bluff, a perpendicular upjut in the land cloven through by the ravine. Tipperton scanned for a way up and, seeing a notch, he turned the pony leftward and rode toward the gap. Yet when he came to it, the defile he found was rubble-filled. He leaned forward and patted the pony alongside the neck. "Well, old friend, I'm not certain a goat could get up that pile of rocks, much less a wagon train."

Turning back, he rode easterly, and finally espied Vail coming toward him.

As they came together he said, "There's nothing west but a steep bluff."

Vail turned and pointed east. "Yon, a third of a league, there is a way across. 'Twill be arduous, yet the train can pass."

"What about farther down?"

"I rode a league past, and there I met Arylin riding west along the rim. She says that there is no crossing for at least three leagues farther on. Hence, the one I found is the best to be had."

Tip canted his head noncommittally and said, "Then there is nothing for it but to ride the back trail and set the guide markers."

And together they rode easterly along the rim to the place where they would start tracking back and setting the signs.

The following day, Beau said, "I see what you mean about the land becoming less friendly."

"Aye," replied Melor, his gaze sweeping across the boulder-strewn ledges. " 'Tis the Rimmens reaching out."

"But we're a distance away," protested Beau.

"Still the stone angles forth."

"It won't break the wheels, will it?"

Melor shrugged but did not otherwise reply.

They rode the rest of the day in glum silence, for the wagons behind were considerably slowed by the edges and ridges and juts in the stony terrain.

And as the sun sank into the horizon, the vanguard came to a deep and wide ravine with long slopes down in and back out.

"Oh, my," exclaimed Beau, "surely there is a better way."

Melor looked east and west. " 'Tis steeper elsewhere than here, at least as far as my eye can see."

"But what about farther down—or up, for that matter—farther than your sight?"

Melor shrugged. "The scout markers say this is best."

They waited until the train arrived, and then Bwen came striding forward. "Fyrra!" she barked, peering down the slope and across and up again. "But they don't expect us to take our wagons through that, do they?"

Ruar sighed. "The scouts believe this place is best."

"Feh! Now what would a scout know about wagons? I mean, they believe that if they can ride through a place, then a wagon surely can follow."

Gara turned to her and gestured wide east and west. "If it's worse up and down, Wagonleader, then would you have us turn back?"

"I didn't say that," snapped Bwen. She turned and called, "Hoy, Braec!"

One of the huge men from the wagons came to her side. "*Naofa* Adon!" he breathed, looking at the way.

"Let's go down and across and see how we may get the train through," said Bwen.

Braec cast a skeptical eye at her, but followed Bwen down the slope.

When they returned, Bwen said, "This will be the way of it: we'll harness a team to each wagon as usual—"

"Hoy now," interrupted Beau, "I'm no expert but it seems to me, no matter how good the brakes, a regular team will not be able to hold one of these heavy wagons back on the downslope or haul it out on the far si—"

"Hush, Waldan!" barked Bwen, glaring at Beau. "Let me finish." Then her features softened. "Indeed, a normal team cannot cross unaided. They will merely be used to steer, to guide the wagon down and up. Nay, the real work will be done by six-horse teams, three stationed on each side."

"Oh," said Beau, but nothing more.

Bwen smiled. "On this side, with lines 'tween collar and wain, six horses will be hitched hindward—"

"Hindwards?" blurted Beau, then slapped a hand across his mouth.

Bwen sighed. "Hindwards, Waldan, as if set to pull a wagon by long ropes away from the slope, but while the team itself will remain on level ground they instead will slowly back and ease the wain down into the deep ravine."

Ruar nodded and said, "Ah, acting as a brake."

"You took the words right out of my mouth," muttered Beau.

Bwen glared from Ruar to Beau, and the Warrow smiled innocently up at her. She shook her head and reluctantly grinned and then continued. "Once safely in the ravine, the ropes will be cast off and the six-horse team taken to another waiting wagon. And down in the ravine, the normal pair will pull the wain to the base of the far slope, where more ropes will be attached and that wagon pulled up and out by another six-horse team above."

Bwen fell silent but Braec added, "With three teams here and three opposite, as each wain is eased down or hauled up, two teams on each side will be standing by and ready for the next. The work can go no swifter."

"Well and good," said Ruar, "on the morrow, then."

The next day, on the near side, even as each wain was eased down, two other teams were already roped to wagons and standing by. And as that wain reached the bottom and was loosed from the ropes to proceed across and the braking team led to another wagon, the next was started down. And on the far side, ropes were attached and wagons draw upslope by the six-horse teams opposite.

Even so, but two wagons passed through the ravine each candlemark, eight wagons every four. And the sun rode up the sky and across as one by one the wagons were eased down and pulled through the bottom and then hauled back up. And as the day aged, the teams on the ravine sides were relieved often, for the work was arduous.

It took the entire day and then some to move the full hundred wains through the ravine. And as the last one was drawn up by lantern light and by the waxing light of a gibbous moon, Bwen said to Gara, "Well, Chieftain, we went all of a ravine width today. If there are many more of these in our path, the snows will be flying ere we gain Mineholt North."

Three days later under lowering skies, late in the day Tip and Vail came riding unto the encamped train, for Coron Ruar had summoned them in. Once again they were directed to the war council. When they arrived, Ruar said, "On the morrow I would have ye ride far point, for we have reached the halfway mark and Mineholt North is but twenty leagues hence. Take a remount as well as a packhorse, for should the need arise, I would have ye unhampered by weary or lame steeds."

Tip glanced at his pony and then at a nearby steed and sighed. "I would ride my pony, Coron."

"Thou shalt do so, Tipperton. Yet shouldst thou and Dara Vail need flee in haste, thou must abandon it for a swifter mount."

Tip frowned but nodded in agreement.

"Shall any ride as courier?" asked Vail, glancing at Eilor, then back at Ruar. " 'Tween us and thee?"

"When we are nigh enough to the mineholt—say, ten leagues or so—I am of mind to send Dalon," said Eilor.

Sitting opposite in the circle, Phais looked at Loric, then cleared her throat.

"What wouldst thou say, Dara?" asked Ruar.

"Just this, Alor Ruar: Loric and I have been given the charge to see that the Waerlinga reach King Agron safely, and this mission thou hast given Sir Tipperton—"

"Hold on, now," objected Tipperton. "I asked to be a scout and a scout I'll be."

Phais held out a hand to stop his words. "I am not objecting to thee riding far point, Tipperton. Instead I am saying that thee should be accompanied by Alor Loric or me."

Tip glanced at Vail, and Phais said, "Dara Vail as well."

Tip looked at Beau. "What about—?"

"I say, I could be a scout, too," piped up Beau.

Ruar shook his head. "Nay, I'll not send ye both. Should ill befall one, the other must survive to carry on."

Beau frowned, and Phais said, "If thou wilt have me, Sir Beau, I will stay at thy side."

"And I shall ride with Sir Tipperton," said Loric.

"But that means you and Lady Phais will be separated," said Tip.

Loric shrugged and said, "Such is war."

The rain began that night, with lightning and the rumble of thunder in the mountains to the west, and the dawn came grey and dismal, with water yet falling down. And as Vail and Tip and Loric saddled their mounts and two remounts and laded a packhorse as well, Beau came splatting through the puddles, Phais at his side.

Tip started to reach for the thong and coin, but Beau shook his head. "I told you once and I'll tell you again, I'll not take the coin. It's up to you to remain safe and deliver it yourself. So you take care, bucco, and that's an order."

Tip grinned and shook his head. "Well then, my friend, perhaps you should take my lute and keep it safe in a wagon."

Again Beau shook his head. "Look, Lady Jaith gave you that and told you bards always carry their lutes and such wherever they go, and if having it with you will make you more cautious, well then, I'm all for it. Besides, it hardly takes up any space."

"Beau, you would have me creeping about and jumping at my own shadow, yet in this mission there may come a time when boldness is called for and not timidity."

"Well, bucco, if you're going to be bold, then do it timidly," said Beau, and looked up in surprise as Vail and Loric and Phais burst into laughter.

And finally all was ready, and Tip and Beau embraced; then Tipperton mounted his pony and followed Vail away, the buccan pulling the packhorse behind. Phais and Loric held one another tightly and kissed gentle and long; then Loric mounted and reined his steed about and, drawing a swift remount after, he followed Vail and Tipperton away into the blowing rain, while still in the mountains thunder rolled.

And Phais and Beau watched them go, and when they were gone into the blowing grey, the buccan reached up and took the Dara's hand and together they walked back along the train as the rain fell down and down.

On this day of unremitting rainfall, the wain drivers deliberately spread the train laterally wide, such that none followed directly in the tracks of another. Even so, in the rain-softened ground and in spite of the wide rims on the wheels, wains became mired, and extra of the massive horses were hitched to bogged-down wagons to haul them free. Still, progress was slow, and when evening came they had gone but six miles altogether, and the last wagons came to the encampment long after the first.

The rain continued to fall, and as Beau sat under a canvas awning strung between his hospital wagon and two poles— "Huah. And here all along I thought armies swift across the land. But we've been at it, what, eight days now? Yes, eight days since we started overland, and we've gone but some seventy miles—"

"A third of a league short of twenty-three," amended Phais.

"Right, then, sixty-eight miles. And so I ask you, are armies always this slow?"

"They are when they drag a great train behind," said Melor.

Phais nodded in agreement, then said, "Yet I have heard from Loric that the Vanadurin—"

"Who?" asked Beau.

"The Vanadurin, riders from the Steppes of Jord."

"Oh."

"Loric says that they can cover enormous distances in a remarkably short time."

"Like what?"

Phais looked down at the buccan. "On open plains, fifty miles a day for days on end, without remounts."

"Fifty—?"

"I have heard it, too," interjected Melor. "Something to do with varying the gait. It's called a long-ride, I believe."

"Aye," agreed Phais. "Loric says that they have superb

horses as well, and they keep them in fine trim—rich grass and choice grain, good water, and they ride them into splendid fitness and school them well in the ways of war."

"Fifty miles a day," said Beau, yet dwelling on the figure given by Phais. "And we go, what, ten?" He looked up at Melor and grinned. "We need a new army, eh what?"

Far out front, another twenty-five miles or so, Tip looked with dismay at another ravine, this one with a raging stream racing through. "Oh, my, they'll never get the wagons across at this rate."

Loric stood and glanced at Vail. "They are yet two or three days behind, given the softness of the soil."

"Mire, you mean," growled Tip. "A regular Muddy Flats."

"Muddy Flats?" asked Vail.

"A crossing along the Wilder River: a ford when the banks are dry, a quag when it rains."

Loric gestured southward. "The land behind is not quite as bad as you would have it, Tipperton. Even so, by the time the train arrives, this river will yet be raging, for it comes down from the Rimmens, where the bulk of the storm fell, and will take days to run dry again."

"On the morrow we will look for a crossing place, a ford," said Vail, "and wait for outriders to come and show them what we've found and let them bear word back to the train."

"But what if there's no crossing?" asked Tip. "What then?"

"Then we and the train will wait together for the water to subside and cross as we did at the last gulch."

Tipperton growled in frustration.

Loric scanned about. "Let us look for a place to set camp out of this weather."

And so they mounted up and rode toward the mountains, where perhaps they would find a cave, a woodland, an overhang.

The rain let up during the night and by next morning was reduced to a blowing mizzle. And when the wagon train set out, the wains well separated laterally, the cavalcade and vanguard rode even farther wide. As Bwen had barked at Ruar, "It's troublesome enough rolling across these drenched hills without having you churning it up ahead."

And once again the spare great horses were harnessed in six-horse teams to hale any mired wagons free. And ere they had gone half a mile the first of the wains became bogged.

Above the roar, Tip shouted, "Lor', I think I could jump my pony over this."

He looked across the gap of the narrow stone gorge, no more than twenty feet wide. Fifty feet below, a rage of water thundered through the long, narrow slot.

Loric turned to Vail and called, "Can we find timber, this is the place to cross."

"A bridge, you mean?" shouted Tip.

"Aye. The timbers will have to be sturdy."

Vail peered 'round. "There is none heavy enough easterly. Mayhap among the valleys of the Rimmens we will find a stand."

"Trees need water to grow tall," called Tipperton. "And if this stream flows each time it rains, then somewhere near the headwaters is where I'd look."

Loric grinned down at the Waerling and nodded. And the trio mounted and rode westerly up the land.

Nigh mid of day the mizzle stopped, and Beau looked up in gratitude and cast back his hood. And as the day wore on, the grey skies lightened and were finally riven with slashes of blue, and when the train came to a halt for the evening, puffy white clouds drifted overhead.

Even so, through the soggy land the train had covered only five miles in all.

As they ate, Phais said, " 'Tis Autumnday this day, when dark and light are in balance. A night we celebrate."

From across the fire, Melor looked up and nodded, but Beau at her side blanched. "Oh, my, but what a sinister thought."

Phais looked sideways at him in puzzlement. "Sinister?"

"Oh, Lady Phais, it's just that from now on, the dark will outweigh the light. I do hope it's not an omen of things to come."

Phais reached over and hugged the buccan to her. "Fear not,

wee one, for it marks but the change of seasons and the celebration of harvest."

Beau nodded, but the frown between his eyes slackened not.

That night the Baeron watched in wonder as a thousand Dylvana and one Lian stepped out the stately rite of Autumnday. And down among the gliding Elves, the pausing Elves, the turning, chanting Elves, there paced and paused and turned and glided one wee Warrow as well.

And some twenty miles farther on, in a stand of tall pine cupped in a mountain vale, three others stepped out the ritual 'neath the three-quarter waning moon.

"A bridge?"

"Aye, Lady Bwen," replied Ruar, "if within these wains there is the wherewithal to construct such."

"Oh, we have the axes and saws, right enough."

Ruar turned to Gara. "Thy horses are better suited to drag the timbers unto the narrows."

Gara nodded. "I will gather a company and we will follow Lady Vail back unto the stand." He turned to Bwen. "By the time you reach the gorge, the bridge should be in place."

Bwen scratched her head and glanced at the sun overhead, then patted the side of the mired wain at hand. "Make it sturdy, Chieftain. Make it sturdy."

Within six candlemarks, and following Vail, two hundred Baeron rode out, the company bearing axes and saws and awls and augers and ropes as well as other tools.

By that evening the train had moved only another six miles in spite of the heat of the sun.

And the next day they moved another seven miles altogether.

The following day they moved seven miles again, hindered primarily by stony, rugged terrain rather than by soggy land. And when evening came, they had reached the gorge.

A bridge awaited them there.

"Coo," breathed Beau, standing with Tipperton, surveying the span.

Great logs, nigh forty feet long and bound together with

ropes and crossbeams, bridged the gap. All was pinned with long, heavy pegs driven through augered holes. Atop the logs and pinned as well was rough-hewn planking thwartwise. Shallow ramps led up and onto the bridge on the near side and down and off opposite. Some fourteen feet wide was the bridge, with no side rails whatsoever.

And a torrent of water yet raced through the ravine below.

"Lor'," called Beau above the rush, "how did you do it so fast?"

Tip smiled. "With two hundred of these great huge Baeron plying axes and saws and other such, how could we not?"

"How did you get it across?"

"Easy, Beau: up at the headwaters it was shallow enough for some of the Baeron to go over on their tall horses, and they simply rode back down on the far side. Then with ropes and those same huge horses, they spanned the ravine one log at a time. After that it was easy. —Well, easy for the Baeron. If it'd been Warrows, we'd still be up there in the valley cutting wood."

The next morning turn in turn the wagons rolled onto the span and across, hooves clopping and wheels rumbling on the rough-hewn planks, the great timbers groaning and creaking under the weight of horse and wain and cargo and driver. One by one they passed across as two Warrows watched, Tip and Beau on the far side, having crossed over with the vanguard. The remainder of the cavalcade and the train escort came between wain crossings, while the rear guard and trailing scouts waited to come last of all.

The great placid horses of the Baeron seemed not at all disturbed by the narrow span above the long drop, but when Tipperton on his pony had crossed, he had ridden as close to the center of the bridge as he could, and while on the span had refused to look down.

And now as he and Beau stood side by side and watched, Beau gestured down into the depths below, where water yet ran, though less wild. "Well, here's another ravine we've managed to foil. Let's hope there's no more in the miles between here and our goal."

"I hope so, too, Beau. There's ten leagues left to go, thirty miles to Mineholt North. Vail and Loric and I should be within sight of the Dwarvenholt before this day is done, or by early next morn at the latest."

"Hmm," mused Beau. "At the rate the train has been moving, it'll be winter before we come."

"Winter?" blurted Tipperton.

Beau smiled. "Well, maybe not winter, but three or four days at least."

In that moment Loric and Vail came riding unto the Waerlings, the Lian and Dylvana trailing a packhorse and two remounts. "We must hie, Tipperton," said Loric.

Tip mounted his pony and took the tether of the packhorse. He turned to Beau and drew in a deep breath and blew it out. "So long, Beau, I'll see you in three or four days, eh?"

"You take care, bucco."

With a salute, Tip wheeled his steed, and together with Loric and Vail rode away north. In moments, it seemed, the trio passed the rolling wagons and then elements of the cavalcade and finally the vanguard farther on to disappear beyond the shoulder of a small tor.

Beau sighed and turned to mount his pony, only to find Phais waiting and watching as well.

"Hist," whispered Loric. "I hear movement below."

A quarter moon stood overhead, and by its light and that of the stars Tip looked down the eastern slope.

They had ridden some twenty-two miles through rugged land, and when night had fallen they made a fireless camp atop a hillock some eight miles short of the mineholt.

And now a faint ching of armor and clop of hooves could be heard in the long, twisting draw below.

"Muzzle the steeds," hissed Vail. And they scurried to the animals and whispered soothing murmurs, Tip's pony accepting strokes and soft sounds as if they were its due.

But of a sudden the packhorse jerked up its head and nickered.

The movement below juddered to a halt.

"Weapons," sissed Loric, drawing his sword, while both Tipperton and Vail took bow in hand and nocked arrows.

"Be ready to flee," whispered Vail.

Back toward the overlook they crept.

And Tip's heart leapt into his throat and he softly groaned, for below a full mounted column, armed and ready, twined beyond seeing through the draw and stood quietly, as if listening.

33

*I*n the fore is a banner," whispered Loric.

"What sigil does it bear?" breathed Tipperton.

"A circle—"

Tip's stomach clenched. *A ring of fire?*

"—a silver circle—"

Not fire!

"—on a field of blue."

Vail stepped forward in the moonlight. "Hál, men of Riamon!" she called. "We are of Darda Erynian, the Great Greenhall!"

A single arrow was loosed and hissed upslope wide of the mark—Vail stood fast—and someone nigh the head of the column barked a harsh command: *"Staande houden!"*

Weapons were lowered yet remained in hand.

"Show yourselves all!" demanded the voice.

"We are but three," called Vail.

Now Loric and Tipperton stepped forward.

"You have a child with you?"

"I am no child," cried Tipperton, raising his bow in one

hand overhead—and below like weapons were whipped up and aimed—"but a Warrow instead."

"*Ik zeggen staande houden!*" roared the voice, and all weapons below were lowered again, Tipperton hastily lowering his own.

"Did you say one of the *Volksklein*? Smallfolk?"

"I don't know whether I am one of those, but I *am* a Warrow."

There was a whispered word or two, and then: "I did not know that Waldans lived in the Blackwood."

Now Loric spoke. "They do not. Sir Tipperton is from the Wilderland beyond the Grimwall, and I am of late from the Hidden Stand, while Dara Vail is a Dylvana from Darda Erynian—that which thou dost name Blackwood."

"And your name?"

"He is Lord Loric, Lian Guardian," said Tipperton, then added, "And just who by the millstone are you?"

"He's a Waldan, all right," said someone below, "like those in Springwater."

Tip's heart clenched to hear that name, for Springwater had been Rynna's village.

"I am Lord Loden of Dael," replied the man.

"Well, my Lord Loden," said Dara Vail, " 'tis meet thou and thine army have chanced upon us this eve, or we upon ye, for mayhap we have common cause 'gainst a dark foe."

"If you oppose Modru and his ilk, then our cause is indeed shared. We welcome you three into our ranks, for though we are but a brigade, we go to harass a Horde, and all are gladly received who would take up arms against the foe."

"Rather than a trio, wouldst thou prefer fifteen hundred instead?"

"Fifteen hundred? Lady, do you jest?"

"Nay, Lord Loden, I do not."

There was a hurried conference below, and several figures dismounted and started up the incline, while the rest of the column moved on through the draw and away.

Tipperton could see that one of those walking upslope stood a head shorter than the others, yet had shoulders half again as broad. "That one's a Dwarf," he murmured unto himself.

"Aye, he is at that," said Loric.

* * *

"Good!" said Loden, the man in chain mail, his helm at his side, his chain coif cast back, revealing honey-gold hair cut short. His pale blue eyes glittered in the light of the waning moon. " 'Tis Fortune indeed that brought us together, for with the joining of our forces we can take the Spawn head-on."

"My Prince," said one of Loden's escorts, an elder man with a white beard.

Prince? His eyebrows raised, Tipperton glanced from Loden to Loric, and the Elf merely shrugged.

"Yes, Tain," replied Loden, turning to the aide.

"My Prince, they are a full Horde—ten thousand Spawn—and even with the joining of our forces we will be but one hundred ten score."

"You forget the Châkka," growled the Dwarf, taking off his plain helm of black-iron and smoothing back stray strands of his dark brown hair from his dark eyes. "With the army of Elves and Baeron and Daelsmen attacking from this side, and the Châkka from the other, we'll trap them between and shatter them like rotten rock."

"And how would you coordinate such an attack, Lord Bekki?" asked Tain.

A guarded look came over Bekki's features and he clapped the helm back onto his head. "There is a way, never fear."

Into Tipperton's mind flashed the memory of the identical look on Raggi's face when Ralk had ordered him to guide the party to the Walkover, a Dwarven secret.

Tip turned to Loric and whispered, "Remember va Chuka."

Loric looked at the Waerling and smiled, then turned to Bekki. *"Bekki, en ke, det ta a Châkka na?"*

Bekki's eyes widened, and he replied, *"Det ta."*

Loric turned up a hand. *"A na ke ein, ti?"*

Bekki nodded, saying, *"Ti."*

"Kala!" exclaimed Loric, then turned to the others. "Indeed, when we strike, so will the Drimma."

"How do we kn—?" Tain started to ask . . .

. . . but Loden held up a hand to stop the oldster's query. "The word of a Dwarf, the word of a Guardian, 'tis enough."

"But—"

"Accept it, Tain."

Tain bowed his head. "As you will, my Prince."

Loden turned to Vail. "We must get word of our alliance to your Coron and to the Chieftain of the Baeron."

Vail glanced at Loric and then said, "I will ride back, for I am swiftest ahorse."

"What about Arylin?" asked Tip. "She should be coming soon."

"Not until late on the morrow," replied Vail. "I can be back there before then."

At a raised eyebrow from the Prince, Tip said, "Arylin is our go-between, that is, between us on far point and our army."

"Ah," said Loden, "a runner." Loden turned to a young man at his side. "Brandt, I would have you go with Dara Vail as my emissary."

"But, brother, I would be at your side," protested the youth. Even as he said it, he looked about, his eye passing over Tain and lighting on Bekki. "Let Bekki go instead, and then he can explain how he'll arrange it so that we crack them like rotten stone. We've plenty of horses he can use."

Bekki blenched and threw out his hands. "Nay, Prince Brandt, I'll not ride a horse."

Tip looked at Bekki in puzzlement. *Here is another Dwarven warrior who will not ride a horse. Surely they are not afrai—*

"Brandt, I have spoken," snapped Loden. "You will go in my stead, for you know our strengths and the way to our hidden camp. Too, these wains they bring, you can guide them the easiest course to a rendezvous with us."

At dawn, Vail and Brandt set out southward, trailing two horses apiece. Standing atop the hill in a brisk autumn wind, Tip watched them go, and when they reached the bottom of the hill and rounded the shoulder of another, Tip turned to Loric. "What now?"

Loric raised an eyebrow at Loden, and the Prince said, "Now, Waldan, we go to our own hidden stand."

Drawing the packhorse behind, Tipperton and Loric rode after Loden and Tain and Bekki down the north slope of the hill and into the draw, and together they followed the shallow

gully as it wended northwesterly and into the reaches of the
Rimmen Mountains.

As they rode, Bekki fell back alongside Loric. "You speak
Châkur." His words were a statement and not a question.

"Aye," replied Loric. "The result of a shipwreck long past,
where the only other survivor was a Dwarf named Kelek. He
taught me Châkur; I taught him Sylva."

"He must have trusted you well."

"*Ti.* Ere the wreck we had traveled together for a number of
years, and often we fought back to back. He saved my life
many a time."

Bekki looked at Loric intently, as if to gauge something
deep within. "*Og at da haun ve vam efil dat?*"

Loric laughed. "We saved each other so many times we lost
count."

"How did you get off the island?" asked Tipperton.

"Ha, now there's a tale:

"The island though moderately large was limited, with
little wood, and we spent most of our time foraging in the sea
for food: spearing in tidal pools or netting in surf that which
we would eat—nets which I made from rock-beaten fiber of a
thorny island weed. Birds, too, we netted, and on the high
rocky cliffs we raided their nests. Kelek was a splendid
climber, and did most of the fetching of eggs. And there was a
side-walking blue crab we favored, yet it was a treat most rare.

"One day in the deepest of the pools we came across a
trapped shark, and it provided us with meat for many a meal,
though shark jerky is not the best of food.

"Yet it was the skin which we prized the most, for if we
could fetch several more like it, we could use the hide to make
a boat, could we find something with which to make the
frame.

"And luck was with us, for no sooner did we see our need
than within a moon or two, we found beached on one end of the
island the remains of what the Fjordlanders call a 'nâhvalr.' "

"A what?" asked Tipperton.

"A nâhvalr: 'tis a kind of whale, with a spotted pelt and
each male has long, spiral-twisted tusk jutting out from the
left side of its head. They live in the icy brine of the far north.
What this one was doing in the waters of the Bright Sea, I

cannot say, yet there it was, what remained of it, that is, rolling in the surf."

"Oh," said Tip. "—Was this one a male?"

"Aye, for its tusk jutted out like that of a horned horse, only longer, much longer."

Tipperton's eyes widened. "Horned hor—?"

"Hush, Waeran," growled Bekki as the wind swirled 'round. "Let him finish."

Tipperton cocked an eye at Bekki, but held his tongue.

"As to what had slain this nâhvalr, I cannot say, for the evidence was gone, there being little left but ivory bones and shreds of rotted meat. —The fish and the crabs had done much of their work, though there was yet some to do.

" 'There is our boat,' I said to Kelek, and down to the skeleton we ran. The stench was quite noisome, yet gulping our breaths we dragged it well up out of the water and into the grasses above. I couldn't have done so by myself, but Kelek was strong beyond his stature.

"For the next several days we dined on crab meat, for they couldn't resist the redolent reek on the air . . . and neither could the birds. And we let them finish the task of stripping the remains to the bone.

"It took another year altogether to lure enough sharks one by one into the deep tidal pool and slay them for their skins, though the meat was not wasted.

"Finally, with nâhvalr bones for our frame, bound together with thongs of sharkhide, and with sewn-together shark skins stretched over all and lashed onto the frame, and with a caulk made of bird guano and fish oil and fiber, we were at last ready to set sail, rainwater and jerky and a few live crabs and an egg or two as our supplies.

"No sooner had we shoved off than the craft began to leak badly, but bailing with frond cups and rowing with weed-woven oars, and with Kelek cursing at the top of his lungs in Châkur, we paddled our sinking, shark-skinned, whale-boned boat below the bird cliffs and 'round the headland only to find Aravan's great ship, the swift *Eroean*, anchored in the small inlet on the southern end of the isle."

Loric burst into gales of laughter, Tipperton joining in. Bekki looked at them for some moments, and then burst into laughter as well. Riding in the lead, Prince Loden looked over his shoulder, and Tain at his side put his fingers to his lips in a shushing motion and snapped, "Do you want to bring the Spawn down on us? They can hear you all the way to Mineholt North."

This only caused Bekki to laugh all the harder, Loric and Tipperton as well.

It was some time ere they got control of themselves, and even then they broke out into suppressed chortles.

"So the boat did you absolutely no good, eh?" asked Tip after a while.

"Oh, no, to the contrary, Tipperton, it did us a wealth of good: not only did it keep us busy for a year or so, it also proved to be quite profitable, for when Aravan hauled us aboard, 'Nâhvalr ivory,' he said upon seeing the necklace Kelek had made of the teeth. 'Have you the tusk as well?' And when we showed it to him, he marveled at its length and perfection, and told us the horn and the remainder of the ivory would bring a small fortune in the city of Janjong, there on the Jinga Sea, his next port of call, it seems.

"And so, rather than rowing across the Bright Sea in a leaky, sinking boat, we sailed with Aravan and his forty men and forty Dwarves, the crew of the *Eroean.*

"In Janjong, Kelek signed on with Aravan as a member of the Drimmen warband, but I went my separate way. In the succeeding seasons he rose to be second in command, I believe."

"Did you ever see him again?"

Loric sighed. "Nay. He remained with Aravan and sailed on the *Eroean*'s last voyage. It was in the time of the destruction of Rwn, and Kelek acquitted himself most honorably in the final battle, though he did not survive to reach his beloved Red Hills again. There at the place of his death, they set a great pyre burning, and he and his other fallen comrades were sung up to the sky."

They rode onward in silence, the laughter of moments before lost on the swirling wind.

Gradually the land turned to stone, and crags jutted up all 'round. And they came to an opening between two bluffs, and here Loden signed for all to stop and he whistled as would a meadow lark; there came a call in return, and Loden spurred forward, the others following, and they rode through a short canyon to emerge on a wide slope. Up the slope Loden led them, and they came to a broad plateau ringed 'round by mountains, where they found the seven hundred armed and armored Daelsmen ensconced in a fireless camp.

Near midmorn, as he fared in the vanguard, Beau saw three riders approaching from the north. And as they drew nigh, he could see that one was Vail, one was Arylin, and the other someone unknown.

With his heart thudding, "Oh, my," he said to Melor at hand, "Tip's not with her and neither is Loric. What do you suppose has gone wrong?"

"Mayhap nought," said Melor.

"Mayhap everything," replied Beau, his knuckles white 'gainst the reins, and he turned to make certain his medical satchel was affixed to his rear cantle.

And Melor said, "Seek not to see through muddy waters, my friend, but wait until the bourne runs clear."

"What?"

"I merely advise that we not—"

"Oh, I see," said Beau. "As my Aunt Rose always said, 'a bridge is easiest trod when underfoot.' "

Melor smiled. "Aye."

Beau shaded his eyes with a hand and peered northward at the three oncoming riders. "Can't their horses go any faster?"

Again Melor smiled, but worry brooded deep within his gaze as well.

Vail swung out wide and 'round, the others following, until all paced alongside Ruar. "My Coron, may I present Lord Brandt, son of King Enrik of Riamon, and emissary of his brother, Lord Loden, Prince of Dael." Now she turned to the man. "Lord Brandt, I present Coron Ruar of Darda Erynian. Too, I present Lord Gara, Chieftain of the Baeron of the Great Greenhall."

Beau looked at the youth dressed in light chain, a sword at his side, his coppery hair cut short.

"We bring good news, my Coron," continued Vail. "Thirty-five score warriors of Dael wait to join us to free Mineholt North."

Beau's eyes widened. *Thirty-five score! Seven hundred men! Oh, my, that is good news indeed. And here I thought something gone wrong—Tip lying wounded or worse.*

"Kala!" declared Ruar, his face breaking into a smile. "And welcome, Lord Brandt, son of Enrik, the help you bring most welcome as well."

Loric and Tipperton spent the remainder of the morning telling what news they held, and of Tipperton's mission to King Agron, and Loden and Bekki traded their news in return:

The Foul Folk, it seemed, had come into the ring of the Rimmen Mountains through the wide breech at Bridgeton, there on the southeastern quadrant of the circular mountain range.

Loden glanced over at Tip and Loric. "Though they bypassed Bridgeton, 'tis apparent now by your account that some marched on to Rimmen Gape, where they razed Braeton, while others came to set siege to Mineholt North."

"What of the town of Dael, did they do no harm there?"

Loden shook his head. "They marched right past, as if it held no interest whatsoever."

Loric frowned. "Hmm. 'Tis not like Modru to leave such in his wake. Something foul is afoot, I ween. Mayhap he hopes to draw ye out of the town, and when it lies defenseless, then he will strike."

Again Loden shook his head. "My sire and other brothers yet command an army within that walled city. It is well protected."

"What of Trolls?"

"Flames await them should they come. Caltrops too."

Loric nodded. Oil fires was one defense against the behemoths. The spikes another.

"Say," said Tip, looking at his sheaves of hand-drawn maps, "if they came through at Bridgeton, that means they came into the ring from the east."

"Aye," said Loric. "They would not approach from the west, for there Darda Erynian lies, and they think it a bane."

"No, no, that's not what I was getting at, Loric. Instead it is this: if they came down from the Grimwall and in from the east, that means they swarmed through Aven."

Bekki turned up a hand. "And. . . ?"

Tip let out an exasperated breath. "Oh, Bekki, it's Dendor in Aven where I am bound, and if it's full of maggot-folk . . ."

Bekki leaned over and touched a finger to Tipperton's sketch. "They could have come from the Skarpal Mountains instead—east and south of the ring."

"Adon," growled Tipperton, "down from the north or up from the south, how are we to know?"

Tip looked across at Loric and Loden, and Elf and man both shrugged, but Bekki said, "Waldan, you will discover whether or not the Grg are in Aven when you finally go there to deliver the coin."

"But there's nothing that way except mountains," said Arylin.

"Not so, my Lady," replied Brandt. "Beyond that craggy uplift is a passage through, one the wagons can manage. And though we will swing back nigh a league, it will save half a day overall."

Arylin glanced at Vail and then Ruar, but it was Gara who said, "Lead on, Lord Brandt. The wagons will follow you." Gara turned to a Baeran at hand. "Durul, ride back to the train and tell Wagonleader Bwen we follow this man."

Durul shook his head and grinned. "Oh, but won't we learn new words from Bwen, words hot enough to blister a hide when she discovers we need curl back a league to reach this passage."

Nigh eventide, Bekki and Loden came to Tipperton and Loric, and Loden said, "I would have you accompany us to see the foe. Then you can both advise the Dylvana Coron and Chieftain of the Baeron whenever they come."

Tip set aside his lute. "When do we go?"

"Now," rasped Bekki, clapping his plain black-iron helm onto his head.

Tip reached for the lute bags. "I'll have my pony saddled in a trice."

"We go afoot, Waldan," said Loden.

Tip nodded as he cinched tight the velvet bag.

"We go armed and armored as well," added Bekki, hefting a war hammer, its poll face blunt, its peen a spike, and a thick blade in front for stabbing.

Moments later, they headed easterly up the slope of the flanking mountain.

It was twilight when the last of the wagons finally emerged from the long canyon, and Beau sighed in relief, for it had been nothing but a long trap should the Foul Folk have fallen upon them.

Yet both Ruar and Gara had sent scouts through, some up on the flanks above; Brandt had said they could ride atop the walls, though in places it would be somewhat perilous. But he assured all that he had hunted ahorse up there, and indeed it could be ridden . . . and so it was.

And now as the wagons trundled out and to a camp in the valley, where pickets warded all 'round, a crisp breeze sprang up and swirled Beau's cloak, and he shivered in the chill air.

It was nigh midnight with a quarter moon rising among scudding clouds, when Tipperton and Loric and Loden and Bekki came through a scattering of pines and to the top of the last rough ridge, while all 'round a cold wind twined.

"There," growled Bekki, pointing at the dale below. Yet his words were unneeded, for hundreds of fires burned in the lowland. "The Grg."

Tipperton could smell smoke from the campfires clinging to the curling air, and now and again when the breeze blew just right he could hear the beat of drums.

"A full Horde," gritted Loden, "in Riamon."

"Where is the mineholt?" asked Tipperton.

"Leftward, at the root of the vale," said Bekki, pointing again.

Tip's gaze followed Bekki's outstretched arm. Against the stone of the mountain he saw—"That dull gleam, what is it? The mineholt?"

"Aye," replied Bekki. "The shut gates cast back the light of their fires."

"Tell me, Bekki," said Tipperton, "just how did you come to be outside when all your kindred are shut within? I mean—"

"Hist!" shushed Loric, and he cocked his head this way and that in the twisting wind, drums now and then sounding. *"Down!"*

Along with the others, Tipperton dropped to the rugged ground where moonshadows lay. His heart in his throat, he listened intently, but heard nought but the wreathing air and the sound of his own pulsing blood. He turned to Loric and breathed, "What is it?"

"Rûpt," replied Loric, pointing down the ridge, "a patrol, and they come this way."

Tipperton looked rightward, and just topping a rise no more than thirty paces off and advancing toward them came trodding an armed squad of Spawn—a dozen altogether.

Down beside Tipperton, Bekki growled and hefted his war hammer, and Loric and Loden drew swords. With trembling fingers Tip fumbled for an arrow as the maggot-folk came tramping on.

34

*T*ipperton turned to his comrades and hissed, "Save me from behind," and then leapt to his feet and shouted "Yahhh!" and loosed an arrow at the oncoming Spawn. And even as the shaft sissed through the air to fell the Rûck in the lead, Tipperton, shrieking, dashed toward the startled maggot-folk and then veered in among the sparse pines.

Bekki, cursing, started to rise from the moonshadows, but Loden grabbed him by the arm and hissed, "No! The Waldan's plan is sound."

Yawling, the Rûpt darted after the fleeing Warrow, and then Loric and Loden and Bekki sprang in pursuit, Loden, with his longer legs, racing before the Dylvana and the Dwarf, though they flew right on his heels.

In the moonlight ahead, howling Rûcks and Hlôks dodged among the pine trees, chasing their small quarry, the buccan shrieking and drawing them after. And one of the maggot-folk hurled a short spear, the shaft flying at Tipperton's fleeing form to fall just short and stab into the ground.

And as the yawling Spaunen patrol hurtled past the embedded

spear, the Rutcha who had cast it slowed to snatch the shaft up, and Loden's blade ran him through from behind.

His scream was lost among the howls of pursuit, as Loric and then Bekki ran past, now at the tail of the yowling pack.

Loden wrenched his blade free and sprang after, to pass by Loric and a beheaded Drôkh, and then to overhaul running Bekki just as his war hammer crashed through a Wrg skull.

But the eight howling Spawn yet chasing the shrieking Warrow noticed naught at all. Even so they had nearly caught up to the wee buccan, short-legged as he was. And as victory seemed within their grasp, three more of the Rûpt were felled from behind, one of them shrieking in death.

And at this shrill cry from the rear, the next one in line looked over his shoulder and screamed in alarm, his squeal of terror lost in the howls of his four kith, yet intent upon catching the foe at hand.

And the Hlôk running in the lead yowled in victory as snatched the buccan by the collar and wrenched him up in the air, the kicking Warrow flailing away as the Hlôk turned to the others to display his catch, only to find that of the Spawn he alone was yet standing . . . and he faced an Elf and a man with blood-slathered swords and a Dwarf with a grume-clotted hammer.

And then Tipperton twisted and kicked him in the face, and the Hlôk dropped the Warrow and reeled back, a long-knife to tumble through the air and take him in the throat.

Panting and puffing— "Oh, my. Oh, my. Oh, my"— Tipperton looked up at Loric as the Elf retrieved his long-knife and wiped the blade clean. "I thought I was a goner when he snatched me up off the ground."

" 'Twas a foolish thing you did, Tipperton," said Loric.

"But clever," amended Loden.

"And honorable," growled Bekki, "even though you did run."

"It was the only thing I could think of," said Tipperton. And of a sudden he burst into tears.

Bekki looked down in consternation, but Loden said, " 'Tis relief, Lord Bekki."

Bekki frowned, then clenched a fist and grunted in agreement. "As sometimes sweats the steel of a sword in the forging."

Loden raised an eyebrow, but Loric, kneeling beside the buccan, looked up and nodded at Bekki and said, "Just so."

Loden looked back at the string of corpses sprawled along their route. "We must hide the evidence of this ambush, else the patrols will double."

"Ambush?" queried Bekki.

"Aye, a running ambush from the rear."

"Nay," growled Bekki. "It was a full frontal attack from behind."

In spite of his tears, Tipperton began to giggle.

Two days later at midday, with Brandt in the lead, the vanguard and cavalcade and wagons finally arrived at the Daelsmen's hidden stand.

At last Tipperton saw Beau come riding up the slope on his pony, and he set aside his lute and ran down to greet his friend. Beau leapt to the ground and the Warrows embraced, glad to see one another again.

"I say, Beau, follow me. I'll show you where to corral your steed. They've plenty of grain and water, these Daelsmen."

As they started up the hill and across the plateau, Beau asked, "What about food, Tip? I mean, I could stand a good hot meal."

" 'Fraid not, bucco. We're too close to the maggot-folk for fires, you see."

Beau groaned, then said, "Jerky and crue, I suppose."

Tip nodded, then his eyes lit up. "Oh, but they do have some early apples, it being nearly October and all."

"A bit green?"

"Some. I wouldn't recommend eating very many."

They came to an overhanging bluff, and in a simple rope pen holding the horses of the Daelsmen, Beau corralled his pony next to Tip's and one other.

As Tip unstrapped Beau's bedroll and medical bag from behind the saddle, he said, "I'm glad to see you, Beau. How was the trip? Anything exciting along the way?"

Beau sighed and shook his head. "The trip? Ploddingly slow. Excitement? Oh, we did see a bear, but that's it. Although it did seem a bit strange, the bear ambling along as it did on a course paralleling our own. The Baeron seemed to think it was special, though it was nought but a bear." He lifted the saddle up and away, the pony shaking side to side to be free of it. Beau rummaged through his saddlebags and retrieved his curry comb. "But how about you, bucco? Any excitement on your part?"

Tip fetched his own curry comb and started on the opposite side. "Not much," he replied, "a minor tangle with some Spawn. And, oh, we did see the Horde in their siege on the mineholt. In fact, there's to be a war council this afternoon, after the wagons and all get settled in. Bekki says he'll find me when it's ready to begin. We three, we'll go together."

"Bekki?"

"A Dwarf, Beau, and a fine one at that. That's his pony behind you." Of a sudden Tip stopped currying and looked at one of the nearby horses. Then he resumed combing knots and tangles from the pony's hair, there where the saddle and trappings had ridden. "You know, Beau, just like the Dwarves at Annory, Bekki won't ride a horse, either. What do you think it all means?"

Beau looked across at Tip and shrugged.

Ruar gazed 'round at the war council. "We are gathered to decide on how best to deal with the Horde setting siege on Mineholt North.

"We are one thousand Dylvana, five hundred Baeron, seven hundred Daelsmen, two Lian, two Waerlinga, and one Drimm: altogether, two thousand two hundred and five."

On the left of the circle, one of the Daelsmen laughed. It was Brandt.

Loden scowled at the youth. "You have something to say, Lord Brandt?"

"I am sorry, my brother, but I found it amusing. —Oh, not that we were two thousand two hundred, but rather we were two thousand two hundred . . . and *five*."

Loden started to speak, yet ere he could say aught, opposite across the circle Bekki growled, "Jeer not at the five, bratling, for two are Guardians, and their swords worth five hundred each; two are Waerans, one of which I have seen in battle, and I would not trade him for a full regiment of Daelsmen; and

lastly, bratling"—Bekki's hand dropped to his war hammer—
"one is me."

Brandt flushed red in the afternoon sun, in anger or embarrassment it could not be told, but then he held his empty
hands forth in surrender and, grinning, said, "I yield, Lord
Bekki, I yield."

Beau looked wide-eyed at Tip and whispered, "What did
Bekki mean, he's seen you in battle? And what's all this about
being worth a full regime—?"

Beau's words were cut short by a rumble from Gara, the
Chieftain among the Baeron and sitting across from Ruar. "We
are not here to bandy words at one another, but to plan the
defeat of the Horde."

"Just so," replied Ruar. He turned to Bekki. "I have num-
bered the forces without. Wouldst thou number the forces
within?"

Bekki nodded. "We Châkka in Mineholt North cannot
match your number, yet we can field nine hundred or so."

Ruar took in a breath and expelled it. "Then together we
number thirty-one hundred."

"Thirty-one hundred and five," breathed Beau.

At Gara's side, Bwen raised a hand and was acknowledged.
"Your count is short, Lord Ruar, for you omitted me and my
drivers—one hundred more Baeron altogether."

"I stand corrected," said Ruar. "Our total then is thirty-two
hundred."

Beau looked at Tip and mouthed, [and five].

"Yet the Horde numbers ten thousand," said white-bearded
Tain, shaking his head. "Long odds indeed."

Loden turned up a hand. "Then we need a plan to shorten
those odds."

"By Fyrra's fuzzy teats," swore Bwen, "how can we plan a
campaign without knowing the placement of the Horde? How
are they set before the gates of the Dwarvenholt? And the terrain: what is it like? Not all of us here have seen these things,
and the mere fact of telling us exactly what we face will suggest several courses of action. Then perhaps we can list our
choices and pick from among them the very best plan."

Ruar smiled at Bwen and said, "Exactly so, Wagonleader.
That is the very next step." Ruar then turned to Loric, the Lian

sitting with the Dwarf and the Warrows. "Guardian, I wouldst have thee render thy report to all."

Loric released Phais' hand and took up a long pointer stick and stood and stepped to circle center, where a patch of loamy soil lay bare. "This is the way of it:

"Mineholt North lies at the northwest root of a broad vale, just beyond the shoulder of yon mountain. The vale itself runs down to the southeast thus." With the pointer, Loric began drawing a truncated wedge in the loam. "Here at the head, where it fetches up against the mineholt, the vale is wide, a third of a league or so. The vale grows even broader as it runs down into low foothills and rolling plains south and east. The slopes to either side of the vale are quite steep nigh the mine-holt, yet they dwindle rapidly and within a league are entirely gone, and there the vale has ended. A road courses from the mineholt along the easterly side of the vale."

"It is the tradeway to Dael," rumbled Bekki. "Not used this past year."

"The fault lies not at our end," said Tain, "but at yours instead."

Bekki growled but did not reply.

Loric looked from one to the other, and when none said aught, he continued. "Here where the vale ends, the road turns due east for that city." His pointer scribed a line in the soil and then jogged sharply.

Bwen scowled at the broad markings in the loam. "That's all well and good, but where is the Horde?"

"Here," said Loric, and he drew a swatch across the dirt. "Here before the very door of the mineholt."

Beau raised a hand, but ere the buccan was recognized, Loric said, " 'Tis a full Horde: ten thousand Rûpt strong."

Beau groaned and lowered his hand.

"And their makeup?" asked Durul, the Baeran sitting on the other side of Gara from Bwen.

"Thousands of Rucha, mayhap a thousand Loka, a hundred or so Ghûlka on Hèlsteeds, and a handful of Trolls."

"Ogrus? They have Ogrus?"

"Aye, Durul, they have Trolls."

Durul shook his head. "Ogrus, Trolls, by any name they are a terrible foe."

"Do not discount the Rukha," said Loden, "for although one alone is craven, in great numbers they are formidable, and here there are many."

"Pah!" exclaimed Bekki. "The *Ükhs* are no threat."

Fuar cocked an eyebrow. "Do not belittle the Rucha, my friend. Else thou art like to find thyself among a multitude in battle and in dire straits."

Bekki glared yet held his tongue.

Bwen frowned at the markings in the dirt. "And where are their wagons? Surely they have supplies."

"Indeed," replied Loric. His pointer moved toward the center fore of the vale. "Their wagons are off the road and gathered here." He jabbed the stick to the earth, and then drew a circle in the center of the swath marking the location of the Horde. "They are well warded by all the Foul Folk. Ghûls on Hèlsteeds are never far, and this is where linger the Trolls. Too, nigh each wagon stand water barrels, no doubt set there to deal with any small blazes a foe might set with fire arrows ere they become critical."

"*Blæ!*" spat Eilor, the leader of the outriders at Ruar's side along with several other Dylvana. "Could we get to the wagons and fire them with burning oil, then we could starve the Horde out. Yet central to the Horde as they are, 'twill be uncommonly deadly, especially if the Ghûlka on Hèlsteeds and Trolls are at hand, to say nought of the Rucha and Loka in between, and whether or no we could fire them all or even enough to be meaningful is dubious at best."

"Aye," said Loric. "Still, by the same token, if their main task is to protect their supplies, then many will be somewhat nullified in any battle."

A murmur of agreement muttered 'round the circle. When it died, Ruar turned to Loric. "Is there aught else thou wouldst say, Alor Loric?"

"Just this, Coron: perhaps the Trolls we cannot defeat, but all else we can, given a clever enough plan. As to the Trolls, should we destroy the leaders, the Ghûlka, and after them, the Loka, then mayhap the Trolls will return unto their mountain haunts. Hence, I say we should avoid combat with them unless there is no other choice."

At Tipperton's side, Bekki nodded in agreement. And then the Dwarf said, "Fifty Châkka have been known to bring a stone-hided Troll down, and if necessary the Châkka of Mineholt North will divert them, but only if necessary."

"Oh, my," said Beau. "At fifty Dwarves an Ogru, five of them will require two hundred fifty Dwarves in all. And out of nine hundred Dwarven warriors that only leaves six hundred fifty to join in the main battle against the Rûcks and Hlôks and Ghûls on Hèlsteeds."

Bekki nodded. "Believe me, Waeran if not diverted, five Trolls will *be* the main battle, and the Ükhs, Hrôks, and Khôls on their Hèlsteeds nought but a distraction."

As Loric resumed his seat by Phais, "Well, then," said Gara, "if the Waldan is right, and only six hundred fifty Dwarves join in engaging the rest of the foe, then two thousand five hundred fifty stand against ten thousand. Their advantage is four to one."

Bekki growled, "But nine thousand of them are Ükhs."

Ruar looked at Bekki and shook his head, yet now it was he who held his tongue.

"Argh," growled Bwen, scowling at Elf and Daelsman and Warrow and Baeron and Dwarf. "Enough of this back-and-forthing about Ükhs and Rûcks and Rutcha and Rukha and Rucha, of Loks and Drôks and Hrôks and Hlôks and Lôkha, of Guuls and Ghola and Ghûls and Ghûlka and Khôls, of Hèlsteeds and Trolls and Ogrus. What we need to do is talk about how to take on the foe while holding our own losses few." She glared 'round the circle as if daring any to dispute her. When none did, she said, "Now then, is there any way to draw them into a trap? An ambush?"

Loden frowned and pursed his lips. "But for their small patrols, none else has strayed from before the mineholt door."

"Perhaps we could present them a tempting target as we did at the Rimmen Gape," said Bwen. "Only in this case it would be a wagon train bound for the mineholt on the road from Dael."

"I think they would not fall for that ruse," said Loden. "Given that the Horde marched past Dael on that very same road, it is not likely any innocent caravan would be foolish enough to blindly follow."

Gara reluctantly nodded. "Aye. At Braeton we duped them into believing we had had no warning the Rimmen Gape was held, whereas in this case they would know any train would have been warned of the Horde by those in Dael. Nay, the foe would not likely fall into such a trap."

Phais held up a hand and was recognized by Ruar. "Can we not divide our forces?" she asked. "Some of us could strike at the Rûpt and then flee, drawing many if not all into the foothills after, where the remainder of us would lie in ambush."

"What of the Dwarves?" asked Counsellor Tain, sitting at Loden's right hand. "Where would they be during all of this?" He turned toward Bekki and sneered, "Hiding in their hole?"

"*Yahh!*" cried Bekki, snatching up his war hammer and leaping to his feet, his face black with rage, and he started across the circle for Tain, the white-haired man quailing back.

And Daelsmen leapt to their feet and drew blades, Tain not among them. And Coron Ruar also sprang up, his own blade in hand. Yet, "Hold!" he called and cast aside his sword, and, unarmed, he stepped between Bekki and the men.

Bekki glared at the Dylvana blocking his way and gripped his war hammer with both hands, his knuckles white, and he started around. But Ruar stepped before him again, and spread his empty hands wide. "The foe is yon and not here within this council, my Drimmen friend." Now Ruar turned to the Daelsman and repeated, "Not here within this council."

The uncontrolled rage left Bekki's eyes, to be replaced by simmering anger, and he glanced down at the blanching man. "Faugh!" he growled, and spun on his heel to return to his place beside Tipperton and Beau.

And a whisper of steel sounded as the Daelsmen resheathed their swords.

And Tip released his pent breath and looked up at Bekki as the Dwarf sat back down, to note the jumping muscles in Bekki's jaw as he yet ground his teeth in ire.

Loden turned and glared at Tain, and the counsellor flinched. And Loden, his voice low and angry, said, "That we have a lingering trade dispute with the Dwarves is no cause for insults, Lord Tain. In this war we are allies, and the quarrel between us can wait till we are quit of Modru."

Tain lowered his eyes. "As you will, my Prince."

Ruar took up his sword and sheathed it. Then he too sat down, and he gazed 'round the circle, where an uncomfortable silence pressed down. Yet finally Phais raised her hand to speak.

"Ill-said remark aside, still Lord Tain has raised a point: how will the Drimma engage in this plan?"

Sitting on Loden's left, young Brandt said, "Bekki has promised the Dwarves will act in concert to any plan, yet he does not say how."

Bekki shook his head but did not speak, and a low murmur whispered among the Daelsmen.

Loric cleared his throat and turned to Bekki and said, *"Bekki, da unst tak dek au va na ke ein."*

Bekki looked at Loric. *"Nid pol kanar vo a Châkka."*

Loric now shook his head and gestured 'round the circle. *"Nad skou dek va ke ein, ut tak dek au det."*

Bekki sighed and nodded, then turned and glared at Brandt. "There is a secret way in, bratling, but I'll not show it to any Daelsman."

Again Brandt flushed red, yet he held his tongue.

"Ah, a secret path," said Durul among the Baeron. "Then if the Dwarves are to join in this ambush plan as proposed by Lady Phais, the Dwarven army could come out along this way."

Bekki pushed out his hands in negation, a stubborn jut to his jaw. "No, no. We Châkka will not allow a Horde to stand between us and our holt, for should aught go amiss and they somehow breach the doors and enter, then we will not be there to stop them, and all of our—"

Abruptly Bekki stopped speaking.

The Daelsmen looked at one another, puzzled, and Brandt sneered, "All of your *what*? All of your treasure would be exposed? All of your gold for them to loot? Your jewels to plunder? Your—?"

Bekki snatched up his war hammer and shouted, "Silence, bratling, else this time I will not stop!"

Now Brandt's hand fell to the hilt of his sword, but Loden grabbed his wrist and would not let him draw the blade.

And Loric called out, " 'Tis not treasure of that sort the Drimma would protect." He looked at Bekki and said in a quiet voice, " 'Tis *Châkia* and younglings instead."

"Châkia?" asked Beau.

"Female Drimma," said Phais.

Bekki's shoulders slumped and he nodded. "Aye. And we would not abandon them in the Châkkaholt."

With concern in her eyes, Phais said, "If we go forth with my plan, then we must do so without the aid of the Drimma."

"Then we would be nine hundred short," protested Tain, "shifting the odds even further against us."

A silence fell among those in the circle, and from the encampment they could hear in the distance someone singing.

Finally Coron Ruar sighed, then said, "Well then, what of another plan?"

Long the discussion lasted, as plan and counterplan were put forth, and often ire flared between Bekki and the Daelsmen, for they had been entangled in a bitter dispute ere Modru's war had come raging, and hostile words came easily unto their lips.

And always each plan turned on whether or no the Dwarven army could be brought to bear.

The sun set, lanterns were lit, and still the allies came to no resolution.

Finally:

"Kruk!" exclaimed Bekki. "I say we array ourselves on opposite sides of the horde and attack them head-on."

"We've gone over that a hundred times, Dwarf," said Tain, "and it seems the best way to lose all. They will simply shift their forces to meet each of us with overwhelming odds."

But then Tipperton's eyes flew wide and he blurted, "I say, Bekki, that's a splendid plan."

"Waldan, haven't you heard a single word we've said?" snarled Tain. "They outnumber us four to—"

Tip pushed forth a hand, palm out. "No, no. Listen to me. What Bekki said is right, but with a small change: can we hold their attention, we take them head-on from hindwards."

Bekki frowned. "Head-on from—?"

"Yes, yes, Bekki. You said it yourself when we defeated that squad of Spawn. And what you said applies here as well."

"What are you getting at, Waeran?"

"Just this, Bekki: a full frontal attack from the rear."

It was after mid of night when Tip and Beau finally unrolled their bedrolls and prepared to bed down.

"I say," said Beau, yawning, "what's all this about you and Bekki defeating a squad of Spawn? And what did he mean when he said he wouldn't trade you for a full regiment of Daelsmen?"

"Ah, Beau, it wasn't just me and Bekki, but Loden and Loric were there, too. And though I didn't know it before tonight, there's bad blood between the Daelsmen and Dwarves, and I suppose Bekki was just feeding off that ill will when he said a Warrow was worth a regiment of them."

Beau sat on his blanket and yawned again, then pulled off his boots and said, "Oh, I dunno about that. He seemed sincere to me."

Tip shucked his own boots as well and drew his blanket up to his chin. Now Tip yawned. "Perhaps so, Beau, perhaps so." Tip yawned again.

"Tell me about this fight with the Spawn squad," said Beau. "I mean, this noontime you merely said that it was a minor tangle, but now I find out it was more."

Beau waited, but Tip remained silent. "Well, bucco," said Beau, "if you don't want to—" Beau looked across to discover Tipperton fast asleep.

The council met again the next morning to make final the plans, and much yet needed deciding, but at last in early afternoon their war plan was finally set.

Ruar looked 'round the circle. "Is there aught else to do?"

"Just this," said Tain smugly, "and that is to choose an emissary to accompany Lord Bekki to his DelfLord and represent all of us."

"What?" exploded Bekki, glaring at Tain. "You must be a

fool to think I would take anyone, much less a Daelsman, through the secret way."

Tain smiled disdainfully. "But someone must go and represent Prince Loden, Coron Ruar, and Chieftain Gara."

"I need no representative," rumbled Gara.

"Nor I," said Ruar.

Again Tain smiled. "Then that leaves—"

Loden started to shake his head, but Bekki said, "I will take Tipperton Thistledown." Tipperton's mouth fell open as Bekki went on. "He is neither man, Baeron, nor Elf, and so can represent all the Lords and Ladies here."

Bwen guffawed and exclaimed, "Well done, Bekki. Well done."

"A Waldan?" protested Tain, turning to Loden. "My Prince, this is unreasonable—"

Loden threw up a hand to stop Tain's words. "Bekki is right, my Lord Counsellor. The Waldan is the best choice of all. It is his plan we follow, and he can explain it well. Too, he has no advantage to gain as would someone of Dael."

Loden looked 'round and received nods from Ruar, Gara, and Loric and Phais, and even a nod from Beau.

And so it was decided: Tipperton Thistledown would go with Bekki and speak for all Dylvana, Baeron, Daelsmen, Lian, and Warrows . . . as well as explain the plan.

As twilight settled over the plateau, Tip finished packing that which he would take with him.

"Well, Beau, it seems I'm ready. I'd feel a bit better though if you'd but take the coin."

Beau shook his head. "Look, bucco, you know how I feel about that. Besides, the coin is likely to be safer with you than with me. I mean, you'll be in a fortified mineholt, whereas I'll be out there in front."

"Yes, I know. And I'm worried about you."

"Well don't be. And I won't worry about you in return. All right?"

"All right," replied Tip, "though I won't take an oath on it."

Beau laughed and said, "Neither will I."

Tip strapped his quiver of arrows to his thigh and slung on

his pack and took up his bow. He hesitated a moment and looked at his small lute packed in velvet in a leather bag, then caught it up as well, saying, "After all, Jaith said this lute should go wherever goes this bard."

Beau grinned and helped him fix it to his back, and then they walked toward the place where the council had met.

As they strolled for the circle, Vail stopped Tipperton long enough to embrace him. "Take care, my small friend," she said, then turned away, her hands brushing her cheeks.

"I will, Lady Vail," replied Tip. "And you take care as well."

Sighing, Tip watched her stride away, then turned to Beau. "Let's go."

At the council circle they found waiting Bekki, Loric, Phais, Gara, Loden, and Ruar. Phais knelt and kissed Tip on the cheek and said, "In a twoday we ride, in a threeday we cast our lot 'gainst the foe. May Fortune turn Her smiling face upon us all. Till we meet again, keep safe, my small friend, for thou hast yet a mission to fulfill beyond."

"You keep safe as well, Lady Phais," replied the buccan.

Now Loric embraced the Waerling. "We shall see thee in the days after."

Tip nodded to Ruar and Loden and Gara, and then embraced Beau. "Take care, bucco."

"Keep well, Tip," replied Beau, returning the hug, "and remember, as Lady Phais has said, you've a coin to deliver."

Bekki cleared his throat, and Tip turned to the Dwarf. Bekki glanced at the sky. "It is time, Waeran."

Tip drew in a deep breath and then said, "All right. I'm ready."

They set off up the beringing slopes on a northeasterly tack, and just as they reached the crest of a low ridge, someone called out, "Good luck, Waldan! Good luck, Dwarf! May Fyrra amble at your side."

Tip turned to see Bwen waving, and beyond, Vail and Brandt and Durul and a host of others watching, even Counsellor Tain. And Tip held high his Elven bow, and those below held high clenched fists in response. And then Tipperton looked down to the council circle, where Beau stood waving. Tip waved back and then turned to follow Bekki over the ridge and down, the buccan wondering if a mere three days from now he would survive what was coming. Would he be alive to see any of these folks again, and if so, how many of them would yet live?

35

*B*eau waved as Tipperton held high his Elven bow and then waved back to him. Then Tip turned and disappeared beyond the ridge, and Beau wondered if he would ever see his friend alive again . . . or if he himself would live beyond the next three days.

Phais stepped to the Waerling. "Come, Beau, let us see if we can find aught worthwhile to eat." And together with Loric they set out toward the mess wagons, where perhaps some meal better than jerky and crue and plain water could be had . . . mayhap a green apple or two.

The following day Beau spent time with Melor, surveying the medicks in one of the hospital wains, making certain they knew all that was there. Too, they assessed those in Beau's bag and added a few for treating wounds in the field.

And when that was done, Beau walked along the base of the cliffs, and at every stream he searched out round pebbles to add to his slingstone supply, for even though they were not lead shot nor steel, still they would do in a pinch.

And he practiced slinging at targets, and in this he was not alone, for many an archer practiced at targets as well.

And Daelsmen and Baeron and Dylvana and Lian drilled with swords and long-knives and lances and spears, and maces and flails and morning stars and hammers.

And horses were groomed, tack checked, for it would not do to have a rein or cinch or other strap give way at a critical time.

And they bundled campfire wood, kindling and billets to take with them.

And in these two days scouts came and went, and the plateau was alive with activity . . . until in early afternoon of the second day, when at last it was time for the first wave to go.

And with no wagons among them, the Daelsmen set out.

After they were gone, Beau fidgeted and paced for eight candlemarks and it seemed as if the signal would never come. But finally a trumpet sounded, and Beau mounted his pony and along with the Dylvana he set out in the second wave.

And the Baeron stood and watched them go.

Down from the plateau they rode and out through the narrow pass, and in the lead of the cavalcade rode Ruar and Phais and Loric, all others coming after, with Beau and Melor far back among the ranks riding to war.

East they turned for Mineholt North, the gape of the valley lying but a mere two leagues away. Wending among rolling hills and crossing stretches of plains they rode, scouts to the fore and showing the way.

And Tipperton was not among these scouts, for 'twas other duties he filled.

Two miles they rode and then another, and 'round a mountainous flank, and in the distance ahead stood the wide mouth of the vale. And Beau's heart hammered to see its yawning gape.

Will it but chew us up and spit us out?

He did not know.

Within four candlemarks they had crossed the remaining league and turned northwestward into the gap. And from the slopes ahead there sounded a distant blat of a Rûptish horn, yet what it signified . . .

" 'Tis an alert from the Spaunen sentries," said Melor. "They have seen us."

"Oh, my," said Beau, but no more.

On they rode and on, up rising slopes and down, riding through swales and over crests across the valley floor.

And from the fore they could hear a growing noise, as of a thousand voices or more yawling wordlessly.

At last they topped the final rise, and they could see out before them a mile away ten thousand Rûpt jeering and japing at the mere seven hundred Daelsmen standing silent on the slopes below but a half mile away.

"Oh, my," said Beau, his heart pounding as he scanned the breadth and depth of the enemy lines. "There are so very many of them and we are so few."

Yet the jeers of the Foul Folk diminished somewhat as the Elves came down the rise, but when the Spawn saw again how few were the foe, their voices rose once more in taunt.

All was going according to plan.

The Dylvana rode down the hill to join the Daelsmen, and from within the Swarm a signal sounded, and the Horde stirred.

Oh, my, are they going to attack?

Yet it was a shifting of Foul Folk, as more took up positions to the fore of the Swarm.

Indeed, all *was* going according to plan.

Now the Elves dismounted to stand by the Daelsmen, and Beau dismounted as well. And he stood looking at the foe; they seemed without number. And toward the rear of the ranks of the Horde and towering above all stood the Ogrus, six altogether, spread out along the wagons.

And still the Rûcks and Hlôks howled in glee, for although the severely outnumbered Daelsmen had been joined by an array of hated Elves, still all the advantage was with the Horde, their count at least five to one.

And the Elves and Daelsmen yet stood silent, unmoving, as if waiting.

Beyond the Horde and set into the stone face of the mountain, Beau saw the iron of two great gates. There stood the shut doors into Mineholt North, and he wondered if Tip and Bekki were within.

Candlemarks passed and the day grew old as the sun ran after a slender crescent moon fleeing down the sky.

And yet once again the Rûptish sentry's horn sounded.

Within another four candlemarks, over the crest behind came riding the Baeron, huge men on huge horses. And the jeering and japing wavered at the sight of these formidable foe.

And with the Baeron trundled some thirty wagons, fully half of which were hospital wains, while the rest held food and water and weapons.

Within the Horde, Ghûls on Hèlsteeds rode together and dismounted, and from a tent and among them came a Ghûl afoot and he led what appeared to be a shambling man into the center of them all. And one of the Ghûls sounded a horn, and the Horde fell silent.

The Ghûls stood quietly, and moments later in their midst the man turned and surveyed the slopes where now stood seven hundred Daelsmen, a thousand Elves, and five hundred Baeron. And then the man turned back to the Ghûls, and it seemed as if they listened closely.

Now the man was led away from circle center, and again he shambled. A horn sounded, and as the Ghûls rode among the Swarm, Rûcks and Hlôks took up positions facing the foe standing silent on the slope before them. And no longer did they jape and jeer.

Twilight came, and within the ranks of the allies a clarion called, and the Daelsmen and Elves and Baeron broke into small groups and set wood for campfires to the ground.

Beau sighed contentedly when he saw the flames come to life. "Oh, good," he said to Melor, "at last we can have some hot tea."

And as darkness fell in the vale of the mineholt, the fires of the allies burned on the hillside, and a half mile away the fires of the foe burned as well, as the two armies faced one another and waited for the coming of dawn.

36

Beyond the crest and down a shallow slope went Tipperton, following Bekki as the eventide swept over the world, and glimmering stars began to emerge in the indigo sky above. Through whin and pine they trudged and then upslope again, the land becoming steeper the farther they trekked, neither Dwarf nor Warrow speaking, but saving their breath for the climb.

North Bekki turned, due north, up the steep face of a high-angled ridge barren of all but rock, and by the time they reached the top, Tip was panting heavily, Bekki a bit less so. As Tip came over the rise, Bekki pulled him behind a great rock and said, "Here we will pause awhile."

"But I can go on," puffed Tip. "I mean, Lady Phais often pressed us this hard and harder as she taught Beau and me the skills of climbing."

Bekki only grunted and stood in the darkness at the edge of the huge boulder and looked back the way they had come.

"What is it?" sissed Tip, clutching his bow and reaching for an arrow. "Are we being followed? By Rûcks and such?"

"Nay, Waeran, it is not the Grg I look for, but sly Daelsmen instead."

"Sly Daelsmen?"

"Aye. It would give them advantage to know where we are bound, to know of a secret way into Mineholt North."

"But surely Loden wouldn't send some—"

"Not Loden, Waeran, but grasp-handed Tain instead."

"Oh. —Are we going to be long?"

"A candlemark or so," said Bekki.

Tipperton shucked his pack and sat down. After a while Tip said, "What is it that Dwarves and the Daelsmen have lying between?"

Bekki growled. "They would charge us double tariffs: one to move our goods through their city, another to use their docks."

"Docks?"

"Aye. On the Ironwater."

"The river," said Tip, remembering his maps.

"Aye. By boat and barge, it is the swiftest way to reach the city of Rhondor or the wide Argon Sea beyond, for river legs never tire, but run all day and night."

"What's in Rhondor?"

"A good market. It is there we trade for much we need in our crafting, particularly in our forging: *siarka, foran, zarn*—"

"Whoa, Bekki, these are things beyond my ken. What is, oh, say, siarka?"

"The yellow rock: like chalk, it crumbles. We use it to make an etching liquid. In Rhondor it is plentiful, for it lies on the floor of Hèl's Crucible for the taking, as do many other ores, nearly pure."

"Ah," said Tip.

Now Bekki sat down, yet he kept an eye on their backtrail.

After a while, Tip said, "And this dispute between your people and the Daelsmen is over tariffs? So you can reach the docks?"

Bekki grunted but otherwise did not reply.

"Well, why don't you just not use their docks? Go south from the city and launch lower down."

Tip could hear Bekki's teeth grind. "King Enrik claims the

whole of all rivers in Riamon, and no matter where we would set in he would charge us the double fee."

"Oh?"

"Aye. And even though Prince Loden himself pled with his father to return to the old way—to charge but the single docking fee—King Enrik listened instead to Lord Tain."

"His advisor instead of his own son?"

"Aye, for Enrik is besotted with Lord Tain's youngest daughter, Lady Jolet, though she looks coldly upon him. It is Brandt she casts her smiles upon. But Brandt favors another, Lady Pietja, though she leads him on, for her eye follows Druker, second in line after Loden. —Kruk! Humankind! A pox on all their petty intrigues."

"Um, Bekki, how do you know this?"

"Because, Waldan, as the representative of my DelfLord, I was in King Enrik's court demanding the recision of this unwarranted tariff when the Horde marched past. I then asked the King to gather a great force of Daelsmen to help us slay all the Grg. He refused, saying that he would not lay Dael bare in these troubled times, and instead marshaled his army and set them to guarding the walls of the city instead of aiding allies.

"In the weeks after, Prince Loden pled with his father, saying that if the Daelsmen did not aid the Châkka and if as a result Mineholt North fell, then surely Dael would follow. Yet once again it was Tain's voice Enrik listened to.

"But then Loden declared that with or without his father's leave, he would gather a force and harass the Horde if nought else.

"After many a bitter argument, King Enrik suddenly changed his mind, and gave Loden leave to command a token brigade and harass the Horde. King Enrik sent Brandt as well. And he assigned Tain to go with his sons. Tain objected, saying that he could best serve his king by remaining in court, but Enrik commanded that Tain accompany Loden and give sound advice to him.

"Bah! The king merely wanted both Brandt and Tain out of the way—to have Lady Jolet to himself."

"Goodness, Bekki. Are you saying that King Enrik sent his sons and Lord Tain into peril just so he could have a tryst?"

Bekki turned his dark gaze toward Tipperton, then looked

back down the ridge and muttered, "Again I say, a pox on all humans, with their ungoverned appetites and petty intrigues!"

Tipperton sighed, and sat without speaking. After long moments more, Bekki said, "We can go now, for it seems Lord Loden prevented Counsellor Tain from sending agents skulking after."

Tipperton stood and shouldered his pack and lute. "Lead on, Bekki. Lead on."

Together they set out along the ridge, and wended their way among the ever increasing boulders and crags while, behind, a dark figure slipped through the shadows and after.

"We turn here," said Bekki, and he stepped into a rushing stream.

Tip's eyes widened, yet in the starlight he followed Bekki into the rill, the water clear, the bottom rocky.

Upstream they trod and up, with stone slopes rising left and right, the chill bourne cascading down ledges and steps from the high snows above. Finally, in the depths of night, Bekki turned aside and scrambled up a stone rise. As he came to the top he halted, and guardedly peered over the ridge.

" 'Ware, Waldan," he cautioned as Tipperton came alongside.

Carefully, Tip raised up just enough to look beyond the crest, and far down below in the wide vale burned the fires of the besieging Horde.

Bekki pointed leftward and up, where immediately at hand a ledge ran along the mountain face to disappear into a wide, dark crevice. "We must go a short way in the open. Take care, for I would not have any of the Grg spy us."

Moving slowly so as not to draw enemy eyes, along the ledge they sidled, Tipperton alternately puffing and holding his breath, for although he had practiced at climbing in Arden Vale, still he was unsettled by heights.

On the slope behind, a figure in shadows watched.

At last they entered the fissure, and in the blackness Tip hissed, "Wait, Bekki, I can't see a thing."

"Here," grunted Bekki, "take my hand." And he reached out and grasped the buccan's fingers.

Leading Tipperton, Bekki stepped along the passage, and after a hundred Warrow-paces or so, he stopped.

"Why are we—?"

Tip's words were interrupted by a soft rhythmic tapping on the stone.

Silence.

Again sounded the tapping, the rhythm changed.

"Kha tak?" came a whisper.

"Shok Châkka," murmured the response.

Stone on stone grated softly, and Bekki tugged Tipperton forward several strides.

Again stone whispered against stone.

There came a click of metal on metal, and of a sudden a phosphorescent blue-green glow lighted all, and Tip saw that he was in a carved chamber of stone, and a handful of armed and armored Dwarves stood glaring at him, the edges of their axes glinting wickedly.

"Lord Bekki," growled one in the fore, "to our secret entrance you bring a—"

"He is Sir Tipperton Thistledown," interrupted Bekki, "Waeran of the Wilderland, and emissary of the Lian, the Dylvana, the Baeron, and the Daelsmen, and I trust him with my life. Take heart, Kelk, for this Waeran brings an army to our aid."

A time later, a shadowed figure came over the ridge and past the pickets and down into the encampment, quietly making its way to where the Elves were bedded, in the midst of which slept Beau.

Removing his boots, Loric slipped under the blanket with Phais. Awakened, she turned and looked into his eyes.

"They are safely within the Drimmenholt, chier," he said. "I followed all the way."

She smiled and kissed him lingeringly, a kiss which soon burned with heat. And they made heady love as in the east the sky grew pale in the dawn.

37

An army?" growled Kelk, cocking an eye at Tipperton.

"Well, it's not exactly *my* army," said Tipperton, "though they did appoint me as their representative, did the Elves, the Baeron, and the men of Dael."

A mutter of approval rumbled among the Dwarves, and Kelk grunted, "Good. At last we will drive the Grg from our doorstone."

As Bekki caught up a brass and glass lantern, Tipperton glanced behind where stood the secret entry, yet he could see nought but a blank stone wall with no evidence whatsoever of a doorway in the rock. Tip's gaze swept on about the chamber. Through an archway immediately to the right stood a carved room, and among the shadows therein Tip caught a glimpse of cots and chests and a table and chairs.

The guards' quarters, I would say.

Straight ahead and beyond another archway a dark corridor clove into the stone of the mountain.

"Come," said Bekki, raising the hood on the lantern, and though no flame was kindled, a phosphorescent glow streamed forth. "We have a ways to go."

Kelk held up a staying hand and said, "Lord Bekki, tell your sire we would join in the fight."

His statement brought a chorus of *Ayes* from the others.

"I will," replied Bekki.

Kelk smiled and slapped the blade of his axe and then stepped aside, as did those arrayed behind, opening the way into the dark passage and the mountain beyond.

Through the archway strode Bekki, Tipperton on his heels, and from behind, the buccan could hear the voices of the warders speaking to one another in Châkur as they moved back into their quarters. What they said he knew not, though he supposed they talked of the coming battle.

Down a gentle slope Bekki and Tipperton went, fissures and splits branching left and right as well as an occasional corridor. Down carved stone steps, and 'round sharp turns they tramped, and in one place they followed alongside a dark chasm, a cold drift of air upwelling and smelling of dampness and stone. Through carved chambers they trod, and archways stood darkly here and there, passages bored away to unknown destinations deep within the mountain stone. They strode down a long tunnel, and somewhere water fell adrip, its tinking echoes sounding within the shadowed hall. And Tip knew if something happened to Bekki, he would be hopelessly lost, and his chances of ever finding his way out would be completely in the hands of Dame Fortune and not within his own.

"Lor', Bekki, my head is spinning with all these twists and turns and I can hardly tell up from down. Do you truly know where we're going, or are you lost and confused as well?"

Bekki laughed and stepped onto a low bridge made of square-cut blocks of stone, and Tip could see they were fitted together with no mortar between. Below raced a wide stream of water.

"We Châkka cannot lose our steps, Waeran," said Bekki.

"Cannot lose your— What do you mean by that?"

"It is a gift from Elwydd. When She made the first Châk, She—"

"Elwydd made the Châkka? The Dwarves?"

Bekki paused at the cap of the bridge, his face eerie in the blue-green light of the lantern. Water tumbled beneath.

"Aye, we do believe it so."

"Oh. Hmm. You know, Bekki, as to who made the War-rows, I haven't the faintest idea. Perhaps Elwydd . . . or Adon . . . or someone short."

Bekki laughed, and they took up the trek again.

"You were saying, Bekki, about not losing your feet . . ."

"It is a gift all Châkka have: wherever we travel on or within the land, be it on foot or by pony or even in a drawn cart or wagon, we can ever after retrace that path exactly."

"Exactly?"

"Aye, exactly. Be it in driving rain or blinding snow or even total darkness, whether or not we can see, still we can step out the path again, without error. Elwydd wove this gift into the very fabric of Châkkacyth, for She knew without it, we could not dwell within the living stone."

Tipperton looked at the crevices and corridors splitting away from the path they followed and driving into blackness. "Well I for one am certainly glad of it, as twisted about as I am."

They trudged up a short flight of steps and through a long delved corridor, then down a stony slope through a natural cavern.

"It does not work on water," said Bekki, "nor when Châkka are fevered."

"The gift, you mean?"

"Aye. In boats, on barges, on rafts, or racked with ague, we are just as bewildered as other kind." Bekki snorted. "I deem we also would be confused were we somehow conveyed through the air."

Now they came to a high ledge along a wall of a huge cavern, and the light of the lantern faded away in the distance ere reaching any other walls or a floor unseen far below. To the left along the ledge Tip saw a long flight of stairs set in a carved hollow cut into the stone of the wall at hand, the narrow steps plunging into darkness and down.

There was no rail.

"This way," grunted Bekki, and he crossed the ledge and started down, his footsteps echoing back from the distant dark.

Tip followed, his heart racing. And he clung closely to the

carved wall hollow on the left, away from the precipitous black fall to the right, a bare three or four feet away.

And his breath came in short, sharp puffs.

Count the steps, bucco, it'll take your mind off it.

His count had passed two hundred when he thought he could hear a far-off singing drifting along unseen faces of stone.

His count had not quite reached three hundred when he became certain of the singing: a soaring voice in solo.

Finally they reached a level floor below.

"Three hundred ninety-seven," said Tip, his voice a bit quavery.

Bekki looked at him in the blue-green light. Tip gestured at the steps and repeated, "Three hundred ninety-seven."

Bekki shook his head. "Four hundred twelve."

Tip shrugged. "I was a bit of the way down before I began counting."

They started across the floor, and still the singing echoed.

"I say, Bekki, who is that singing?"

Bekki tramped onward and did not answer.

Striding along at Bekki's side, Tip frowned up at the Dwarf but did not repeat the question.

Now several voices joined that of the singer, a chorus, and there was not a deep voice among them. Somewhat like Elven Darai they sounded, or perhaps as would Warrow dammen.

Are these the voices of female Dwarves? What did Phais and Loric call them? Châkia? Yes, Châkian.

They came to an archway where stood a pair of guards, with others asleep in a nearby chamber, and after but a brief exchange and a salute, Bekki and Tipperton went onward, the warders' surprised gazes following the Waeran. What Bekki had said to the guards and they to him, Tip did not know, for unlike the exchange at the secret door, this time the Dwarves spoke entirely in Châkur.

"Why do you have guards here deep in the holt?" asked Tip.

"We are coming to the core, Waeran, and the holt is on war footing."

Tip cocked an eye at the answer, yet asked no more.

Down long hallways they strode, turning left and right, Bekki not hesitating in choosing their path.

Now they passed by arched openings into corridors where

portcullises barred passage, the black-iron rods socketed deeply into holes.

The way blocked? Is this just because of war?

At one of these barricaded archways, Tip saw the glimmer
of phosphorescence gleaming 'round a distant turn, and it was
from this corridor the singing came. Twenty or more voices he
gauged, Châkia voices, Châkia singing together.

As he crossed the opening, Bekki's footsteps lagged, yet he
did move onward. Tip, too, trailed, listening to the song, yet
he could not tell if it was a choral of joy or sadness, though a
thing of splendor it was.

Now Bekki's steps hastened, and Tip trotted to catch up.

They passed among Dwarves moving through the hallways
on errands of their own, warriors in black-iron chain mail, axes
and hammers at hand. And most, if not all, saluted Bekki, and
curious gazes followed the pair.

Finally, through open iron doors and into a large chamber
Bekki went, where he stopped at the edge of a polished granite
floor. At the far end Tip saw a dais, three steps up to a black
granite throne, ebon stone padded in red velvet. And on the
throne sat a Dwarven warrior, dark beard, dark armor, dark
helm. An axe leaned against the arm of the stone chair.

This was the DelfLord, no doubt, yet it was not he who captured Tip's eye. 'Twas instead a willowy figure sitting on the
steps below, a figure all swathed in veils, a figure in deep converse with the DelfLord.

"I bring an emissary," called Bekki, and at these words the
DelfLord looked up, and the figure on the steps turned toward
them and then stood in a gossamer swirl of feathery lace and
silk. She was no more than four feet tall.

*Is this a Châkia? But she is so slender, and Dwarves so very
broad.*

As Bekki and Tipperton waited, the figure moved down and
away, across the polished floor and toward a recessed alcove,
and Tipperton thought he saw delicate bare feet under floating
layers of diaphanous concealment.

As soon as the figure had vanished, the DelfLord stood and
motioned for Bekki and Tipperton to approach, and he moved
down the steps toward them.

"Det ta kala da ta ein, Bekki, ea chek," said the DelfLord as he quickly closed the distance and embraced Bekki fiercely.

"And I am glad to be back, Father," replied Bekki in the Common tongue.

Tipperton's jewellike eyes widened. *Bekki is the DelfLord's son!*

Stepping back, the dark-eyed DelfLord glanced down at Tipperton, and then looked to Bekki and in Common said, "We thought you trapped in Dael."

"Nay, Father," growled Bekki. "The Horde passed it by, marching directly here. I remained behind to muster the men of Dael, yet King Enrik sent only a token force."

Again the DelfLord looked down at Tipperton. "This is the force? One Waeran?"

Bekki exploded in laughter, joined by the DelfLord, and Tipperton's own giggles were lost under their roars.

Finally Bekki managed to master himself and, smiling, said, "DelfLord Borl, may I present Sir Tipperton Thistledown of the Wilderland, emissary of Coron Ruar of the Dylvana, Chieftain Gara of the Baeron, and Prince Loden of the Daelsmen. Sir Tipperton brings to our aid an army of two thousand two hundred."

"And five," added Tipperton. "Two thousand two hundred and five."

Borl looked to Bekki, and then back to Tipperton, the DelfLord's puzzlement clear. "Five? And five?"

"Yes, sire," replied Tip. "If you let me count Bekki, that is."

Again Bekki broke into laughter, and at his father's wildered look, he said, "Two Lian, two Waerans, and me."

Shaking his head, DelfLord Borl threw an arm about Bekki's shoulders and said, "Come, you must tell me of these five as well as the two thousand two hundred. Are they here to aid us, and do they propose a way to rid us of the Grg?"

As Borl led his son and Tipperton to a side table and called for bread and tea, Bekki said, "Aye, Father, on both counts. If you will permit, we will summon the captains to the war room, where Sir Tipperton will lay out his plan."

Perhaps it was yet night or dawn or even day when the discussions with DelfLord Borl and his captains ended; here in the undermountain realm Tip could not tell. Yet whatever the case, day or night, he was bone weary when at last he was shown to his bed.

As he slept he dreamt he awakened for but a moment to see a slender figure in swirling veils standing at the foot of his cot and looking down upon him, yet he dreamt he immediately fell back asleep . . . or at least he thought he was dreaming, though as weary as he was, who could say?

He had no memory of the dream when Bekki came and awakened him.

"Time to break fast, Tipperton," said Bekki, using the Warrow's given name in the familiar for the first time. "Hot-cakes and maple syrup and rashers. Then we will take a long soak in a hot tub."

Tip bolted up and began scrambling into breeks and jerkin. "Oh, my, I don't know which sounds better: a hot meal or a hot bath."

After break of fast and the tub, a messenger came to Bekki and Tipperton and informed them DelfLord Borl had called another meeting of his captains. Tipperton and Bekki hastened to the war chamber, to find the others assembled 'round a large stone table on which was spread a large map showing the wide dale before the gates of the Dwarvenholt. Figures and tokens were spread over the map, each to represent an element of the Horde or others. Borl looked up from the map when the two came in, and as they took their places, he said, "Last night I called upon all to consider the plan and auger out any weaknesses, and to devise tactics to overcome them. What say ye?"

Across the table a yellow-bearded Dwarf, Captain Dalk, cleared his throat. At Borl's gesture, Dalk reached for one of the figures representing a Dwarven company and began: "DelfLord, there is this . . ."

Throughout the remainder of the day they moved figures over the face of the map, trying to account for every contingency. Yet when the meeting came to an end at last, the DelfLord's gaze swept across each and every one assembled and he said, "We have tried to foreglimpse every turn of events, yet there is only one adage in combat and war: the moment the battle begins is the moment all goes wrong."

Tipperton left this meeting much less certain of the merit
of his plan.

With his lute of light and dark wood and of silver strings
and frets, Tip looked for an empty chamber in which to practice. And given his unfamiliarity with the caverns, and given
he did not wish to become hopelessly lost, he finally wandered
into the throne room, to find it empty.

Sitting on the steps of the dais, Tip began chording the
Elven instrument, and after a while, fingering individual
strings, he attempted to duplicate the melody he had heard last
night when he and Bekki had trudged through the confus-
ing ways of the mineholt, a song he thought of as "Châkia
Singing."

He did not know how it began, yet he did know a deal of the
middle, and hesitantly at first, but with growing confidence,
silver notes cascaded through the air, yet he came to the place
where once again he no longer knew the melody. Faltering, he
tried to find a way to finish the song and he tried to find a way
to begin it, yet all he essayed sounded wrong to his ear, and,
sighing, he stopped.

Yet as he did so, from somewhere within there came a
sweet voice in song.

Startled, Tip looked about, seeing no one. And so he listened, enchanted.

The singing stopped.

Tip waited.

The singing began again, repeating the aria, yet this time it
slid into the song he had been playing . . . but stopped again.

Now Tip took up his lute, and he played the aria as best he
could, then paused.

The voice sang a passage and paused; Tip repeated it.

The voice sang again, another passage.

Tip again repeated; it was the song's beginning.

Now singer and player alternated, Tip following the voice
through the aria and chorus, and all the while he looked for a
place the singer might be, yet he could not discover where.

At last Tip realized that he had come to the end, and then
he began at the beginning and played the song all the way
through, the sweet secret voice singing in harmony to his

silver-stringed tune. And when all was done and the echoes had died, he was met by absolute silence.

Tip stood and walked on polished granite all about the great throne room, looking behind every pillar and within each alcove to see where the Châkia had been, yet he found nought but mute stone.

Finally he called out, "Thank you for the gift."

There was no answer.

Sighing, Tipperton took up his lute and trudged through the doorway and into the passage beyond, leaving an empty chamber behind.

That night he slept without waking, and if someone in veils of gossamer stood at the foot of his bed, it was a thing he did not know.

All the next day the Dwarvenholt was alive with preparation, and Tipperton made ready as well, for he was determined to join the Dwarves in this plan of his.

Sometime in the day Bekki and Borl came to fetch Tip, saying, "The Grg signal has sounded." And they led Tipperton up a long stair that twisted and turned within the mountain. Finally they came to a chamber furnished with a table and four chairs, and on the table was pen and ink and sheets of vellum. Bekki turned to Tipperton and said, "Take care and let no gleam escape."

Both Bekki and Borl divested themselves of their helms, and they laid aside their chain-link armor, though it was made of black-iron and not likely to glimmer. Tipperton, though, had no armor, no helm, and so he simply stood and watched, wondering what was afoot. Bekki and Borl inspected one another for aught that would glitter and inspected Tipperton as well, and then they turned to a blank wall and Bekki clamped down the hood of the lantern, shutting its light away. In the darkness Borl slowly and quietly slid inward and aside small stone panels.

Daylight streamed inward and Borl beckoned Tipperton to look.

But the Warrow was too short, and so Bekki fetched one of the chairs and Tipperton stood thereon . . .

... and looked out over the vale before the mineholt door ...

... where stood the Horde ...

... Rûcks and Hlôks and Ghûls on Hèlsteeds ...

... and monstrous great Ogrus mid all.

"Oh, my," said Tipperton, his voice hushed as his gaze swept over the vast array, "but they look so much more formidable standing this close than when viewed from the heights above. —There are so very many of them."

Borl grunted. "It will not be easy, Sir Tipperton."

"Tip," said Tip.

Borl turned. "Eh?"

"Just plain Tip will do, DelfLord, that or Tipperton."

Borl grunted and turned back to the viewing port.

"Here they come," he muttered.

Tip looked out.

Over the crest of the near-distant hill came riding the Daelsmen, their numbers paltry when compared to those of the Horde.

At first the Horde drew into a defensive position, but when it became clear that there were but seven hundred of the Daelsmen, hoots and jeers drifted up from the Foul Folk, and Rûcks japed about.

The Daelsmen arrayed themselves, and segments of the Horde made ready to do battle, yet Ghûls rode among them, the corpse-foe hissing orders and the segments stood fast.

Time passed and time more, and Bekki and Borl sketched out the dispositions of both men and Spawn.

Now Tip heard the blare of a Rûptish horn, blatting much like the one Vail had sounded above Braeton at the Rimmen Gape.

And at last over the hill rode a thousand Dylvana. Down they came and down, down to stand alongside the men of Dael. And among them Tip saw a wee figure astride a pony.

"Oh, Beau," he breathed. "What have I done to you?"

Once again the Horde shifted about, and the japing and jeering diminished, yet when there seemed to be but a thousand of the Elves, the taunting began again.

*   *   *

The day waned as four more candlemarks passed, and once again the Rûptish horn blatted, and finally over the hill came riding big men on big horses as five hundred Baeron came, and with them rolled thirty great wagons.

These huge warriors came down the hill on their huge horses and arrayed themselves alongside the Elves and men.

The jeering stopped and again the Horde shifted about, and this time the Ghûls rode together in the center. And from a tent they drew out a shambling man, his head angled askew, and he stumbled along as if witless and would have fallen but for the strong support of the Ghûl at his side.

Borl sucked in breath between his teeth.

"What is it?" hissed Tip. "Who is this man?"

"Modru's eyes," gritted Bekki.

"Modru's voice," growled Borl.

Frowning, Tip looked once again at the man, just as one of the corpse-foe stepped forward, and the buccan could see the Ghûl's lips move. What he might have said Tipperton could not tell, for not only were they entirely too far away to hear, they probably spoke in a Foul Folk tongue, none of which would Tip know.

The man straightened, his head snapping up, and Ghûls shifted back as if afraid, while the man with his fists on his hips arrogantly turned about. Now the man looked at the force standing on the hillside before the Horde. And then he turned to the Ghûls gathered about and seemed to speak, and they listened attentively. And of a sudden the man sagged and would have collapsed but for the Ghûl at hand catching him under the arms. And shambling, his head askew, the man was led back into the tent.

"Was that, is that Modru?" asked Tip.

"Nay, Tipperton," replied Bekki. "It was his surrogate."

"Surrogate?"

"Aye," replied Borl. "A witless man that somehow Modru possesses even though Modru himself sits like a spider in his iron tower in Gron, or so we believe."

Tipperton shuddered.

Bugles sounded below, and Tip looked out to see the Horde redeploying, Rûcks, Hlôks, and Ghûls on Hèlsteeds moving about to face the foe.

Quickly Borl sketched this new array, and then turned to the others.

"The plan seems to be working," he grunted.

"For now perhaps," said Tip, "but not for long."

Borl frowned at the buccan.

"You said it yourself, Lord Borl: the moment the battle begins is the moment all goes wrong."

Grudgingly Borl nodded, then turned again to the portals as twilight drew over the vale. On the hillside the Daelsmen and Dylvana and Baeron broke ranks along with two Lian and a Warrow, and soon campfires were burning in the moonless dark of night.

And in the high mountain chamber, Bekki and Borl slid the stone panels back into place, and when they were firmly set, Bekki raised the hood of a fireless lantern. In the phosphorescent glow the Dwarves donned their mail and helmets, and with Tipperton down the steps they went.

Time eked by, Tipperton waiting, along with nine hundred Dwarves. And sometime after mid of night, he along with the others took up their weapons and roped clay pots and stone-grey blankets and stood before the side postern, and throughout the entire Dwarvenholt all lights were extinguished.

Tip's heart hammered within his chest and his knuckles were white on his bow. And through his thoughts ran a single thread:

Come the dawn, bucco, your reckless plan will fail. Come the dawn. The dawn.

38

*I*n the last candlemarks before dawn, Beau was awakened from a fitful doze by Loric's gentle hand. "The time draws nigh," said the Elf.

Beau scrambled to his feet just as Phais came leading the buccan's pony. "Hast thou thy bullets and sling?"

"Yes, but I shouldn't need them back at a hospital wain."

"Thou dost never know, wee one," said Phais.

"Aye," added Loric. "Remember the plan: should the Rûpt attack up this slope, then thou must flee before them as will we do."

Beau glanced down at the vast Horde of Foul Folk, nought but shadows stirring 'round nearly extinguished campfires, nought but hot coals in the predawn marks. "Oh, I know the plan, all right. Still, do you think they'll attack?"

"Nay, I do not," replied Loric, "yet one never knows."

"We have tried to account for all," said Phais. "Nonetheless, events oft run in directions unforeseen."

"Don't worry," said Beau, taking up his medical satchel, "I'll be prepared for all." And he lashed the kit firmly behind the pony's saddle. He looked up at Phais. "I'll get some extra sling bullets from one of the armory wains."

Loric glanced eastward, where faint light glimmered in the sky. He turned to Phais. "The herald of dawn creeps toward this vale, chier."

Phais nodded, then knelt before Beau and embraced him. "We shall see thee after."

"Oh, Phais, do take care," whispered Beau, and he looked up at Loric. "And you, Loric, you as well."

"Aye," replied Loric, and then he glanced at Beau's pony. "And thou, my friend, be ready to run."

"Don't you worry, Loric. I'll fly like the wind."

Phais then stood, and she and Loric strode away from the buccan and toward where their horses were staked.

With a sigh Beau watched them angle through a bustle of activity, then turned to find Melor at hand holding out a warm cup of tea. "Drink up, Beau, for it may be the last we will have for many a day to come."

Beau gratefully accepted the brew and took a sip and then another. "I say, shouldn't we get to the hospital wain? I mean, things will be starting soon, and I want to be ready should they bring any wounded."

The light in the east grew, struggling against the dark, but even as the shadows yet clutched the vale, Daelsmen and Dylvana and Baeron mounted.

In spite of Tain's objections, Loden signed to Brandt, and the youth raised a bugle to his lips and blew a mighty blast, and echoes rang and slapped among the mountain stone.

And Loden drew his sword and shouted a war cry and rode out from the allied array and galloped alone toward the Horde. And he skidded to a stop partway between and in the dimness raised his sword on high and shouted out a challenge. And turning his horse he rode up and down the line and called the challenge over and again.

He was met by catcalls and jeers.

And in the east the sky grew lighter with the slow approach of dawn.

Now all the Daelsmen rode forth, and the Horde braced for

an attack, a Rûptish horn blatting among the swarm. Yet the men rode back and forth along the line with their leader, and cheered as he taunted the foe.

And still the sky slowly paled.

Now the Elves joined the Daelsmen, and finally the Baeron on their huge horses rode forth.

And among the ranks of the Horde, Rûptish horns sounded and more of the Foul Folk stepped to the line and awaited the attack, Ghûls on Hèlsteeds now riding at the fore, while Rûcks and Hlôks jeered behind.

And Coron Ruar glanced at the sky and then raised a silver horn to his lips and a clarion call rang out over and over again: *Ta-rah, ta-rah, ta-rah . . .*

Along with the others, Tipperton sat with his back against stone and listened to jeering and catcalls, and he jerked at the blast of a horn—no, no, it was not the signal, but a horn nevertheless. And there followed the sound of hooves thudding upon the sod and a calling out of a challenge.

Tip did not look, he dared not look, but remained perfectly still. Even so, he knew it was yet dark in the vale; perhaps they had started too early. Oh, surely not.

The jeering increased, and more hooves thudded, and now came a Rûptish blat and the ching of armor and tramp of feet as Foul Folk moved.

He heard the hammer of even more hooves racing back and forth, and even more still, and midst the Horde horns sounded— Rûptish blats, not the signal—and he remained motionless, waiting, waiting, three roped clay pots at his side, his bow in hand, arrows in the quiver strapped to his thigh.

And then it came, the clarion call—*Ta-rah, ta-rah, ta-rah . . .*—over and over it rang.

The signal had come at last.

Beau stood upon the wain seat and peered through the glimmering pale light in the east, trying to see through the dimness which yet clutched the vale.

Horns sounded, those of the Daelsmen, those of the Rûpt, and he could see a swirl of movement as horses galloped to and fro. Now there were more horses, and the dawn crept upward, yet gloom still cloaked the valley. Even so, his amber gaze could make out more detail, and he saw the Elves riding with the Daelsmen.

The wan glow in the pale skies eased upward but a scintilla, and now the Baeron joined in, and within the Horde horns blatted, and more Spawn shifted to the front.

Beau glanced at the sky.

Come on, come on, we can't let it get too light, else we are all undone.

In that moment came Ruar's signal: *Ta-rah, ta-rah, ta-rah, ta-rah . . .*

And in the shadow-wrapped vale, the stone behind the enemy came to life and silently crept down the slope and toward the unaware foe.

Ta-rah, ta-rah, ta-rah . . .

His back to the rise of the mountain, Tipperton lowered his stone-grey blanket and peered through the dawning dark, then stood and started forward along with the others, creeping down toward the wagons of the Horde, while in the vale, with horns ablare, Daelsmen and Baeron and Elves thundered back and forth and called out challenges and held the eye of the foe.

Now the Dwarves quickened the pace and Tipperton ran silently with them.

The moment the battle begins is the moment all goes—

RRRAAAWWW!

A bellowing roar wrauled out above the thunder of hooves and blare of horns and shouts and jeers of foe and foe, as one of the hulking Trolls turned to see a stone-grey-blanketed Dwarven army with clay vessels on ropes awhirl and rushing down upon the wains at the unprotected rear of the Horde.

And at this thunderous howl a number of Ghûls looked behind and toward the mountain to see the onrushing foe, and they yowled and pointed and raised horns to lips and blew blasts, and spurred their Hèlsteeds into their own ranks, fighting to get through.

Among the Horde confusion reined, for wasn't the foe before them and not to the rear?

Again the Troll bellowed, and other of the great Ogrus turned to see the Dwarves. And the behemoths lunged through Rûcks and Hlôks and bashed them aside in their rush to head off the assault.

Yet there were nine hundred Châkka and only six of the massive Trolls.

Amid the assailing Dwarves, Tipperton ran down and hurled a clay pot to smash upon a wain, and a volatile yellowish liquid splashed outward. And he hurled another and then his last, each to crash upon the wain. And all up and down the line, Dwarves did the same. And as they did so, yet other Dwarves hurled hot clay vessels to crash upon the wains, smoldering firecoke shattering outward.

PH-PHOOM! Fire bloomed upward as wain upon wain exploded in flames, lighting the vale a garish red.

And then the Trolls were among the Dwarves, their great war bars smashing to and fro even as the Châkka withdrew. But two of the Trolls came between the Dwarves and the distant side postern into the mineholt, and the scurrying retreat was cut off.

Dwarves fell back and formed into Troll-squads to attack the monstrous foe. And Tipperton loosed arrows at the Ogrus, only to see his shafts shatter against the stonelike hides.

Yet now the western flank of the Horde turned and, howling, hurled themselves at the Châkka, the segment of Rûcks and Hlôks and Ghûls on Hèlsteeds also to come between the Dwarves and their sanctuary and prevent their escape. And scimitar and tulwar and cudgel met axe and hammer and flail in a great clang of steel, howls and shouts and war cries bellowing forth.

With the roaring fires raging behind, those in the fore of the Horde could hear and see the fighting at the wains and with foe before them and foe behind many milled about in disarray, even as Ghûls on Hèlsteeds blew horns and yawled orders and Hlôks flailed about with whips. Confused elements of the Horde turned and struggled toward the rear, while others behind attempted to reach the fore.

And then the Baeron on heavy horses slammed into the line, their maces and hammers and morning stars smashing and shattering, while Dylvana loosed arrows in among the foe, black-shafted arrows flying in return, shrieks and screams and roars and the clangor of metal filling the air.

With Loden in the lead and Brandt right after and belling the bugle, the Daelsmen thundered down the line to circle 'round and come to the aid of the Dwarves, to help them break past the Trolls to reach the mineholt side postern.

And even as they were smashed down, Dwarves hurled clay pots at Ogrus, the vessels to shatter on three of the stonelike hides and spew yellowish liquid out. Now a Dwarf with a fire-coke vessel hurled his clay pot—

—Yaaaahhh . . . !—

—and that monster caught fire, and he whirled about like a living torch and shrieked in agony.

But there were no more fire-coke vessels, and so the other two Ogrus who had been drenched with the yellowish liquid were yet roaring and crunching their great war bars into the warriors of the Dwarven Troll-squads, and, along with the remaining three Ogrus and the Rûcks and Hlôks and Ghûls on Hèlsteeds, they extracted a dreadful toll on the desperate Châkka.

His arrows ineffective against the Trolls, Tipperton was driven aside, and he fled toward a burning wagon. Upon reaching his goal, he snatched out one of his red-fletched arrows—a signal arrow, a Rynna arrow—and set it to string and jabbed the head into the flames.

Fsss—! the scarlet collar caught fire, and he turned and loosed—*ssss . . .*—a long crimson streak to flash through the air and fade behind as the arrow flew—

—to strike the foe—

—a Troll—

Ph-phoom! flames to explode on the monster.

And atop the hill at the hospital wain, as the burning arrow scored a crimson line through the gloom, Beau cried out, "Oh Lor', that was Tipperton's arrow. He shouldn't be there. It's all gone wrong!" and he leapt from the wain and hurled himself onto the back of his pony and spurred down-slope, Melor calling out, "Wait, Beau!" but the buccan was down and away.

Tipperton jerked a second red-feathered arrow from the quiver at his hip, and as he lit it he heard—
—a shriek of rage—
—a shout: " 'Ware, Tipperton!"—
—and the thunder of hooves, and bearing down on him came a Ghûl, Hèlsteed in full gallop, cruel barbed spear aimed at the buccan's breast. Yet the buccan drew his bow to the full and loosed again, a second crimson streak to fly through the shaded air and strike—
PHOOM!
—the other soaked Ogru—
—yet the Ghûl came on and—
—Tipperton dropped to the stony ground and rolled under the burning wagon and out the far side—
—as Bekki, howling, hurtled down the slope and leaped through the air to crash into the Ghûl—
—while Tipperton, scrambling, ran onward, his wee form lost down among the enemy—
—Bekki and the corpse-foe to smash down into the bed of the furiously burning wain—

As Beau galloped down the hill and toward the distant melee, a second crimson streak flashed through the air. "Hang on, Tip!" he shouted, fumbling at his waist to open the pouch and extract his sling while racing downslope. And as he sped down, a lone rider thundered up the hill toward him, running the opposite way. As they hammered past one another, Beau saw the white hair and white beard of Counsellor Tain as that man fled from the field of combat, his eyes wide with fright.

And onward raced Beau, down toward the mighty struggle, his sling now in hand as he fumbled in his pouch for a bullet.

And he saw combat directly before him, an Elf 'gainst a Ghûl, barbed spear 'gainst flashing blade, though a bow-bearing Rûck ran nigh. Down galloped Beau as the Elf closed on the Hèlsteed rider ere he could bring his spear to bear. Fire-light flashed from the sword as it swung forward to take off the corpse-foe's head, yet ere it clove, a black-shafted arrow slammed into the Elf, and just as Beau hammered past she crashed to the ground—

—It was Phais, pierced through.

As three of the Ogrus burned shrieking, two of their kindred scrambled up the slopes of the mountain and away, the monsters howling in fear of red-streaking arrows which caused Ogrus to burst into flame. The sole remaining Troll yet battled Châkka, and Grg closed in to aid him, just as shouting Prince Loden and the yawling Daelsmen rounded the flank of the Horde and thundered in among the foe, swords reaving and lances piercing, to be met by blade in kind.

And at the fore of the Horde, the Baeron had bludgeoned in among the Spawn and now were completely surrounded, while Dylvana strove to break through the entrapping ring.

Tipperton ducked and dodged down among the swarming enemy, and darted this way and that, his bow, though strung with an arrow, now useless against foe too close at hand. And a Hèlsteed slammed by in the shouting struggle and bashed the buccan to the ground. His arrow lost, on hands and knees Tip scuttled among trampling feet and thrashing legs to be kicked up against a canvas wall.

Under the edge he scrambled to come up inside a tent.

And therein stood a man—

—who slowly turned toward him—

—and in dim lanternlight gazed vacantly at the Warrow.

Tip snatched at an arrow as he looked into the face of a man whose eyes were empty and whose drooling mouth hung agape.

It was the surrogate and he smelled of feces, and urine stained his breeks.

Nocking the arrow, Tip drew the shaft to the full and aimed at the man's breast.

Outside, battle cries and screams and shouts and shrieks of the dying and the wounded filled the air, horns blowing, steel clanging against steel, sharp edges cleaving into muscle and sinew, blunt iron shattering bones.

Yet inside, the man just stood there, uncomprehending, spittle running down his chin as he stared vacantly at a Warrow with a full-drawn bow. And then the man grinned an idiot's grin down at the wee buccan, his gaping mouth smiling wide, grunting, "Uhn, uhn, uhn."

Sighing, Tip relaxed the draw—

—and in that moment the tent flap slapped aside as a dark figure hurtled in and crashed a hammer down and into the man's head, the iron smashing through the skull as if it were nought but a ripe melon, blood and brain splashing wide as Tipperton—"*Waugh!*"—leaped backward and drew his bow against—

"*Bekki!*" shouted the Warrow, seeing who it was as the dead man crumpled.

Bekki stood above the corpse, the Dwarf's beard and hair singed, his armor soot-covered, his clothing scorched.

Shrieking in rage, Beau loosed at the bow-bearing Rûck, the sling bullet to slam into the Spawn's throat, the Rûck to drop the bow and clutch at his crushed neck, unable to breathe, and he fell to the ground, his feet drumming in death.

But now the Ghûl turned on the buccan, and Beau loaded again and let fly, the missile to crash into the Ghûl's skull, dark matter to splash outward. Yet the Ghûl merely grinned and bore down on the Warrow.

Jerking his pony aside as the Ghûl thundered past, Beau fumbled for another bullet, while the Ghûl wrenched his Hèlsteed about, the beast squealing in pain.

Beau loosed another missile, and it struck the foe in the shoulder, bones to crack. Yet still the Ghûl grinned and bore down. But in that moment a rider flashed by—Loric!— and his blade sheared through the Ghûl's neck, the creature's head flying wide to bounce on the ground as the Hèlsteed galloped past Beau and away, the headless corpse yet astride.

"Loric, it's Phais!" cried Beau, and he sprang from his pony and jerked free his medical kit—

Oh lor', oh lor', don't let her be dead.
—and ran to the side of the downed Dara.

Bekki looked up. "Tipperton! I thought you slain."

"We will be if we don't get out of here," cried Tipperton.

Bekki nodded and looked at the corpse, its head smashed into an unrecognizable shape. "I came to kill Modru's eyes and ears and voice, and that done, we can leave."

As Tip stepped toward the tent flap he said, "You're all burnt, Bekki—"

"Not as bad as the Ghûl," growled Bekki. "I am alive; he is not."

Gripping his war hammer, Bekki cried, "Follow me," and he charged from the tent and in among the shouting foe, his maul smashing left and right. And with Tipperton on his heels, Bekki battered his way to the line of burning wagons and out.

Yet just as he passed a blazing wain, a Rûck leapt at his back, long iron spike raised to stab.

thuk!

Tipperton's shaft slammed through the Rûck's back, the arrow head to punch out through his breastbone, and he looked down at the out-jutting, grume-covered point as the spike fell from his nerveless fingers to clang upon the stone, the Rûck to collapse after.

Bekki whirled in time to see, and grunted his thanks.

"I told you Rûcks were dangerous," shouted Tip above the roar of battle.

The last of the Trolls scrambled up the mountain slopes after his fleeing kindred, his war bar abandoned in his haste to escape, for although he was but barely scathed by axe and hammer and flail, he too feared the crimson streaks which could set his kind afire.

And seeing the Trolls fleeing, the Rûcks turned tail and ran, and though Ghûls on Hèlsteeds shouted and Hlôks flailed about with whips, shrieking in fear the Rûcks hurtled away from the Daelsmen and Dwarves.

Through the remainder of the Horde the wailing Rûcks ran, and their kindred, seeing panic, fled with them as well, and the battle they were winning instead became a rout, as toward the east and the road the Swarm fled.

The field they left behind was littered with the dead and wounded from both sides.

And dawn finally came to the firelit vale, pressing the shadows back.

39

*T*he carnage was horrific, the dead and the dying scattered across the field, the wounded crying out in agony, calling for aid. Riderless horses limped midst the slaughter, though other mounts lay dead. And mid the butchery a squealing Hèlsteed thrashed with broken legs.

O'erwhelmed by the sheer magnitude of the task, healers moved among the casualties, rendering what aid they could. Comrades also were afield, giving comfort to their brethren. Still others gathered the stray mounts and led them aside, where they, too, could receive aid.

Squads of warriors with knives or spears in hand strode among the felled, their work bloody and grim.

"Come," gritted Bekki, "we have a task to do."

Tipperton looked up at the Dwarf, an unspoken question in his eyes, yet he followed Bekki into the field.

They came to a downed Rûck, hamstrung by someone's blade, the Rûck feebly scrabbling at the ground and trying to crawl. Bekki grabbed the foe by the hair and jerked his head back and—

"Bekki, don't!" cried Tip above the Rûck's piglike squeal.

—slit his throat, blackish blood to spew outward.

Bekki dropped the now dead Rûck and looked at Tipperton, the buccan pale and trembling and on the verge of vomiting. "Would you have me let him live, heal him?"

"I, uh—"

"He is one of the Grg, a creature of Gyphon," said Bekki, as if that explained all.

"Oh, Bekki, it's not right. He couldn't even defend himself."

"Nevertheless, it must be done," growled Bekki, moving on.

"I can't go with you, Bekki. Not to do this," said Tip, turning away.

Bekki paused. "Did you not tell me on our journey to Mineholt North, Tipperton, that when your mate was slain, you wanted them all dead—all the Ükhs, Hrôks, Khôls, Hèlsteeds, Trolls, Rivermen, Kistanee, Chabbans, Hyranee, and aught else who sided with Gyphon?"

Tip turned once more toward Bekki. "Yes, Bekki, I said that once. Yet I have since found it gives me no satisfaction to kill Foul Folk. Vengeance does nothing to ease a wounded heart. And no matter how many I slay, it will not bring Rynna back." Tears ran down Tipperton's face. He gestured about the bloody field. "To kill in battle is a necessary thing. But this, this thing you do, this cutting of throats of those who cannot defend themselves, this is murder . . . just as was the case of the surrogate, for he was without wit, an innocent victim of Modru, and could not defend himself . . . and neither can these felled foe."

Bekki ground his teeth. "You have much to learn, Tipperton, for in war the object is to win."

"Even at the cost of the innocent, the defenseless? Does a lofty goal excuse the deeds, no matter how evil they are?"

Bekki did not answer, but instead he stared beyond Tipperton, his mouth falling open, agape.

Tipperton turned, and up the slope the gates of Mineholt North swung wide, and beings covered from head to toe in concealing veils came forth, guarded by fierce Dwarven warriors.

And Tipperton knew these were the Châkia, the protected, the sheltered, the shielded, the cherished.

And they moved into the slaughterground, kneeling here and there to aid wounded allies, their deft hands bandaging, applying unguents and salves, and washing clean and stitching closed the cloven wounds.

Bekki hastily sheathed his dagger and took up his war hammer. "I must go with the Châkka and ward the perimeter of this field."

And moving as one, Dwarven warriors set an armed ring of steel about the battleground, for they would have no enemy come upon their beloved Châkia. And in this they were joined by the Dylvana.

"I will aid the healers," called Tipperton after Bekki. And as he turned, he scanned the slope for sign of Beau. And then Tip's gaze found him—"Oh, no!" Tipperton began running among the wounded and dead and dying, down toward the buccan carrying his satchel and trotting through the field alongside Loric, who bore Phais cradled in his arms, the Dara, bare to the waist, not moving at all.

While all about the bloody work of squads of Daelsmen and Baeron went on, making certain all Foul Folk were dead—all Rûcks, Hlôks, Ghûls, Hèlsteeds, and even the burnt Trolls.

"Beau, Beau, Lady Phais, is she—"

"No, Tip, but she might be if we don't get some gwynthyme in her. I think the arrow was poisoned. "We're taking her to the Dwarvenholt."

"Follow me," said Tip. "I know a bit of where we need to go: the kitchens, they'll have hot water."

"Hot coals, too, I would think," said Beau. "We need to cauterize."

Up the slope and through the gates and into the mineholt Tip led them, and then through corridors and to a kitchen.

Veiled Châkia were within.

Loric gently lay Phais on a table, while Beau dragged a chair alongside. As he climbed onto the seat, he called for hot water and a clean teacup and a small bowl, and he rummaged through his bag and drew out a short, thin iron rod with a leather-wrapped fired-clay handle. "Here, Tip. Find some hot coals and stick this in. When the iron glows yellow, let me know."

As Tip turned, a Châkian came to the table, bearing a basin

of hot water as well as a cup and bowl. Too, she bore soap and towels. "You must thoroughly wash your hands," she softly said through her concealing veils, "as must all who will tend this Lady Elf."

Beau looked up, his amber eyes widening slightly. "Are you a healer? I could use some help."

Silently the Châkian began to wash her hands, and she set the soap before Beau.

Beau took out the small silver case from his breast pocket and extracted a portion of the precious golden mint, and dropped it into the cup. He poured hot water in after. A refreshing fragrance filled the air.

While it steeped, he washed and dried his hands. He turned back to Phais. "She's bled a lot," he muttered. "Pray to Adon it was enough to leach the poison out." Beau took up the cup and looked at the Châkian. "Yet the wound is deep and so we've got to get this down her."

The Châkian reached out and took the cup and stepped away and fetched a small spoon, then crossed back to the table and began carefully spooning limited amounts into Phais, the Dara swallowing reflexively.

"How's that cauter coming?" Beau called to Tip.

At the stove Tip said, "It's just now turning red."

"Well then, you heard the Lady: get over here and wash your hands," snapped Beau.

Moments later, Tip, with beads of sweat on his brow, handed the yellow-glowing instrument to Beau, and Beau nodded to Loric. "Uncover the wound."

The Alor lifted away the bandage from her chest.

Beau looked closely and glanced across at Loric. "If I use this, she'll never breathe with ease again." He stood in pensive thought for a moment and finally shook his head and handed the glowing cauter back to Tip. "We won't need this."

Tip sighed in relief.

Beau looked at the Châkian. "I need you to spoon a bit of that gwynthyme tea into the wound . . . ah, yes, a bit more, good, that's enough.

"Now give her the remainder, and when it's gone, put the leaves into the bowl. I need them as a poultice. Now where's my gut and needle?"

A short while later, Beau tied the last knot on the bandage and said, "There, all done." He looked up at Loric and then over to the Châkian. "Her wound will bleed even more if she is not still, and she's lost enough as it is. We need a place where she can rest and remain quiet."

"Thel, Sol Châkian," murmured Loric.

The Châkian turned to Loric, her head canted. *"Da tak Châkur?"*

"Ti," replied Loric. *"Kelek at skal ea. Ea ta Loric."*

The Châkian clapped her hands and called out to two Châkia, and they fetched a litter. "Fear not, Guardian," she said to Loric, "for along with other wounded females, we shall bear her to our healing chambers, where she will rest in quiet."

"I will help," said Loric.

The Châkian shook her head, her veils swirling. "Nay. The chambers are in our quarters." She turned to Beau. "Only healers are allowed."

Beau plunged the still hot cautering rod into a basin of water to cool it, then dried it and dropped it in his satchel. Taking up the bag, he said, "Lead the way," and he hopped down from the chair.

Tip and Loric watched them go.

"Come," said Loric at last. "Let us help fetch the steeds, including our own."

A time later, Beau emerged from the Dwarvenholt and moved into the battlefield to help with the injured. And he found Melor on the slopes, deciding who would be next: there were those who could wait, and those who could not, and those yet alive but beyond all help.

It nearly broke Beau's heart to pass these latter by.

From the field, after initial treatment, the wounded were borne into Mineholt North, males carried to one set of quarters, females unto the chambers of the Châkia and given over to their care, for Phais was not the only wounded Dara. Female Baeron, too, were taken unto the Châkia, even though some protested. Yet the Dwarves would have it no other way, for this was their Châkkaholt, and herein females lived in quarters apart.

Chieftain Gara and Coron Ruar accepted this arrangement, for as Gara said, "When in Rhondor, one must live as a Rhondorian."

Throughout the day and into the night, along with the other healers Beau worked feverishly. But when he collapsed into bed at last, all who could be saved had been, and all who could not were not.

Altogether, nearly three quarters of the allies had been wounded—many but minor scathings, others major blows—and of those taking the greater wounds, nearly half had died in battle and more would die in the days to come.

Ruar took a count of the battlefield dead; three and two hundred Daelsmen; twenty-two and one hundred Baeron; forty-six and two hundred Drimma; eighty-four and one hundred Dylvana.

Of the foe, some three thousand of the Foul Folk had been slain altogether, two thousand killed outright during battle, another thousand on the field after.

All the next day funerals were prepared for the dead: the Châkka to be burned on pyres with the broken weapons of their enemies at their feet, while mourners would wail and warriors would swear vengeance; the Baeron to be borne to a wooded vale and in absolute silence be laid to rest 'neath woven bowers; the Daelsmen to be interred in the earth as their feats were shouted to the world; the Dylvana to be burned while their kindred sang.

As he and Tip watched the Daelsmen cutting sod and digging the pits for the burial mounds, "It's not right," muttered Bekki, his hood cast over his head in the Châkka gesture of mourning.

"What's not right?" asked Tip, peering up at Bekki's red face, Tip wondering if the Dwarf were angry or if it was simply the flush from his burns. He had been treated with aloe to hasten healing, yet his face and hands were still ruddy.

"Clean stone or purifying fire is the only true way to honor the dead. Else it will be overlong ere the soul gains freedom to be reborn. This interment in earth, why, roots will catch the soul. No wonder Châkka and Daelsmen are at odds."

Tipperton shook his head but remained silent, even as he noticed that the Daelsmen looked with disfavor upon the building of the great funeral pyre of the Dwarves, and the making of the pyre of the Elves, as well as the Baeron lading wains with their dead to take them into a forest, and muttered of the error of their ways.

So, too, did the Baeron look upon the others and shake their heads as well.

Only the Dylvana seemed to ignore the varying customs in their preparations to sing all souls to the sky.

As to the dead Foul Folk—all three thousand one hundred twenty—though the Dwarves objected, Ruar insisted they should be burned as well. At last Borl assented, for though he believed fire would honor the Grg, still he could not see any other swift way to rid his dale of these dead . . . and he did not want to leave them to rot upon his very door.

Tip looked over the field of slaughter and sighed. "So many killed, Bekki. So many killed. It seems somehow unfair."

Bekki grunted. "War is not a pleasant game, Tipperton, not a diversion of sport. Fairness has nothing to do with it. There is only the 'rule,' if rule it is, and that is to slay as many of the foe as you can."

"I thought the only rule was to win."

Bekki nodded. "That, too."

"And if you can win without slaughter . . . ?"

Bekki looked down at the buccan. "Not easily done in war."

Tip sighed. "I think that to win a war without slaughter, the victory must come before any battle is fought."

They watched long moments more. Finally Tip said, "Of all who fell, only a few were those I knew."

Bekki's eyes turned grim as flint. "All Châkka who fell were my brothers."

On this second day as well, Beau visited many of the wounded, including Phais in the Châkia. healing chambers. When Beau, escorted by a Châkian, came into the infirmary, the Dara was fevered and thrashing about as poison coursed through her veins. Châkia attended her, some bathing her brow with cold spring water while others attempted to hold her still.

And her bandage was seeping red.

"Oh, my," whispered Beau, "I should have burnt the wound."

"Shall I ready a cauter?" asked the Châkian at his side.

Beau shook his head. "It's too late now, for the poison has spread."

"We have tried a sleeping draught," said another of the Châkia. "But the fever gains the upper hand now and again."

Beau nodded and reached into his breast pocket for the silver case. Shortly, and with the help of a Châkia, he managed to get the gwynthyme tea into the Dara. Partway through, she settled into an uneasy sleep.

"I'll be back later," he whispered to Phais as he bandaged the wound again, a fresh poultice laid on. The Dara made no response. And with tears in his eyes, Beau left her side.

The following day, the funerals were held: Châkia wailing, hooded Châkka tearing at their beards and swearing vengeance as smoke twined into the sky; Daelsmen marching 'round mounds and calling out of brave deeds done; Dylvana standing by the roaring pyre and singing; and somewhere in the still woods, Baeron standing silent, while Loric, who had gone with them, stood a distance away and softly sang.

That night the corpses of the Foul Folk were burned, and no one whatsoever grieved, though many there shouted curses.

And in the infirmary Beau spent another dose of his precious gwynthyme.

The next morning Coron Ruar called a meeting of the war council, DelfLord Borl and an elder Dwarf, Berk, attending as well. They met in the great war room of Mineholt North.

"There are yet seven segments of a Horde in Riamon," said Ruar. "The scouts report that they now drive southeast."

"Not toward the city of Dael?" asked Bwen, her arm in a sling. "I am somewhat surprised."

Loden shook his head. "Dael is a walled city, well protected. They passed it by on the way here. The numbers of the Spawn are even less now; hence they pass it by again."

Borl growled and gestured about. "Mineholt North, carved as it is in the living stone, is even more protected than your city, Prince Loden. Why they came and set siege here instead of there is a mystery to me."

The elder Dwarf cleared his throat. "Once long past in the First Era, Modru proposed an alliance to Breakdeath Durek of the Châkka. Durek turned him down. A time later, Foul Folk cast Durek into the Vorvor, there at Kraggen-cor, some say at the behest of the Enemy. Yet Durek survived, perhaps by the hand of the Utruni. I think this yet galls Modru and he seeks revenge."

"Would he do so after all these years?" asked Tipperton.

"Who knows the mind of Modru?" replied Loden, shaking his head. "Not I."

Brandt cocked an eyebrow. "What would Counsellor Tain have said?"

Loden turned up his hands. "We'll never know, Brandt; Tain's slain body was not found."

"He wasn't slain," blurted Beau. "He ran."

Loden looked at the Warrow. "He what?"

"He ran," repeated Beau. "Fled the conflict—up the hill toward the hospital wains. I saw him as I charged downslope to get to the fighting."

Loden looked about the table, muscles twitching in his clenched jaw.

Melor cleared his throat. "When Lord Tain reached the top of the hill, he turned eastward, toward Dael."

Rage blazed in Loden's eyes. "Fled from the field of battle, and here I thought him dead, his body hacked apart as were many of those we buried, as were many of those you burned." The Prince clenched a fist and gritted, "But now I find he ran." Slowly Loden unclenched his fingers. "Nevertheless, I will deal with him when next we meet." The Daelsman turned and looked at Ruar. "There is a Swarm within the Rimmen Ring we must deal with first."

"I say we take their toll as they run," said Chieftain Gara. "Hit them hard when they least expect it and then withdraw."

"Harass them, you mean," said Bwen, her words a statement and not a question.

Bekki growled. "I like not this striking from ambush. It has the ring of dishonor."

"How is it different from what we did here?" asked Tip. "I

mean, behind their backs we slipped out through the postern in the middle of the night, shrouded in blankets like stone, while their attention was drawn toward those before them in the vale. And then as dawn crept toward us and their regard was full upon the riders and challenges and feints, well then, we struck from the rear. And if that's not an ambush, or the like, well then, I don't know what is."

Bwen burst out in laughter. "Ah, Bekki, he's got you there."

Daelsmen and Baeron joined Bwen in her laughter, while Dylvana and Lian smiled. Even DelfLord Borl cocked an eye at his son and grinned.

"But we were grimly outnumbered," protested Bekki.

"As we are still," said Ruar. Now he looked 'round the table and asked, "How many are fit to ride, and have we enough horses?"

"I tally some thirty-eight and four hundred Daelsmen," said Loden. "As for horses, five hundred twelve."

Gara glanced at Bwen, then said, "Ten and three hundred Baeron, with horses to spare."

And Bwen added, "There will be another five and sixty of us driving wains."

Ruar nodded, then added, "Twenty-five and six hundred Dylvana, and we, too, have the mounts."

"I will pledge two hundred Châkka," rumbled DelfLord Borl, "on ponies, of course. The rest of the Châkka must stay and care for the Mineholt . . . the wounded as well."

Ruar looked to the right, where sat Tipperton and Beau and Loric. "Ye three and thy wounded companion have done well in our campaign, but ye yet have a sworn mission to fulfill. Even so, ye may choose to ride with us, and we would be glad of it. Still, we know not where the Swarm will lead us, toward Dendor in Aven or away. What say ye?"

Both Beau and Loric turned to Tipperton, and Beau said, "Well go on, bucco. Which way will it be?"

Tip took a deep breath and blew it out and peered down toward the floor. Finally he looked at Bekki and then to Ruar and said, "These past days I've come to realize that no amount of killing of Foul Folk will ease the ache in my heart. I slew all

I could in Rimmen Gape, twenty or more, I believe. Another dozen or thereabouts fell to my arrows here—"

"Including two Trolls and a back-stabbing Ükh," said Bekki.

Borl's eyes widened. "You are the one who loosed the red-streaking arrows?"

Tip nodded.

"Elwydd," breathed Borl. "That alone saved the lives of many, mine among them, for I was before one of the Trolls the moment your arrow came and he burst into flames."

Tip threw up a negating hand. "DelfLord Borl, I didn't do it alone. The Dwarves who drenched the Ogrus with the liquid of fire deserve most of the credi—"

"Heed!" called out Borl. "I, Borl, son of Berk and DelfLord of Mineholt North, do here and now name you *Châk-Sol*. Let all within hearing carry the word forth unto those who should know. So I have said, so shall it be."

"Châk-Sol?" asked Tipperton. "What is—?"

"Dwarf-Friend," said Loric. "Thou hast been named Dwarf-Friend, as was I long past in the Red Hills Drimmenholt."

"But what does it mean?"

Borl smiled. "All secrets, councils, and counsels of my Châkkaholt and of my kindred are yours for the asking."

"Oh, my," said Beau, looking at Tipperton wide-eyed. "Does this mean you'll grow taller and broader in the shoulders and carry an axe?"

Tipperton burst out laughing, his giggles to be joined by guffaws of the entire council.

Finally, Tip held up a hand. "I thank you, my DelfLord, even though I do not think I deserve such an honor. I'll try not to let you down."

Bekki leaned over to Tipperton and growled, "Not likely, Sir Tipperton, not likely."

And Borl's sire, Berk, took up his axe in a gnarled hand and flashed it on high and cried out, "All hál Sir Tipperton, Troll-slayer and Châk-Sol!"

And thrice came the collective shout: *Hál! Hál! Hál!*

Tipperton's face flushed red. "Really, I don't—"

"Nonsense," snapped Berk. "You do."

Tip held up his hands and said, "I yield," which brought a satisfied murmur of approval from all 'round.

Finally, Ruar cleared his throat and called for quiet. Then he turned to Tipperton. "We await thy decision, Sir Tipperton, named Troll-slayer and Châk-Sol: wilt thou and thy companions ride with us to harass the Swarm, or will ye three bear instead toward Aven?"

Tipperton looked about the circle, then said, "Coron Ruar, though these past weeks I did set it aside, we are sworn to go to Aven. Too, there is one other who is sworn to our mission as well, and that is Dara Phais, sorely wounded. I cannot—we cannot—leave her behind, no matter which course we would choose. Yet my mind is clear now: we will wait for her to heal, and then ride on together: to King Agron in Aven we go; to Dendor if he is there; or to wherever he may be if not."

Bekki's brow furrowed at these words, but Ruar nodded and said, "Ye will be greatly missed, my friends, yet a sworn duty calls ye to go one way whereas we go another. We can do nought but wish ye success. Yet stay, for we have much to decide here today, and thine advice would be most welcome."

Ruar now turned to the remainder of the war council. "I count us thirty-eight and six hundred and a thousand strong, those of us who can ride. We are yet outnumbered 'tween four to one and five. Even so, the Swarm is on the run, and that gives us advantage. . . ."

The council lasted the rest of the day, but in midmorn Beau left, whispering that he had Phais and other wounded to tend. Tip and Loric remained in the council, though neither had much to say.

In midafternoon Beau returned and whispered to Loric and Tip, "No change."

Beau had no more than taken his seat when Bekki turned to Borl and said, "Sire, I must accompany Sir Tipperton into Aven."

At the raised brows of his father, Bekki went on: "Apprenticed as I was to DelfLord Valk in Kachar, I have traveled throughout Rimmen and Aven and know well both of those realms."

Borl held up a hand. "What of our debt to the Dylvana and Baeron and Daelsmen? And who will command here as I ride with them?"

"Sire, that we owe our allies, I cannot dispute. Yet we owe Sir Tipperton as much if not more, for not only did he save your life, but he saved mine as well. And had he not slain the Trolls, the battle would likely have gone the other way. It was his plan we followed which broke the siege. And this last: he is Châk-Sol of Mineholt North and needs aid. I am among our best warriors, hence I ask leave to go. As to who will command in Mineholt North, my grandsire, your sire, is yet hale."

Berk turned to Borl and said, "He is right, my son, a great debt is owed. As for me, I was DelfLord before, and though it is a burden, and though I would rather ride to battle, if you so choose I will take on the task of holtwarder until you return."

Borl clapped his hand on the shoulder of his father and said, "None better, sire." Then he turned to Bekki. "Aye. You are right, my son, and I give you my leave if he'll have you." He looked at Tipperton. "Will you accept another into your service, Châk-Sol?"

Beau leaned over and whispered to Tip, "Seek the aid of those not men." When Tip turned to his friend with wide eyes, Beau grinned and added, "It's all connected, you know . . . even to insignificant Warrows such as we."

Tip shook his head and turned to Borl. "Gladly, my DelfLord. Gladly will I have Bekki at my side."

Bekki grinned fiercely as Borl declared, "So he has said, so shall it be."

Over that day and the next, in spite of all the healers could do, more of the severely wounded died, and more funerals were held.

But on the third morn, the Dylvana, Daelsmen, Baeron, and Dwarves rode out on the track of the Swarm, all upon horses but the Dwarves, and they upon sturdy ponies.

Following after went Bwen and her wagons, and though the pursuit of the Swarm would far outstrip her wains, still she and her drivers would be on their trail at need.

Behind in the Châkkaholt remained the wounded, under the protection of the Dwarves until they were fit to ride. As to when that might be, 'twould be sooner for some than others was all Beau and the Dwarven healers would commit to.

And just ere they left, Vail and Melor came to see Tip and

Beau, to wish them good fortune and farewell, for Vail was riding with the scouts and Melor as a healer in the vanguard.

Too, came Prince Loden and Prince Brandt, and Chieftain Gara and Wagonleader Bwen, and DelfLord Borl, and lastly Coron Ruar. And they all bid Tip and Beau and Bekki and Loric good-bye, and asked that their regards be conveyed to Dara Phais as well.

And then they were gone, warriors riding and wains rolling down the road toward the city of Dael. And when they had passed from sight, Tipperton, Beau, Bekki, and Loric, along with others, stepped back through the side postern and into the Dwarvenholt, shutting the gate behind.

The following day, as Beau stepped out the door of the chamber he and Tip shared and strode down the hall to make his rounds, behind him Tip called out, "I say, Beau, wait for me. I'll take my lute and go with you to see Lady Phais."

Beau paused until Tip caught up and then strode onward, saying, "Uh, I dunno, Tip. These Châkia, they are mighty close."

"You mean thick with one another?"

"Oh, they're that, all right. But I mean shut to out-siders. —Like the Bosky in troubled times, though instead of a Thornring they are hedged about with iron bars. Only in this case, the Châkia, they don't let males in."

"Well, I think I'll try regardless. The most they can do is turn me away. Besides, you've other patients to treat—male patients, that is—and I might be able to cheer them."

And so when Beau made his rounds Tipperton went along-side, and he played his lute in each of the infirmaries where Beau took him, and all the wounded were glad of it.

As they finally walked toward one of the portcullised halls, Tip said, "I think I'll do this from now on, Beau. It seemed to give them heart."

"My Aunt Rose always said that good spirits make the healing go faster."

Tip sighed. "Perhaps I ought not to play and sing for them, then."

Beau looked at him in puzzlement. "Why ever not?"

"Because, Beau, the faster they heal the sooner they go into battle again, and this time they might be killed."

"Oh."

They rounded a turn and before them stood a portcullis. Beau pulled on a cord at the grille. Somewhere a bell rang.

As they waited, Beau said, "Well, I think you ought to play for them regardless. I mean, perhaps someone who heals faster will prove to be the someone who saves the world from Modru and his ilk. It's all con—"

"—nected," finished Tip. "Yes, Beau, I know."

On the far side of the portcullis, a figure concealed in layers of gossamer veils moved down the hall toward them, silken fabric floating behind.

She stopped at the grillework.

"We have come to treat my patient," said Beau.

"You may pass, Sir Beau, but your friend—"

"I've come to help with the healing, too," said Tip, and he held up his lute. "In my own way, of course. This kind of healing is needed as well."

Now Beau said, "Tip's right, you know. It will help."

Silk shifted leftward as the Châkian canted her head to the side. "Tip? Sir Tipperton? Troll-slayer? Châk-Sol?"

Tipperton swept a wide bow, as wide as a three-foot four-inch Warrow could make. "At your service, my Lady."

Without further word the Châkian stepped back down the hall to a niche-held lever which she threw and a wall-mounted crank which she turned, and silently the portcullis rose in its track.

Beau ducked under when it was high enough, Tipperton following.

Quietly the grille was lowered again and the lever lock thrown once more.

They followed the Châkian through corridors to a large chamber filled with cots, where wounded Dara and female Baeron lay. Here and there veiled Châkia moved among them, administering to their needs. Now Beau came to where Phais lay abed, drifting in and out of consciousness, virulent poison running in her veins. Thin and pale and barely awake, she wanly smiled at him, and her eyes slightly widened at the sight of Tip, though his own heart fell to see the look of her.

"While Beau has come to poke and prod," said Tip, outwardly grinning in spite of his inward dismay, "I've come to play and sing."

"Poke and prod?" huffed Beau, rummaging through his bag. "Poke and prod, indeed."

"Never mind him, Lady Phais," said Tipperton, taking up his lute. "What song would you have?"

Phais paused, her eyes closed, and Tip thought she had fainted, but then she whispered, her voice weak, "Dost thou know 'The Dancing Sprite'? I deem it would lift the hearts of all."

Tipperton grinned. "As you will, my Lady." He looked about and spied a chair and jumped upon its seat. And then his fingers ran across the strings and he began to play, silver notes filling the infirmary with lively sounds, Tipperton raising his voice in song to all:

> There was a Sprite, a lovely Sprite,
> Who danced within her ring.
> And when she danced her lovely dance
> She didn't wear a thing . . .
> . . . And danced around in sport.
>
> There came a lad, a handsome lad,
> Her very own kind, you see.
> He peeked through leaves and watched her dance,
> And fall in love did he . . .
> . . . Or something of the sort. . . .

When Tipperton came to the end of the song, laughter echoed throughout the chamber, ranging from weak to hearty. In a bed across from Phais, a Baeran woman with her leg in a cast guffawed and called out, "Served him right, it did," and this brought on more laughter.

Even the Châkia tittered behind their many veils.

As Beau spent his last dose of gwynthyme and prepared a cup of tea, Tip played and sang another song and then another. And he sang several more as a Châkian slowly spooned drifting Phais her drink. And another still as Beau laid on the gwynthyme poultice.

And after each of his songs he was greeted by applause and calls for more.

Finally, though, Beau said, "Come on, bucco, I've more patients to deal with elsewhere, and they can use your songs, too."

And so Tipperton called out, "I must now leave"—his announcement to be met by a chorus of disappointed *Ohs*— "yet I shall return on the morrow," and many called out, *Please do.*

Tip sprang down from the chair and went to Phais. "Get well, my Lady, oh please."

Phais, her eyes closed, whispered, "I fully intend to do so, my wee friend."

As they strode away, a Châkian at their side, Beau said, "I dunno, Tip. That was the last of the gwynthyme, and if it doesn't work . . . Oh, I should have run the cauter into the wound, even though the scars would have done ill things to her breathing ever after. I should have. I should have."

"This gwynthyme, Beau, don't the Dwarves have any?"

Striding beside Tip, the Châkian said, "Nay, we do not. Gwynthyme is a rare thing, and we have none."

"Elwydd," said Tip, a one-word prayer.

Late in the night, Tip was awakened by Beau coming into the chamber they shared. Beau was weeping.

Sitting upright, Tip asked, "What is it, Beau?"

"Lady Phais," said Beau.

"Oh, no," moaned Tip.

"No, no, Tip, it's not that she's dead or anything. It's quite the opposite: finally, finally, her color is good and her breathing truly not labored. Oh, Tip, she's sleeping peacefully. The gwynthyme has burnt out the poison at last."

The buccen embraced one another, tears running down their faces.

"Come on, Beau, let's go tell Loric."

The next day Tipperton again accompanied Beau on his rounds, each buccan in his own way administering to the wounded. When they came to the Châkia infirmary, they found Phais sitting up in her bed, a veiled Châkia at her side and feeding the Dara her first good meal in days, meting out small spoonfuls. Even though Phais was eating, she was yet weak, exhausted. Still, as Beau had said, her color was much better.

The Dara spied the Warrows nearing and smiled, and Beau said, "Oh, my, Phais, but you are looking quite splendid."

Phais reached out and took Beau's hand, her grip weak. " 'Twas thy ministrations, Beau."

Beau looked down, shaking his head. "The credit is due to Lady Aris."

"Aris? In Arden Vale?"

Beau nodded. "Yes. she is the one who gave me the gwyn-thyme. Without it I don't think you'd have survived. The arrow was poisoned, the wound deep."

"It was Vulg poison," said the Châkia, her voice soft.

"Vulg poison?" asked Tip. "How do you know this?"

"Nought else is so baneful, and this was delivered deep."

"Oh," said Tip, looking at Phais, the Dara nodding in agreement.

Now Tip took up his lute. "What will you have, my Lady?"

Phais sighed. "I would see my beloved."

"Loric?" asked Tip, then slapped himself in the head and growled, "Of course it's Loric, you ninny." He turned to the Châkia. "Surely you can allow Alor Loric in to see his beloved."

Her veils shifted as she looked at the buccan. "Nay."

"But it would do her a world of good," protested Tip.

"He is male," said the Châkia.

Tip's mouth fell open and he gestured at Beau, then tapped his own chest. "You let these two males in."

"He is a healer; you are Châk-Sol."

Tip's eyes widened. "But wait, Loric is Châk-Sol, too."

The Châkia stopped her spooning of the thin stew and looked at Tipperton. "Which holt?"

"Um, the Red Hills."

Now the Châkia resumed her spooning. "I will speak with Lord Berk."

The following day, Alor Loric visited his love, and he held her gently, tears streaming down his face.

*　　*　　*

Days passed, and mid-October came and went, and even as the hillside trees turned to gold and scarlet and orange, the healing of wounds progressed and the number of funerals declined, until there were no more who would die from this battle, the survivors on the mend. Even so, the wound of Dara Phais healed slowly, as sorely damaged and poisoned as she was.

And still Tipperton made the rounds with Beau and played his silver-stringed lute.

And came the waning days of October, leaves now russet and brown and falling to swirl in the chill wind. And still Phais lay abed. Yet in this time under the ministrations of Beau and the healers, others improved, some slowly, some rapidly. And some were declared fit, and these asked for horses and arms and armor, and they rode away to join the allies in harassing the Swarm. And as each or several rode away from the mineholt, Tipperton stood and watched them go, wondering if any would prove to be a linchpin and bring Modru tumbling down. After all, perhaps Beau was right, for it truly did seem, like ripples on a pond, a given event led to other events, all intermingling. As Beau would say, all is connected.

And so Tip would watch them ride away and wonder what the future would bring. And when they were gone from sight, he would turn and enter the mineholt once more, the warders closing the side postern behind.

The final day of October came, and with it the first snow-fall, lightly powdering the ground, but it was melted away by midafternoon. On this day as well, Phais was allowed to rise from her bed for the very first time.

Weak and trembling she did so, Loric at her side. And he escorted her to the privy, for she swore that e'en had she to crawl, she would no longer use the pan.

In celebration Tip took up his lute there in the infirmary and played the song he only knew as "Châkian Singing." And when the Châkian heard him, they gathered 'round and sang, their sweet voices filling the chamber and echoing down the halls, and folk stopped to listen wherever they were.

Loric wept to hear their words, for in Châkur did they sing, yet he never spoke of it in any of the days thereafter.

*   *   *

Autumn marched into November, and more snow swirled down, yet in the Dwarvenholt all was snug and secure.

And no word came from the allies as to how fared the war.

In mid-November Phais began reaching and stretching and bending, her body pulling against scar tissue, and in late November she was fit enough to leave the infirmary. On the same day she was discharged, after moving her goods into Loric's quarters, she took up her sword and followed him to the great exercise room, where she drilled with her lover at blades.

On the first day of December a great blizzard flew.

By Modru's hand, some whispered *He is the master of cold, and it is his season.*

Yet in the Dwarvenholt all was warm.

Some ten weeks after she had been wounded, Phais declared she was fit to ride, and nigh dawn three days later, she and Loric, Beau and Tipperton, went to the infirmary to bid the Châkia good-bye. And as they did so, Tipperton stood on a chair and played one last song, and when he was done he jumped down from the seat and stooped to place his lute in its velvet bag and then into the leather one. One of the Châkia came to Phais and turned her back to all others, and she drew aside the veils at her face to kiss the Dara good-bye, and that was the moment when across the bed Tip stood with his enwrapped lute . . . and Tip's eyes widened at the sight of the Chakian's face. "Oh, my," he said. "Oh, my."

As they passed from the Châkia quarters and into the main Dwarvenholt, Tip said, "She was so beautiful and didn't look at all like a Dwar—"

"Hush, Tipperton," admonished Phais. "Speak of this no more."

Beau looked at Tipperton's yet surprised face. "Huah," grunted Beau. "I wonder what this is all connected to?"

Phais frowned at Beau, and he, too, fell to silence.

They came to the main gate chamber, and there stood Bekki

and his grandsire, Berk. At hand were three saddled ponies and four horses, two saddled and two laden with goods.

Berk looked at the two Waerans as they drew on their quilted-down winter gear. "Take care, little healer," he said to Beau. "You, too, Troll-slayer, Châk-Sol." Now he turned to Phais and Loric. "Farewell, Guardians, may Elwydd keep you all."

Lastly Berk embraced Bekki and slapped him on the back, yet all he could manage to say was, "Châkka shok, Bekki, Châkka cor."

"Aye, Grandsire, holtwarder," replied Bekki, wiping his eyes.

Bidding farewell, the five of them led the animals out through the side postern into the frigid air, their breath blowing white in the chill.

Pulling on his gloves, Tip mounted, as did they all.

He looked about at the snow-laden peaks rearing into the frozen sky, ice glittering in the diamond-bright cold winter sun. It was the fifteenth of December and a scintillant blanket lay over all.

Taking up the reins of his pony, he said, "Come on, my friends, let's ride. We've a coin to deliver."

And down from the mountain they rode.

It's all connected, you know.

ABOUT THE AUTHOR

DENNIS L. MCKIERNAN was born April 4, 1932, in Moberly, Missouri, where he lived until age eighteen, when he joined the U.S. Air Force and served four years spanning the Korean War. He received a B.S. in electrical engineering from the University of Missouri in 1958 and an M.S. in the same field from Duke University in 1964. Dennis spent thirty-one years as one of the AT&T Bell Laboratories whiz kids in research and development—in antiballistic missile defense systems, in software for telephone systems, and in various management think-tank activities—before changing careers to be a full-time writer.

Currently living in Tucson, Arizona, Dennis began writing novels in 1977 while recuperating from a close encounter of the crunch kind with a 1967 red and black Plymouth Fury (Dennis lost: it ran over him: Plymouth 1, Dennis 0).

Among other hobbies, Dennis enjoys scuba diving, dirt-bike riding, and motorcycle touring—all enthusiasms shared by his wife.

An internationally bestselling author, in addition to the HÈL'S CRUCIBLE duology,[1] his novels include *The Dragonstone, Caverns of Socrates, Voyage of the Fox Rider, The Eye of the Hunter, Dragondoom,* THE SILVER CALL duology,[2] THE IRON TOWER trilogy,[3] and the story collection TALES OF MITHGAR.

Never one to sit too long idle, Dennis has also written *The Vulgmaster* (a graphic novel) and several short stories and novelettes which have appeared in various anthologies.

He is presently working on his next opus.

1. HÈL'S CRUCIBLE
   Book 1. *Into the Forge*
   Book 2. *Into the Fire*
2. THE SILVER CALL
   Book 1. *Trek to Kraggen-cor*
   Book 2. *The Brega Path*
3. THE IRON TOWER
   Book 1. *The Dark Tide*
   Book 2. *Shadows of Doom*
   Book 3. *The Darkest Day*

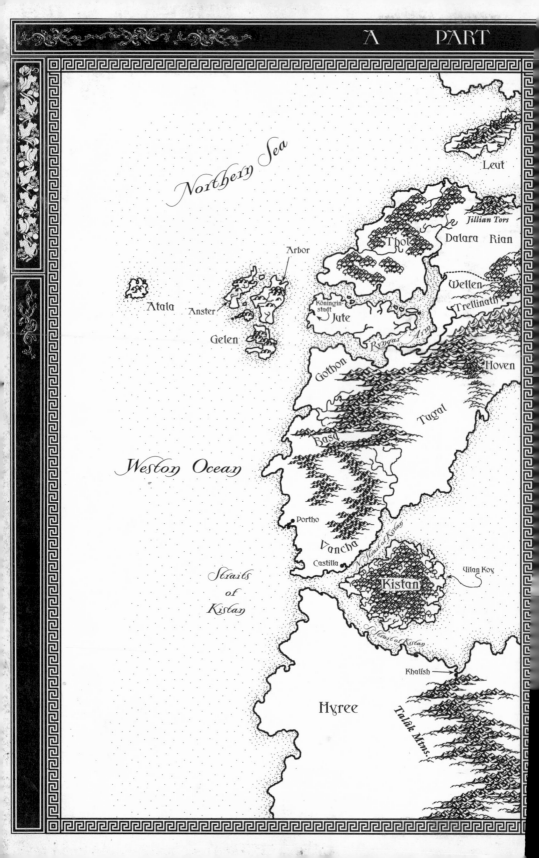